To Ben

12 ROUNDS

Thanks for the Support

By

Mark Stubbs

Mark Stubbs

12 ROUNDS

Third Edition Published
By
Bonkerbooks

A catalogue record for this book is available from the British Library

ISBN 978-0-9929144-1-7

www.Bonkerbooks.com

For the preservation of World Wildlife

Mark Stubbs

A big thank you to all those involved with 12 Rounds and of course a special thank you to the love of my life, Ronnie Stubbs!

Thanks

Mark

CONTENTS

Chapter *Page*

0 Preface 1

1 A Recipe for Disaster; Just Add Water 5

2 Meet Billy 55

3 Haley 96

4 The Living Dead 139

5 Any Pills? 170

6 Like Lambs to the Slaughter 181

7 Do You Think I'm Sexy? 218

8 Pear-Shaped 247

9 Wrong! 288

10 Cherubim Collide 327

11 Taxi! 370

12 Thirteen 399

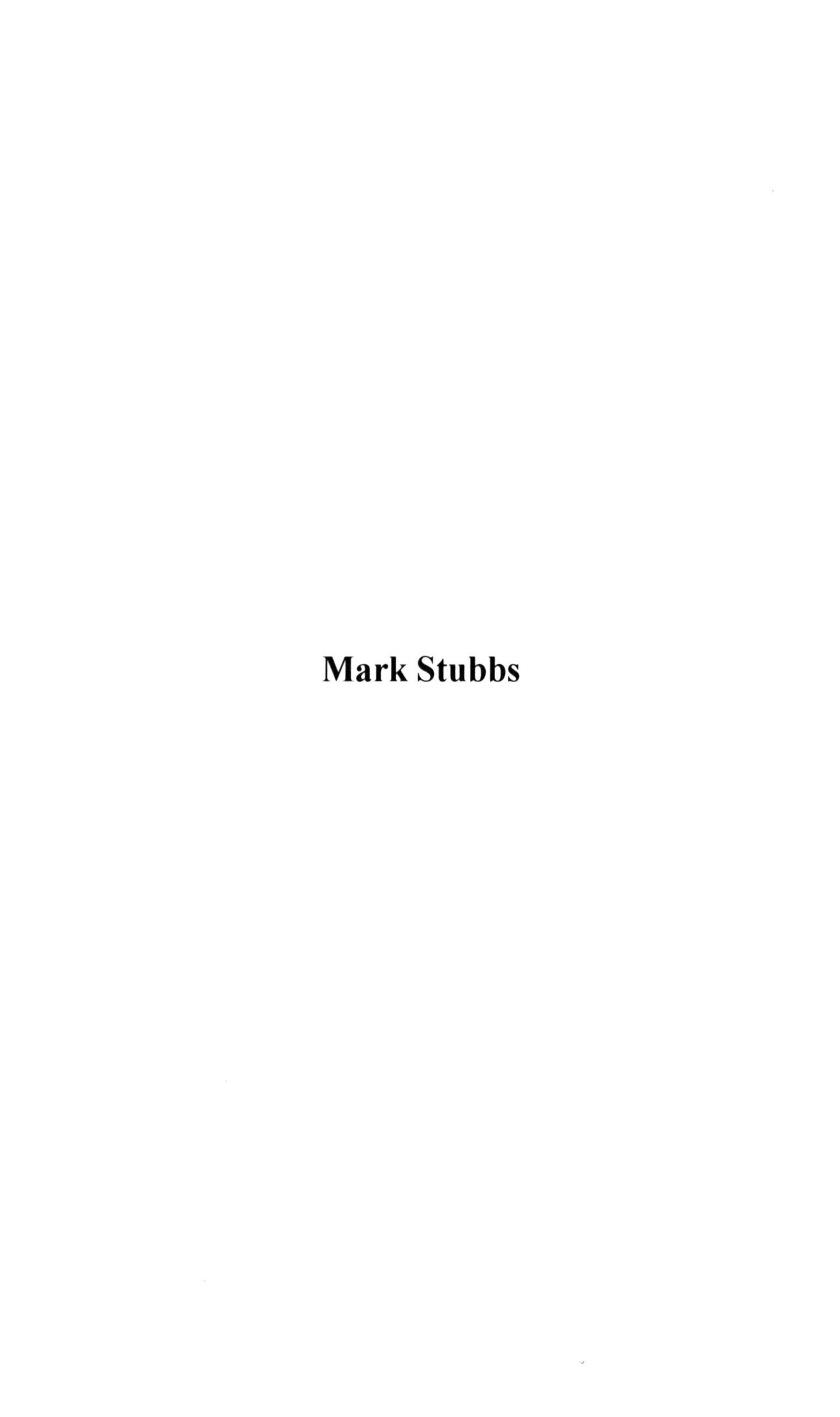

Mark Stubbs

Preface

"I have a dream!" a famous chap once said. Yeah, cool, but I bet it wasn't as fucked up as the two that I had the other night.

Now, for some reason I'm not normally one for dreaming. And for me to actually remember a dream that I've had, is remarkable in itself. But then having said that, if you'd had dreams like these, forgetting them would be more of an issue than remembering them! I'll run the first one by you quickly, so you can see what you think.

God and the Devil are sitting in the pub. It's a normal boozer and the London location brings the scene to life. The Devil gets them in, after some light banter between him and our creator over whose round it actually is; or more importantly, who keeps pulling a fast one when it's his round. Anyway, Lucifer, red in colour, horns, pointy tail, the works-takes two pints over to a table with a view, located just opposite the bar, and the two of them set to work. This is like a weekly review meeting, of course, they try to hold it weekly, but with the pressures of their jobs it ends up being more like fortnightly. This particular meeting, though, has been called only four days after the last one. The reason for this was that they had a problem: a big fucking problem.

Anyway, God, white attire with matching hair, including facial, opens the debate.

"We've got a problem!"

The Devil nods in acknowledgement because this is a fact, albeit somewhat understated.

"A fucking big problem..!" God adds for emphasis, noting the Devil's expression. "You have an angel out of control, you know that and I know that, but what I want to know is, what the fuck, are you going to do about it? Because it's getting out of hand..."

Our Lord tells it like it is, pulling no punches. This question seems to make the Devil feel uncomfortable. Yeah, he knows he's got a rogue angel, but as for what he can do about it, he hasn't the faintest.

"Well, what do you expect me to do about it? He's special, we know that, and the children of God will not be able to stop him. It happens - I can't be responsible for every mortal I recruit! If I could stop him, then I would - you know that! Okay, I've made a bum call, but it's what we do about it now that's important. Quite frankly, my hands are tied, because I can't destroy my own!"

The Devil puts his case across bluntly; he's washed his hands of this problem as far as he's concerned. Let God sort it out. After all, that's what he's there for!

God nods in agreement with his fallen angel because he does have a point. The ball has now landed in the Holy One's court and he has to deal with it.

"I'll have to send a Cherub down, then. There's nothing else I can do, is there?" God offers, the tone of his voice indicating that any alternative suggestions would be welcome. God, the Devil was a pain in the arse sometimes!

"Well, you'll fucking have to then. But if you do, send Gabriel. Don't send any monkey down because this one's a bad boy. He's a wrong'un, mate!"

The Devil offers his response while making it clear that this situation was not really his fault. He picks them and sets them off on their merry way to evil, but sometimes he picks a Pup! It happens; down there is a world so fucked up now that gone are the days when you could inject a little evil into someone and they went and did your work. No mate, these days you sometimes ended up injecting evil into evil, because too many people are fucked up in the head. And when that happened, this was the result! When such beasts were unleashed, there were very few people down there these days who were equipped with the skills to fight them. Oh, how the times were a-changing!

God agreed with his former employee: Gabriel was the only one of his Cherubim who could deal with this situation. He agreed that the Devil did seem to have his hands full these days, but like he had told him before, tell him when we've got a wrong'un, and God would deal with it. The Devil had done as he was asked, and hopefully in time to rescue the situation. By working together, they could still prevent a catastrophe. In this day and age, shit like this was going to happen all the time, and it was definitely becoming more frequent. Evil was the nature of the business, but some people were starting to take the piss!

"Okay then, I'll send Gabriel. But you just keep out of the fucking way while he works - you know you two don't get on!"

The Devil nodded in agreement. He would keep out of Gabriel's way. Fuck, nothing would give him greater pleasure because that angel wasn't the full ticket, he was a fucking lunatic, but then, that's why he was so good at getting things done and taking care of situations like this. So that was it then, meeting closed. God was sending down his right hand man. May God fucking help us all!

Bit weird, yeah? Sorry to anyone religious about all the swearing and all. I don't mean to cause offence, because of course it was only a dream, and I'm sure God wouldn't use such language. Anyway, I woke up at that stage, a bit perplexed to tell you the truth. I went downstairs and got a quick glass of water, but this dream would not remove itself from my memory. After a quick trip to the lavatory, OK, more information than you really need, I went back to bed, as it was the early hours of the morning. I started to drift off to sleep again, still with the dream on my mind, until another took over. And if you think the last one was weird, then fucking try this one!

Enjoy 12 Rounds!

Chapter One

A recipe for disaster; just add water!

"Well, he looks fucking dead to me, man!" the acne-scarred Asian teenager commented. It was an understandable remark, although a little premature in view of the fact that dead people are not usually breathing. "Na, he ain't dead, he's just smacked up," the streetwise youth corrected himself.

The rest of the onlookers thought the cleaner was probably right. Anyone responsible for the cleanliness of one of the most frequented toilets in London would tend to become familiar with this sort of scum. Mr Mop had seen it a thousand times over. Somewhere between twenty-five and thirty, the cleaner labelled the unconscious white male who was causing an obstruction upon his floor. He was apparently glued to the cold tiles by his own vomit; yellow bile laced with red globules of blood. Adhering to one side of the man's gaunt complexion, it looked as gross as it smelt. The janitor's training had served him well on this occasion; to prevent further disasters, he had been proactive enough to make good use of his 'slippery floor' and 'cleaning in progress' signs. Their metal frames were sizeable enough to warn unwary customers of the dangers that lurked where they dined.

So, who was he then? Who was this man who lay there shaking on the cream-tiled floor of one of Britain's leading fast food restaurants? Sanj did not know, and he did not want to know if it meant rooting through his pockets. Well, with the needles and all that, you can't be too careful these days, can you?

It was business as usual as far as serving food was concerned. An odd glance from the multi-racial staff was about all the concern shown from behind the safety of the busy counter. Six in the morning was often entertaining - wide-eyed clubbers, piss-heads, homeless vagrants sheltering from the cold - a recipe for disaster, one might say. There were also the night-crawlers dining after their shift had finished and people of the day dining before their shift began. Saturday morning was always particularly special.

If the smackhead's soul had departed his body and risen above the action, the sight that met it from below would have been almost as comical as it was tragic. Some old bag stuck her two penneth in - youth of today and all that old bollocks. She was all dressed up for winter; it was just a shame that she was three months too early, or three months two late, depending on which way you looked at it. The woman fucking stank an' all - but they do, don't they? Old cabbage and piss! They did as far as Sanj was concerned, anyway.

The young blonde seemed to agree with most of the old waffle that the dear old lady felt the need to share. Polite, she was, the blonde, that is, very well-mannered. A teenager? Sanj thought not, although she weren't far off it. Nice, an' all. Sanj could see down her top when she knelt over the unconscious man, trying to get his attention with her soft voice. A black lace bra, and well filled at that! The blonde's words of kindness and encouragement were having little effect.

The restaurant seemed to be functioning pretty normally with not many people put off their food – well, why should they be? After all, it was just another fucking smackhead - filthy fucking scum! At the end of the day, it was just as well for him that he hadn't made it outside before collapsing, because let's face it no one would have helped him out there. He'd have had to wait for the road-sweepers while passers-by robbed him of whatever valuables he carried.

The dimly lit street outside was suddenly illuminated by orange flashing lights as a siren indicated that people should get out of the way, bringing a sigh of relief to the compassionate blonde. Two men got out of the ambulance, the younger carrying two bags while his senior put out a half-smoked cigarette. The blonde got the once-over; our knight in green-clothed armour couldn't help wishing it was her who needed his attention. Kiss of life, loosen the clothing and all that.

"Come on then, give him air, let us in," the head of the rescue team requested. They all obeyed, and the old lady started to fill them in on the situation up to press, but to be honest it needed little explanation. Sanj used his mop for support while managing to sneak one final glimpse of bulging flesh encased in lace as the blonde got to her feet, causing her admirer to study her arse instead. She clocked him, though, as she pulled her jeans back up over her skimpy underwear, so he had to be a little more cautious about it than he had before.

The ageing paramedic knew his stuff. He diagnosed the victim's poison in a matter of seconds: eyelids pulled up, torch in the eyes, pupils examined.

"Give him a shot, then."

His junior wasted no time in carrying out the order. Opening a green case, he produced a frightening-looking piece of equipment. The needle was enough to make the majority of the population go weak at the knees. The paramedic in control of the situation stopped his colleague before he started to remove the needle from its packaging.

"Hang on, strap him up first in case he goes into one."

The junior rushed out to the ambulance and fetched a stretcher on which to strap their project. It was light and easily carried, being made from modern fibres, but nevertheless strong. When you're strapped into that, you aren't going anywhere!

The senior paramedic had to get his hands dirty for a change, assisting his colleague in lifting the shallow-breathing patient. Clothing loosened around the chest; straps fastened together where they were needed; now it was time to set up the needle. The barrel was already loaded - it comes like that - you simply have to fit the needle, take aim and fire. Bang, it enters the skin like a knife cutting through butter, into the blood stream and then straight into the heart. It takes the skill of a madman to administer the life-saving drug; just take aim and stab your subject as though you want to kill him; it's not hard.

Once NARCAM had been pumped into the patient's body a reaction was only a few seconds away. If he had been unrestrained, he would have sat bolt upright; that much was clear. As it was, cocooned in the red space-age stretcher, an expression of sheer surprise was about all the reaction that he was able to show. The patient suddenly became overwhelmed with panic, his silent thoughts evident only from the strain in his eyes and the contorted muscles of his face.

What the fuck is going on? Why can't I move? Who the fuck are you?

When you overdose on heroin, it's your breathing technique that kills you, or rather your lack of it. Palmer ordered his patient to breathe, shouting the command at the man in his care in several sharp bursts. The man in shackles seemed too concerned with the fact that he was restrained to worry about breathing, although he needed to, as you could see from his face. Palmer offered his patient some oxygen but he wanted none of it. He just wanted his freedom. The paramedics looked concerned, especially the younger of the two, his expression indicating that he was not used to his patients reacting in this ungrateful manner. Palmer, however, was familiar with these displays of confused paranoid delusions. He knew he was the good guy, but one had to see it from his captive's point of view.

"Out of the way!" Palmer knelt beside his patient and placed a rubber-gloved hand over the weeping mouth of their patient.

"Okay, okay son, let's calm down a bit shall we? And start breathing. I'm gonna release you, don't worry about that, I'd just suggest that you get your breathing in line while I do so." Palmer adjusted the position of his hand carefully to avoid being bitten.

The patient did calm down slightly, not just because he had been asked to, but because he seemed to be getting his marbles back.

"We're going to let you go, all right son? So let's just keep calm; we don't want you hurting yourself. Are you ready?" Palmer asked.

Silence from the man beneath his hand indicated that he was.

"Unfasten him," Palmer ordered his colleague in a matter-of-fact manner. Soon the straps were unfastened and the protective jacket was opened. The audience half-expected the paramedics' prisoner to react with violence and make a break for freedom, but for now all seemed calm. Palmer helped his patient sit up with one hand while the other remained firmly over the young man's mouth until he was upright enough to sit by himself.

Like a foal making its first stand, the star of the show struggled to his feet as best as he could. Confusion was written on his face and he coughed as though in pain. There was something restricting his breathing so he deposited it onto the floor, almost causing others to follow suit in disgust. The vomit appeared to be the least of the addict's worries; the dark substance mingled with it was greater cause for concern. The mucus or vomit clearly contained a large quantity of blood, at least half and half. Palmer had seen this before, usually in patients who had had one too many ciggies, but not in a man of his age; this should not happen. The paramedic wanted to share his knowledge; offer some advice - but what was the point? Smackheads don't listen. Oh well, one had to go through the motions.

"You should come with us really," he said. "That drug won't last long and you should really have a constant supply of oxygen. I know you aint gonna, but the offer's there if you need it." He knew full well that the suggestion was falling upon deaf ears.

Still unsure of his footing, the man suddenly made an announcement to his audience that seemed a little strange, indicating possible delusion.

"I've been to hell!" He declared.

The Asian cleaner and the pretty blonde sniggered in embarrassment, but the elderly lady and the paramedics failed to see the funny side and were not so quick to mock. Maybe he genuinely had seen something that he thought was hell? Let's face it, he may well have died at some point on those cold tiles and who knows where you go and what you see when your life is taken from you? It's pretty much uncharted territory really, because very few people have the pleasure of returning once they have left us. Never knock the unknown, they say! Paramedic Palmer certainly didn't and he had witnessed a lot of strange shit like this; far too much for there to be nothing in it.

"Go on son, on your way!"

The human waste clung desperately to his gaunt skin as poisoned water failed to wash it away. He was unsure if it had been raining before he had entered the restaurant. He doubted it, but then he was in no position to remember really. Our hero had been named Anthony at birth, still was, but not Anthony Howe any more. He was now Anthony Jenkins due to a change in father figures. You would hardly ever hear Ant answer to his real name, though, because no one ever called him by it. Apart from his mother, that is. He was known to most simply as AJ, for obvious reasons. He was a slim lad but not through choice, his habit was in control of his build. He would probably have been much bigger if it hadn't been for the regular medication, but as it was his size was chemically controlled.

The streets of London don't look their best in the heavy rain, especially in the dark. It was not bitterly cold, just cold enough to wish you were on the inside of those expensive walls rather than traipsing around outside them. Soho stinks in the morning. Does rain make the smell more pungent? The smells of food preparation dominated the air, which was the last thing he needed, considering that he was now wearing most of the contents of his stomach down the front of his not-quite-fashionable leather jacket. People sharing the street with AJ seemed more concerned about getting wet than he was and took any available opportunity to dodge the rain. That was fine by him, because it simply left his path clearer. Let it rain, the harder the better, fuck it, because Anthony Jenkins didn't give a fuck!

*

So, you want to know more about AJ, do you? Okay, after all, he's a fascinating character. Twenty-seven he is, well, in a few weeks anyway but, he doesn't look it. Twenty-four would be a safer bet if you were guessing. London had been his permanent home for those twenty-seven years; not always Soho, though his family had never lived far from it. Mum? Yes, she was still around. Not a very nice lady by all accounts, but then it was all down to who was judging. If it was AJ, he would be honest and say that there was a little love there.

Unfortunately, though, there was not a lot of tolerance between them. If you looked at the bigger picture, Mum had made her fair share of mistakes in life and her son was a sick drug addict. And when I say sick, I don't just mean medically ill, because there had been a few mental problems as well. So, chuck into that the cocktail of drugs that Anthony had consumed throughout his life and the mayhem that came with it, and you didn't really have a recipe for a happy household there.

Dad was dead; he'd been burned and urned about six years ago and now sat in a little pot at the crematorium, but then he had been dead twenty-one years before that as far as AJ was concerned because he had never seen him, hadn't known anything about him for all that time. Mother had only come clean about his father when he died. There was some money involved, you see, and you know what sort of secrets money can bring to the surface. Dad didn't want his son to know he was doing two life sentences with no parole almost as much as Mum didn't want to tell her son where his father was, but money brought the issue out into the open.

Dad was a bad boy. He had always protested that he was not a killer, but even if he hadn't actually pulled the trigger he had been part of a crew that had carried out a brutal robbery in which two people had died. One was a woman, a post office worker, this being the reason why the case caused particular outcry. In fact this caused more attention than the fact that a policeman had also been shot dead, but when you tie it all up life sentences were on the cards no matter who was convicted. Maybe they got the wrong man, maybe they didn't, at the end of the day it was justice. Dad died of cancer.

Anthony's share of the inheritance was only six grand, but then six large is six large, which mother took care of. Two reasons really; to stop her heroin-loving son killing himself with it and to invest it in the family business. The shop wasn't doing great. It was doing all right, but not well enough to feed its owner's habit. Mr Jenkins was in the business of smut. He ate, slept and drank smut, as well as two bottles of whiskey a day. The shop sold just about everything to do with sex, as adult shops generally do. To be fair, it was quite a bit more advanced in the variety of its stock than most. The new partner was to thank for this, because as well as himself and his money, he brought youthful visions with him. Granted, they were a little distorted. Mr Jenkins senior may well have owned the business but he had had little interest in it; drink, prostitutes and the gee-gees took priority in his reasonably happy little life. The fact that he was an embarrassment to his wife and two stepsons was never an issue to him really, because what you can't see doesn't hurt you.

Oh yes, sorry, nearly forgot. OJ, Oliver Jenkins, AJ's brother. He was also inside, so maybe it's hereditary. Seven years, possession of cocaine with intent to supply. But then, with three thousand pounds worth of the gear found in your flat, you'd be taking the piss to claim it was personal, wouldn't you? He was in Woodhill, Milton Keynes, and had done two years with only another one and a half left to do realistically, if he kept his nose clean, in more ways than one, that is!

He was a nice bloke really; it was just the lure of the big money that outweighed the legality of his chosen career path, not to mention the need to feed his habit, which ultimately fucked him up in the end, sad, but common enough. AJ went to visit him quite a lot, well, once a month, but then it's a fucking long way, you know? He looked okay. He was banged up with a load of his mates and former colleagues, plus he was being looked after by the screws, which was financed by his former employers as a token of goodwill. See, these drug dealers are not all bad!

There's nothing remarkable to say about OJ really, except he was twenty-three and a big cunt; seventeen stone at least, just like his dad, who was AJ's stepdad. He was tasty too, a real hard fucker, again, just like his dad, and so not too many people gave him shit. Having said that, though, he was generally labelled quite a placid bloke really, but then he was coked-up most the time. As far as AJ could remember, outside of work the only real thing that was certain to set him off, and would almost definitely make him chuck his toys out of the pram, was if you called him Orange Juice, or Simpson, he fucking hated that! During business hours was a different matter, but then business is business, isn't it? The brothers got on quite well under the circumstances, but then with dad being a cunt and all, one would imagine that they'd had to stick together.

*

Time was getting on and AJ was wet, predominantly about his legs and head. Leather protected his midriff, but a change of clothing was a must for someone in his condition. You could always hear AJ before you saw him, he coughed like he was suffering from lung cancer or something, a painful, barking cough, almost a grunt you could call it. What was wrong with his chest, then? He didn't know. The quantity of blood stained phlegm that he constantly brought up and shared with society was cause enough for concern, but he wouldn't see a doctor; he had lost faith in the National Health Service many moons ago. That's why he prescribed his own medicine.

The Jenkins family lived on the third floor of a block of six flats. It was fucking horrible, I'm not going to lie to you, but to AJ it was home. Not a happy one, but a home nevertheless. AJ had only moved back with his mum a year ago; he had lived with a girl for about five years before that, but I'll cross that bridge in a minute because that's the Golden fucking Gate!

London was getting busier as the soaked youth reached the staircase to the flats that he called home, and there they fucking were again, vagrants! The young man should have felt at home with them really, considering the state he'd been in tonight, but they were really not welcome, the fucking bastards! They were all sitting together asleep, one of them mumbling gibberish, having taken advantage of the shelter afforded by the brick enclosure of the staircase. A dead cat lay next to them. Bastards, they always did that. It was a game to them; they would entice the cat over and then catch and torture it. This one had its eyes missing, and for what? AJ didn't know, but he was more angered by the vagrants making a home under his stairs than about the death of a cat.

The tramps had to pay. AJ had told them before and they were taking the piss now. If his stepdad saw them, he'd kill them. He'd tried before, poured petrol on them and set light to them, no bullshit! That was for nicking his clothes off the washing line, though.

With a surprising amount of residual energy, AJ ran at the vagrants and trampled on them, jumping up and down on them as if using them as a walkway. The human trampoline seemed confused, grunting and babbling foul language at its attacker. AJ was not finished yet, though. Quickly he ran up a flight of stairs, unzipped his trousers, released the beast, and let loose a stream of urine that rained down upon the guilty. The ones, who'd almost gone back to sleep again, despite their drunken rage.

That felt better; a lot better. The assailant enjoyed the feeling of victory as he climbed the remaining two flights of stairs. Piss-soaked tramps were no longer on his mind as he fumbled with his key in the lock; he was more interested now in who would be greeting him on the other side of the heavy-looking door. Well, there was only one way to find out!

Thankfully it was mum. She was dashing about, fag in hand getting ready for work. Cleaning was Mrs Jenkins game, until twelve o'clock that is, then she changed professions. From twelve till six she worked in finance, well, she worked as a money changer in an amusement arcade.

Sue asked her son where he had been and received a brief account of the night's events. Her response was as expected.

"Yea well, you fucking better be up to open the shop at ten or your sodding father will bloody kill you!"

Nice! She was right, though, and AJ appreciated the warning although Allen was not actually his father, thankfully. It was not worth correcting his mother on this point, though, she would only go off her tits as usual, 'who brought you up and all that?' Brought him up? AJ had to laugh. The only thing Allen brought up was his dinner after a night on the piss!

Mother was not happy. It was Saturday morning, and no one likes working Saturdays at the best of times. Also, she knew that Saturday morning would be when her husband, if you could call him that, would be at his worst. He would be pissed up beyond belief, having drunk constantly from yesterday lunch time to, well, he probably hadn't stopped. The sad case would have spunked all his money and would probably be with some old tart right now. Yes, that was her husband!

Anthony promised that he would be up in time.

"Yeah, you bloody better. And clean yourself up, will you? You look like shit. I see you're still coughing, it's all that shit you pump into your body. I don't know why you don't just go and see a doctor, but then you know what he's going to say don't you, you fucking druggy! Going out and getting soaking wet like that doesn't really help either, does it?" Mrs Jenkins nagged.

"I'm all right," Anthony lied, which received exactly the response that he had expected in the form of foul-mouthed sarcasm. He had heard it all before.

"Right, I'm off. If he brings any little tarts in here, you better warn him that I'll fucking kill him when I get home, do you hear?"

Anthony did hear, although as far as he was concerned it was not, the done thing to go warning your stepfather that your mother may object to him bringing prostitutes back to the family home, but he agreed for argument's sake and promised that he would issue the warning. Mum knew he wouldn't, but she had to put on a front in order to try and reclaim a little of the self-respect that her husband was inclined to piss up the wall.

*

Mum wanted to get away from her husband but there was one thing stopping her. Well, two things really I suppose. Firstly, there was the threat of violence from her husband. It was the usual situation when you're married to a bully or an alcoholic bully in this case. She may curse the man behind his back, but never to his face; that only resulted in bruises. The second was losing everything she owned. Anthony's father had been reasonably well set up before he went down, and on his death bed he had kindly offered his wife the remainder of his wealth. Unfortunately for all concerned, money hidden away does not tend to make much interest. He had updated the currency, but that was about it. So when Sue went to collect the money, it was not a lot really, barely twelve grand, which was a lot in its time, but not by today's standards. She gave half to AJ as she had promised her husband and then hid the rest away for a rainy day. Mrs Jenkins was simply biding her time. She didn't work every hour God sends to finance her husband's activities out of stupidity, oh no, she knew that the more he could drink, the more his liver would perish, and the more he would get himself into trouble, hopefully removing himself from the equation eventually. AJ knew how she felt and he could not really blame her because she had more love for the tramps downstairs than her husband. One thing neither of them knew, however, was the fact that Sue was not the only one financing her husband's habits. Someone else was too, and they were not as gullible as his wife. Neither were they to be fucked with. If only she knew!

Mother soon left for work with another cigarette in hand, lit and all ready to help her cope with the stairs, tramps and initial burst of Soho street mayhem that she was sure to face as she left the safety of her own home. AJ was on his own now, which was how he liked it. Standing there soaking wet, he had to agree with his mother's comments on the state of his appearance while studying himself in his bedroom mirror. He had not really cared at the time, but he cared now. Stripping to his shorts, AJ coughed heavily into the filthy clothes that he held and deposited what was blocking his throat. Again, mother was right; his illness was getting worse. But then it was going to, he reminded himself while filling the washing bin with his damp, heavily-soiled clothing. It was time for bed, after the briefest of showers, just for a few hours, just to take the edge off this tiredness. AJ never slept much as a rule; or rather he slept quite a lot, but it was never real sleep. A drug-induced slumber was a better description. He could rest his body, but never his mind.

The bed was cold, like the damp, dull room. Mum had said that he could decorate if he wanted. That was nearly a year ago, mind, when he had moved back home. He would get round to it one day. Yeah, one day. It would have been nice to watch television and nod off gently to sleep. If there had been a television, that is. The room had actually seen about seven or eight in the past few years but they were simply collateral for when things got a bit tight and 'gear' required purchasing. He hadn't bothered replacing the last one; it just seemed like a waste of time. The video went the same way, and the stereo, it was lonely, but at the time the need was urgent. So, AJ was left with nothing but his thoughts. Whenever his twisted mind had nothing else to ponder on, it thought of Haley. Where she was, what she was doing, what condition she was in. It was bad news whichever way you looked at it. She was a lovely girl; 'was' being the operative word, because she was not so lovely anymore and never would be again, due to her illness. Yes, she was sick all right. Haley was so ill that she was about ready for a box. She was in a hospice now until it was time to meet her maker, or, as she said, until the maggots were wriggling through her body. Yes, she was bitter. Pneumonia would be on her death certificate, maybe on her gravestone as well. Whatever; it was better than AIDS. Society generally had some questions to ask when those four letters come into the conversation: did she shag a queer? Was she a druggy sharing needles with others of her kind? Funny, though, no one had asked if she had been given contaminated blood by the National Health Service, or whether perhaps she had been raped by a sufferer. Maybe she had simply had unprotected sex with a heterosexual male, which in fact was the truth of the matter. Well, she had actually been a prostitute and she made no bones about it. Let's face it, it was an occupational hazard and there was a lack of awareness back then. As a result she got caught; HIV caught her. Haley had had a good innings, apparently. They say that seven years after diagnosis is pretty good, and they had been good years up to the last six months, but only because of AJ.

When her lover had been to see her in hospital the evening before she'd looked bad; thin and gaunt. As always, though, she was more concerned about the only person who was dear to her. She had no family anymore; no real friends. They had known each other for about six years now. There was nothing romantic about it when they met; he was buying and she was selling. Not sex, she had given up selling her body a year or so before. No, she was selling heroin on this occasion, although she also kept a stock of every other drug that had a street value. AJ vaguely remembered their meeting. They had shot up together in a dead drug dealer's flat (long story) back in the days when AJ used to inject his medication, which he couldn't any longer. They just seemed to click; they were both fuck-ups, AJ was fond of saying. Things moved on like they do, and their relationship flourished. AJ moved in and everything was okay. Not brilliant, but it was tolerable. Until Haley started collapsing, was admitted to hospital, and basically never came out again. Hospital to hospital to hospice. When Haley became full blown, AJ moved back to his parents' flat because he couldn't afford the rent without his lover's benefits. So the flat had to go, just like her business and everything she had ever owned; all gone. With these thoughts, AJ began to drift off to the anaesthesia of sleep.

Anthony was back again, on the floor of one of the world's most popular burger restaurants. In fact, it was exactly the same one that he had lain upon just hours ago in reality. But why was he back? What he remembered of the audience was also there, surrounding him. Just colours, though. No faces, just colours. The paramedics were just arriving, like well-built green angels coming to save him. AJ recognised them, and the recognition created an explosion of fear inside the poisoned youth, to the amazement of the audience. Panic stricken, AJ repeated the word 'no' through trembling lips. The witnesses were bemused; after all, it was just a paramedic for Christ sake, not the angel of death or the reaper! No, it was neither of them. In fact it was worse than that; the one thing that AJ feared most in this world was reaching out for his throat and there was absolutely nothing he could do about it. The assailant's fingers soon began to grip his throat and squeeze with all their might against the veins in his neck. As the strangulated victim gasped for air, it was finally time to awake and face the music.

"Get up, you bastard!"

In a haze of confusion, AJ opened his eyes, the lids struggling to break the seal of yellow solvent that had glued them closed. He squinted in pain as it became clear that he was not actually on the floor of a fast food restaurant. He was actually in his bed, and judging by his father's reaction he had overslept. He was pissed, dad, that is, not paralytic, but not far from it. AJ tried to keep the peace by apologising for his mistake while attempting to pry his stepfather's hands away from his jugular. The grip was tight and the assailant seemed intent on harming his victim. As the colour faded from his face, he noticed that he did in fact have an audience and knew her well. Her name was Tara. She said nothing, although her face spoke volumes. She looked frightened, petrified in fact, although she knew her client, Mr Jenkins, well. It would have been stupid to make any comments on the scene she was witnessing, so she didn't. Anthony's determination not to be strangled in his bed was winning over his alcoholic stepfather's attempt to bring his life to an early close. He managed to loosen the grip on his throat, causing his attacker to fall on top of him. AJ managed to push his seventeen stone stepfather off the bed and make for the door, Tara having moved out of the way. But Mr Jenkins was not finished yet. He shuffled about unsteadily before creating a human barrier in front of the door way. AJ received punches to his head and knees to other parts of his body. He managed to break away from the brawl.

"All right you cunt, leave it out. I'm fucking up now, so fuck off with your whore and let me get on with it!" AJ ordered as he stared into his stepfather's wide open eyes from the other side of the room, watching the saliva drip from the drunk's mouth. What a mess, what a fucking mess! Breathless, with vomit threatening to make an appearance anytime, Mr Jenkins emitted one last warning now that he begun to feel extremely unwell.

"You fucking better," he spat, before leaving the room. AJ breathed a sigh of relief and bent down slightly to get his breath back, his hands supporting his midriff. He was cooling off now, the damp air making his breath misty as he panted heavily to recover from the attack. Dressed only in thin shorts, he soon needed to protect himself against the cold by dressing. Blue Jeans, a blue t-shirt and a red cardigan were at hand. In the background he could hear his name being cursed in between the sounds of vomit hitting water-filled porcelain. Nice! That's his dad, that is!

Tara watched with disgust as she witnessed the vomit leaving her customer's body through the same orifice that had first imbibed it in its earlier form. Feeling like she might follow suit, she stuck her head back into AJ's room and said hello before inquiring about his girlfriend's health.

"Well, you know?" AJ replied. "Busy?" He asked with a hint of piss-take in his voice.

"Oh, you know?" The reply came with irony.

AJ smiled. He actually liked Tara, which was saying something. She was a pretty girl; she just looked dirty. Tarty, I suppose. You could spot her trade a mile off due to the way she dressed. She was not high-class, it was fair to say, but with the right trappings she could have been.

"Good luck, anyway," he said, as he went out. Walking past the bathroom where his stepfather still crouched with his head down the toilet, AJ hoped that Tara would have the chance to fleece her punter, clear him out of cash and at least get a half decent price for such dirty work. He also hoped that his stepfather would choke on his own vomit and die slowly. London smelt a bit better than his flat. Dazed by the energetic start to the morning, AJ slammed the front door shut and began to climb down to earth. The piss-soaked tramps were still out for the count, but he left them in peace this time.

"I'll be back!" He joked in a foreign accent, not knowing that he actually would be back a lot sooner than he thought. His tired eyes ached and he needed his 'breakfast', which he generally took in the form of a powder. It was not a major problem yet, he just felt tense and uncomfortable, but the shop was only just around the corner.

Why do people persist in fucking in the shop doorway? AJ asked himself when he arrived at work, especially on a weekend. He didn't so much mind them fucking, go forth and multiply, but it would be good manners to take their expelled bodily fluids with them. What sort of wanker leaves used, recently-filled condoms in his doorway? Could they not dispose of them in a civilised manner, like in a lavatory or a bin, or maybe fuck somewhere else? Just because the doorway was a little secluded, it wasn't an invitation to copulate within it. AJ would like to fuck someone in his doorway; fuck them with a bat, he fantasised, as he hooked two used condoms out of the way with his foot and launched them into the gutter for someone else to deal with.

Fort Knox was thankfully still fully secure. How people got through a solid steel outer front door or a fully-caged front window AJ could not explain, but they did, quite frequently as it happened. It amazed him why anyone would put so much effort into stealing magazines, videos, vibrators or a slick lips pulsating pussy. Some people must just be desperate. Surely if the thief put this much effort into a bank, then he would never have to steal again. Whatever; they had not struck last night, which was a bonus. Having opened three locks on the outer door, AJ was soon inside his shop because the inner door was already open. This was due to the fact that it had still not been repaired from the previous break-in, but then what was the point?

He switched on the luminous red 'sex shop' display sign that was situated in the front window. This created a fabulous red glow which brightened up an otherwise gloomy room and gave it the illusion that the shop was fitted with a sophisticated alarm system. The mornings were always quiet, as the need for marital or sexual aids was usually not so great mid-morning. It tended to pick up in the afternoon and evening as boredom set in. The shop was as big as an average family front room, but could do with being a bit bigger really in view of the rapid growth of the sex industry. But without going through all the rigmarole of offering a mail-order service and all that palaver, you were pissing in the wind and getting wet trousers. Especially with Britain's turn-of-the-century views on the industry causing the majority of sales to take place under the counter. What was the Government doing? Think of all that tax!

The outer walls of the shop were lined with magazines and videos catering for various tastes; a pervert's library. Heterosexual, Gay, Bizarre, TV, Fetish, it was truly an eye opener if nothing else. With such inspiring titles as 'Shaven Girls,' 'Big Boobs,' 'Pregnant Vicky,' 'TV Times,' or 'Big Boys and their Toys,' Christ, you were spoilt for choice! Having said that, AJ had never seen most of them move off the shelf since he had worked here; he'd be able to move them to the classic section before long! If your preferences were against the law, say, for instance, for our four-legged friends, then you got a more personal service in the back room. And believe me, if you thought your tastes would offend then think again. The middle of the shop contained just about everything you needed to get your rocks off: eighty seven different dildos, all-purpose built to entertain any orifice; twenty three different

Pulsating Pussies, including the world famous tight-lips 2000, which speaks for itself if you feel like paying through the nose for a chat with a palpitating plastic fanny; and no less than sixteen blow-up dolls, four of which spoke. One spoke Chinese, one French and the others English. Not that it really mattered to AJ what language they spoke since he had never had a conversation with one, other than to perform a product test. Quality control was a must in Soho-people had been killed for less than the sale of an illiterate rubber doll with a speech impediment.

If you liked dressing up, or dressing up your partner, then you'd come to the right place. All tastes were catered for, so customers could feel free to sift through the vast range of tacky uniforms, market stall underwear and basically anything that you really would not like to be wearing if you ever got rushed to hospital. If your dick didn't work or you had a problem with its size or performance, then worry no more, you simply need the power pump, vibrating penis developer or the miracle spray that prolongs an erection. Well, so it says on the box! Being a store of the nineties, the shop had a policy of promoting safe sex, as well as making money of course. It stocked more condoms than you could use in a lifetime, some safe but all very profitable.

With the shop open, the only thing left to do was have a spot of breakfast. An ancient-looking opium pipe was hidden under the counter for the sole purpose of allowing AJ to administer his medicine, the days of foil and a plastic pen casing being long gone. Needles were also a no-no; you could only do that to yourself for so long before needing micro-surgery to repair a rapidly decaying limb. AJ's leg had been saved from amputation and it seemed the lesson had been learnt. Shorts on the beach were now out of the question, though.

The opium pipe was simple enough, you just added the powder to the metal bowl situated midway along the pipe, lit it with a lighter, inhaled on the exhaust at one end, and then there, you had it, breakfast! As AJ's lips sucked on the drug-taking implement, his eyes closed in anticipation of the relief that he was about to receive. He was not disappointed either as a seepage of red Saliva trickled from one corner of his lips and down his cheek. The pain that withdrawal had inflicted upon his body was beginning to heal. Anxiety was beginning to take a back seat and life once again began to feel bearable; the wonder drug was indeed wonderful! AJ sat back in his chair after his final inhalation. It was now time to relax for as long as the punters let him. He hoped for a quiet morning as he made himself comfortable with his feet up on the desk. His drug-fuelled mind thought only of Haley. It didn't seem fair that he was enjoying this wonderful high while she was lying in hospital as good as dead. He should be with her really, by her side, but he knew that he could not. He would visit her later, though, because he always did. She hadn't looked too good at last night's visit, she was weakening as the days went by and it was only a matter of time now, precious time. AJ began to nod off into a drug-induced slumber. The door had a bell and was unlikely to ring for a few hours, so for the time being he was free to enjoy life in another dimension.

His mind sent AJ back to school, to the playground to be precise. The very school of which he had left with pretty much the same as he had entered it with, nothing! Except that he could now recite at least fifty names for female genitalia and could speak the English language in its contemporary form by inserting a swear word after every other word, quite an achievement, really. He had also mastered certain social skills, including the ability to skin up, jack up, chase, spike a vein, chop one up, drop one and bomb one. Yes, the skills he had learnt at school had certainly trained him for life.

Anyway, back at school someone kept ringing a bell. There were two blokes, both of them African origin, standing at the classroom entrance, a bit out of focus although well within range. The one on the left was ringing the bell while the one on the right was just staring at AJ as if waiting for him. None of the other kids seemed to notice them. Haley was also in the picture, although in a more youthful form. She was so pretty back then, even though AJ had not actually known her back in those days. It was definitely her, though, there was no doubt about that, and she seemed very keen for AJ to follow her through the doorway. AJ was running but it was as if he were on a conveyer belt or treadmill or something, he could run as much as he liked but he was going nowhere, apart from closer to the teacher-like figure and that tosser who was beginning to irritate him with his constant bell ringing. Soon AJ was so close to the men that he could smell their expensive cologne. The bell was so loud by now that it was beginning to pound on his eardrums. Anxiety swamped his body, poisoning it to the point where he was forced to awake in a fit of panic.

"Fuck!" AJ swore as he opened his eyes, the perspiration dripping into them and stinging his eyeballs. He almost fell off his chair with fright, especially when it registered that his 'teachers' were actually in the shop, standing there staring at him. Fucking hell, had his past caught up with him?

"Arh, hello, sorry about that. Heavy night, you know? Err, can I help you with anything?" AJ asked, still dazed by his schoolyard experience as he coughed in pain. Bleeding mucus had been drawn into his mouth and there was no way he could expel it in front of customers, so AJ simply swallowed the semi-solid mass.

"Er, hello! I'm awake, my friend, so you can stop the chimes now, if you would be so kind!" He said, as the ringing sound continued. It was by now well and truly beginning to get on his tits. The well-dressed black guy swung the door towards AJ and then back towards its frame a couple more times before his colleague gave him a knowing look that instantly put a stop to the monotonous ringing in AJ's ears.

"Right, good, thank you, that's better, isn't it? Now, what can I do for you gentlemen?"

The two men were extremely well-dressed in tailored trousers, Italian loafers and designer shirts, partially concealed by thin leather jackets. A tasteful amount of jewellery completed the look; silver, to match their heavy watches. The bell ringer had nothing to keep his mind occupied now, so crossed his fully extended arms in front of his body as if protecting his manhood before walking towards the counter to join his colleague, who had not yet said a word and did not look as if he were going to. He merely stared at AJ in an intimidating manner. He certainly looked like a tough guy, being well built but not ridiculously pumped up, athletic, rather, and just enough to put him a size above most. His hair was in dreads, but they were very small ones. His colleague had opted for a completely shaved head. Mr Dreads continued to stare at the shopkeeper unnervingly. Although AJ had never seen the men before, he had his suspicions as to who they were, or more importantly who they worked for, and he was not particularly in the mood to be fucked around by a couple of messenger boys.

"Mr Jenkins, please." Mr Dreads asked with surprising politeness. AJ was not surprised by the request, although a little intrigued to find out why they wanted his old man.

"That's me!" He said truthfully. The man laughed.

"No. Mr Jenkins, please," he repeated. AJ shrugged, before informing him that the man they wanted was not in today. It was Saturday, and he didn't do weekends.

"He has left something for me?" Mr Dreads asked with in an exaggerated Jamaican accent.

"Not that I know of, what did you order?" AJ enquired innocently. He thought he had worked out what was happening here. His stepfather had seemed a bit flush over the last few months and the answer to the mystery surrounding his sudden wealth was beginning to become clear. The visitors were Yardies, or from a similar organisation with a similar objective. *Oh no, Cunt, what have you done?* AJ silently enquired of his stepfather. There was no maybe about it; there was fucking definitely trouble ahead.

Dreads went quiet for a moment and began to look around the shop with interest as he pondered.

"He is late for payment," the gangster informed in a strong accent. Straight off the boat, AJ suspected, because that was how this organisation operated. They came in and played the game for a while until they were either, arrested, killed or deported. It made good business sense. AJ didn't feel too threatened as yet, but he could really do without this start to the day.

"What's he owe then, what's he overdue?" He asked at last, hoping it was a sum he could clear straight away, like half a monkey perhaps.

"One and a half…!" Mr Dreads informed him.

"A hundred and fifty quid…?"

The debt collector laughed.

"A hundred and fifty quid?" He repeated. "No, no, larger man. One and a half large..!"

AJ coughed as usual, but with more vigour due to the sudden surge of anxiety that rushed through his body. A dark, half-solidified, blood-contaminated lump of phlegm was propelled into his mouth, requiring urgent expulsion into the bin. One and a half grand. How the fuck did he get into this?

"What's it for? How much has he borrowed?"

The Jamaican seemed to tire of the questions. He was not here to discuss the ins and outs of his client's account.

"The money, please…" AJ was asked again. He simply could not deliver. The mood was going to turn nasty; blind Freddy could see that.

"Well, I ain't fucking got it, have I? It's my dad that owes you it anyway, not me, so you'll have to speak to him, won't you?"

Dreads went frighteningly quiet, apparently taking great interest in his surroundings as he walked around the shop. A smile lit up his menacing stare as he glanced over the rubber female department. AJ knew that the silence meant trouble. Baldy was still standing between him and the front door. He had not moved. Dreads had now started picking the odd thing up in a bid to intimidate him further, and in all fairness it was working. The Jamaican started putting the stock to the test. It started with the odd dildo being thrown across the room and into the video selection mounted on the wall. And didn't they fall? It was amazing how much devastation a dildo can cause. It said on the box that they had explosive powers, and it wasn't wrong because the videos leapt off the wall in a sort of domino effect. AJ was shocked, although unsurprised, at the sudden turn in events, especially when the silent one flicked the latch on the front door closed.

"Oi, what the fuck do you think you're doing? Fuck off!" AJ cursed automatically, the destructive over-reproduction of adrenaline beginning to poison his body and make him volatile. It was a bit like the 'Incredible Hulk', you know at the start when he starts to go green and shit, although AJ didn't suddenly look like he'd just eaten something he shouldn't have and start to rip his clothes to shreds. No, AJ showed no physical symptoms, he just got mad, real mad. Okay, everyone gets mad, it's part of life, but when your body is being completely flooded by the very substance that evolved to protect you, then, things are bound to go tits up!

Mr Dreads looked on with interest, his face showing an element of surprise as well as admiration for his client. Baldy just made his stand more pronounced, forcing his shoulders out to emphasise that he was a big man and relied on the fact to induce fear.

"Get out of my fucking shop," said AJ quietly.

Mr Dreads seemed intrigued by this order. AJ had just earned himself a Black Mamba, but fortunately it missed. The Mamba is a big rubber dick, by the way; the type of big rubber dick that you don't want hitting you in the face in any circumstances. The man who had launched the imitation penis now accepted that a confrontation was inevitable. His client was game, it seemed, and that inspired him. It made him smile. How could this thin, weak man be so foolish? The Jamaican in charge of this operation, sent another missile flying across the room. It caught AJ on the side of the head. Fortunately it was only a butt-plug, therefore not too heavy, although the box did have sharp edges. The man in charge walked towards his client with a menacing look on his face.

AJ was beginning to feel sick as the two different poisons in his body began to mix. The heroin had only a mild effect now as the adrenaline took over. Clearing his throat, he reached under the counter and groped wildly for his insurance policy, but fuck! It was not there. *Fucking piss-head old twat!* AJ swore to himself. It was there yesterday, and his business partner was definitely not playing rounder's today. Okay, he was going to have to deal with this the old-fashioned way, in accordance with the old adage that attack was the best form of defence. With surprisingly few cracks showing in his confidence, AJ squared up to his opponents. One on one, AJ was confident that he could have taken the Jamaican but they came in pairs for a reason. The pleasantries were now well and truly shelved as they set about their work.

Reaching into the back of his trousers under his coat, Mr Dreads removed a small baton which, when flicked, extended itself to three times its original length.

"Shit!" Was about all AJ had to say. The odds were suddenly stacked highly in his opponent's favour now that he was tooled-up.

"You, fucking bastards…!" AJ swore as he set to defending his territory. Dreads looked a bit shocked as their supposedly easy target turned into a fucking lunatic. Baldy was also confused, and too slow to make a move as AJ ran past him towards his target. Once he was in range, Dreads swung the baton wildly at his attacker. The tide seemed to turn as AJ charged at pace towards his target, keeping his head pulled back as far as he could while still in transit. Once within range of his opponent, he suddenly came to a halt straight in front of his victim and let his head naturally catch up with the rest of his body. There was a crack, followed by a gargling scream, and Dreads hit the floor like a heap of shit. Baldy looked gobsmacked as his colleague writhed on the floor in pain, his nose not just broken but smashed to fuck. The man in charge had made a number of critical errors so far. Firstly, he had underestimated his opposition, always a bad thing to do. Secondly, he had trained his colleague, who was pretty much brain-dead, only to attack on his command because he liked to play the big man and do the bullying himself. Baldy was basically just a meat-head who was lost without leadership. Finally, Dreads had bought into the shop a frighteningly dangerous weapon that was now in the hands of the enemy.

AJ had so much poison shooting through his veins at that moment that he was dangerous, fucking lethal, in fact! The trouble with an excessive supply of adrenaline is that it stops you from thinking straight, so smashing a confiscated baton down repeatedly on your victim's head might seem like the right thing to do. The frenzied attack was getting out of hand as blood spattered everywhere. Every strike of the baton created a backwash of red liquid that covered everything in sight. The Chinese vibrating doll looked as though she'd been macheted as the blood splattered on the plastic wrapper that covered her and her friends; the naughty nurse and the policewoman, who now looked as though they had their work cut out.

Baldy had also made a critical error: he had locked the front door when he thought that the odds were stacked in their favour. He watched now as AJ beat the corpse that lay before him without mercy or remorse until he was confident that there was no life left in the body. It was becoming clear to Baldy that they had been handed a bum deal when they were assigned this mission. This skinny little white feller was not your average punter; he was completely out of his fucking tree! As AJ stood up from his murderous crouching position, he seemed to have the look of a madman in his eyes. Saliva dripped from his mouth, mixing indiscriminately with his own blood and that of his victim.

AJ knew his only chance of survival was to get rid of the evidence and move on. Move on where, though? He didn't yet know, but his poisoned mind told him that he had limited options and the only viable one at this moment was to clear up this mess one way or another.

"You, take your friend out the back!" AJ ordered abruptly.

Automatically responding to a direct order despite the change in leadership, Baldy lifted the disfigured corpse by the legs and began to drag it, leaving a thick red line of blood behind it. It was surprising how much damage could be caused by a cosh.

"Take him out the back!" AJ ordered again. His face wore a look of shock as he saw the shattered skull that he himself had just caved in. The bald man dragged the body anti-clockwise around the main central display towards the counter before careful manoeuvring it into the back room, just to the left of the main door and counter. The beaten corpse made a sickening thud as it was dragged down the single step into the rear of the building. AJ followed into the back room, cautiously checking that the front door was definitely locked first. He closed the door behind him and stared at the dead man. Baldy looked at his new boss enquiringly.

"What?" AJ asked, although it was pretty clear what was being asked of him.

The back room was a bit of a shit-hole: no natural light; no windows; a sort of toilet cubical and washroom in amongst boxes of sex aids that weren't really selling. AJ popped out here occasionally for a cup of coffee although the doctors had told him he shouldn't drink coffee because it would make him sicker.

"Do what I say and you'll walk away from this, don't, and you'll go out with your brother!" AJ promised. Well actually, Baldy was going out with his brother whatever the outcome, but AJ needed his help again first.

AJ walked over to a cupboard below a coffee-stained work surface and sifted around in it until he found what he was looking for: a pair of pliers and a six-inch screwdriver. His assistant seemed confused, especially when the pliers were tossed across the room to land at his feet.

"Pick them up!" AJ ordered as he slid the screwdriver into the back of his own jeans pocket, only now realising just how blood-soaked his own clothes actually were. Baldy hesitated momentarily, then reluctantly obeyed and picked up the pliers. Suspect market equipment, cheap without a doubt!

"Good, now I want you to do something for me," AJ continued. "First I want you to remove all his jewellery, his wallet, and any other identification. Then I want you to remove his teeth, all of them."

Baldy's jaw dropped. He was joking, right?

"I can't do that!" he started to say, before a metal baton changed his mind.

"You will do it. You'll do what I fucking well say, or I'll be removing your teeth next!" AJ corrected him. This was easy.

Slightly dazed by the metal that had just struck the top of his head, Baldy set about his task. Rifling through his former employer's pockets, AJ's new recruit bore him gifts. A mobile phone, a couple of silver rings, a chain, a wallet and a envelope packed with the spoils of their last three customer liaison sessions. AJ received the offerings with bloody hands and a smile.

"Three and a half large…!" Baldy hastened to share the information with his new boss.

Right, just the teeth then. The front ones seemed a logical place to start, but they seemed to shatter too easily so he began with the thicker, stronger-looking molars instead to practice his technique. With a crack and a look of disgust on Baldy's face, the first one was removed.

"In there!" AJ ordered, dropping a plastic bag onto the floor next to his colleague. "Come on, hurry up," he instructed. If he only managed to pull out one tooth every couple of minutes this was going to be a lengthy task. "Come on, you cunt, wrench them out. They're only teeth, they won't bite!"

AJ cleared his throat and spat the contents onto the corpse, just as a mark of respect. He had started to shake. The poison in his body was no longer as strong as it had been but it was still keeping him active. He would have to rest soon, calm down and come back to reality, and he would, just as soon as he had taken care of his visitors.

"Look, stamp on the fuckers!" He suggested, bringing his foot down hard on the dead man's mouth. There was a sickening crunch as the hard-soled shoe made contact with the gum tissue and enamel. The teeth began to crack and become wobbly, all nicely pushed back into the mouth enough to allow for easy removal.

"It don't matter if you leave bits in, just as long as all the crowns are snapped off." No one could identify you by the roots of your teeth, could they?

As Baldy tugged hard on the final tooth, he was sure the body twitched. With a nervous cough and a look of horror on his face, he stepped back from the corpse. It was probably just the nerves twitching, weren't it? But whatever the reason, it caused him to cough up a mouthful of vomit.

"You dirty bastard!" AJ joked as he crouched down by the body and watched bile drip from the corner of Baldy's dark-skinned mouth. He made a sickening noise as he cleared his pain-riddled throat and rotten lungs of the fluids that restricted his breathing and emptied the contents of his mouth onto the dead man. AJ laughed as he stood up again.

"Beat that fucker!" he challenged, while Baldy stared in disbelief at the filthy mess splattered across the dead man's blood-soaked clothing.

"What's your name?" AJ asked his crouching helper. He was not really interested, but was ready to move on to phase two.

"George," the man replied, with hope in his voice.

"Well George, we're going to have to dispose of your friend there now and I'm gonna need your help to do that. But first, I think it would be wise for you to take your clothes off. No no, George, you got me all wrong," he added, seeing the look of shock on the man's face. "What I meant was, how are you going to walk away from this if you're covered head to toe in claret?"

George began to remove his jacket and shirt before something occurred to him.

"Hang on though, what about you? You covered in blood, ain't you? What about you?" he asked.

"Look behind me, George," AJ requested.

George did: a sink, a cupboard and a load of old crap basically. George looked confused.

"The cupboard, George. I've got a whistle in there for when customers and shit come around, innit!"

"A whistle?" asked George with caution.

"Suit, you twat. Whistle and fucking flute! Forget it; I've got a suit in the cupboard, okay? A fucking suit! Now forget taking your clothes off. If you want to look like you've been gang raped by a pack of virgins then that's up to you, but I personally want to clear this mess up, and quick!"

AJ had played his cards right and George removed his shoes, socks and trousers, folding the clothes up as if expecting to wear them again.

"Right George, let's get to work. We need to get our mate's clobber off, don't we?"

George looked blank.

"Clothes, George, get his fucking clothes off. We need to get rid of them!" George understood now. Clobber! Right, off with the clobber it was then. George went down on one knee in the pool of blood and started to disrobe his former employee. AJ watched on while his hand crept around his back and into the back pocket of his jeans. The screwdriver was located and gripped.

"That's right, George. Get them off mate, because we've got to clear away the evidence or its curtains for us. The end, George, the end…!"

George laughed: his new boss spoke in funny riddles. Curtains…? How did they ever come up with that one? Unfortunately for George, he didn't get much of a chance to ponder on it because, as his new buddy had just said, this was the end. With the handle of the screwdriver switched from the retrieval grip to one suitable for stabbing, AJ went into battle. The element of surprise won the fight: cowardly, but nevertheless effective.

The screwdriver entered George's right ear as if it were cutting through butter. There was a bit of resistance on the skull, but pretty soon the handle met the side of the screaming victim's ear. And scream he did, although no one could hear him because AJ had taken the precaution of sticking his hand over George's mouth just before the screwdriver broke the skin.

You sometimes hear about people getting things stuck in their brains yet still remaining alive, and George was not going to sleep as easily as one might have expected. AJ pulled the screwdriver out of his victim's skull and took aim for another strike elsewhere in the body. Claret? Fuck me, yes! You've probably never seen anything like it. Thankfully, after a couple more stabs, in the heart, hopefully, but more likely the lungs, there was silence and George no longer resisted.

Two dead men lying together on the floor; one with his face caved in, the other with his brains peering out through a head wound and blood seeping out from a broken heart. Fuck, how did it come to this? AJ didn't know really; he had just been pushed too far. Never mind, though, because there was a way out of this for him with the help of a little role playing. The debt collector without teeth was going to play the part of AJ. He was going to be left on the floor as he was, but with his hands tied behind his back. Beside him would lie George. This scene would hopefully create the impression that AJ had been the victim of an attack, especially as a fire would take care of the problem of skin colour.

Okay, simple. AJ used a bit of cord to tie Dreads' hands behind his back and George was laid next to him with the metal cosh placed strategically in his hand for full effect. AJ stripped his own clothes off, which was a pleasure because the once-warm fluid that stained them had now become cold and uncomfortable. Okay, Baldy was a few sizes too big for our skinny hero, but in this world beggars can't be choosers! The clothes didn't look too bad, well, not bad enough to make Londoners bat an eyelid, anyway. AJ cleaned the odd spillage off the clothing and searched the pockets, finding a wallet and another phone. Terrific, there's never one around when you need one and then when you don't need one, you've got two! He chucked Dreads' phone onto the floor. Baldy's was better, it was a better colour and a bit slimmer. Dressed in clean clothes, AJ looked presentable once again as he studied the shop that had been his money-maker for more years than he cared to remember. It had to go, though, and it was going now!

Right then, what did he have at his disposal that was capable of creating the final scene of this little production? Gas and candles - what more do you need? The candles were ideal: they would be used as a timer and the gas would be the incendiary device. It was simple, the gas was piped to the central heating boiler which heated the whole shop. AJ studied the appliance, being somewhat ignorant in such matters. He was just going to have to break the pipework, but first he had to set the detonator. Candles in hand, he made his way to the main shop and calmly lit one of them, watching with interest as the substance became hot, melted and dripped onto the floor. He seemed almost mesmerised by the flame and dripping wax but snapped out of it once there was enough hot wax on the tiled floor to enable the candle to be glued to it. The other candles were dealt with in the same way until there was a circle of them like wax monoliths, waiting to fuel devastation.

AJ left the candles burning while he ventured back into the store room. A moment later, he came back into the shop with a look of excitement on his face. Behind him he had left the sound of hissing gas, having fractured a pipe on the central heating boiler. The fuse had now effectively been lit and it was time to leave the scene. The arsonist looked around the shop one last time before he unfastened the heavy metal door; pausing for a few seconds to take one last mental photo.

"Good riddance!" Anthony Jenkins rejoiced before leaving the shop, closing the door behind him for the very last time.

London was busy; but AJ cared not that in a matter of minutes the winners of his personal lottery would be announced. Those bouncing little balls were all floating around in the air at the moment, waiting for those unlucky winners' numbers to come up. Who would it be, then? The train-spotter with the anorak? The poverty stricken mother and her two children? The Asian fellow, traditionally dressed? The Turk? The fuck knows what? AJ was not prejudiced about who would perish in his quest for vengeance; they would all be welcome if it were up to him. Not long now, just seconds away from the final draw. AJ crossed the road, trying not to look too conspicuous in his oversized clothes. He needed a podium from which to watch his handiwork, and the pub over the road seemed the ideal place. The plan was to enter the pub, buy a pint and then sit at the front of the drinking establishment on a bar stool to view the explosion. Unfortunately this was not to be, because the fuse was not long enough to allow for such luxuries. Arthur picked the winners just as AJ reached out to open the pub door and London lit up like a fire cracker as the winning numbers were drawn.

AJ actually felt the blast push him forward with a force that was phenomenal, considering he was 70 metres or more away from it. The blast helped him through the door of the rather rugged drinking establishment, where AJ was sheltered by the untouched glass windows behind which he was now able to stand and watch. Thankfully the screams of terror and the smell of burning flesh remained at a safe distance behind the toughened glass. Shocked? Yes, AJ was shocked as he cleared his throat and swallowed. The numbers had been drawn and were being announced. The papers would soon write about the number of innocent people who had been killed, but then to AJ, no one was innocent any more. Anyone and everyone who got in his way were guilty because they were society, they had created this monster, and so here he was.

AJ took a seat on a bar stool, the comments from the people around him bringing a smile to his face. He was happy with his secret. No one recognised him because this pub was frequented by drunks and social misfits and it was early in the day. So AJ just watched the havoc he had wrought on his own doorstep, concentrating first on a bleeding mother who was searching for her missing child. Obviously suffering from severe shock, she stumbled backwards into an Asian gentleman, turban half unwrapped, who was searching for his glasses. Had he not realised that he had no fingers left on the hand which he was using to feel around for them? Probably not with shock affecting his ability to think rationally. Behind the couple at the front of the stage, a motorcyclist searched for a way out of the rubble, having somehow survived part of a shop falling on him. A noise diverted AJ's attention to a man crying with despair as his partner of the same gender lay helpless in the street.

"Fuck 'em!" the killer cursed. "Fuck 'em all!"

The scene never became boring in the whole ten minutes or so that AJ watched. He was thirsty, so got a pint to keep him company. He was not generally a drinker, as his illness made it difficult for him to tolerate alcohol, but in moderation it calmed his nerves and right now they needed calming. He gave a nervous grunt, which released a deposit of mucus from the back of his throat. He allowed it to slide down his gullet with a smile. It wasn't so bad, you tended to get used to the flavour of your body rotting away from the inside after a while. He carried his pint to the front of the pub with shaking hands and wobbly legs, spilling some as he went.

The pub was a shit hole: pool table; fruit machine; an assortment of tables with an assortment of chairs, none of which matched each other. Whatever, it sold alcohol, and what more did the hardened drinker require? This was an establishment catering specifically for those special cases, except for AJ's father, that is, because he had got credit problems here.

AJ took his rightful place, front stage, and watched as the fire brigade turned up at last. Just in time, it seemed, because the hairdressers' shop next door to AJ's was steadily burning away. The police had been a lot quicker in responding, but they were only around the corner. The boys in blue kept people back, presumably in case the nutter responsible for this disaster had any further devices waiting to go off. That's what AJ would have done anyway; wait for the emergency services to turn up to deal with this little drama, only to have another explosion take care of the helpers.

The police were mainly uniformed, although a couple of suits assisted them until CID arrived on the scene. Cunts In Disguise, AJ liked to call them. Only now did it dawn on him that these men would soon be hunting him if his plan failed, but hopefully it would be hailed as a gangland killing. Baldy would almost certainly have form, he was too thick not to have, so his dental records would link him to a gang, and there you have it. But even if they did see through his plan they would never take him alive. And if they did, well, at least he would get to see a doctor!

The pint tasted good as AJ studied the scene of carnage, hugging his secret knowledge. It looked like four dead, well, four pretty fucked up at the very least from where the bomber was sitting. One was a child, but he felt no remorse. The enemy was the enemy, men, women and children as far as AJ was concerned. The paramedics cleansed the rubble of flesh while the fireman dealt with the flames and the police took a closer look at what lay before them. One detective peered into the open front shell of what used to be AJ's shop, then retreated with a handkerchief covering his face. He was accompanied by a fire-fighter with an air of seniority about him. It looked like they'd found AJ's mates: Barbecued Baldy and Char-Grilled Dreads! AJ watched the scene with interest, although occasionally his thoughts drifted away to lunch because he was hungry, or rather his lungs were hungry for their medicine.

Somebody of obvious importance had now arrived on the scene, looking not at all fazed as he led a party into the building to carry out an examination. He was quite a big man but his features were delicately chiselled, indicating to AJ that his size was manufactured rather than natural. The man had shortish dark cropped hair, a messy crop, though, a bit of an indie thing. He wore dark trousers and a knee length coat. Wearing his serious face, the top cop removed his coat and handed it to the fireman, who said nothing as a well-toned set of biceps flexed in front of him, poking out of a tight black T-shirt. He wore a lot of jewellery for a copper: rings; a chain; all silver. Both his arms were decorated with body art from the elbow joints up in an intricate design that looked like some kind of tribal markings. The detective looked well hip: a cop with attitude. AJ wasn't sure that they really existed. He admired this man and felt drawn to him.

"Come on!" AJ lip-read what the guy was saying to the uniformed police officer. He ordered the back-up to man the front line, on strict instructions to let no-one else into the wreck without authorisation. Fireman Sam received one more glare from the opposition before the man in charge led the uniforms into the burnt out shell of AJ's shop. The scene became quite boring from then on: bag 'em and tag 'em, so that you can burn 'em and urn 'em! The copper in black looked familiar to AJ, who spent the next five minutes trying to think where he had seen him before.

William Tap was the man in black. Known as Billy out of uniform, or Tapped to his friends, who were few and far between. Billy Tapped; it spoke for itself really! Although not technically the top dog, he was quite high up the ladder but still had a small way to go before he made chief. He was certainly leading this little mission, though, there was no doubt about that! Less than half an hour before, Billy had been in the office listening to a police broadcast about the explosion when he was informed that the fire brigade had found a couple of crispies on the scene. So, here he was, Detective Sergeant Tap! Crude, ill-mannered and easily irritated, William had been in the force for seven years or so now. Unpopular as he was, he got results. Billy hated the system; he hated the way people who he had painstakingly chased and arrested just simply walked from justice due to a piss-poor system. So, to counter the courts and the do-gooders he made sure that anyone he arrested didn't walk. Of course, senior officers were well aware of his crude methods of policing but they turned a blind eye because William always got his man, and got the right man as well.

Tap had been in the army for a spell before joining the police, and had reached his goal of making it into the SAS. He was one of the youngest blokes ever to have done it, and some say the fucking meanest. Now, these SAS fellers don't say a lot about the shit they do and they never disclose details about their colleagues to anyone, but some of Tap's comrades had broken their silence since his departure from their unit because this bloke weren't for fucking real! Okay, hypothetically speaking, they're at a job, a relatively easy hostage situation in, say, Africa. There are some rebel characters playing up and they've got hostages and all that palaver, so their government buys the services of the SAS. The boys go in, do their dirty work and then the clear-up process takes place afterwards. Certain findings are made, and there are bodies with multiple stab wounds or fifty plus rounds in what's left of them. The SAS had a rogue amongst them, although they had trained him and he did the job better than most. The trouble was, he liked the job too much. In fact he was a fucking liability and people were starting to ask questions. Of course, he had been disciplined for his behaviour on many occasions, but time and again his colleagues would find him ripping the guts out of the enemy with the aid of a sharp knife and his fingers.

Anyway, Tap was forced to seek medical help after he went paranoid on his last job, having convinced himself that his colleagues had been instructed to take him out of the equation. According to his mental health evaluation he was just a cocaine addict, nothing more. They all liked a little toot now and then but, things had got just a little out of hand for the golden boy of the brigade. So Tap was out of the elite force and off to drug rehabilitation. Afterwards, the police welcomed him with open arms; dishonourable discharge or not, he was clean now as far as his habit was concerned and he had the paperwork to prove it. It didn't take long for Tap to work his magic once he was on Civvy Street. Of course, he didn't have to go in as a monkey; he went straight into the gorilla cage, CID and from then on he never looked back. It was a fucking brilliant life for him, almost like the army, and once he had reached a high enough position they gave him a gun and a licence to kill! As far as the scars on his arms were concerned, those were the results of his having removed the tattoos indicating his membership of the SAS. Apparently he cut them off with a knife, but there was one on his back as well and there were various rumours about how he dealt with that one. There was a prostitute with a blow torch, a prostitute with battery acid and another with fucking sandpaper! The list was endless and just got sillier as it went on. The brake-fluid variant was Tap's particular favourite, well, it takes the paint off cars!

The actual truth was that Tap had burnt the tattoo off himself. One night, after a particularly heavy night on the old Charlie, crystallised in base form so it was Crack, if you like, Tap had burnt all his army memorabilia in his mother's garden and watched it burn until it became a bed of hot ashes. While staring at the fire, completely off his tits, Billy started coming out with this crazy-arse speech about this and that before proclaiming himself as a devotee of his creator, the absolute Judge, and all sorts of crazy shit. The way he was talking, according to the neighbours anyway, he seemed to believe that he was some kind of higher being sent by Our Lord to rid the world of fallen angels, whoever they fucking were. A bit odd, you could say, especially when he suddenly turned his back to the fire and allowed himself to fall down onto the hot coals as if he were simply falling onto his bed! No bullshit, he just fucking lay there for a few seconds before the cocaine's anaesthetic properties wore off and he tore himself off the burning embers and rolled about in the grass in agony. The next door neighbour had to put him out with a garden hose because the lunatic was actually on fire. One thing was for sure, though; and that was that Tap had managed to disfigure the symbol of allegiance to his previous employers so that it was no longer recognisable. A good while afterwards Tap had a fair amount of surgery to repair most of the damage. As for the arms, there was not a lot that could be done for them and it wasn't just down to the removal of the tattoos.

The skin on Tap's arms was disfigured with three to four inch slashes because he had had strange habit when he was in the SAS. Before a mission he used to cut himself with a knife, usually on his arms, just above the elbows, and then leave the wounds open under his uniform. Bizarre though this may seem to normal people, it made perfect sense to Tap at the time. Why did he do it? Maybe he had to feel some pain before he was able to do what he did, or perhaps he was releasing some of those demons that had overrun his body. Who knows what the madman was thinking before he did what he was trained to do? Those were dark times for Billy.

*

So, to give an example of William's unique method of policing, imagine that you do a raid on a house known to be a key point in the movement of drugs. You raid it, and catch them with twenty five grams. They'll walk because most of the gear is sold as quickly as it arrives, so there's never a main stash. What do you do to bring them to justice? Easy. When you raid them, you bung them a kilo of gear retrieved from previous raids and it's bye-bye for five years plus. The court won't chuck that fucker out, and you have your justice.

The only problem with William's tactics was that there was a risk involved as he was forced to work with low-life's to get results. They knew he was a copper and were not big fans of the police, but they respected him for his ability to switch sides as and when necessary. This made him dangerous, or useful, depending on which way you looked at it. Being dodgy, he had to mix with the underworld; the criminal fraternity, as it were. To add to all of this, Billy was bisexual and not afraid to show it. He had probably been fiddled with as a kid or something because his sexual preferences were not the norm, if there is a norm these days. Married, never. Serious relationship never had one. Let's just say he had hurt a number of people on his way through life, in more ways than one. The uniformed police officer held a handkerchief tightly to his face as they inspected the inside of the burnt out shell of the former sex shop. Lumps of dried, cooled plastic floated in a sea of dirty water. Detective Sergeant Tap's expensive loafers were ruined, much to his dismay, as he splashed around in the polluted water that surrounded the two corpses. A nice job! Tap had to commend the work of their killer. Yes, killer. There was no pulling the wool over these eyes; this was murder! Establishing who they were would be the hard part of this detective work. With the old choppers missing, the identification of one of the gruesome twosome would probably never be formally proved. To find out who the other was would take a pathologist. One had to sit back; sit back and wait for the clues to emerge. Later, though. It was lunch time now and Tap had a few errands to run.

"Fuck!" AJ swore to himself. It had only just dawned on him that he had probably burnt his pipe in the blaze. Bastard; he wished he had remembered the pipe. What the fuck was he going to do about lunch? He studied the bar anxiously. Foil, no, nothing was made out of foil any more. Glass it was, then. AJ left his position at the front of the stage in favour of the pub lavatory. It was, as expected, as shit hole, filthy, with a stench of piss that burned the back of his throat. AJ felt no remorse as he urinated on the floor instead of in the urinal. If they cleaned the fucker, he would be more than happy to piss in it. As the fluid drained from his body, creating steam as it hit the milky substance beneath the urinal, he spat out the residue of disease from the back of his throat and into the porcelain in front of him.

The room was lit by a solitary, standard household light bulb, so AJ stole it. Fully clothed, he sat on the toilet seat lid and carefully twisted the metal element off the end of the bulb. You had to be gentle; twist it backwards and forwards quite a few times and it works loose in the end; rush it, and you'd better make sure that there's some bog-roll handy! This one was easy; piece of piss to remove. Once the cap was off, AJ tipped the bulb back up the right way, and there we have it, a new pipe! A makeshift packet filled with powder was soon located and the contents tipped into the light bulb. Lighter at the ready, fingers strategically placed, AJ heated the powder until it vaporised as required. With his mouth placed over the end of the smoking device, AJ inhaled the vapours that rose from the glass cauldron and once again everything became better; everything made sense.

AJ left the toilet as if in slow motion. Everyone was staring at him. The whole room watched him leave the toilet, steadied by a hand against the wall. They all knew what he had been doing. Didn't they? Did they fuck; one too many at thirteen hundred hours was perfectly normal for a Saturday - as long as you didn't piss on the floor and steal the light bulbs, that is! AJ could feel the warm glass in his pocket. The bulb was worth holding onto for possible future use. Thankfully no one had stolen AJ's front row seat, because he needed it. His drink, rapidly warming in a pint glass, did not seem so appealing any more as he stared out of the window.

Nothing much happened for a while. DS Tap picked up his coat, which someone had hung on the fire engine's wing mirror, the bastard! He stood staring towards the pub and then allowed his gaze to drift slowly back towards the wreckage. What he was looking for he had no idea, but the act gave him time to think. Eventually, he spoke to the plain-clothes officer next to him.

"Door to door, both sides of the street. Find out who owns that shop, who rents it, who works there, who shops there? Get a match on the stiff with teeth and don't spare the horses on this one, Slug. This fucking stinks; stinks to high heaven. Hurry up, all right? I'll be back in the office in a couple of hours. Things to do, people to see!" His right-hand man knew better than to argue.

The plan up to now was running smoothly; the basic ingredients had been added and things were beginning to take shape. Some props were required for stage two, but where the fuck AJ was going to get them from at such short notice he had no idea. Guns, I'm talking about; AJ could get one easily enough under normal circumstances, but now, being marked and pretty soon to be at the very least wanted for questioning, he was not going to be able to knock up the kind of friends that could deliver such special orders. Saying that, though AJ had made some new friends lately. They were dead now, but perhaps they could still be of help. AJ still had Baldy's phone. Baldy and Dreads had been dodgy geezers; surely they must be able to get hold of shooters. There was only one way to find out, so he checked out the address book in the phone. Lenny, Babs, Mr K, Baby C, Tyrone, who the fuck, were these people? AJ had no idea, but Tyrone sounded safe. It was time to give our old friend Tyrone a call, just for old times' sake. What was Baldy's real name again? Oh yeah, George. AJ and George go way back. No conversation would take place on this mobile though, because AJ was going to have to act as though he had been given the number by George as a kind of recommendation. So, the pay phone it was rather than risking George's name coming up on Tyrone's display and giving the game away.

AJ left the safety of the pub to use the phone box outside, away from prying ears. It was down the alley along the side of the pub. It was mind-blowing trying to get the number to come up on the screen of the mobile phone without it ringing the chosen digits, but with patience AJ finally beat the system. Twenty pence a call, fuck me, it had doubled since AJ had last used a public phone. No wonder people were always ripping them off; they must be more lucrative than a bank on a good day! AJ rang the number before letting the twenty pence drop into the machine and then fourteen rings before someone finally answered. Tyrone?

"Waasssuppp!" Someone asked down the phone in a funny accent.

"Tyrone?" AJ asked, causing everything to become silent for a matter of seconds.

"Who dis?" A heavy accent enquired suspiciously.

"You don't know me. I'm a mate of George's," the impostor replied. "You may be able to help me with a little something?"

Silence reigned once again. People often rang him out of the blue, but not a white boy!

"And how do ya know my man 'G'?" The phone quizzed.

"Habits my friend habits. Now, this, 20 pence ain't gonna last forever, so can you fucking help me or what?" AJ's patience was by now beginning to wear thin as the silence crept in again.

"Well what do you want then, tools?"

AJ concurred. Heavy tools, to be precise!

Tyrone was cautious; he had to be in his line of business and to be honest this prospective customer had not yet won him over. It was the white thing that threw a spanner in the works.

"And where is George then, is he with you?"

Fuck no, he's more like with God, AJ joked to himself, although this was no joking matter; some serious bullshit was required.

"Nah man, he's in fucking hospital, ain't he?" Shit, well what else could AJ say? Tyrone was surprised, he hadn't seen George for over a week but news of a brother in trouble soon gets round.

"You what, he's in hospital? Why?"

"Well, he's sick, man. He collapsed with something the other day and was rushed to hospital straight away. He's got a bit of a fever sort of thing; his whole body's burning up. He's in a right two and eight apparently. I went to score off him the day before and he didn't look too clever, but I had no idea that this shit was coming."

"Okay, look, your number is coming up withheld. Give me it and I'll call you straight back, all right?" It sounded good to AJ.

"Okay 0208 521 4522. I'm waiting, but I haven't got all day. I need my goods and I need them sharpish." The phone went dead way before he had finished his commands; he just had to wait now. He stayed in the phone box because the last thing he wanted was someone who recognised him coming up and reminding him that the shop which had just blown up over the road was actually his. There was silence until a tune played from AJ's, or rather George's pocket.

"Shit, who the fucks that?" AJ swore as he frantically searched through the pockets. "Ah bollocks…!" That was the light bulb cutting his fingers. Other pocket, that's the one. With bleeding fingers held out of the way, AJ read the phone display. Fuck, it was Tyrone! Okay. He pressed the green button and spoke into the plastic miracle in his best Asian accent, which in fact made him sound like he was from Manchester, but that was all he had. Tyrone's voice asked for a Mr Belazaire.

"Hello there, I'm afraid your friend is unavailable, sir. He is in ward fifteen and this phone cannot be used in the wards because it causes interference with the equipment. Can I take a message and I will be glad to pass it on as soon as he awakens?" AJ shook his head in despair. He knew his Indian impression was shit, but at least his story was plausible, just! Hopefully Tyrone was as thick as his friend.

"What's wrong with him, then?" Tyrone asked.

AJ flicked droplets of blood from his lacerated hand onto the plastic window.

"Sickle-cell is a possibility but we are not one hundred per cent sure yet. The doctors are still doing tests."

Tyrone ended the call and AJ switched off the mobile, waiting for the public phone to ring. It didn't take long.

"Okay, what do you want?"

"Nothing too heavy, something you can hold with one hand." AJ pretended he knew what he was taking about. There was silence from the arms dealer as he assessed just how big a Muppet had been cast in his path. Fucking hold with one hand! What was he expecting, a tank?

"Okay, nothing too heavy, fine. Yeah, I can help you. It's a bit of an old dog but it serves its purpose if you're only going to wave it around and that."

"Does it kill?" AJ asked bluntly, having no time to play games.

Tyrone chuckled and explained that, yes, indeed it did kill. 'Course it did, it was a fucking gun; but he felt compelled to remind his customer that it was the finger on the trigger rather than the gun itself that committed the act. They got round to discussing the price.

"Name it" AJ challenged, conscious of the three large in his pocket.

"A grand…!" Tyrone replied firmly, as if bracing himself for ridicule, and was surprised when AJ simply agreed. Easy work as far as Tyrone was concerned distracted by the smell of easy money.

"Where then…?"

"The back of Lady Compton's, one-thirty?" AJ suggested, causing Tyrone to chuckle again, but agree nevertheless. Okay, Lady Compton's it was, one-thirty, and the phone went dead. Cunt, AJ labelled his new friend. Cunt was the only way to describe him. Until one-thirty!

AJ returned to the pub. Nothing had changed; the sorry old crew who had inhabited the pub earlier were still there, as well as some new faces that posed no real threat. *It was fucking incredible!* AJ grumbled to himself as he bought another pint from the barmaid, before cautiously carrying his beer back to the pub window, reprising the front row seat that he had given up in order to move his plans on. One-thirty was just around the corner.

The clock on George's phone moved on slowly. AJ studied the two cuts on his hand; they had started to heal a bit now, or rather they had stopped bleeding now that they had had chance. Now that there was time for thought, AJ thought about Haley. It would be a surprise for her when he went to get her later, to break her free, because usually he never saw her on a Saturday afternoon; normally he had to work and wait until he could sneak into the ward at night before he could see his loved one. How surprised she would be to see him.

Chapter Two

Meet Billy

Time soon became of the essence; he needed to get out. There were two options: walk out the front door, around the side and up the alley or use the fire escape at the back, next to the toilets. AJ had seen it when he was eating his lunch earlier on and it looked like a viable option. He made his way to the lavatory, slipped out of the back door and into the alley. There was nothing there but a few wheelie bins, a silver BMW and the stink of shit, courtesy of blocked drains and a general lack of maintenance. Oh London, you can't help but love it! A number of back entrances were linked together by this rather small access. No one was about, even though they should be. AJ cleared his throat in anticipation and sat down on a metal construction designed to foil ram-raiders. It was not comfortable, but the wait was not long because Tyrone was already there; you just couldn't see him.

The noise of a whirring motor filled the air and AJ caught sight of a prestigious sports car, the driver's side window of which was being wound down. At first it looked like there was no one in the car, but then Tyrone's head appeared cautiously. He had been keeping a low profile.

"Hi!" He said, watching his client walk over. AJ nodded by way of greeting and the two shook hands. As he released AJ's grasp, Tyrone opened the door and climbed out of the plush silver sports car. Whoever said crime didn't pay was wrong; Tyrone looked the part in leather trousers, boots and a black shirt. He was also liberally adorned with gold, including half his teeth.

"Well, you got it?" The buyer asked.

"'Course I's fucking got it. What do ya think I is, on a picnic?" Tyrone was about as Jamaican as he was tea-around-the-lake, but he persisted with the fake accent nonetheless, presumably for the good of his image. Whatever though, as long as he had the goods! Tyrone got back into his car, signalling to his guest to do the same with a single quick nod of the head. AJ obeyed: leather seats, nice! Before long the powerful engine roared with bags of low end grunt, or a rotten exhaust sang out of tune until I.C.E showed it who was boss with a pounding of drum and base. The music blared out from within the car as it reversed back onto the main road at pace before speeding off. Tyrone seemed unaffected by the noise, which resembled a mobile disco, as he studied the rear view mirror for signs of pursuit. All was clear, though. It looked like AJ was genuine, but one had to be sure. AJ asked where they were going.

"Nowhere!" Came the brief reply as the vehicle pulled up outside a music shop, the noise now turned down to a sensible level. From the shop emerged a youth of similar age and dress as the driver, just a different colour. He was carrying what looked like a record case, which was deposited in the boot of the car. No words were exchanged, and Tyrone started the engine again and drove off at a sensible pace to avoid drawing attention. They continued for about ten minutes up this road, down that one, across roundabouts, through traffic lights. AJ was glad that he hadn't needed a car up to now. He could drive, but preferred to take his chances on the trains instead.

So where were they now, then? Not too far away, just another dirty back-street alley, but this time below a set of flats rather than businesses. The flats looked in pretty good nick, but they were up for renovation according to the huge billboard attached to them. The smell of the Thames was in the air. The advertisement showed a picture of the buildings in their future glory, overlooking the Thames. The flats were boarded up for their own protection pending their renovation.

AJ would have liked a flat like one of these under different circumstances, but he was aware that a padded cell or wooden box, were about as good as it was going to get from now on. It could have been different with better health and a bit of help; he could have made something of himself. Okay, he wasn't the most academic guy in the world, but this was basically due to a lack of enthusiasm and hope at school rather than a lack of intelligence. What he did have, though – a gift of nature that could not be learned - was common sense. He was sharp, a decision maker.

Tyrone continued to drive through a maze of alleys until the car pulled up in a courtyard set in the middle of the flats. Only now did it become evident that the flats were built in a kind of circle, surrounding what would once have been fountains, paths and gardens consisting of borders and small lawns. There was fuck all there now, though, dry mud with man-made intrusions such as bricks and concrete all flattened down tightly as a base for future projects. Someone had been kind enough to rip off the recently-fitted, but totally inadequate, security fence and gate, leaving it lying on the ground.

"Show time…!" Tyrone bragged as he got out of the car, indicating with a slight head movement that AJ was to follow. AJ opened the door, coughed and spat. Before climbing out, however, he hesitated and pressed a button on the glove box that allowed a huge portion of the dash to swing upwards before his curious gaze. He sneaked a look back; Tyrone was opening the boot and fiddling around inside it. Turning back to the glove box, he found a pair of leather gloves, tissues, CD boxes, and then an object that almost caused his eyes to pop out of his head. *That's the one! That fucker will do nicely, Tyrone my son!*

AJ took his prize from the treasure chest and slid it into his jacket, fumbling slightly until the heavy metal object slipped nicely into the inside pocket on the left side of the jacket, the one that did not contain the money. It sat there reasonably comfortably, he thought with surprise as he pushed opened the car door that had fallen shut again.

"I need a piss!" AJ lied, not waiting for an answer as he walked towards the nearest wall twenty metres or so away, coughing wildly to expel the latest obstruction clogging his throat.

"Nice!" Commented Tyrone sarcastically, as AJ turned his back and unzipped himself.

Forcing the fluid out of his body, AJ retrieved from his inside coat pocket the firearm that he had stolen from his new companion. Like a kid with a new toy, he fiddled with every button and switch, other than the trigger, until he found what he wanted. At the press of a small lever, the magazine containing the bullets popped out into its new owner's hand. It was quickly removed and the ammunition content assessed before the clip was refitted and ready for action. Excellent stuff - he now had the power to command!

AJ zipped himself up again and relocated the firearm in its makeshift holster, turning back towards Tyrone again to do business. Tyrone was ready; the stall was set up inside the boot of the beautiful car and it was time to shop.

"Right then, let's get on with it!" AJ suggested to his supplier, who nodded in agreement. The case inside the boot contained three guns, but they were not exactly what AJ had had in mind. The one with the brown handle was from the First World War or something, well past its sell-by date. He reminded Tyrone that he was looking for a gun that made holes in people, not a fucking antique.

"Do you think I'm fucking stupid? Do you think I'm some kind of cunt?" he asked, menacingly.

Tyrone stepped back from his suddenly unfriendly client and reassessed the situation. Clearly, he had underestimated this particular Muppet.

"So you want a fucking nice modern automatic, do yah?" The dealer asked, rapidly switching to Plan B. Tyrone was not used to dealing with people who actually wanted to use his supplies for their designated purpose, usually they just wanted to frighten someone, take a post office or simply show off, the weapons were not really reliable enough to use in the field. As his client had quite rightly stated, they were antiques, wall hangers, or heaps of shit. Never mind, Tyrone did have what his client wanted inside the car, although there was no way that he was going to part with it, not to this madman. No, it was simple: get his personal weapon from the glove box as though he intended to trade it, wave it about a bit and then take off into the sunset leaving his unsatisfied, brain-fried client eating the dust created from a fast getaway.

"You want a nice shooter? Then a nice shooter you will have, my friend. Sorry to piss you off and all that, but you hadn't made it clear that you wanted a professional weapon. Take a look at this, brother. This is the bad boy that I think you require." Tyrone went to retrieve his piece from the glove box, leaning across from the driver's side to do so as he was not keen to cross into his customer's territory. AJ may have been small, but his sudden mood change and quiet stare, the muscles taut in his face, were enough to unnerve anyone.

Realising that he was beaten when his groping hands found nothing, Tyrone climbed out of the car again and leaned against the open door for support. For some reason he was laughing, an annoying giggle that rose from a combination of nerves and stupidity. He had made an oversight; a fucking huge one. Tyrone held his hands up playfully, as though the whole business was just a joke.

"Okay, you already got it, yeah?"

"Yep, I already got it!"

"Oh man, you got me there! You're a tricky sort of feller, you are. Oh well, you got the goods. Just pay me and I'll be on my way." Tyrone now dropped his hands nervously. His survival was in the hands of this grinning madman.

"How much do you want for it?" AJ asked as he removed the silver object from inside his jacket, holding it high in the air for the loser to see. Tyrone knew that this Muppet was going to take the weapon whatever, but he still had some pride to uphold.

"Well, we said a grand didn't we?" A grand was a good price; that was a proper shooter. AJ had to agree; it was indeed. Waving his new toy, AJ signalled to Tyrone to sit down on the ground some distance away. Tyrone obeyed, sitting uncomfortably on the ground like a scolded school child.

"Okay Tyrone, a grand it is, but I feel as one of your loyal customers I should at least get a bit of background knowledge on the weapon that I'm buying. What is it?"

Tyrone was pretty certain that this white boy knew exactly what he was holding. What was he - police, ex-army? Fuck knows, but he wasn't just an ordinary bloke. Whoever he was, he didn't look well. He had a cold or something as far as Tyrone could make out; in fact he looked extremely ill for someone of his age and the shit that he kept coughing up and firing into the wind was a definite cause for concern.

"What is it?" AJ asked again.

"Look on the side, man. See those letters? BDA-380. That's a fucking Browning, man, that's what it is. A lovely piece, worth well over a grand, so just pay me and then I can fuck off and you can do whatever it is you want to do. You're happy, I'm happy, we're all fucking happy and can you please hurry up because I can feel arse grapes growing as we speak?" Tyrone begged, causing his customer to chuckle.

"So how do you use it?" AJ enquired, coolly. Tyrone, twitching nervously, was not keen to answer.

AJ reached into the boot of the car. Two of the guns in there were revolvers, just like the cowboys had used. AJ lifted out the simpler-looking of the two. He could see straight away that it was loaded with six bullets; six rounds of destruction.

"Webley, eleven something millimetre." Tyrone offered, pre-empting the next question. AJ had not actually been going to ask, but it was nice to know anyway.

"Ah ah ah, don't fuck with that my friend," Tyrone continued. "Over eleven mill point forty five of an inch, we're talking sleeping elephants here. That's nearly a hundred years old, man, that's what you white boys used to round my brothers up with. Seriously man, if that don't blow up in your face the recoil will chuck you over that car. It's fucking noisy as well. Bad move firing that!"

AJ was impressed with Tyrone's engineering and history knowledge, delivered under pressure and thankfully without that ridiculous Jamaican accent that he now seemed to have lost. One thing was for sure though; the old fashioned weapon that he held in his hand was a killer, and by cocking the hammer the gun had now became lethal; maybe as lethal as the piece of modern technology that he held in his other hand. He put the Browning automatic back into his inside coat pocket, just for now, and kept the Webley in his right hand just in case the need arose to put Tyrone's theory to the test. The Webley seemed to have newish bullets loaded in it, however, and AJ wondered whether Tyrone was full of shit because you didn't sell guns to the likes of him only to have them blow up in the customer's face.

The next gun AJ picked up was similar to the Webley, but according to the writing on the side of the weapon this one was an Enfield. While the weapon was still concealed within the boot he fiddled with a few buttons and levers, causing the round thing holding the bullets to fall out from the side of the device, dropping the ammunition out onto the carpet of the boot before closing the barrel again. It was time for a little fun. He dropped the empty weapon back into the boot and removed the last one. He knew this one: a Luger.

"The Jerries used this one in the war, didn't they?" Anthony commented, showing that his days in front of the idiots' lantern had not been wasted while he gave the weapon his devoted attention "I suppose this blows up in your face as well, does it, and is better hanging on a wall?" AJ enquired, tucking the Luger into the waistband of his jeans.

Tyrone laughed nervously and shrugged, tiring of these games.

"It's up to you man, but I have a responsibility to warn you."

"Well, tell you what. I'll take these three for a grand, but I don't want this one. Like you said, it's getting on a bit," AJ commented, removing the Enfield from the boot as though doing his dealer some sort of favour. He tapped the Browning through the stolen coat pocket with the barrel of the antique Enfield as he suggested the deal and tossed the gun so that it landed just in front of Tyrone. Tyrone seized his chance, picked up the discarded handgun and cocked the hammer.

"Right, don't fucking move!" He ordered, climbing to his feet and pointing the weapon in his opponent's direction.

AJ laughed as the air was filled with the metallic noise of a firing hammer attacking empty chambers. Tyrone pulled the trigger again and again but the chambers were empty, their contents sitting neatly in the boot.

"What are you going to do now, Tyrone my friend? I can't believe that you were going to end our beautiful friendship," AJ asked, pausing briefly to suck the snot up from his aching lungs and expel it. He was going to have to hurry up because pain was starting to rise again within his failing body. AJ needed to medicate himself within the next five minutes or so. It was not a matter of dire urgency yet, but the games had to commence or there would be trouble.

"Well, what do you fancy then? Webley, Luger or Browning automatic. It's your execution, so it's only fair that you get to choose the bullets that are gonna end your sorry arse life. Go ahead and take your pick!" AJ ordered as Tyrone began to shuffle backwards with fear, having lowered his weapon to his side.

Tyrone was shaking with fear but believed that he still had a chance. His opponent had limited experience of the weapons in his possession: one of them would take several minutes for him to fathom out how to fire it and the other was a hard-gun, to aim with. Even experienced handlers struggled to hit their targets with the Webley because the weapon was simply too powerful and only effective at close range. So Tyrone had to open up the range. He was a fast runner and AJ did not look like he was much of an athlete, so Tyrone made his choice.

"I'll take the Webley, but you'll have to fucking catch me first, you cunt!"

Tyrone ran for his life, tossing the useless handgun as far as he could in anger. His opponent laughed. Okay, a chase it was. Tyrone was a fast runner, but with nowhere to go his efforts were wasted. The brick construction surrounding them was like an amphitheatre, except it was missing the jubilant supporters of the gladiatorial contest about to begin.

The Webley was the only weapon simple enough to operate without the time to self-train. With the weapon ready, AJ closed the boot and made his way to the driving controls. The engine fired with a roar and the car leapt forwards.

Meanwhile, Tyrone was jumping up at the boarded windows to see if any of the panels were loose, but there was no such luck. The chariot of death drew closer as the hunted turned to meet the hunter and it looked like a kill was inevitable, but suddenly the silver beast slewed to a halt in a cloud of dust.

The first thing that Tyrone saw once the dust had settled was a right arm stretched out with the fingers wrapped firmly around the grip of the handgun, and it was not a pretty sight! The gunman smiled as he pulled the trigger. Tyrone had not been joking; the kick back from the weapon was harsh. It was like, well, AJ could not describe it, even when he sampled the feeling again and again and again. The first shot had sunk the target to the ground somewhere off in the distance, the ground that Tyrone had covered since he had accepted his fate. The salesman had in no way exaggerated the power of the weapon. The first shot had done the damage, but the next five were wasted due to a lack of skill and strength, and a heart full of hatred. The latest victim of the cause was dead, he fucking had to be, but now it was time to leave. AJ held his arm out of the window and waved to the imaginary crowds, who shared his jubilation; he was their hero, he had sated their need for blood, everybody loved AJ!

The scene of the latest killing was left far behind as the silver sports car manoeuvred through the alleyways which had led him there. He should have taken the time to savour the damage that he had inflicted on his victim, but there was no time. There had been a nice spray of blood, but AJ had not had the opportunity to really study his handy work. Maybe next time. The first people AJ saw was a group walking dogs; two couples and two hounds. They would find the body within minutes because they had heard the noise of the gunshots, that much was clear. They all stood back as he drove past them at pace. It did cross his mind to silence the witnesses, but at the end of the day it didn't matter what they knew. Find the body, why should AJ give a fuck? The streets that the alleyway fed into were alive with suspicious eyes and although gunshots were not the norm within the capital, people knew them when they heard them, thanks to the Idiot's Lantern that took pride of place in nearly every home. One shot could be mistaken for a car misfiring, or two even, but six huge bangs was definitely a firearm at work. So what do we do, act discreet? Do we fuck! Madmen have no discretion. AJ simply drove like a madman with his horn bleeping as living proof that the man at the wheel really did not give a fuck.

*

Slug was getting the arse. He had been sitting on a bench outside a very well established burger restaurant in Leicester Square for nigh on twenty minutes, and he had had enough. The plot behind their latest case was thickening at a rate that DS Tap could not imagine, because no fucker could get hold of him! Slug had rung his colleague three times since his disappearance in order to warn him, but kept getting his answer phone. So what was he doing? Satisfying his lust, which was primarily aimed at the younger members of society, males on this occasion. How a detective could be so successful when he only thought with his dick was beyond the junior partner. Slug could see him through the window, wining and dining some young lad on burgers and cola; he obviously knew the way to a young man's heart! Sixteen, he guessed, probably foreign or from out of town, having escaped to London for a new start and in search of adventure. Whatever, he had somehow landed in William Tap's path - not the best of places to land, really, but it could be worse.

The young lad, who had blond, shoulder-length hair, was dressed in the uniform of the restaurant in which they dined. He was clearly benefiting from a sort of unofficial lunch break due to the fact that Tap had ordered his time off. The management knew better than to deny it, because if Billy Tap gives your staff orders, then that's fine, he was as good as management. Anything to keep him sweet! Slug wondered what was taking so long to discuss, but didn't much like the images the thought conjured up. The pair had worked closely together for a number of years and were well matched because what Slug lacked in ability to catch criminals, he made up for with his ability to turn a blind eye to Tap's behaviour. The duo was a small ecosystem within themselves, each needed the other to survive. Symbiosis they call it. Tap once described his relationship with his partner to a few close colleagues while drinking in a bar one afternoon. He was the North American sea otter and Slug was a sea urchin - one of those ugly things with spiky hair that sits at the bottom of the sea - and they all lived in a field of kelp. Now if the sea otter eats the urchins, all well and good because otherwise the bastard urchins eat all the kelp. So to keep the urchin numbers down and the kelp fields alive, you need the otters. Kill all the beavers, then the urchin population grows and eats all the kelp, and then everything that lives in the kelp is fucked. The urchins are also fucked because they have nothing left to eat.

"That's me and you, my friend, the beaver and the urchins!" Tap bragged. "It's amazing, that Discovery Channel!"

Taking another anxious peek through the glass, it looked like the meeting was coming to an end as the couple stood, and Tap handed over a thick-looking envelope to the pretty young boy. Tap nodded to the manager with a smile as he left the burger bar; he had visited the boy on a daily basis throughout the whole of the last week and the manager's co-operation in this matter was much appreciated.

"Right, Slug, let's have it then!" Billy demanded briskly, in response to the look he received from his colleague. But Slug would not get into a debate; he preferred to be led and to follow. That's the way they got results. Slug? Steven Leslie Urquhart Goddard, a right fucking mouthful, and so to his friends, of which were many because he was quite a nice bloke, he was known as Slug. Always had been, and probably always would be. It was dad's fault, he was very well-to-do. Mum was dark-skinned, Italian or something. Whatever the DNA said, Slug still looked about as British as you can get really, average height, dark brown hair combed sensibly, no facial hair, nondescript dress sense, no jewellery or body art - he just liked things low key and didn't want to stand out too much from the crowd. Slug just smirked as he arose from the bench on which he had been sitting his numb arse perched against the backrest. He supplied his boss with a few of the missing parts of the jigsaw.

"We've got some information regarding one of our two crispies found in Compton Street. George Belazaire was the giver!"

"Belazaire eh? Well that's a bastard, ain't it? If the giver was Belazaire, the taker was almost definitely Jay Alleyne then, weren't he?" Tap replied enigmatically. He was actually referring to the position in which the two bodies had been found. Although the pair had been blown across the room, the corpse with its teeth missing and hands tied behind its back had been found entwined together with the other, and let's face it, it did look a little bit dodgy!

To be fair Alleyne had had it coming. It looked as though Belazaire had murdered his colleague and then something had gone wrong and the killer had blown them both up, whether it was an outsider or Belazaire himself. After all, he was a shining example of incompetence. A good theory, but Tap would swear that Belazaire hadn't done it; he didn't have the balls to kill. So who had done it then? Tap didn't know yet.

"I suppose we'll have to sort this fucking mess out for Her Majesty then? And I was looking forward to a quiet day today; got a few errands to run, Slug, you know what I mean? Where to, then…?"

He knew Slug would have a basic plan of attack drawn up, that was his part of the deal. He thought and Billy acted; it was called team work.

So who were Belazaire and Alleyne? Bottom of the ladder boys, collectors of debt, deliverer's of goods to the order of the bigger boys. General gofers equipped with enough brains to survive but, not enough to climb the ladder to another level. As it happens, they had survived pretty well up to now for foot soldiers, but Tap could bet his bottom dollar that Alleyne had caused their extinction. He had a gob on him, although he was generally harmless enough; spineless he was, but definitely goby and it would seem that his mouth had probably got him into trouble this time. Tap had nicked him only a couple of times before but he did have a name that kept popping up. George, though - he was just a small-time dealer like his colleague, but he was often ordered to chaperone the man with the mouth around in the hope that his sheer size was enough to inflict fear on a customer and gain the payment through intimidation rather than violence. It usually worked.

Whoever had put an end to the two men's careers was brave because what they lacked in brains, they made up for in muscle. Although they were not fanatics, they did have strong links with the Yardies, and the Yardies took the loss of their staff very seriously. Most forces to be reckoned with in London could negotiate a death, you know, take one of ours in retaliation and we'll leave it at that, anything to prevent a war and a disturbance in an otherwise reasonably quiet existence, but not with the Yardies. A death was an insult, an excuse for a war, and war was good. War allowed territories to be taken, land to be gained. Unlike the underworld figures of old, a Jamaican leader did not expect to live long. In fact the most common killer of a Yardie gang member was the heir to his throne, or a rival gang of the same creed and colour, but they refused to unite and thus become stronger as one. Being a policeman had a number of advantages a few disadvantages too, of course, but the advantages certainly outweighed the negatives.

One advantage was the way you could talk to people, and Tap took full advantage of this little perk.

"Put a ticket on that and I'll fucking stick it right up your arse, luv!" The pretty young traffic warden looked stunned, especially when Slug removed a plastic I.D card from within his coat's inner pocket. C.I.D, he explained, on official police business. The traffic warden had reached for her walkie-talkie and was about to call for the assistance of the police, but there now seemed no need. Fucking rude bastards! Slug had parked the car in a bus lane, but so what? He had to pick his mate up, they were in a hurry, people were committing crimes all around them and parking was not much of an issue to them.

"Shit!" The phone was ringing in Slug's pocket as he replaced his ID.

"Fuck off, then!" Tap instructed the traffic warden while his colleague answered the phone.

"Wanker!" the uniformed one replied as she walked off in disgust to set to work on another victim, as the two officers discussed the phone call which Slug had quickly concluded.

"Shooting down by the water, IC3. Worth a look…?" Slug inquired. Tap agreed, but didn't they already have something pencilled in the diary for this afternoon?

"Yeah, we did, Billy, but you took a bit of an overextended lunch break, didn't you? So I sent Sid and Doughnut. They'll check out Mr Jenkins, have a chat with him and that, and keep him busy until we've got the positive IDs of Belazaire and his buddy." Slug explained the plan up to now, paying special attention to the times when Billy had found it hard to concentrate on anything but his dick.

"Well we've got IDs now, get Doughnut to pull Jenkins in?" Tap suggested. His mind was not entirely on the job at the minute; he had things on his mind, like a sixteen-year-old blond and a fair bit of homework to get done this afternoon.

Slug was surprised; Tap was usually on the ball. Driving swiftly towards the docks, Slug concentrated mainly on dodging the traffic but was able to share the basics.

"We can't pull Jenkins in yet because we can't find him. He's a piss-head by all accounts, but he's not at home. Or if he is, he's not answering, so I've sent Doughnut and Sid to check out the local drinking establishments to see if he's about. We're looking for his son as well; he should have been at work this morning, at the shop, that is, but apparently no one knows if he opened the shop or not. Well, it's all blacked out, innit? The windows and that so you don't really know if it's open or closed. I've just arranged the paperwork to do the door and then we'll search the flat. Might as well take this call first though, eh?" Slug asked as the traffic once again came to a standstill. Tap put the sirens and blue light on to aid their advancement through the crowds and a path cleared as if by magic. They were only around the corner from all the excitement and it was worth a look. After all, it was a shooting and so more interesting than the majority of calls. Just how interesting it would prove to be, though, William Tap had no idea. So, we've got the wheels; we're all tooled up and hungry for it; so where do we go? To get Haley? No, not yet; we've got someone else to visit first. We're going back home now, back to pay AJ's stepfather a visit; a visit that's been owing to him for some time. Dad was going to be the next victim. Dad had been chosen for his sins because his behaviour could no longer be tolerated.

Sirens could be heard in the background, possibly attending to the mess that AJ had just created. The dog walkers would have found the body by now; maybe they had a mobile phone with them. So what! AJ felt indestructible. Home was not too far away; the traffic just made it a bit difficult to get to. Ten minutes of mayhem to reach home turf. He drove the stolen sports car up the alleyway leading to the back entrance of the flats, but first he paused at the entrance, having been waved down by Rigger, the newspaper salesman.

Rigger? Yes, that was his name: Rigor mortis. The poor man was getting on a bit and looked as though he had the disease; he had done for the last ten years or so to be honest, salt of the earth bloke, though, and all that! He had lost several fingers – "frostbite from climbing Everest," the rosy-faced character was fond of saying, as well as: "they got bit off by a tiger at London zoo," and so forth. What a Geezer! Rigger was the eyes and the ears of the street; if you wanted local news, you saw him. AJ had grown up with the joker right through his childhood.

"Nice motor!" The old man commented as the electric window slid down.

"Yeah, thanks mate, just nicked it. The bloke who owned it wasn't too keen to let it go though, so I had to shoot him!"

The old man laughed because young Anthony was a card at times.

"Sorry to hear about your shop, son. You were lucky that you weren't in it!" Rigger sympathised.

AJ's expression turned to one of concern. "The shop…? What's happened to it?"

"The explosion, I thought you were in it! Well, there was bodies found in it. I just thought you'd have been there today. The police came here and went into your house to tell your father, I was thinking. But I'm happy to see you're all right, son."

AJ smiled, thinking fast. He hadn't considered that the police might have been around already, asking questions. They could even be sitting there waiting for him. Then again, though, the old man had thought it was AJ's corpse that had been found in the shop and the police might think the same thing at this stage. That had been the original plan, but it had never been exactly watertight.

"I didn't open up today," he lied. "I don't know who was in the shop. There shouldn't have been anyone. Are the police still here?"

They had gone. They had not actually been there long, a few minutes at the most, the old man explained. AJ was not surprised at this, because with Dad as pissed as usual, he had probably slept right through the knocking on the door. That is, if he hadn't just ignored it; after all, he was an ignorant cunt!

"I'll see you later," AJ bid farewell to his spy, who had served his purpose.

The corner by the bins seemed a logical place to store a stolen car, next to the fence that backed on to the Chinky. It fucking stank, always had done, but then AJ was used to it because this was home. The stairs had two entrances to them which met at the bottom next to where the tramps still lay, clearly not having taken heed of various warnings. Never mind, they posed no real threat and would be left alone for now. AJ's main concern was what lay above them, third floor to be precise, and there was only one way to find out exactly what that was. He mounted the stairs cautiously, having no idea what to expect. On reaching the top he found the front door open, clearly forced. Reaching into his narrow waistband, he groped for the Luger. The Browning was still located snugly within the inner pocket of the jacket but AJ had not used it as yet, he didn't even know if he could, so the other piece of German technology was his chosen weapon for now.

Technically, the weapon was not actually a Luger; it was in fact the follow up to the Luger, its replacement, if you like. The gun was actually a Walther P38. They look similar, but the latter has a longer hammer, that's the bit on top that hits the end of the bullet, indicating that it was a police weapon rather than a service model. It had a safety catch for the hammer, but in this case it had not been activated so the weapon was ready to kill. Tyrone was right about the warnings he had issued about a gun as old and mechanically complicated as the Luger, but this was in fact a lot newer than it looked, possibly mid-fifties. It looked well-maintained as well. Whatever, it could kill, and was ready to do so as AJ cautiously pushed the front door open a little wider, listening carefully to the voices that he could hear inside as he did so. There were two men that much was clear, and they were definitely foreign, Jamaican, at a guess. Their conversation was suddenly punctuated by an ear-piercing scream and the sound of gasping breaths, the sound of some bird in agony. AJ had his suspicions as to who it might be; Tara seemed a likely candidate, Dad's whore. What the fuck were they doing to her, though?

AJ had no chance to ponder over his last question as it suddenly became evident that someone was walking down the hallway towards him. He could see the dark-skinned intruder walking towards the front entrance of the flat through the gap between the door and its frame. *Shit!* AJ had to hide himself, and fast. The stairs that had taken so long to climb took merely seconds to run down. AJ was surprised that he had moved so fast, but not surprised that he now could not breathe. He stood in the street for a few minutes, out of sight from the enemy, clearing his throat and attempting to regain his breath as blood and something else - bile or pus or something - dripped from his lips. It was only then that AJ realised he was standing in the street with a loaded handgun, although fortunately very few people actually noticed.

"Fuck!" He swore with regret as he ducked back into the small room beneath the stairs, which someone was now descending. There was no time for a plan, so AJ took the first course of action that came into his head. He pulled the tramps' filthy covers back and climbed in amongst them, much to their surprise as they moaned and groaned.

"Shut up, you cunts!" He hissed at the tramps, who seemed too pissed to know what was going on. All was silent except for the footsteps coming down the concrete steps. Four heavy feet sounded on the steps, so it looked like whoever was in the flat had decided to leave. It fucking stank, in amongst the filthiest bastards that AJ had ever had the pleasure of snuggling up to. It was damp too, the moisture seeping through the arse of his stolen jeans. Piss! AJ knew as much without even checking. Snuggled up cosily between the tramps, AJ was completely hidden under the covers. The stench of urine made him gag, but there was no time to change venue. Besides, this was a good hiding place; he was completely out of sight but at the same time could still view his targets through a hole in the blanket. The intruders were Jamaican. AJ had been right, dad's friends, no doubt wanting to know where their foot soldiers had got to. Or worse still, they might know the score already because this sort of information flows through the criminal world a lot quicker than it does in the real one. Maybe they were here for revenge, in that case! Well, good, because we can all have some of that!

The two men appeared on the last few steps. They were dressed in a similar style, just with different coloured ski jackets. They were decked out with gold teeth, the works and their eyes lit up as they saw AJ's car, or rather, Tyrone's.

Bollocks! Only now did AJ realise he had left the keys in the ignition. *Shit!* Oh well, that was his wheels gone! He cursed his own stupidity as he heard the car's doors close and the well-tuned engine light up with a roar. Having accepted his loss, AJ decided that his new friends must not leave. Although they were not really part of the cause, they had hunted down his father so it was clear that they would almost certainly attempt to find him. It was better to have it now and be done with it, attack being the best form of defence.

Ready to do battle, AJ quickly jumped up from his bed of piss and excrement and went in pursuit of the two men, who had begun to turn the car around in a three point turn. The passenger of the groaning sports car tapped his friend on the arm in concern and they both stared at the skinny white boy advancing towards them. Suspicion turned to alarm as AJ produced the P38 from behind his back, spit and blood drooling from his lips, and ran almost right up to the glass of the driver's side window before pulling the trigger. The glass shattered almost instantly and a wave of blood drenched the exploding, razor-sharp shards. Again and again the trigger was pulled, a total of eight times, before it clicked empty.

Blood trickled from the killer's face as he paused for breath, breath that was not easily come by as he spat into the car both his own bodily fluids and those of his victims, who twitched in their seats while their brains adjusted to death. As AJ studied his handy work, it amazed him how much mess a gun made at such close range. It was weird, really, because instead of exploding, one of the heads had sort of imploded so that he looked like one of those blokes who pull those funny faces up North - you know, Gurners, I think they call themselves. AJ could not deny that the killings had been rather enjoyable. He had aimed at his victims' facial features as if conducting some kind of experiment; an eye, a mouth, an ear; and the bullets had shredded each one as he had commanded them to. Maximum effect from minimum effort. He remembered more than anything else the looks on his victims' faces before they died: surprise, then terror, followed by pain.

AJ had crossed the line now, en route to his own grave. It was only a matter of time before he would be brought to justice and would join his victims, he knew that. Who was going to stop him, though? Now that was an interesting question. He had never believed in an afterlife you live, you die, you rot or you burn there was no better place, no great meeting place in the sky. People were just like cars, and when they were switched off, wrote off or scrapped, their existence was simply terminated. Today, however, Anthony felt differently because something was not right; something had changed inside him. It was as if it had suddenly occurred to him that there were a whole number of different worlds out there, but as for specifics he could not say.

With blood dripping from his clothes, AJ backed away from the destruction he had caused. It was time to move on again, but first he had to see for himself whether these two gentlemen had done him the favour he suspected. He saw Rigger in the distance, staring. AJ put a finger to his lips, signalling to the newspaper man to keep quiet because this was not his business. A nod from the old man signified his complicity. AJ was in two minds whether to kill him, but what was the point? The old man could not assist AJ in his mission so it would be a wasted bullet, and his ammunition was rapidly depleting. He would live today. The gunman tossed the spent handgun onto the floor before climbing the stairs again. The tramps had not even stirred; they had no interest in the outside world, just the world within their tent of blankets.

*

Sirens blazed in the distance as well as on top of the car.

"Down there you cunt!" Tap gave directions and he was right this time. They had got a little lost, to be fair, but this was definitely the right turning. The alleyway was tight and Slug eased off the gas a little, because between them they had already wrecked four cars this year. Not bad in five months.

"Shit, Paras are here. Fuck, shit and bollocks I was hoping to have a sniff around there before those Cunts turned up."

Their vehicle entered the former gardens of some derelict flats where it had been reported that a young male had been shot with a firearm. The old brick flats had an eerie air about them, Slug thought, studying the old walls as they drove through the middle of them. The whole construction reminded him of one of those old theatres in Rome where they used to have plays and all that old nonsense or Gladiator fights. Yeah, you could easily see one of them taking place in here. The car skidded slightly in the dust as they pulled up at the scene. There was one ambulance and two paramedics attempting to work their magic. You could see the looks of disapproval on their faces as one of them just managed to make out the figures in the police car through the sun-drenched front window screen. Billy Tap!

Tap opened the door and climbed out into the dust. He had just put a new pair of loafers on, from stock. The others got ruined back when he had been investigating the explosion in Soho. The paramedics gave Tap a look of concern as he walked over, sunglasses in place, dressed as though he was about to attend a showbiz gathering as opposed to a shooting incident. The patient had been put on a stretcher and he looked in a bad way; still breathing he was, but it seemed to be hard work.

"What we got then, chaps?" Tap asked as he drew in close and looked over a shoulder, so that the paramedic could smell the minty odour of over-chewed gum. He looked up at Tap as though he was taking the piss.

"A fella with a hole the size of my fist in his left lung. He's unconscious and probably will never regain. He's very poorly indeed, so can you please leave me alone so I can try and save him?"

Tap smiled as he turned to see where Slug had got to.

"Tyrone Banks!" He said as he turned back to the paramedics who looked confused.

“Your chap there, his name is Tyrone Banks.” Billy repeated.

Oh right, it was nice to know who you were working on; obviously their patient had been up to no good so it should be no surprise really that the police, especially Billy, knew him.

“So we looking at a box then or what?” Tap enquired. The paramedic working on the man simply shrugged.

“Slug? What are you fucking doing, you madman?” Slug was kneeling on the floor as if he was looking for something under the car. He was, and he had found it, but it was awkward retrieving the object with the aid of a tissue. Slug stood up awkwardly and held the prize high for all to see.

“Bloody run over it, didn’t I?” He exclaimed. Thought I saw something. Only I could fucking do that, couldn’t I?” He brought the weapon over, holding it carefully with the tissue with one finger poked through the trigger guard.

“Webley…!” Tap knew it at a glance. “Big fucker an’ all, point forty-five. So our friend on the stretcher shouldn’t really be here, or certainly not in one piece. It must have been fired at long range, fucking fluke, though, hitting his target at long range.” Tap wondered if they were dealing with a professional marksman.

Tap walked back over to the patient and the paramedic working his magic looked over his shoulder enquiringly.

“That’s definitely a bullet done that, ain’t it?” Tap asked.

“Definitely, why…?”

Tap looked more closely at the wound before answering.

“Well, my colleague back there has just located a suspect murder weapon but it’s a forty-five and by rights, if you got hit with a forty five, you’d have a bigger hole in ya than that; you’d lose the arm.”

The paramedic was warming to Tap.

“Yeah, you’re right in one way,” he replied. “The bullet only did the damage indirectly because that hole was made by his mobile phone, which at present is sitting in his left lung. There look, you can see it!"

Tap could indeed see it as the paramedic lifted up a flap of skin. This was bizarre, and needed to be shared.

"Slug come and have a look at this! The geezer's got a phone sitting in his lung. Come and have a look."

Slug declined the offer; he didn't like looking at gunshot wounds, or phone shot wounds for that matter, because that was probably the way he was going to go in the end.

The paramedic continued with his work, pissed off by the circus behind him, until he was interrupted again.

"Whip it out, then!" Tap suggested, referring to the phone.

"Are you serious? Remove the phone?"

Tap was. He needed the SIM card from the phone, and urgently, so they could trace who he had last been doing business with.

"Go on, whip it out then. You could just say it was in the way or something. You'll be doing him a favour, won't you?" Tap wheedled.

"If I remove that phone, he'll die, because it's about all that's keeping him alive at the moment. It's blocking arteries that need blocking, so it can't come out until he's on a life support machine. Forget it mate, it's not happening!"

But Tap did not like taking no for an answer. The men in green suits lifted the stretcher into the back of the ambulance with care while Billy Tap watched like a scolded schoolboy.

"Just get the SIM card out of it, that's all I need," he tried again. "You can leave the casing in there." His voice began to register his growing impatience now. "Slug!" He called, signalling to his partner with a simple twist of the head

Slug nodded, understanding that he was required to keep the lead paramedic's colleague busy for a minute while Tap got what they wanted. They had to have the SIM card; the patient could be in surgery for hours while they fucked about getting the phone out, and those were hours they simply didn't have. They had a more important case to get on with, as well as a little private work to take care of en route.

Tap climbed into the back of the ambulance and pulled the doors shut, sirens in the background meant time was limited.

"Now, Peter!" he read the name from the paramedic's name badge. "I want that SIM card. I need it to find the person who did this, so I really need your assistance, okay?"

It was not okay, and Peter refused point blank at first but began to look a little less certain as Tap removed his persuasion tool from inside his jacket. The hand gun had an amazing effect because the paramedic suddenly lost his attitude problem. Although he was certainly not keen to assist, the gun pointed at his head ensured compliance.

"Now, you are going to remove that SIM card. You can leave the rest of the phone in, but I want that SIM card and if you don't do it, I will, okay?"

Peter finally agreed to carry out the operation and picked out a few hand tools from his bag of goodies. The medic put a light on his head, lit it and stared down at the patient, who was all but dead. He could see the phone's battery easily enough and knew that that had to be out of the way in order to facilitate the removal of the SIM card. It had become slightly dislodged, so he carefully picked at the back of the phone before attacking it with a pair of long-nosed pliers. The battery was then lifted out, accompanied by a huge gush of blood that fired out into the paramedic's face, causing the light to turn red momentarily until Peter located and crimped the offending artery. He carefully swabbed blood from both his face and the rapidly-filling wound.

"Can you see it?" Tap enquired.

Peter nodded.

"Good, well fucking pull it out then. Chop-chop, though, because we've got company…!"

The medic obeyed as cars began to pull up outside the van. Within seconds Peter had succeeded in his task as the plastic clip retaining the SIM card was unhitched and the card was handed over to its new owner with a pair of tweezers. The two men could hear Slug outside making excuses for what was going on in the ambulance, so it was time to leave.

"Nice one, Pete. Right, story is, battery was leaking into blood stream. Look at it, it's all cracked and shit, yeah? You had to remove it to prevent poisoning, right?" Tap warned Peter not to fuck with him as he re-holstered his hand gun, because he was not a man to be fucked with. "You pulled that off a treat; just stick to your story and all will be well. Do you understand, Peter?"

Peter did; it was crystal clear. There would be no bad press regarding DS Tap's assistance in the matter.

Tap and his main man left the donkey work to the donkeys. They had their potential murder weapon and they had the SIM card, but the gun was no use to them so they gave that to one of the Muppets to bag and tag. Not the SIM card, though, no way! Buzby was going to take a look at that. Yeah Buzby a nickname acquired by the telecommunications expert back at Scotland Yard. He had earned it due to his expertise in anything that rings, is picked up and answered. Buzby was sort of shared between the secret service and the police. Top bollocks he was by all accounts, takes weeks to get an appointment as a rule, but not if you've got dirt on the man, which of course, Tap did. Well, it was the only way to do business these days!

The story went that a year or so before, Buzby needed a favour doing of the slightly illegal type. It was something to do with his ex missis and Tap did the necessary, but instead of payment the standard favour was left open. But the plot thickened. When the favour was called in, Tap had a mortgage, same as everyone else; he'd had it about ten years or so by all accounts. Anyway, one day Billy got a letter saying that his endowment policy was not going to make the full amount at the end of the term. Slug had been on duty with Tap at the time and tried to calm him down, but he was well pissed off. So, to cut a long story short, he found out who was in charge of the building society top man, no fucking about and Buzby and his little task force bugged his phones. Tap found out where his man was going to lunch, turned up and put it straight to this bloke that he had forty-eight hours to sort this mess out and make sure his endowment policy matured just as it should. He demanded no extra, no extortion, he just wanted what he considered had been promised to him, failing which the excrement would hit rotary motion.

One thing about William Tap was that you could call him every name under the sun, but as crooked as he was, he still had his own moral code. So, did the man pay up? No, foolishly he didn't. When the forty-eight hours were up, true to his word, Tap ruined the poor man's life, properly ruined it and all. He broke into the guy's mansion with a bag full of goodies and downloaded kiddie-porn onto his computer, e-mailing some particularly evil shit to his office. His video collection suddenly grew considerably with the addition of some pretty nasty productions, plus a photo collection of the same variety was hidden in various places. Was that enough, though? Oh no, if you fuck with Tap, you will know about it, and so for the grand finale, the icing was truly added to the cake and the whole lot was passed onto the nonce squad, anonymously of course. Tap felt no remorse, even when the poor chap topped himself on remand, because if you fuck with people's lives, then Billy Tap will fuck with yours.

So, Buzby would look at the SIM card, it went without saying, really, but just to confirm, Tap rang him just to ruffle his feathers a little. Slug drove at a more sensible pace back to the Yard. They had had to stop a few times to carry out a number of errands; anything to stop Billy moaning on about how tits-up the day had been. He had important homework to take care of and as always when you're busy, the phone didn't stop ringing and the stiffs just kept piling up. And there it went again.

"Yeah, go ahead Slim!" Tap sighed into his mobile, before falling silent. "Well how did you let him get away, you useless fat fucker?" Billy intended to cause offence but didn't achieve it because Doughnut was used to such abuse, being one of Tap's foot soldiers. Being fat in the police force was worse than being ethnic or gay as far as harassment went.

"Well, you've got a fucking gun, ain't you? That's no fucking excuse. Slug, you hear this he got away, we couldn't catch him he had a gun!" Tap adopted an effeminate voice. Slug preferred not to get involved unless he had to. Tap continued speaking into the phone.

"Wankers…! Sit tight, Doughnut, but mind where you fucking well sit. We'll be there in five. Make sure you've got a Jam Jar an' all, 'cos you're nipping off to see Buzby for me, all right?" There was a brief silence before Tap spoke again. "What, more? You fucking better not be winding me up, Doughnut. Okay, take the mother in. What about the old man?" Tap could hardly believe his ears as he listened to the rapidly-thickening plot. "Shitty death don't fucking touch anything. Anyone else know yet?" It appeared that it was their little secret at the minute, causing Billy to express his delight. "Good! Don't fuck up, Doughnut!"

The big man promised he wouldn't, although everyone knew it was impossible for him not to. A fuck-up he was, but you had to love the man, especially when he delivered news like this. "Five minutes, Slim!" Shouted Tap as the phone went dead.

Eight minutes to be precise, eight long-arse minutes, but they got there in the end. During this time Tap shared his new found knowledge with Slug: two dead gangsters found shot in a car outside the Jenkins' family home. Now isn't that a fucking coincidence? Mum's in cuffs; she had just arrived back at the house. Dad was dead, tortured badly along with a young woman, probably a Tom but she was shot in the head as well. Messy, very messy, but it showed that they had their man in Slug's eyes.

"It's the son, then?"

"Maybe, unless he turns up slightly chilled…!" Billy joked, although to be honest, he didn't really know for sure because nothing made much sense at this moment in time. The SIM card and Tyrone's fight for life would be the key to the case, but in the meantime, it looked like Anthony Jenkins was their man. This was their little secret though, just for now.

Uniform had turned up at the scene but Doughnut and Sid had done a good job at keeping them away from the heart of the matter; CID ruled on this site, unless you wanted to go and have a word with Billy. Uniform did assist with the matter of policing the area, though, under the orders of CID Sid, who was making sure that no one got past the blockage and damaged the evidence. Neighbours and passers-by had heard the gunshot and had called the police; the whole fucking force it looked like! As Tap and Slug pulled up at the scene, the plastic strip denoting that this was a crime scene was removed to allow them to enter. As soon as Tap got out of the car, Sid approached him to give him a briefing of the area and what lay within it. Sid was of course, not really called Sid; no, that would be ridiculous. Sid was of Asian descent and his real name was something unpronounceable to Billy, so he was christened Sid when he joined up; it was for the best. Now, Sid was not the brightest of lanterns ever to shine, but apart from adding to political correctness within the task force, he was pretty well connected in the Asian community. He spoke the lingo, he looked the part, and he knew how his people worked. Having made his way up the ladder with the help of this knowledge, he had proved himself in the CID. Of course he was also bent, crooked, that is, but that went with the territory.

Sid pointed out the murder weapon.

"Luger!" he smiled, hoping to impress. "You'll like this!" he promised eagerly as he pulled a sheet away from the top of the death-filled silver sports car. "Point blank. Right fucking messy!" Sid boasted, and in all fairness he was right, although he knew that his main-man would be unfazed by the gory sight. Unfazed he was, even to the point of sticking his head inside the car and having a good look around. Sid liked a bit of gore to get the old adrenaline going, but fuck! Not to the extent of putting his head in the car.

"Whose motor?" Tap quizzed. He had an idea, but needed confirmation that his theory was correct. Sid had not got that far yet and he confessed as much, anticipating the bollocking which duly arrived in Tap's next breath.

"Well fucking find out, then! It's Tyrone Banks', though, I'll tell you that for nothing, but run a check anyway. I take it you've searched it?"

Sid shook his head.

"Nah, man, not yet. It's been kicking off, innit? Reporters, uniform; fuckers won't keep their noses out, will they? I've been fucking them off ever since we've been here, bastards!" Sid whined convincingly.

"Chop chop then, get searching!" Tap ordered, before enquiring where Doughnut was? Sid nodded towards the top of the stairs, to the third floor where the man in question was waving down at them, signalling towards the space at the bottom of the stairs and its inhabitants, the tramps. As Tap sauntered over to them, Sid set to work searching the car of death. He planned to start with the obvious places, like the glove box, so he opened the passenger door of the silver and red sports car. Unfortunately, he was in for a little surprise.

"Oh, for fuck's sake!" the appalled officer exclaimed as his shoes were dyed to match the car's interior. "Bollocks!" Blood, snot, piss and body tissues had drained into the foot well, filling it up well above the door seal. Having opened the door, Sid now wore the excess on his shoes - nice! And after all that, the glove box was empty, apart from some leather gloves, CDs and odds and sods. Funny that, finding gloves in the glove box! The boot told another story, though, because in there Sid had found a number of loose bullets - point thirty-eight they looked like, big fuckers, as bullets go! What gun would fire them, though? Only ballistics would be able to tell, so Sid bagged them and tagged them ready for shipment. Unsurprisingly, the car offered no real evidence as to who its owner was, so Sid rang it in. Lo and behold, it was indeed Tyrone Banks car; how the fuck did Tap do it?

The tramps were having a bad night, made worse by Billy Tap's threats to have Doughnut sit on them if they didn't get out from their tent of blankets and offer some form of story regarding what had taken place tonight. For fuck's sake, they were key witnesses!

"You…!" Tap pointed his finger at a young officer, who looked surprised but happy to oblige. "Here's a score, find a corner shop or something and get a bottle of whiskey and some cups, or fucking beakers or something. Hurry up though, yeah?" He handed over a crisp new twenty pound note. "Good man, nice and quick, eh?" Tap added as the youth left to run the errand. "You keep an eye on them!" he ordered another of his colleagues before setting off up the stairs.

Doughnut was waiting at the top. The flat door was open and the lights were on. There was no smell of death in the air, but it was early days yet.

"Sure it's safe?" Tap asked, pulling out his handgun to be on the safe side. In accordance with his cool image, Tap carried a Glock, unsurprisingly acquired by means of friends in high places. With a practised movement he pulled the top of the weapon back so it was ready for action as he led his crew, into the flat. Slug followed as they edged into the shabby dwelling and Doughnut hot on the trail behind him, although unarmed on Tap's strictest instructions.

There were several sets of footprints on the paisley carpet, all apparently leaving the apartment. They looked like they had been made by trainers. The hallway they entered was eerily silent. On checking for undesirables in the kitchen, front room and toilet, it seemed that all was clear. Mr Jenkins was discovered all carved up in bedroom one. The whole room stank like a brewery. Fucking hell, what a mess! It looked like the middle-aged man had been cut to ribbons with something, more than likely the smashed whiskey glass on the floor and possibly a knife as well, because some of the cuts and stab marks to the body were too clean. The bottle had definitely done his face and stomach though, you could see that clear as day as the victim lay naked on the bed. That must have been painful, especially what they'd done to his bollocks. Fucking animals! Tap simply stared at the corpse. And they said he was a sick bastard! Mr Jenkins obviously had something that these fellers wanted, or was this a revenge attack? More than likely the latter after seeing what had taken place in the shop.

"The bird's in here!" Doughnut called out, diverting his attention.

Slug had seen it already and was looking rather faint.

"Outside Slug, if you're going to throw your guts up," Tap warned him. "Don't mess the crime scene up." Evidence was vital at this moment in time and Slug had a habit of vomiting on it. "Clear up downstairs mate and then go and get a few hours' kip; we've got a long night ahead of us, son. Fucking make sure that you keep in touch with the hospital though to see how our friend Mr Banks is doing, all right? I want you down there as soon as he's awake!"

Slug struggled with the long hours, and the gore for that matter, and he had been on since four this morning. It was different for Tap; he simply didn't require much time at home, or sleep, not when there were plenty of stimulants available.

"I'll be off then!" Slug said as he made his way back through the hallway and down the stairs. As long as everything was under control down there, he could fuck off. He knew the procedure.

"They've fucking raped her, ain't they? And then they did that. Can you believe that?" Tap asked Doughnut, who shook his head in amazement. Tap was referring to the damage inflicted on the naked body spread out in front of him, in particular to the genitals. It looked as though she had been raped at some point because there were two condom wrappers on the floor, although there were no used condoms; these guys were cleverer than that! The young girl probably thought that once they'd had their sick fun they'd leave her in peace to pick up the pieces, but unfortunately this was not the case. It appeared that the sex attack had only been the beginning of it. No one would ever know for sure, but it looked as though this girl had suffered in ways that were beyond the imagination of most. The murderers had forced the knife into their victim's genitals before pulling the weapon through the body and all the way up to her throat. The sight was horrific; even Tap was moved by it! Not the blood, you understand, he could dig that, it was just the thought of the pain she must have suffered throughout the ordeal, and the fact that she had possibly still been alive before someone shot her in the head.

"Doughnut, ring Sid and ask him to check our friends downstairs for weapons; we're looking for shooters and blades!" he ordered briskly.

Outside, Sid was busy washing his shoes as his mobile went off. The order did not go down too well.

"Oh, you're having a fucking laugh. I'm already covered in claret!" Sid moaned.

Tap and Doughnut searched the room while trying to ignore the female corpse and the blood-soaked bed. It stank of shit, and piss, come to mention it. It was those clothes on the floor; someone seemed to have had an accident or something.

"He's a big cunt! Thirty six waist..!" Doughnut commented.

"He may be a big cunt, Doughnut, but he's fucking anorexic compared to you, ain't he? Imagine if you shit your pants, eh? Fucking Jesus, we'd have the environmental health in before we could search this room!"

This was Jenkins junior's room that much was clear. There wasn't much in it apart from clothes. Drawers were opened and their contents thrown across the room. Tap held up evidence of drug use for his colleague's inspection: tin foil, pipes, no brown stuff though, our man had obviously collected his stash. It didn't look like they were going to come up with anything useful until they dug deeper under the bed and found some photos and a sort of diary.

Tap put the diary on the bedside table for a moment while he scanned through the photos.

"Here he is, that's him, I reckon. Must be because his face appears in most of them, looks like a right arsehole though, don't he?"

Doughnut had to agree. The man in the pictures had shifty eyes; smackhead eyes. It figured that they were dealing with a user because he'd have to be off his tits to have kicked off this mess.

"I'd give her some, though!" Doughnut made his colleague stop at the next picture, a picture of a really pretty girl. Tap disagreed.

"No you wouldn't mate, because she'd be swinging on my dick. Don't matter though, because I've just seen one for you buddy, although I don't fancy yours much. Here she is!"

Tap located a picture of a really skinny woman: ill-looking, malnourished and thin.

"Well, it's the same bird, innit?" Came Doughnut's surprised response. "Go back to the other; yeah, that's her. She must have been ill or something then. It's definitely her, though!" Tap shuffled back through the pack a bit until he found the previous photo.

"Fucking hell, lard arse, you're right; they are the same bird. Well who the fuck is she?"

Doughnut didn't know, but his keen eye had already made up for the whole week's fuck-ups.

"Right, here's the plan!" Tap began, just as his colleague's phone rang. It was Sid. Doughnut listened for a few moments before bringing Tap up to date.

"Yeah, they were armed, couple of knives and a couple of handguns. Shooters haven't been fired recently but they're both fully loaded. What do you want to do?"

Tap took the phone.

"What you got, Sidney?" He asked. A smile appeared on Tap's face as he told Sid that he would like to keep the Glock, but the other things could be left because they weren't worth shit. "You know what to do with it, Sid, don't you?"

Sid did: bag it, tag it and put it in the boot of his boss's car ready for sale. Billy would bung him a few drinks for his trouble.

"Come up here when you've done," Tap continued, "I've got a little job for you."

A top-of-the-range weapon like that was worth big money to the right people, but in this case Tap intended to use the weapon to repay a favour. Usually, though, he would nick it if he could get away with it and top up his pension a little. If he didn't supply the criminal fraternity with guns, then someone else surely would. The reason for having the weapon bagged and tagged before it went in his boot was a sort of safety net, so that he could say he was just taking it over to forensics himself if anyone tried to question him. The knives and the other handgun would be properly bagged, tagged and logged before being taken over to forensics.

Back upstairs, Tap gave two photos to Doughnut. One was a picture of the man who they suspected was Anthony Jenkins and the other was a picture of this ill-looking women in her former glory.

"Right Doughnut, get back to the yard and get missis Jenkins to fill us in on a few things that don't add up. I wanna know about her son, whether that's him in the photo. I wanna know what his fucking problem is, where he is, or is likely to be, and who that bird is. Make it snappy, though, because I want to catch this fucker." Billy warned before remembering the diary and picking it up from the bedside table. It was not actually a diary as such, more like a list of appointments: appointments that Jenkins had attended, it would seem, along with thoughts that he had collated about the doctors or care-workers who had treated him, or not. It outlined what Anthony Jenkins thought of the treatment he had received in all its inadequacy. The bits that Tap picked out at random expressed hatred, misery and especially frustration. He tucked it away in his pocket for bedtime reading as Sid entered the room.

"Nice innit?" Tap commented.

"Not bad! She keeps it neat though, don't she?" Sid continued with reference to the woman's pubic hair, which was heavily trimmed.

Tap had to agree.

"Yeah, that's a tidy little piece. I might have a quick go on it myself actually while you pop this SIM card to Buzby and wait for the results. After all, she's still warm." Tap confirmed this fact by touching the woman's hand.

Doughnut shook his head as if in disgust, laughing in spite of himself. They were sick bastards, but perhaps when you worked with corpses every day you became immune to it. If there was no funny side, then you had to make one, otherwise you'd lose it.

Billy settled down on a chair in the lounge to read through the diary he had found back in the bedroom while his two little helpers set about their tasks. The peace and tranquillity was soon broken by the phone ringing in his pocket.

"Yes, Slug!"

Slug reminded Tap that there was a policeman downstairs with a bottle of whiskey and his change.

"Oh fuck, yeah, I forgot about that. I'll be down in a minute."

Leaving the building with the diary under his arm, Tap negotiated the stairs to the bottom and praised his new apprentice; he could keep the change.

"Wakey, wakey, rise and shine!" The tramps were surprised to find their nemesis in a strangely hospitable mood.

"Look what we've got for you, you smelly little fuckers!"

Tap pulled back the blankets, pausing for a breath as the stench of piss and shit burnt the back of his throat.

"Fucking hell, you cunts stink. Fancy a drink, my little darlings?"

He squatted beside them. Behind him, there was a flurry of activity as the uniforms swarmed into the flat now that Tap had finished, accompanied by white suits and blue overalls, each according to their own particular function in the proceedings. Tap chuckled as he watched them. He already had his man; he just had to net the fucker now.

"Who's the leader then? Who's the daddy, the Mayor of this little community?" Tap enquired. The tramps just moaned and one reached for the tent of blankets in order to cover up this nightmare. Tap opened the bottle and half-filled a transparent plastic cup, snatching away as a filthy hand reached for it.

"What's your name?" Tap ran the neck of the bottle along in front of their noses.

"James," replied the drunk in a Scottish accent.

"A sweaty sock, eh? Here, have a drink my son; get that down you." Tap offered the tramp the cup of whiskey, which was gratefully received and gulped down with urgency. Tap enquired if anyone else fancied a drink and poured the same amount into three more cups, sharing them out.

"Another?" He asked, taking a clean cup and half filling it. "Another coming right up for my main man James. But first, what's been going on here tonight, James? There's been some pretty weird goings on by all accounts. What did you see?"

"Some lad woke us up earlier on. I woke up and he was in the sheets with us, hiding from someone. Black fellers, I believe. I think they came downstairs and went outside. The lad followed them if I remember rightly, heard some banging, then you lot woke us up. Can't get peace and quiet anywhere these days?"

James had pretty much filled in the missing gaps and was duly rewarded with a bevy. His mates were also soon refreshed.

"Any guns James, did you see any guns? And this lad, was he this chap from upstairs, third floor?"

The tramp reached out with his cup, silently demanding a refill. Tap obliged.

"That bastard upstairs it was! Aye, I remember now. Keeps pissing on us, you know? Fucking did it this morning an' all. Didn't see a gun, though, but saying that, he did have something in his hand when he…. Yeah, that's right he went upstairs then come down again almost straightaway because them blackies were coming down too. He went out front before running back in here again. Yeah, I think it was a gun as it happens, and he was definitely fiddling with something when he barged back in here!" James babbled, leaving his listeners to do their best to decode the harsh accent. Tap had got the gist of it anyway, and it was twenty quid well spent.

From what Tap could make out from the evidence so far, it looked like Anthony had intended to go up the stairs but the Jamaicans had already been on their way down. So he went to do a runner but changed his mind or something like that, and then hid with the tramps. The Jamaicans had come down the stairs, not knowing he was there, and had somehow ended up in his car. Maybe the keys were in it and they'd just decided to nick it? Tap didn't know, but it looked like Jenkins had capped them both for their sins regardless. Probably for killing his dad, one would imagine. Although he wouldn't have known that at the time because he hadn't had a chance to go in the flat yet. Or maybe he had; maybe the tramps had the times all fucked up? He could have gone up, seen them in action, and then come down to lie in wait for an ambush. That sounded more likely. Then again, why hadn't he just capped them in the flat? It didn't make sense. Nah, Tap was pretty sure that Jenkins Junior had not gone upstairs and had been planning to kill the Yardies anyway. They might have been after him because he owed them money, or had dissed them in some way, like killing their buddies in the shop. Why Tyrone, though? To buy guns or drugs, Tap knew that much but what the link was, he didn't know.

Tap filled the tramps' cups with the remainder of the bottle and tossed it into the corner with the others. He knew that the tramps saw a lot more than they let on, watching the world go by; the world from which they'd cut themselves off. Tap kicked the tent of blankets back towards them; the smell was hideous, like the smell in Jenkins Junior's bedroom. The shit-stained clothing tied in nicely with the tramps' version of events. It would all link up eventually; just the diary to consult next so that he could create a profile of the madman he was chasing.

"Anthony Jenkins, I'm going to take you down!" Tap promised out loud as he winked at the rookie officer who was standing by. "Look after yourself son. Aim for the top, because that's the bottom!" He nodded towards the tramps as he left.

Chapter Three

Haley

Blood trickled onto the perfect white sheets and separated into rivulets as it wove its way through the crumpled expanse of well-washed cotton. The blood was fresh; fresh from the mouth of the young man who slept quietly at his lover's bedside. She was also asleep, although she had woken at some point to touch her visitor gently and feel the comfort of his warm hand entwined with her own. He had laid his head on the bed level with his lover's waist while remaining seated in a chair next to the bed. It had been a busy day and he had a lot to tell his soul mate, but she had taken her medication just over an hour before and would be drowsy for a good while yet. It was a bit risky coming into the hospital before eight o'clock, but the nurses knew that this patient was only going to be keeping her bed warm for a matter of weeks now and their compassion allowed them to turn a blind eye.

The patient herself was clearly sick; thin-faced and gaunt in complexion. She had once been a pretty girl, though; you could clearly see the remains of it in her face, particularly those gorgeous bright blue eyes that were now so full of pain and suffering. Her ill-health had stolen most of the colour from her skin and if you knew no better, having seen her out and about, you would guess that she suffered from some sort of eating disorder. Her hair was mousy brown in colour, apart from the ends hanging around her shoulders, which bore testimony to the fact that she had once been blonde. To Anthony she was still beautiful because he was lucky enough to know her inside as well as out. He loved her like no other and it broke his heart to watch her rotting in her bed. And people had the nerve to tell him that there was a God up there who cared. Bullshit!

The room where Haley lived was small, but accommodated a bed, a chair and a cabinet. It had a built-in wardrobe and a wall-mounted TV and video combination. One window looked from the room into the main lounge of the complex, or would have done if the blinds had not been closed, and the other looked out into the streets of London. Haley had been in the hospice for about six weeks now. Before then she had been in various hospitals, fighting against pneumonia, but now the end was certain and she had been lucky enough to land this place in the hospice. It was no consolation for the fact that she was dying, but it was comfortable.

Time moved slowly for Haley, her fate sealed. She thought a lot, although she tried not to. Haley told Anthony her dreams of how their lives could have been if things were different. They would have lived in a white house, their house, and they would be married because that's what married people did, they owned nice houses together. She didn't want to die in the hospice and Anthony wasn't going to let her; that was one dream of hers he could make real for her.

He only awoke when he felt a grip tighten on his hand. Haley was communicating with him now that she had the strength to do so.

"Hello, Anthony." A soft voice greeted him. He lifted his head from the bed and smiled at his best friend. Haley looked tired, but even so she was able to summon up a smile for him, the same smile that lived in AJ's mind every time he thought of her when they were apart.

"Hello, Haley, brought you a present." He pointed over to the side cabinet where a small brown Teddy Bear peered down at the patient. "It farts when you press its stomach, and then if you press it again it says, 'Oh pardon me!' I thought it might cheer you up," Anthony lied, because he hadn't known the

Teddy farted until he had squeezed it on the underground after buying it. Fucking nearly shit himself to be honest, a talking Teddy. Last thing you want after a toot on the old brown powder in the underground toilets. Haley laughed. A Teddy that farted and then apologised whatever next…?

"Have you been busy today? Are you all right? You seem troubled," she enquired. She could see that Anthony was not himself; he kept looking around and his hand kept tightening upon hers. He was obviously anxious. He was fine, he lied.

"It's just been a bit manic today, usual Saturday stuff. No, no, I'm fine. What about you though? You look well, better than this morning."

Haley had to laugh. She felt like shit but as always she played it down.

"I just had a bad night, Anthony. They've upped my medication a little now, though, so I'll be okay for a while." Haley lied, well sort of lied, she was going to deteriorate rapidly over the next few weeks so they would keep increasing the medicine until the end. A thing they didn't speak about too often, the end.

"Is it cold out?" Haley asked. She couldn't see through the window. It was pissing down, AJ informed her, before asking her if she would like to go outside. Not now, obviously, but sometime soon?

"I would, that would be nice. The nurses take me out occasionally but I feel a burden to them. If you come tomorrow, you could take me out. Only in the courtyard, though. It would be nice, if you want to?"

AJ concurred immediately; of course he wanted to. The room was silent for a while as Haley studied the nervous figure sitting beside her. He was hot - he always was, but he was particularly hot tonight; she could see the perspiration on his frowning brow. The bed rocked gently, turning the rattle of metal equipment into a steady rhythm that never missed a beat.

"Anthony, your legs are shaking. You'll wear your kneecaps out. You know what the doctors said!" Haley reminded him as the bed went still and the rattling metal fell silent. "What's wrong?"

AJ jammed his feet firmly under the metal frame of the bed at the point where it met the floor to restrain the tension being forced out of his body. Damaged kneecaps were the least of his worries at the moment! He smiled at Haley. She was so clever, cleverer than him by a long shot; she could tell exactly when something was troubling him. He couldn't tell her yet; he had to lie, at least for now.

"Look, we don't talk so much about the… well, about the end, do we? I know what we decided, but I feel it's time we discussed it. Look, right, you don't want to die in here, do you? Things are going to be different from now on. I want to give you what you deserve, what you should have been given a long time ago. You might not have long to enjoy it, I know that, I understand that, but I've sorted something out for us. Money, a place, somewhere we can be together until the end."

Anthony spoke from his heart. He would get what he had promised for Haley, although he didn't know exactly how he was going to manage it yet. He had three grand. That was the money sorted, now he just needed a place. It shouldn't be that difficult, not with eleven rounds at his disposal.

"It doesn't matter how," he said in response to Haley's inevitable question. "Leave how to me, all you have to do is be ready to leave here tomorrow when I come and take you for that trip outside. You need to do something, though; you need to find out what drugs they're giving you. That's really important, but not as important as keeping our plans a secret. No one must know, or they'll try and stop us."

AJ spoke confidently; he had it all planned. Well, sort of. He cleared the blood-stained phlegm from his throat, but he could not swallow it so he took a tissue out of the box on the bedside cabinet and spat the concoction into it before putting it in the bin.

"That's getting worse, Anthony. Why don't you see a doctor?" Haley asked.

He shook his head in response. He didn't have another three years left for them to find out what he already knew was wrong with his respiratory system.

"Dad's sold the shop," he continued fabricating. "He owes money, and big time. He's been given ten thousand up front because he needs five, like now, and so I've took five as well. With that money you can have your dream come true. Remember, the dream that you have? Well, we can share it!"

AJ almost convinced himself, although in reality there was a little more to it, such as the police, the Yardies, and all the bonuses that come with being one of the most wanted men in Britain. It was all going to kick off tomorrow, AJ was almost sure of it. Tomorrow the media would know just who was responsible for the largest killing spree on British soil for some years. That's why time was limited. Hopefully the police didn't know just yet, although they would have their suspicions and would no doubt have pulled mum in for questioning. She would be none the wiser, though, and would think her son incapable of such violence. Tyrone was dead, so he was saying nothing. There was just Rigger, the newspaper man, but then he had witnessed AJ shoot two men dead at point blank range, so he'd be saying nothing. He hadn't been there when AJ had run from the block of flats after discovering his slaughtered father and the dying prostitute, whom he had finished at her own request with the first round from the Browning, the only firearm he now had left at his disposal. Rigger's stall had been packed away and he was long gone. Shame really, because AJ had changed his mind and was going to kill the man just to make sure of his continuing silence. The old feller had probably suspected as much.

"But that money, you could spend it on yourself! You've got to live once I've gone. It's your future, Anthony!" Haley pleaded, although secretly she welcomed the idea; it gave her some excitement in a life bound for imminent death. But she would refuse the offer for her lover's sake.

"Don't worry about the money, there's plenty more coming. It's now we have to think about, time is precious. So be ready tomorrow, say ten o'clock?"

Haley nodded in agreement just as there was a knock at the door and a familiar face smiled in from the corridor.

"Leigh!" Haley greeted her guest. "Anthony, this is Leigh, one of my nurses. She's going on holiday tomorrow." Haley informed him without a hint of jealousy. She was truly pleased for Nurse Anderson because she deserved a break. Thirtyish she was and a pretty girl.

"I just popped in to say goodbye before I leave, and good luck with your treatment over the next few weeks. I'm flying first thing tomorrow so I've just got to grab a few bits and bobs before the shops shut. Take care!" Leigh embraced her patient and kissed her on the cheek. "Good luck!" she whispered in Haley's ear. Tears filled their eyes before Leigh broke from the embrace and left the room, waving goodbye. The visit had reminded Haley that death was closing in fast. Leigh had obviously called in before her holiday because she thought it unlikely that her patient was going to live until her return in a fortnight. It also sold AJ's offer of her dream being made true, because the moments now were indeed very precious.

"Get me out of here tomorrow, AJ, we'll share my dream." she asked.

AJ squeezed her hand and smiled as he listened to the distant voices in the corridor. He could hear Leigh talking to the night-shift nurse about her flight: three in the morning was a crap time to fly, and so on. Leigh had given him an insane idea, helped him hatch a plan. Unfortunately she was going to have to assist, although indirectly. AJ asked a few questions about the pretty nurse, discreetly of course. She was unattached; recently divorced. Her ex-husband was very well-to-do so she was comfortably off; nursing was just something she loved to do.

"I'm going to have to go soon, Haley, I've got some final odds and ends to sort out before tomorrow." AJ said truthfully, and Haley nodded in agreement. Carefully, he stood and leaned over the metal bed so that he could gently kiss her on the lips. It'll be all right tomorrow; we'll be together until the end!" AJ promised. As long as all his plans went his way they would be, right until the end. Whoever's end came first, that was. He walked slowly away, keeping a gentle hold of her hand until their fingers finally parted. "And remember find out what medication you need. I've got someone who'll sort all that out, but we need to know what to buy."

He left the ward with his head bowed, taking care to avert his face as he passed nurse Anderson, who was still chatting in the corridor. He kept an image of her in his mind as he exited the front door of the ward and entered the maze of corridors en route to the real world. Miss Anderson was wearing a beige woollen coat - well, AJ thought it was woollen, and her dark, shoulder length hair was tied back in a ponytail and secured by a big, flat, silver thing. High-heeled black boots completed the look. AJ sat on a bench outside the hospice next to a news stand and alongside several people who were awaiting a bus to arrive. Apparently it was thirty minutes late. So, tell someone who gives a fuck! It was strange being front page news, and even stranger to be the cause behind all three of the major stories. The articles all appeared close together on the front page, as if the editor couldn't choose a winner for the best spot. The news had never been so interesting! It just remained for AJ to bide his time on the cold wooden bench while he waited for his subject to leave the hospice.

*

It appeared that Billy Tap had a bit of time to himself while his bods did their stuff. He was stuck for a while now. Although the team had an impressive number of clues, the information still had to be extracted from them. Firstly, they needed the SIM card back in order to pursue the main suspect. Secondly, they needed Mrs Jenkins to spill her guts on what she knew, if she knew anything. It would also be handy if Tyrone were to perk up a little so that Tap could interrogate him and extract whatever information he could give. Oh, and that bird, the ill-looking, skinny piece in the photos; Tap could do with knowing what her story was. He wasn't asking for much. It all took time, though. Not a lot of time, but enough to allow the devil to find more work for idle hands.

Over a pint or two, Tap had studied the diary that he had illegally retrieved from the Jenkins' flat. It was a sad story really; a bitter saga of how our health service, once envied throughout the world, had gone to shit. The doctors seemed to have pushed this young man from pillar to post and then finally to the edge: misdiagnosis, six-month waits to see various specialists; numerous cancellations; accusations that he was exaggerating or was a hypochondriac, and so on. It was no wonder they had a fucking lunatic on their hands, Tap thought; he might have lost the plot himself if he had been in this chap's place.

While he was in the pub, progress reports were communicated to him on his mobile. The latest was that Mum was keeping, well, mum! Tyrone was being measured up for a box and Buzby was just awaiting the co-operation of the phone company. So things were moving along, but not at any great pace. There was time for a few hours social life, which was only a phone call away.

"Stacey? You know who it is. Have you got company?" Tap spoke into his mobile. It was about eight o'clock and Stacey did indeed have company.

"Well fucking get rid of him then, I've got something for you."

"Is it big?" Stacey giggled.

"The biggest…!" Tap promised. "And I'll be bringing a friend. He's a nice boy, you'll like him. See you in an hour!" Tap ended the call, laughing.

Tap made one more call, this time to André from the burger bar. They were going out tonight for some fun, he informed the boy. The date was on and Tap quickly finished his drink, snapping shut the diary which had been open on the table in front of him. The diary was important Tap was sure of that, but in what way? Had AJ stolen money from the Yardies to fund his own private war? What had Tyrone sold young Mr Jenkins; what sort of arsenal was he dealing with? Tap had read through the document three times now and he understood Anthony Jenkins' predicament, but what he could not work out was who was going to pay for the poor service. The diary boasted thirty or more possibilities. He decided to leave the data alone for the time being now that he had absorbed it, to allow his subconscious the opportunity to analyse it. For now, though, it was time to have fun: fun in the form of sex. Dirty filthy drug-fuelled bisexual sex. After all, having fun was what life was all about!

AJ kept the image in his head, making sure that the picture stayed as clear as possible until he saw who he was waiting for. Rain dripped onto the newspaper he had been using as camouflage, but it did not matter. Nurse Anderson had absolutely no idea that she was being followed. She had no enemies, therefore, no reason to look over her shoulder. She crossed the main street and disappeared down into the underground, folding away her conspicuous yellow umbrella as she did so. Her stalker followed down the stairs and then used the machine nearest the entrance to buy a ticket. AJ used a fresh ten pound note to buy his ticket to ride; it was the first of the dirty money. As a token gesture he donated the change to a begging vagrant who gratefully pocketed it. It made such a change to assist your fellow man rather than urinating on him! Three minutes of uncertainty loomed until the train arrived, then he boarded the carriage next to the one occupied by his subject. AJ studied her through two pieces of glass; one quarter panel and one door, having chosen the seat nearest to the front of the carriage. She was standing, loosely gripping the red hand rail above her head.

Each time the train stopped he experienced a surge of adrenaline, watching the subject like a hawk. There were four stops in all before she bailed out at the fifth, not far from where Anthony lived, funnily enough. The doors opened and he fought his way through the barrage of inpatient commuters massed in front of him.

Through the turnstiles and back out into the rain, and Leigh was waiting at the traffic lights. Struggling to keep up, her pursuer just managed to catch the lights himself. She stopped at a corner shop and through the window AJ saw tampons, cigarettes and some little drink things in foil containers appearing on the counter: last minute 'bits and bobs, he recalled. Leigh left the shop but the umbrella remained closed this time; AJ correctly guessed that they must be getting close. She stepped up to the main entrance of some smart-looking flats in an old, but well-kept building. It had obviously been renovated recently. Ms Anderson encountered a sofa as she ascended the steps; someone was obviously moving out and she stopped for a little chit chat.

AJ decided that now was not the right time to storm the building. Instead, he went for a walk in the park to clear his head and make a plan. He took a wet seat on a bench and stared at the old building for inspiration. Unbelievably, he got it. Three floors up, third flat from the left, Leigh Anderson was closing her curtains, illuminated by the bright light behind her. So, he knew the flat and he knew that Ms Anderson was leaving the country for two weeks at three in the morning. Excellent! With a bit of luck then, AJ could move in the next morning.

Casually, with a wet arse, AJ crossed the road again, hands in pockets and shoulders hunched against the elements. He cleared his throat and spat into the wind, the majority of the contents coming back at him. That one hurt; they sometimes did, and the pain was always greater in bad weather. He watched with interest as a sideboard came out of the building with the aid of two men who were very soon out of sight in the van. Silly that, leaving your key in the front door; nice one! AJ will have that! And he did. That really was an unexpected bonus, because he'd been planning on having to search Leigh's home for the front door key once he'd taken possession of the flat. Instead of standing around looking suspicious, AJ opted to return to the park, to maybe have a little 'toot' to keep him occupied until Leigh Anderson left for the airport. After all, someone might have spotted him looking a little cagey, pulled him up on it or called the old bill, which might have forced him to do something really naughty, like shoot them and fuck the whole plan right up. Nah, Park life was the way forward.

Two figures, maybe father and son, approached another set of flats. Once again it was an aged, red brick construction with a slate roof. The older man chose the top floor apartment, the home of Stacey Payne, and pressed the buzzer. Miss Payne was expecting her guests; she invited them in and closed the door behind them. Tap was late as usual, but then if you asked him if he gave a shit, you know what answer you'd receive.

Stacey was very attractive indeed, not tarty or home made at all. No, she was natural. Blonde hair tied back, full lips, designer jeans and T shirt; she looked posh. She was also very well spoken, which always gave Tap the right horn, as he put it.

"Stacey, beautiful as ever…!" Tap greeted her.

"Billy, as poorly timed as ever!" Stacey retorted with a smile. "Who's your friend, then?"

Tap kissed her on the cheek and introduced André to their host.

"Pleased to meet you, young man." Stacey said truthfully. And wasn't he young? The age didn't matter as long as Tap had brought with him what he promised, which was the book he carried under his arm.

Tap made himself at home in the flat, but André was obviously nervous.

"Make yourself at home, why don't you?" Stacey joked, since Tap had already removed his coat, hung it up and was sitting at the table ready to dine. Stacey took her younger guest's coat and offered him a seat, taking the expensive bottle of wine from Tap.

The flat was very tasteful. It consisted of two large rooms divided by a huge glass door that was at present open. The table at which they sat at was in the larger of the two rooms. The other room was simply one extremely large bedroom. The kitchen was at one side of the table and on the other side, between the kitchen and bedroom, was a small lounge area consisting of a couple of sofas and two chairs, all made of leather. Tap sat with his back to the main entrance, where a bathroom was situated. As he looked ahead of him he could see right through the large windows to a small balcony. The world of journalism had been good to this child of the seventies; or rather Tap had been good to her, because she hadn't got here entirely by herself, despite her hard work. For London it was a pretty view; you could see right out into the bright lights of the city and beyond. It really was a lovely flat - not a patch on Tap's, but nice nevertheless. Stacey had done well for herself.

"You want to eat now?" She suggested. She had only made chilli con carne, blaming her limited cooking prowess.

"Not really," grinned Tap, "I hope the sweet is a little more imaginative!"

Stacey was obviously keen for some clue as to what information was coming her way in return for her hospitality. All in good time, Tap promised.

"Well, what do you want to do then?" Stacey asked as she brought out the sweet trolley.

Tap pulled her down onto his lap and kissed her, before standing to lead her through the glass doors and into the bedroom.

"Look Stacey," Tap whispered, "André has little or no experience of women. He's convinced he's gay, but I was thinking a night with you would, well, let's say test his theory. He's a good lad, a good friend of mine, but he needs looking after, and that's what I do; I look after him. He loves me, but you know me; I'm not really any good at the old love thing. You see, I saved him from a little predicament one day, you know, work and all that, fucking nonces, and he looks up to me. But I don't want to be the wrong type of influence on him, you know what I mean?"

Stacey did know. She was actually taken aback by such thoughtfulness on the detective's behalf, but this was business and it was time to negotiate the package.

"Okay, so you want me to put him through the paces? It's no problem! What will he like me to wear?" she asked. To Stacey it was merely a sexual act between her and an old friend, via a new one. As for sex with Tap, it was good; better than good; probably the best she'd had. André, though, was another matter. Tap had a bit of a cheek there, but if the boy really had never had a sexual encounter with a woman then it would be interesting if nothing else.

"Dress like you're going out to a club or something, you know what I mean. I watch him when we're out, and he likes it, I can tell."

"And when do I get paid, then?" Stacey smiled.

"I'm working on that now, but don't worry; this one's the big one. The quicker you can take my young friend under your wing and out of my way, the quicker I can get you your story. Keep him busy for a while though, if you can?" Tap pleaded. He really did have work to do, but André was under his feet.

"Club wear it is, then. I won't be long," Stacey promised.

Tap made his way back to the lounge, where André had left the table and was nervously flicking through a women's magazine.

"That'll fuck your head up!" Tap joked, and the boy smiled nervously.

"Stacey's nice, ain't she?" Tap asked casually. The boy nodded. "Yeah, Stacey's real nice. She wants to spend a little time with you - you know, fool around a bit? She likes you, so I'm going to leave you with her for a bit, while I take care of a few things. I'm not going anywhere, I'll be right here, but I won't be much fun for a few hours. She'll take care of you, you all right with that?" Tap asked. "Good lad!" he concluded, just as Stacey reappeared from behind one of the dividing doors to her bedroom. She looked stunning in white knee-length boots, a blue skirt and a bikini top tied at the front, just above her pierced belly button.

"Jesus!" Tap blasphemed. Work no longer seemed so appealing, but it had to be done; society needed him. He would simply join the show a little later on and relieve his frustrations. For now, though, he had a killer to catch and he wasn't going to do it with Stacey standing there in the doorway half naked.

"Run along then, André, go and see Stacey." Tap ordered, and the boy walked obediently towards the bedroom and Stacey.

"Are you not joining us?" André asked.

"No mate, not just now. Maybe later though yeah?"

André nodded as Stacey led him by the hand into the bedroom and partially closed the frosted glass dividing doors behind them, leaving a gap of about a metre. The small opening seemed to align perfectly with the centre of the bed, giving Tap a good view of the action as and when he required it. For now, though, his colleagues needed his attention to try and stop this sick son of a bitch, Anthony Jenkins.

"All right Slim, what's she got to say for herself then?" Tap demanded, speaking into his mobile and referring to the questioning of Mrs Jenkins.

"Nah, she's a right cunt, right hard work. The bird in your picture, though, the ill-looking one, her name is Haley."

"Haley fucking who…?"

"Jenkins says she doesn't know her second name. She's in a hospital, though, sick by all accounts!"

"Sick with what…?"

But Doughnut had no further information.

"You're a fucking fat useless cunt, Doughnut! I want better answers than that; she's taking the piss out of you. Get her away from her brief and get a phone to her, I want to speak to her." Tap ordered as his phone beeped twice. "Hang on, Fat Boy, I've got another call."

With the press of a button another caller came on air.

"Sid? Hang on, I've got your lover on the other line." Tap fumbled with the buttons but Doughnut seemed to have disappeared. "It's all right, Sid, I seem to have lost the Fat Boy. Tell me the good news, then!"

Sid did have good news, as it happened. They had managed to save the slightly damaged SIM card.

"Yeah, Buzby's saved it; cleaned it all up and it's ready to roll. We got the data on Mr Banks' calls for the last week or so, who he's been talking to and so on. And I take my turban off to you, Mr Tap. You were right, it looks like Jenkins has adopted George Belazaire's phone. Belazaire was barbecued this morning in the explosion and there are calls to Tyrone Banks' phone in the early afternoon, and it weren't Belazaire because he was done to a crisp by then! Do you want us to call the number?" Sid enquired.

Tap didn't want the number called, not under any circumstances. He was doing the talking on this little number, because this was his little baby!

"No, bring it down the station; I'll be there at twelve. I want you to get to the station, get some shut eye, and I'll see you when I see you. You know how to work it, don't you?" Tap asked, referring to the state of the art spying equipment Buzby used. The machine could record everything said by both parties and locate roughly where a call was being made or received. It could actually only tell which telephone masts were receiving the calls, and even with the masts being so close together in London that still left a huge area to cover, but as long as the oral evidence was on disc that was the main thing.

"Nice one, Sid, any news on our good friend Mr Banks?" Tap enquired. It was Slug's job really, but Sid was under strict orders not to disturb him so he had chased the matter himself with the hospital a couple of hours ago. The doctors had said that tomorrow morning was about the earliest they would be able to see the patient. They had no option but to wait; the suspect was firmly under police armed guard and Sid would get a call when the key witness awoke. Tyrone was going to make it through the night, the doctors were convinced of it. It appeared that his phone had saved his life.

"Okay Sid, go and get some sleep and I'll see you soon."

Through the gap in the frosted glass dividing doors, Tap could see his boyfriend being educated in lessons of love. He sat back in his chair, put his mobile down on the table and watched. Stacey was still wearing her clothes but her breasts had been released from the bikini top to allow André to explore. Tap felt a pang of envy, having nuzzled between those perfect breasts many a time, but then it was all new to André.

The silence was suddenly broken by the phone. It was Doughnut, returning the call that had been cut off previously.

"Yes, Slim."

"Got Mrs Jenkins here, boss. Hurry up, though, she's only meant to be taking a crap," Doughnut sounded furtive and out of breath.

"You've not been giving her one, have you?" Tap enquired with concern. Doughnut had not, of course, but couldn't think of a witty response.

"The next voice you hear will be Mrs Jenkins!" he managed.

"Mrs Jenkins? Tap asked. "Good. Now, I'm Detective Sergeant Tap and I'm leading this investigation. I'm sorry I can't be with you at the moment, but I'm currently engaged. You see, we've got a bit of a problem at the moment. We've got a seriously ill freak creating mayhem on my streets. It's your son, Mrs Jenkins. So when I'm told that all you have to offer our investigation is crap, feeble information, alarm bells are starting to ring!"

He listened to the angry response, which he had expected.

"By all means tell your lawyer," he continued. "I can take care of your lawyer, don't worry about that, but think about yourself a little. You're a widow now, soon to lose a son as well unless I can catch him alive. Even so, you won't be getting much help from him for the rest of your days, so where does that leave you? Have you heard of the Yardies before?" Tap asked.

The answer was negative.

"Your son has. He's done these people a huge injustice. In fact, your son has killed four of their boys. How would you feel if four of your family members had been slaughtered? You'd be a bit pissed off wouldn't you? Were they collecting money? Did your husband or son owe them money?" Tap asked.

Mrs Jenkins said she did not know, but it was more likely that her husband owed them money than AJ. Tap thought she was probably right.

"Okay then, four dead henchmen, an outstanding debt; how long do you think you're going to last out there, Mrs Jenkins? You're probably top of their hit list by now. There'll be a bounty on your head and more than likely a queue outside waiting to collect. I'll tell you something now: I'm going to catch your son, dead or alive, and the press are going to have a field day. We could promise you police protection - waste of time, you know that. You need me; I'm the only one who can keep you alive. Now I suggest you get back in that interview room and you spill your guts, because otherwise I can't do a lot for you. Help me, though, and I'll help you; I'm good like that. So, do we have an understanding?"

They had a deal.

Tap suddenly found himself with no one left to call. Time was moving slowly, so he helped himself to another glass of wine and sat back in his chair again to think. He scoured the diary again as he sipped. This little book held the key to the downfall of young Jenkins, Tap was sure of it. The National Health appeared to be a major target. So what could he do? What was the worst he could really do? Tap dreaded to think. It was clear so far that arson, explosions and cold-blooded murder were well within his capabilities. At the very least, one would assume that the doctors who dealt with Anthony would be at the greatest risk; surely they would pay first? As a precaution Tap compiled a list of the most likely candidates.

Viewed through the gap between the frosted doors, André seemed to be getting on well with Stacey's tutoring. Stacey was lying on her back and the eager boy was driving his body against hers. He seemed to be enjoying himself so much that neither he nor Stacey heard Tap leave the flat. Time was getting on and Billy had a date with a killer. André would be all right back at the flat; he could find his own way home in the morning if he didn't manage to get back to collect him. Stacey's payment for her services had not been settled yet; she would receive it by email within the next few hours.

*

Tap made his way to the underground en route to the Yard, the light from the streetlamps reflecting off his shiny, black leather jacket. Two stops, easy enough. His shoulders hunched, his hands in his pockets and the diary under arm, the policeman looked around to spot any potential trouble but there was none around. Skateboarders, drunks, tramps, train security and officials, wankers, all of them. Tap felt special; he knew he was better than the rest. Down at the nick, Tap made his way up to the top floor. Sid was there, waiting.

"Shall we give our old mate a call, then?" Tap asked.

The blue button on the technical-looking box of tricks had the number already programmed into it; you just had to press that when you wanted to call. Sid was clearly feeling proud to be part of the first live link-up with their killer.

"The disc records the conversation as soon as you press the button," he explained. "All you have to do is speak into the hand piece and you'll hear him on the speaker, but you must have that red button switched on first because that rings the database that tracks the calls."

Red button it was then, followed by blue. There was a bit of a delay before the database was linked up to the unit, but soon the phone rang. It continued to ring until the timer on the equipment timed the call out. They pressed the blue button again, the phone rang a second time and someone answered eventually.

AJ nearly shit himself as he was forced out of his drug-induced slumber by the tune in his pocket. He was sitting on the bench in the park just outside Leigh Anderson's home. The phone had actually been ringing for a while, much to the annoyance of a nearby vagrant. AJ had heard it, but instead of waking, he had introduced it into his dream. He had had to medicate himself with heroin as he studied his new property from the park bench, and it had been a most pleasurable hit. In the dream, AJ had been in his flat, his new flat, surrounded by white everything. Haley was there, although she was out of focus; just a white blob in the distance. The doorbell was ringing, and it was annoying him so he made his way to the front door. He paused before answering the door, because the tune had suddenly stopped. However, it soon started up again and this time Anthony awoke, fumbling for the phone in his inside pocket. It was next to his wad of cash as opposed to the cold steel killing-machine that lay hidden in the other inside pocket.

What the fuck do I do with it? AJ asked himself. Answer it? He didn't want to really, so he just pressed the green button in order to receive the call before putting the phone to his ear. He didn't have to speak; he could just listen.

"Mr Jenkins, I presume?" a voice filled the earpiece. There was a nervous giggle.

"Forgive me, caller." AJ couldn't resist replying. "But I seem to be at somewhat of a disadvantage. I know who you are. I just don't know your name. You were in Soho this morning, though, weren't you? I hope your shoes dried?"

Tap was impressed; AJ had instantly elevated himself from the position of a jumped-up prick with a chip on his shoulder to that of possible psychopath. Tap realised that he was dealing with a fairly bright individual with an agenda. Anthony Jenkins wanted to play games, and Tap would be only too keen to oblige.

"You're breathing heavily, my friend, did I take you by surprise?" Tap teased.

"Take me by surprise? No, that would be difficult." AJ chuckled confidently. "You don't even know where I fucking am!" 'Am' sounded like 'ham' as blood stained phlegm forced its way out of his throat and out onto the pavement.

"A cold, Anthony…?" Tap asked casually. "What's it all about then, Anthony? Are you upset about something? Someone pissed you off?"

AJ laughed manically, while Tap listened for clues in the background. All he could hear was traffic. The laughter suddenly stopped, and the voice spoke again in an ironic tone.

"You know who's pissed me off officer. You've been bagging them up all afternoon! What's your name?"

"Billy," Tap replied mildly.

"Billy fucking bullshit…!"

The phone went dead.

"Bollocks!" Tap swore. "Cunt, shit, fuck and bollocks…!"

Not good so far, but he was gonna have this cunt! He hit the blue button again.

"Come on, answer, you bastard!"

Anthony Jenkins obligingly answered.

"Sorry Billy. You have to do that, though, don't you?"

"What?" Tap asked, baffled.

"Switch off, Billy. Surely you're recording me?"

"You're on a digital cell phone Anthony. You see the stars above your head? Well, you go all the way up there before you come back to us; how the fuck are we going to trace you? I can find out the area you're in, we've probably done that by now, but you're one in half a million, Anthony, so I think you're pretty safe." Billy spoke as if to a child.

"Yeah right, you would tell me that, wouldn't you?" AJ fired back. I'm not fucking stupid; let's get that straight!" Tap had just earned himself a dead line.

"Cunt!" the policeman screamed. He hit the blue button twice, but AJ was not answering. His phone was engaged, and suddenly the box of tricks on the table in front of them started ringing.

"Well how do you fucking answer it then?" Tap demanded.

Sid had no idea; they hadn't bargained on that!

"Shit, ring Buzby!" Tap ordered. Sid did; no fucking answer.

"Bollocks!" Tap cursed as he gripped the handset in rage, unknowingly pressing the button that allowed his voice to be heard. The ringing stopped and the sound of traffic replaced it. Tap nodded at his side-kick with relief, swallowed hard and exhaled deeply.

"Hello, Anthony?"

"Billy! How the fuck are you? And Billy who, is it that I have the pleasure?"

"Tap, Anthony, Billy Tap, and I'm all fine and dandy, thank you for asking."

"Cool. Hey, can you guys still trace me if I ring you?" AJ enquired, hypothetically it appeared. "Got to go now, bye!" The voice was replaced by the sounds of taxis, buses, beeping pedestrian crossings and trees swaying in the wind. Tap didn't dare hang up but remained glued to the earpiece in case the voice came back. Eventually the phone's battery ran out, at which time the box of tricks read twenty two minutes, thirty two seconds, and so many of those little things that are smaller than seconds. Tap was fucked.

*

The phone was actually sitting in a tree. It was in a small recess within Anthony's reach, and that's where it remained right up until the battery ran out. Anthony was leaning against a corner shop, drinking a can of cola. He appeared not to have a care in the world as he took his time with his drink, but suddenly became alert when he saw Leigh Anderson getting into a taxi. It was twelve thirty and her flight was at three, so she must have been flying from Heathrow. Whatever, she was gone now and Anthony could take possession of his new flat. First, though, he had to gain access to it, and this was to be done in two stages. For stage one he had the perfect solution: the key in his pocket that he had been rolling through his fingers for the last five minutes. As for stage two, he'd worry about that when he got there.

One thing about breaking into a flat in the early hours of the morning was that you had to be quiet. The lock was more solid than AJ had bargained on, but then it would be; this was not some derelict flat in Soho occupied by dropouts, no sir, this was a class joint with good secure locks to keep the likes of the Jenkins family at bay. Anthony hit the door with frustration just as a pair of eyes, alerted by the disturbance, peered from the next doorway. He'd been clocked by some old cunt and now he'd have to kill him, he knew that. He needed this flat too badly. He had put great effort into this project and granddad there was not going to fuck it up. He thought quickly.

"Sorry if I woke you, mate. I've just missed Leigh by a few minutes, I reckon. I'm meant to be looking after her fish and greens and that, and I've gone and lost the keys, ain't I? Well, not me as such, the bastards that just robbed my motor, excuse my French. Thought I'd just catch her before she went but by the time the old bill arrived and checked my car over it was too late."

The old man seemed to be taken in and told Anthony that he had missed her by about ten minutes.

"Really…?" Anthony played the innocent like an old pro. "So, if I could ring her, then I could get her to turn round and drop a key back here, or she could leave me a key at the airport? No, second thoughts, she could give it to the taxi driver to give to me. That's fantastic, you're a genius! Only thing is, they've nicked my bloody phone. I know her mobile number, but I've got no phone. I don't suppose…?"

The old man nodded in agreement and led the way into his flat.

"Maybe he'll charge the battery?" Sid didn't believe that for one minute but something positive had to be said.

"Yeah Sid, that's right, and maybe his arsehole will heal up in the meantime and he'll die of constipation, eh?"

Doughnut, who was actually chomping away on a doughnut, entered the room. Tap pointed at something behind him as he came in.

"Do you know what that is, Doughnut?" He asked, facetious as usual.

Doughnut did; it was a door, but he wasn't going to say that. He'd heard this one before.

"That is a special door," he answered correctly. "That is a 'don't come through me unless you've got some fucking good news to share' door!"

Tap didn't seem impressed, although he was; he had trained Lard well, but he wasn't going to tell him that.

"No, Doughnut; that's a 'if you don't stop eating that shit you're not going to be able to fit through the fucking door,' door!" Tap retorted triumphantly.

Sid coughed up a mouthful of coffee; respect was due, there was no way Doughnut was ever going to get the better of the governor.

"Well, have you?" Tap asked.

Doughnut grunted, no longer sure what he was being asked.

"Good news, Slim, are you the bringer of good news?" Tap elaborated.

Doughnut swallowed the last three mouthfuls hastily.

"Yeah, yeah not a brilliant result but you were right; showing her them pictures of her husband and his whore certainly assisted in the process."

Sid shook his head in disbelief.

"Well what's she say, then?" He couldn't resist asking.

"Well, it weren't a surprise for her that there was a whore there; often was, apparently. She was also saying that her son's not well."

Tap had to stop him there.

"Doughnut, we know he's unwell. He's killed four people so far in one day and blown the chest out of another; he's definitely fucking ill, Doughnut!"

"Yeah, granted he's not playing with a full deck, but he's got something else wrong with him, something wrong with his lungs; bronchitis or something? He's an addict, yeah; all right we knew that, but he's not just a dabbler, he's full on. Hence the lung trouble, mother reckons. She didn't know Anthony had any major problem with the health service, though. He didn't like going to the doctors about his chest and that, but she put that down to the gear he tooted."

Tap sighed.

"Doughnut, tell me something I don't fucking already know, because we know all this. We found his smoking tools at his house, a Tom in his Dad's bedroom, a diary filled with nothing but hatred for the NHS, and you heard him on the phone Sid - he was chucking his guts up, weren't he?" Tap wanted more, or Doughnut was going to be in his bad books.

"The girl, Doughnut, who is she? What's she about?" Billy enunciated slowly, as though speaking to an idiot.

"Again, she's ill. Jenkins has been going out with her for a while now, a couple of years. They lived together by all accounts, in her flat, but now she's in a hospital somewhere. The mum don't know where though; they're not close you see, him and his mum. Anyway, Jenkins visits this bird every day, apparently, so she must be pretty fucked!"

Tap was beginning to understand, although he wasn't going to let Doughnut off the hook that easily.

"So what's her name? Tell me you've got her name? Please fucking tell me you've got her name, and not fucking Haley, we know that!"

Doughnut held his arms up in defence; he didn't have the second name. Detectives had ripped the suspect's room to pieces and found the name Haley everywhere, but not her surname.

"Oh you cunt, Doughnut!" Tap exploded. "Well what's wrong with her then? At least tell me that."

Doughnut merely shrugged.

"Age then?" Tap asked through gritted teeth.

"Mid-twenties?" Doughnut ventured.

"So she's anything from eighteen to thirty. Fucking superb!" Tap had to walk over to the window and stare out into the bright lights of the city for five minutes while he calmed down. He eventually turned to his colleagues again.

“Okay, what we got? Jenkins, he’s an ill man - bronchial infection or something, maybe that smackhead thing they get when their lungs fuck up? Does he get on with Pops?” Tap enquired.

Doughnut shook his head; no, the father and son thing was not good - well, step farther.

“Okay, the bird’s also ill, we don’t know what with, but she’s ill enough to be in hospital. Sick at her age, it don’t make much sense,” Tap ruminated, then his eyes lit up.

“She’s got the lurgy, I bet you any fucking money! She’s got HIV, and him, bronchial infection, he’s on his way out mate. They’re both on borrowed time!” Tap guessed. Exploring the lead was a matter of simple police work.

“Doughnut, go home and get some shut-eye. Be back by tomorrow lunch - our lunch, that is, not yours!” Tap ordered. He turned to Sid.

“People with AIDS are all on a register or something, someone will know where they all are, find it, and find out who and where she is.”

Sid nodded. At least he could get some rest between making the phone calls and waiting for the replies. If none were received in a few hours, he would have to make chase up calls. What was the Gaffer going to do? No one knew but Tap. As his troops went their separate ways, the man in charge sat at his desk and prepared to write an email; he had a payment to make.

*

The old feller’s flat was aesthetically pleasing; it had had a recent revamp, and probably not the first because all the mod cons that one takes for granted these days were at hand. AJ simply followed patiently as the old man led the way down the main hallway and into the open plan kitchen to the right of the front door. As he lifted the cordless phone, the old man offered his guest a cup of tea and walked towards the kettle standing idly on the work surface. To the left of the open plan kitchen there was another room, which Anthony supposed was a bedroom. The corridor then continued down to another door, lounge perhaps?

Anthony didn't want tea. The old man shrugged but put the kettle on anyway. Anthony watched him as he slowly drew the cold steel weapon from within his leather jacket. He stealthily concealed the weapon behind his back, planning to use it as a bludgeon rather than to shoot the old man, in order to keep the noise down.

"What's your name, then?" Anthony asked out of the blue. He felt it wrong not to know a man's name before he killed him, although he had done it twice already the day before. The old man, turning slowly to face Anthony as though startled by the question, replied that his name was Gordon.

Poor cunt, Gordon! Anthony felt pity for him. Gordon was looking a little worried now, as Anthony stood with one hand behind his back and the other holding the cordless phone.

"Are you going to call then?" He asked. Something was amiss, Gordon could see that.

"I have, Gordon, she's not answering. I'll try again in a minute," Anthony replied, handing the phone back to him. Gordon moved to take it, apparently without noticing that the distance between the phone and himself seemed to increase as Anthony drew it towards him, until the prey was within the snare.

AJ moved fast. Using the butt of the weapon, he bludgeoned the old man frantically in the face several times, aiming for the bridge of the nose. His victim instantly hunched forwards and began to make a bit of a racket, so he changed tactics and started to hit him on the temples until the hot wet blood pumped from a wound just above the victim's ears. Another strike just above the temple rendered the victim almost instantly silent, which was not surprising considering the size of the fucking hole in his head. Clearly his frail skull had collapsed under the barrage of blows and now he lay and twitched on the floor like a fish out of water. It never ceased to amaze AJ just how much blood came from a human body; you really did have to see it to believe it! The carpet was fucked; that was Anthony's first thought after it finally sunk in that victim number six had been claimed. Well, it was six as far as he was concerned because the notion that Tyrone had survived hadn't even crossed his mind.

He needed a little rest and some medication to calm his nerves as the adrenaline in his body began to stabilise to a normal level. Normal for Anthony, anyway! He put the gun down on the table opposite the sink, leaving a smear of blood. With the innocent bystanders in the Soho bomb blast forgotten; cast off as coincidental in AJ's mind, this was his first victim to die directly via his hands, who had not really been a threat. It was tough to register. The other key players taken out had had a reason to die, but this little old man for fucks sake! Anthony was going to need some drugs to allow him to think the matter through, or at least to offer some relief from the demons in his head. He wanted to sit with his victim; sit with Gordon for a while and have a chat. First, though, he needed something to sit on in the kitchen because the blood stained carpet on the floor looked far from welcoming. This was the first opportunity Anthony had had to sit and spend some time inspecting his handiwork; spend some time with death and maybe learn to respect it. After some minor exploration of his new residence, AJ found a duvet in the main bedroom at the front of the flat, next to the bathroom, just off the lounge. As he pulled the duvet towards him off the bed, he uncovered something that suddenly made his jaw drop to the floor.

"Fucking dirty bastard!" he swore at the bed, in which were lying several pictures of the "kiddie porn" variety. Murderer he may have been, but he drew the line at that. Distressed, he dropped onto a chair behind him and simply stared at the pictures in disbelieve. Children naked, children naked with adult men, children being… The pictures bought back memories, vague memories, so vague that Anthony didn't even know if the events in the flashbacks had actually taken place. It was years ago. Dad wasn't involved, but something had happened to him as a child. It had seemed that the memories were safely locked away, but the reality was that they were just hidden temporarily. What had happened? The memories flitted elusively through his mind but would not stay still long enough for him to grasp them.

Anthony left the room and spat something against the magnolia wall; a red and yellow thing with black spots. After coughing violently for a few seconds, he set to work dragging his victim towards the main bedroom, in turn diverting his mind from the fire burning in his lungs. This man was now as guilty as any of his other victims, in fact his crimes were about as low as it got in Jenkins' book, and that was saying something. Dragging the body through the bedroom door, he swept the pictures off the bed before heaving the body onto it. He then removed the old man's pyjamas and crossed the corpse's arms. Anthony couldn't help but look at Gordon's genitals as he lay there naked; the sight of the shrivelled member turned Anthony's stomach and made him look away quickly: the fucking filthy cunt! It was time to operate.

Gordon was going to pay: Gordon was going to pay for his crimes, Anthony promised himself as he ran to the kitchen. He had already paid with his life, but the case was far from closed now. Although he could no longer hurt the man physically, AJ was going to create a little artwork for the benefit of Billy Tap and it would serve the purpose of leaving something of himself behind for posterity. He would call it 'effective punishment.' It felt good to be working for a cause again. In a twisted way, Anthony considered that his work would show a measure of moral justice. He had, after all, just rid society of a nonce who, if caught by Billy Tap, would have got maybe two years in prison. Well, Anthony gave him a lot more than that; Anthony gave him the death penalty: it was what the public wanted but the government were too scared to implement.

He took the knife he had found in the kitchen and sliced it easily through the lower abdomen, having protected his hands with a pair of Marigolds first. It was a bit tough cutting around the inner thigh, he kept catching the pelvis, but he soon got his technique and a whole circle appeared around the dead man's genitals. By carefully stabbing underneath or behind the small island of flesh a few times with the sharp blade, the trophy was finally retrieved and placed against Gordon's lips. The knife was then wedged against both sets of teeth and the mouth forced open to receive its last meal. The meat dropped in a treat, with a little help, leaving just the penis poking out from between the teeth and lying lifeless against one cheek.

That was a fucking work of art, AJ commended himself. The operation had not created much blood; most of that was in the kitchen. The final touches were added by collecting all the pictures off the floor and laying them on the body for full effect. Climbing onto the bed, the artist dipped his fingers into the open wound between the old man's legs and, using his hand as a brush, set to work naming the piece. It took several dips into the paint pot to create the name, but he was soon leaning back and admiring his handy work. The words 'effective punishment' appeared large and bright against the background of the beige wall, and below them he had added as an afterthought: 'just doing my bit!' The statement bore the artist's signature, A Jenkins.

Anthony saw himself as a dark crusader rather than a cold-blooded killer. Fuck me, another month like this and the City would be a reasonably safe place if he carried on with his social cleansing! He was, however, slightly unnerved by the coincidence of his victim actually being a paedophile. Out of all the houses and flats in London he had had to pick this one; something wasn't right. He didn't know what or who was driving him, but it was too much to be a coincidence. This had happened for a reason. Somehow, he had turned into a magnet for London's undesirables. And all he wanted was to give his dying girlfriend her final wish; the right to die in the comfort of her own home. She was going to get it, too.

The duvet no longer looked so inviting, so he chucked it on the floor. It was time to leave Gordon in peace now; the police would find him some time and it would be self-explanatory. As a parting shot, he threw the knife at the wall, where it stuck in the plasterboard. With sudden interest, he pulled it out and stabbed it into another place in the wall, which divided this flat from the one next door. These partition walls must have been put in well after the building itself was built. Fucking hell, this was piece of piss. He stabbed repeatedly at the wall until he had a hole big enough to put his head through, and before long it had grown to a hatch-sized hole, then a door-sized hole, and then a well-aimed kick created a vision of heaven: Haley's new home had been found. After a few more kicks and a bit of trimming, he had full access.

This was it; this was the room that Haley had described. This was the house in Anthony's dreams, conjured from his lover's description of her dream home and the place where she wanted to die. Everything was indeed white, just as in the dream. His dirty footprints had already sullied the crisp, cream carpet.

"Fuck!" He swore, as he stepped back into the old man's flat and wiped his feet on the carpet, checking each foot individually. With his feet clean, Anthony once again crossed into the other world. He would find a hoover or something to clean up the mess he had made, because the dream palace was going to remain that way. Haley's tomb would be just as she had dreamed: perfect! Alcohol first, though. Anthony needed a beer; it had been a busy night and it wasn't over yet. A clock in the corner showed three in the morning: time for breakfast. A quick look round the palace and then it was time to self-medicate. After all, he had been a busy boy and deserved a little break; just him, a beer and his medicine in the haven he had found. Tap had spent an hour or so on the email to his tame reporter, who was hopefully still taking care of André. She had struck gold here: Tap had let her know almost everything - everything that he wanted her to print that is. What he was after was information from the public and a reaction from the main suspect, and this early morning news report would hopefully notch up the score in favour of the authorities because losing that phone connection had been a real bastard; a real blow to the case. But the day was still young. Tap had had about three hours' sleep. It was not much, but enough in the circumstances. White powder fired up each nostril seemed to make up for it quite handsomely. He had a cup of coffee, but it made his teeth go numb because of the drugs. That was the bit Tap didn't like. The drug itself was wicked, though. He could become an addict again tomorrow if it weren't for the numb teeth that reminded him of a trip to the dentist. Coke was just about the only drug that one could use discreetly in Billy's profession; everyone was doing it, especially those like Tap who got their shit for free! And let's face it; a smacked-up copper would have been about as much use as a chocolate fireguard. Speed? Gurning and rolling eyes; dead fucking giveaway, so coke it was. Well, if it was good enough for past royalty and Mr Sherlock Homes, then it was good enough for Billy Tap!

"All right Slug, what's the news then son?" Tap enquired as his sidekick entered the room.

"Tyrone's up. Still poorly, but I reckon we could get in there now with a little gentle persuasion," Slug reported proudly. He had slept at the hospital this morning rather than go home to an empty flat. Hospital, flat, what was the fucking difference as long as his batteries had time to recharge? Tap asked if he had tried to question him yet.

"Ah, no…. Well, I tried but there's some cocky cunt on the door, and…"

"It's okay mate, no problem. I'll come down and sort our cocky cunt out. Give me twenty-five. While you're waiting, ring Sid and see what he's come up with."

Tap had to wait three or four minutes for his junior assistant to arrive - a right cunt she was as far as office duties and time keeping were concerned, but she was fucking naughty-looking and a right slapper, which was why she got the job. Tap liked this woman; she was very much like him but in bird form, hence an ideal woman.

Dressed as though she had just come back from a nightclub, because she probably had, via someone else's bedroom, Jo took off her coat and hung it up while Tap ogled her arse, and what a nice arse it was! He could make out the outline of her thong under her skirt.

"You look fucked. What you been up to? Little ones today?" he enquired, just out of interest, referring to the size of her underwear.

His assistant lifted her skirt up quickly to flash her arse at her employer.

"Getting fucked," Joanne corrected, "good and proper an' all, right up the Jacksy and everything."

"So you had a quiet night in, then?" Tap countered, playing with his plaything. Jo agreed: she had had a bottle of wine and a good film. Oh, and she had touched herself a little she admitted, as she knew that would be the next question.

"Good, glad to see you're behaving. Don't want you bringing the side down!" Tap joked, because how the fuck could anyone bring this department into disrepute? Anyway, back to business. Tap had a mission for his petite assistant so he led her across the room daintily by her fingers.

"You see that?"

Joanne did.

"Now, I have a special mission for you today. Sit there!" Tap ordered. His assistant obeyed, while he stared at her bare legs with desire. He especially liked her painted toe nails poking through her strappy, high-heeled shoes.

"All I want you to do today is sit by this box of tricks and call me if it rings. There you are, nothing too taxing! Don't let it out of your sight, though, not for one minute. If you need a shit, shit in that bin. If you need food or drink or anything, tell Monkey-Boy to get it!" Monkey Boy was another of Tap's juniors; an ex-student wanker who pulled information off the computer as and when they needed it: stats, figures and stuff like that, basically what Tap's bosses required but Tap had no idea how to deliver. To give him credit, though, Monkey Boy was the bollocks at it, which was just as well because the main men just couldn't be fucked with paperwork.

"Just don't leave it unmanned, that's all. Fuck everything else, just watch that phone thing and when it rings, call me. Simple!"

"Billy, just fuck off. I'll look after your magic box for you, just go!"

"That's my girl!" He liked Jo, she was a lovely piece. Even better on her back with her clothes off, but nice enough to work with as well. Apparently she also had an attractive personality.

*

All right Slug?" Tap smiled as he entered the hospital with his mobile phone glued firmly to his ear. Slug nodded in agreement. Billy was finishing his special burger, which was twice the size of a normal one. Watching his blatant flaunting of the rules, a new nurse behind the reception desk felt it her duty to inform this man that food and phones were not allowed on the wards. Tap, however, was busy with the juicy details from the night before and kept most of his attention on the phone.

"Hang on, André. Slug!" Tap interrupted his conversation to nod towards the nurse. Slug knew what was being asked of him and signalled an acknowledgement. It was better he silenced the nurse than Tap.

Tap carried on his conversation while Slug set to work on his task, intent on his lover's account of the night before.

"Yeah, it's different ain't it, not as tight, but… you took her arse as well? Top man! She's good, though, ain't she? A top bird. Did she like the story I gave her?"

André was still at Stacey's. Stacey herself had rushed off in the early hours, literally as soon as she had finished servicing André and had read the email of her life. Tap commended this stroke of luck as he took another bite out of his rapidly cooling burger.

"Good, I'll pop round in about an hour, just got some business to do at the minute. See you soon!"

As they waited, Tap asked Slug if he had heard from Sid yet. Slug had; a list existed and Sid had located it, but he was waiting for someone to arrive who could access the computer to read it. The lift opened and two people got out. One of them was a member of security and well known to Tap.

"You're here to see that fellow I suppose, the one that was bought in yesterday. Banks isn't it?" Mark May asked. The two had known each other for many years. Mark was gay, and every time he got into a bit of bother Tap sorted it out, for cash, of course, so now he owned Mark lock, stock and barrel. This came in quite handy for such things as planting bugs on the wards and carrying out death-bed interviews.

"Where is he, eleven?" Tap asked. Of course he was; ward eleven was generally kept for patients with wounds resulting from violent crimes. It was kind of private having only two beds, and was perfect for the policeman's work because there were no prying eyes to watch the action. Ward eleven was on the third floor and Tap thanked May for his assistance as the lift doors closed behind them.

A police officer of similar ethnic origin to Tyrone Banks sat outside his private ward. He stood up as the two men approached him. Tap tried to pass, but the young officer stood in his way and informed them that no one was allowed in the ward.

"Get Stratford on the phone!" Tap ordered Slug, so Slug did as he was told. Stratford was a Uniform Sergeant at their nick, and he was going to get a fucking mouthful by the look of things! As soon as the phone was answered, Tap snatched it.

"Stratford, I've got one of your bigger boys standing between me and Tyrone Banks. If you don't want to be slapping another complaint of assault on my arse, I suggest you step him down, now!" Tap didn't wait for an answer, but simply passed the phone to the uniformed policeman and watched him frown as he received the unexpected information, before passing the phone back to Slug.

"Bye then. Fuck off!" Tap said cheerfully with a wave, as the policeman moved aside. They entered Banks private room to find their man sleeping, only to be rudely awakened as Tap poked a finger in the middle of his chest. Tyrone's face was a mask of fear and surprise as he reached for the panic button, but it was too late; Tap was looking after that for the time being.

"Hello, Mr Banks," Billy greeted the patient, whose eyes were wide with shock. Billy was fucking horrible as far as Tyrone Banks was concerned; he had dealt with him before. Similar situation, just a different era. Having said that, though, their last meeting was small time compared to the shit he was in at the moment, although exactly how deep he was in the shit, he had no idea. Tap's presence, however, suggested he was in it up to his neck. The cunt was eating his grapes now.

"Nasty wound that. Looks like a giant sewn-up fanny!" Tap continued. "Yeah, right fucking mess that was, lucky you got that big arse phone, though, because if you'd had mine you'd be boxed up, son. Burned and urned by now!" Tap showed off his own small, slim-line phone.

"What do you know about a chap called Anthony Jenkins then, Tyrone?" he enquired as if the name did not mean much, trying to prise a grape pip out of his tooth as he spoke. Tyrone said that he didn't know anything; it was the wrong answer. Tap shook his head as he picked up an apple from the fruit bowl on the cupboard beside the bed. He threw it up in the air and watched as it landed with a thud on Tyrone's bandaged chest.

"Tyrone, you sold Anthony Jenkins some guns yesterday, didn't you? No no no, let's change that: you tried to sell him some shooters, but Mr Jenkins was a bad arse, wasn't he?"

Tap liked coloured guys, well, he liked most varieties of men but dark-skinned men of African origin really flicked his switches. Tap removed his coat, laying it carefully on the next bed before rolling up his sleeves in a professional manner. He then took a pair of rubber gloves from the open box next to the fruit bowl. Slowly, he rolled the rubber over his fingers, covering his expensive rings and ornate watch.

"Feel free to talk at any time during the operation!" He offered, as he pulled the covers back from his victim, leaving him totally exposed but for a thin white nightdress with a little green pattern on it. Tap patiently explained what information he intended to extract before he left the room: firstly what guns Tyrone had been offering to Anthony Jenkins for sale, and secondly what ammunition had been stolen. Tap assumed that the weapons had been stolen too. Basically, Tap wanted to know what firepower the psychopath now had at his disposal. Now, what Tyrone had to understand was that the man he had helped to arm was the most wanted man in Britain at that moment. Tyrone must have the answers.

Tap pulled the curtain, on its metal rail, around the bed. Taking a banana next from the fruit bowl, he began to manoeuvre the loose gown up the patient's body. By the time it reached his stomach, Tyrone's last shreds of dignity were well and truly gone.

"Hey Slug," Tap called, "it's all a myth what they say about these black fellers!"

"Really!" was Slug's disinterested comment. He just wanted Tyrone to spill the beans before he spilled something else. Time was getting on; Jenkins would be up by now and probably causing all sorts of havoc.

*

AJ awoke, his shirt covered in blood. He had found an old disposable biro the night before, removed the guts, cooked up on a piece of foil and administered his medicine. He had coughed at several stages throughout his brief, drug-induced slumber and the results were all over his clothes. Stiff-necked from an awkward sleeping position, Anthony stood up slowly. In the bathroom, he ventured to look in the mirror and it was not a pretty sight. Maybe he had better have a bath. After all, it was going to be a big day.

*

"What you doing, man? What the fuck are you doing?" Tyrone asked.

Tap said nothing, but merely smiled as his rubber-clad fingers brushed gently against Tyrone's manhood. Tyrone screamed with terror, but in ward eleven no one could hear you scream. Tap happily informed his victim that his pride and joy had twitched; it was going to rise to the occasion, Tap was sure. Tyrone shrieked once more.

"You're enjoying that, Tyrone; you like that, don't you? I can feel it; it's twitching. Come on get hard for me, Tyrone."

Tyrone did not want to rise to the occasion. He was shocked into speechlessness, his dick firmly in the rubber-gloved hands of this lunatic of a policeman and, unfortunately for its owner, starting to harden. Tyrone was horrified, but Tap just laughed in jubilation. He had done this before to heterosexual men, just for a laugh with a group of friends, and it often worked. It was obviously working for Tyrone.

"You're fucking mental, you are!" he screamed, racking his brains for some information. Tap picked up a surgical wipe and cleaned the end of Tyrone's penis before slowly lowering his head towards his groin.

"No, no, please!" Tyrone pleaded in a fit of panic. "I'll talk! Stop, please! I'll tell you what you want, just don't do that, please!"

Tap raised his head. "Okay, talk then!"

Tyrone was catching his breath, his damaged lung hurting.

"I'll suck this fucker if you don't start talking!" Tap warned, but looked increasingly worried as his patient seemed to have genuine trouble breathing. The rubber glove released its grasp on Tyrone's rapidly-shrinking member.

"Slug, I think he's going into one! Help me here, son!"

Slug's head appeared through the curtains.

"Cover him up, will you?" He asked, then reached across the bed and took hold of an oxygen mask which he placed over Tyrone's mouth. His breathing gradually became regular again.

"Time to give us a few answers now Tyrone, okay?" Tap asked, gently. Tyrone nodded. Playtime was over; the gun dealer was ready to speak.

"Right, okay. The Enfield, we've got that. We found six rounds in the boot of your car. That puts that out of the equation. We've also got the Webley; Jenkins emptied that out. We know that, and so do you mate, you caught one in your chest for us to analyse now, didn't you? I'm sure you'll get your reward in heaven. Now, the Luger; that's spent, and we've also got that bagged and tagged back at the station. Oh, by the way, that claimed two lives last night, two of your brothers. Yardie boys they were, part of Boyd's mob, so you might want to think about dying sometime soon." Tap attempted to inject a little humour into the conversation but Tyrone wasn't laughing.

"It's not really for me to criticise your stock, Tyrone, but have you ever thought about becoming an antiques dealer - if you ever get out, that is? I mean, with the crap you sell, it might be worth a thought. And let's face it, it's a lot fucking safer, ain't it? Now, what else was there? He's got others I know that, otherwise he wouldn't have wasted the antiques. We've got a nine millimetre shell that was recovered from a young woman's head. He's got something special, ain't he, Tyrone? Come on, what's he got?"

Tyrone shook his head. Tap took the oxygen mask away.

"Do you know what Boyd is going to do when I tell him what the crack is? He's gonna come in here and do this!" Tap punched Tyrone straight in the chest. Slug stepped back, cringing with amazement; that was a little heavy. Boyd was dirty; he didn't play by any rules and he already knew where Tyrone was, Tap had told him as much when a couple of his cronies had been sniffing around earlier for information. Tyrone was given a few minutes to think the matter over while Slug and his boss exchanged looks. Tyrone grunted.

"What?" Tap asked bluntly, just as his phone rang. "Answer it for us, Slug."

Slug left the curtained-off bed area to take the call. Tap was not playing games now. He turned back to Tyrone.

"I'll do you a deal," Tyrone whispered.

Tap loved a deal, so he listened with interest.

Slug was still talking on Tap's mobile as Tap drew back the curtains from around the bed, removing his rubber gloves at the same time. He had pulled Tyrone's covers back to their original position. He picked up the unused banana, peeled it and began to eat it as Slug finished the call.

"Me and Tyrone was able to cut a deal, weren't we Tyrone?" Tap said.

They left Tyrone in peace and made for the lifts. The uniformed officer was back on the door of the ward.

"No hard feelings eh…?" Tap half-heartily apologised, tucking the empty banana skin into the rookie's top pocket. As they climbed into the lift, Tap updated his partner on the latest news.

"He's carrying a Browning 9 millimetre, fully loaded, so that's a clip of twelve, right?" A full magazine, twelve rounds this was cause for concern.

"Shit!" Slug remarked, before reminding Tap that the clip was not actually full; it would have one round missing because

Jenkins had shot the prostitute in his bed with the Browning. Tap concurred; Slug was right. So the countdown had begun.

"You promised him the works, then?" Slug guessed as the lift doors opened. Tap nodded.

"The full monty, Crown prosecution deal, protection, the full package, pointless, though, because he'll probably be dead within the hour."

Tap removed his phone from his pocket and pressed a few buttons as they left the hospital.

"All yours…!" He simply stated into the phone. He had just signed Tyrone's death certificate.

Chapter Four

The living dead

Slug knocked harder on the door. He felt a knuckle give, but adrenaline anaesthetised the pain.

"Come on, you cunt!" He swore to himself, examining the joint on his middle finger. There was no answer. He was outside the flat of Stacey Payne, and a pain she was at times - a pain in the fucking arse! He had been sitting in his car for the past twenty minutes, just waiting. Sid had called.

"Slug, this Haley bird. I got her, she's in a hospice called St Mary's. Haley Mills her name is. Where's Tap?" the fastest-talking man in Britain quizzed. He had rung his governor's mobile several times but it just rang until the answer phone cut in. The situation was urgent because Sid had just phoned the hospice and been told that Haley Mills had a visitor right there and then: IC1 male, mid-twenties, skinny in appearance with a gaunt complexion.

"Sounds like our man to me," Sid explained, jubilant. He was convinced that he had struck gold, and was right by the sounds of things.

"Bloody hell..!" Slug congratulated him. It suddenly dawned on him that this could be the end of the case before it had even really started. "I'll get Tap. I'll call you back!" Slug promised as he climbed out of the car and made his way to Stacey's flat. Out of desperation he jumped up three steps at once to reach the door and hammer upon it.

"Tap, open the fucking door! Tap, quick!" Eventually the door opened and Tap appeared, doing up his clothes.

"I just got Sid's message, he's got our man!" Tap greeted him. He was not alone; André followed him out of the flat. They both looked rough; Tap needed a shave and André needed some sleep by the look of things. They'd been on the old nose candy Slug could see it a mile off.

Slug was driving, there was no question about that, and André was getting a lift. He sat in the back, wearing a blank expression. London was a cunt to drive through at the best of times, but someone had inconveniently died and they got caught up in the funeral procession. Tap threw Slug's blue light onto the roof where it stuck fast, and the streets filled with cold blue light and the sound of the siren.

"Get that coffin out of the way! Police business…!" Tap screamed, hanging out of the window. The road soon cleared and they were able to pick up speed again.

"Where we dropping lover boy then…?" Slug enquired.

"At his flat," came a voice from the back, but Tap wasn't having that, they didn't have time. A tenner passed over the back seat changed Andre's plans.

"We'll drop you just before the bridge. You can get a tube from there because it'll be a fucking nightmare to go all the way round, all right?"

Within minutes the car was one person lighter as they reached André's station. Slug turned away while the two kissed their goodbyes. A marked police car drove slowly alongside them as they started to pull off, suspecting kerb-crawling, but a wave of respect acknowledged their recognition of Billy Tap and they slowed to allow the green sports car to accelerate on the inside before speeding off into the distance. It was how it worked!

The hospice was a bastard to find but they found it, though, in the end; it was an old mental institution, apparently.

Discreetly, their unmarked car pulled up on the gravelled car park surrounding the well-kept grass. Somewhat less discreetly, the two officers got out of the car. It was nothing they did as such; they just looked like trouble.

The institution was old, Blind Freddy could see that. It was very well kept, though; obviously nothing to do with the NHS. No way, this place was kept looking the part by charity. At the car park end of the facility there were no doors, just bay windows pouting from between large, well-preserved stone blocks, painted in keeping with the character of the building. The establishment represented a small oasis in the centre of a busy, filthy, dirty, sprawling metropolis. Feeling just a little conspicuous, the visitors walked around to the side of the building and followed the signs to reception. The pond was nice, ducks and things like that rowed steadily up the stream; it was just a shame they had to shit all over the small wooden bridge and the path to the reception.

The reception desk was manned by a pretty young woman.

"Hello," Tap greeted her, staring as if in an attempt to intimidate her. The nurse returned the greeting with caution as Slug provided identification.

"Police!" He stated. "You have a Miss Haley Mills in your care?"

The nurse confirmed as much; she had been in the recreation area the last time she had seen her.

"Down that corridor and follow the blue foot prints," she added helpfully.

Looking at the floor, Slug saw that it was covered in red, yellow, green and blue footprints.

"I believe Haley has a visitor today?" Tap asked. "Do you know who it is?"

It was an easy enough question to answer. The nurse pushed the visitor's book towards them, where the names of all the day's visitors were listed.

"Here, you can look for yourselves," she said.

The information Tap needed was there, clear as day. Haley had a visitor who had signed in but not yet signed out, so Anthony Jenkins was here, they had found him!

"What ward is she in, you know, her room or whatever?" he asked, urgently now.

"The Julie Flanigan suite, yellow footprints!" The white-uniformed nurse answered promptly, and Tap thanked her. That was rare, but her helpful and straight-to-the-point answers had earned his respect.

Tap had found a map on the wall, which showed that the recreation room was right at the back of the building. Billy made a mental note that there was a lake and a park at the back of the complex; very nice. The ward they wanted was just around the corner.

"Come on!" Slug said, fed up of balancing on the two blue feet that were painted on the floor while his boss read the notice boards. Tap nodded. He was coming, but he had just been looking for another approach on his friend Mr Jenkins. What the fuck - if it came down to it a gun fight in a hospice, it would hardly be the end of the world! He took out his handgun and checked it was ready to fire before hiding it away out of sight. Slug felt in his jacket and reached for his own weapon; it too was ready for duty if necessary.

Julie Flanigan's place looked empty, although there was a corpse in the first room on the left, opposite another reception desk. At least they thought it was a corpse until its eyes opened. Fucking hell! Slug's glance asked Tap if he had seen it, and Tap's replied that he had as he made his fingers in to the shape of a gun and pretended to shoot the floor, indicating that he would like to do the women a favour. The reception desk was unmanned. Tap wasn't surprised; imagine sitting there with the living dead giving you the eye all day, fuck that! The next room in the ward had an empty bed. The room was obviously lived in, but the occupant was out. That left two more rooms in Julie's pad, only one of which seemed to be occupied. They could hear the patient in the furthest room away; the one in the corner, coughing their guts up just before an alarm sounded and two nurses ran through. The other room looked empty; maybe a punter had left last night at short notice.

"Haley Mills?" Tap asked one of the two hurrying nurses, pointing to the room where the apparent emergency was happening. She shook her head.

"She's gone outside; Anthony is walking her. That's her room, though, can I help you?"

"We're just friends of Haley's, we've come to visit." Tap lied.

"No you're not; you're policemen. News travels fast in this place. What's he done then?" She asked, tartly.

Tap was checking to see if the nurse had stockings on under her dress; he had a thing about them.

"What makes you think it's him we're here for?" He enquired.

"Well it's not Haley, I know that much!" she replied. They're out the back, anyway, and if you're taking him away please use a bit of decorum; she wouldn't hurt a fly and he's all she's got. Stay there a minute!" The nurse ordered while she turned and checked to see if nurse number one had solved the problem which had prompted the alarm. Fortunately she had been able to drain the fluid out of the invalid's lungs, poor bastard.

"Come on, I'll take you to them!" She offered, obviously having no idea that her place of work presently housed the most wanted man in Britain. As far as Tap was concerned, this was not really the time to bring the subject up. The yellow footprints led the trio to the recreational area; they had reached their destination.

"Where are they, then?" Tap snapped. There was only one old man, looking like a strange alien form amongst the brightly coloured modern sofas. There was also a kid with no hair. Through several sets of natural wood French-style patio doors, Tap could see a number of people outside. Two of them were in wheelchairs under a huge oak tree, just sitting there as if dumped. One was talking to another ill-looking patient with a walking stick. Tap felt like he was walking amongst the living dead.

"So, where are they then?" He asked again. Is that him with that bird out there?" He caught a glimpse of a healthy-looking male deep in discussion with a zombie over by the large pond. The couple were sitting close together on a bench as if in love.

"They're both men, that's not Haley!" The nurse laughed. "They were out there half an hour ago. They're probably walking around the park or something, let's go and have a look."

The policemen followed her to the patio doors and out the back into the warm, breezeless morning. The trio walked along the path towards the huge tree in the middle of the garden. More of the living dead became apparent as they walked; it reminded Tap of spotting animals in a safari park as a child. He started to feel a little nervous. Anthony Jenkins could be anywhere; hiding in the bushes, behind those trees - he could be surveying them at this very minute. But unfortunately he wasn't, and the nurse seemed quite taken aback.

"Well I don't know where they are. Haley shouldn't be this far away from a nurse, she's not well enough, not well enough at all. I'm getting a bit worried, to be honest!" She reached into her pocket and removed a small walkie-talkie device with which she called the main reception and asked the nurse there to check the cameras.

"Gate four by the kitchens, okay thanks!" She announced after a couple of minutes. Gate four was open; Emily had just seen it on the camera, although the alarm had not gone off. "Down by the kitchens, over there!" she pointed and within minutes the trio had made it over to the door in question. It was indeed open, and looked as though it had been opened by force. Tap could see immediately that the wiring for the alarm had been tampered with.

"Stay there!" He snapped, removing his handgun from its hidden holster and preparing the weapon to kill, simply by clicking off the safety lock. Slug was close behind, holding the nurse back with an extended arm while Tap moved silently towards the open gate with practised skill. At the gate, he moved swiftly through the opening and manoeuvred his firearm systematically towards whatever caught his attention. No one was there; there was a gravel car park which gave rear access to the kitchens, but no human presence. Jenkins had been here, though, his trade mark was there on the floor, the dirty bastard! Tap scoured the area for clues while pointing his weapon down towards the ground.

"Why is there no one in the kitchens?" Tap asked. The nurse had no idea; she made to walk up to the kitchen door but Tap held her back and opened it himself. The room was empty. "Who should be in there?" Tap enquired.

Francis, the chef, should have been there; it was strange that he wasn't in by now and preparing the lunches. Sheila did the breakfasts but she went at eight.

"Who's Francis, boy, girl, what?" Tap interrogated further. Francis was an Irish feller, the nurse explained to the detective. Tap nodded.

"A lucky feller then, luck of the Irish? Well, I hope so for his sake. Tell me a bit more about him." The nurse, whose name was Sally, seemed only too pleased to assist. Tap listened as he dropped down from the step to the kitchen.

"About six foot, Francis is, and quite skinny…"

"Does he drive?" She nodded. "What car?"

"An orange car, well not a car as such, it's one of those small bus things." She was trying to be helpful. "It's one of those little beetle van things, you know?"

"Beetle van things?" Tap repeated, just to make sure he was still a part of this planet. "Fucking Kombi-van!" He exclaimed. "Big fucking noisy square thing?" he asked. Sally confirmed his guess; Francis drove a Volkswagon Kombi-van.

"Where does he usually park it?" The small car park was surrounded by trees and beyond them was a wall. There was nothing untoward about the area between the trees and the wall, but on the gravel where the vehicle had been parked Tap could clearly see blood stained pebbles all clumped together. It was definitely claret, there was no mistaking it. It looked like they had another casualty; the lucky Irishman's good fortune may have just run out.

The nurse looked stunned, bewildered at the situation she found herself in. Her walkie-talkie began to shout her name; it was Emily on reception. Some guy had just shown up at the desk looking for the two gentlemen with Sally. It was Sid, and Tap told him to stay put until they came to get him. Slug called the forensic lab for further assistance as they made their way back into the hospice, putting the wheels in motion for a small army of uniformed officers to attend the site and search for evidence while the bigger boys did what they did best. Road traffic units and beat-bobbies would soon be notified and watching out for a orange coloured Kombi-van. Traffic would be checking those details immediately; the cogs were turning. Slug had just sealed Anthony Jenkins' fate. At the moment it was not clear why he had chosen a form of transport that would stick out like a sore thumb, but no doubt Tap would fathom that little mystery before long. Maybe it was just the first vehicle he came across. Slug didn't know, but he doubted that Anthony Jenkins did anything just by chance. There would be a reason behind it, because everything that Anthony did seemed calculated.

“Allright, Sid! Good work here, son!” Tap greeted his colleague as they arrived back in reception. “Jenkins has been and gone by the look of things. It looks like we have a casualty, but no corpse as yet. There’s fucking claret everywhere out back though, so someone’s leaking like a sieve. Come in here and I’ll explain.” Tap ordered.

Sally led the elite team through a door at the back of the reception desk and into the viewing room for the cameras.

“All yours…!” She said.

Tap sat in the leather chair provided and frowned at the array of screens and equipment in front of him. Slug knew it was time to intervene.

“Maybe you’d like to get us some coffee or something please while we play about with it a bit?” he suggested, gently steering the nurse out of the small office and shutting the door behind her. Tap stood up from the control chair and walked away from the desk.

“Get Buzby down here!” He ordered.

There was a picture on the screen, or rather four pictures, each taking up a quarter of the screen. Slug pressed a button on the deck next to a joystick and the four pictures changed.

“Excellent!” Slug muttered. They had eleven cameras by the look of things because the third page of picture shots only had three camera views on it; the one on the bottom right hand side of the screen was blank. However, the shot in the top left corner of this screen was theirs; it was clearly the area at the back of the building where the kitchens and laundry were situated. That was picture nine according to the number in the corner of the screen. By touching the same number on the control panel, the picture they had found grew to full size. Tap praised his main man.

"What do you do now, then? Can you rewind it?" He asked.

Slug tried, but each button he pressed caused the screen to disappear or change colour as he played with the controls in a trial and error fashion. With perseverance they somehow got the picture to rewind. Slug kept stopping the tape because he was unsure just how far back in time they needed to go. After about the sixth interruption, the Kombi van magically appeared on the screen. It was just leaving the scene.

"You got him!" Tap exclaimed with excitement. "Rewind it slowly, mate."

But Slug had reached the limit of his expertise with the machine. Oh well, at least they had the vehicle registration. Sid rang it in as Slug pressed the play button again and they all waited for the orange van to reappear. There was nothing.

"Nah, forward it a bit!" Tap ordered. Slug obeyed, and the van drove straight into the picture and headed towards them. Bingo, good morning Francis!

"Here he comes! Fucking hell, that's a fucking shed, that is!" Tap said in disgust. The Irishman parked the vehicle and climbed out, going about his daily business without a care in the world. Then something caught his eye from behind the vehicle and Tap cursed venomously as Francis disappeared from view behind it and the trio slumped despairingly in their seats.

"We've got action!" Billy jumped from his chair as if his arse was on fire. A wheelchair was being pushed towards the offside of the vehicle, although the faces of the wheelchair's occupant and the figure pushing it were unclear. The figures were out of sight now, but their man had clearly managed to open the side door of the van and was helping his wheelchair-bound girlfriend into the vehicle. Tap realised exactly why Anthony had opted to steal a van rather than a car, conspicuous though the vehicle was. Of course, Jenkins may not know for sure that he had the police chasing him yet.

"Sid, seize the tape and stick around here until all the loose ends are tied. You did good here mate, you did good!" he praised, and he meant it; this was a good lead. "Come on Slug, we've got places to be!" Tap informed his shadow.

*

"Got the fucker, Motherwell Road!" A police helicopter pilot boasted, steadying a helmet-based microphone with his free hand as he skilfully steered his vehicle through a steep descent. "Yeah, definitely, see the reg on it. That's your vehicle!"

Tap received the information a little over three minutes after the discovery was made. About fucking time; he had been sitting there in the car staring at his phone for over ten minutes or so, anxiously waiting for the call until his patience was rewarded. Slug watched as Tap absorbed the joyful news.

"Motherwell Road!" Tap exclaimed joyfully. "That's where it is! What's left of it anyway."

"Torched?" Slug assumed correctly, a moderate fire, rapidly expanding. "No wonder they found it so easy then! I mean, a burning van would tend to send out smoke signals, don't you reckon?"

"You'd think so, wouldn't you? Tap chuckled. "He likes torching things, does our Mr Jenkins, shagged by his old man as kid." Tap did his criminal psychology bit, causing Slug to laugh.

"Leave it out, Billy. Any fuck-up walking the streets has been shagged by his old feller as far as you're concerned!" he countered.

Tap laughed in reply, it was true, it did seem to be his answer for everything. Well after all, look at him!

"Burnt to a fucking cinder," Tap cursed as he drove onto the site. It was all the interior, wooden cupboards and shit, that had caused the rapidly-spreading fire to engulf the vehicle so quickly. That was Slug's opinion, anyway.

"You should join traffic!" Tap praised him as their car dipped sharply into several pot holes on the waste land. "Or perhaps not," he corrected himself.

As the fire continued to smoulder behind an apparently unused warehouse, Tap climbed stiffly out of the vehicle, holding the base of his spine.

"Fucking whiplash. I'm gonna claim off your insurance; advanced driving my arse!" he cursed. They walked over to the melted, but still smouldering, orange beetle van. "Maybe it's all the lard from Francis's arse that's cooking away there. I suppose Jenkins has left him to fry?" Tap guessed. As the fire died, so did Billy Tap's hope of any clues having survived.

The uniform who'd had arrived first at the scene had done a good job of keeping a small audience at bay from the danger area. Having seen the best of the bonfire, those with something better to do now left the scene after giving their names and addresses. Nobody had seen anything of any importance. Tap shook his head in disbelief at the situation he was faced with; no witnesses, no forensics, nothing! He was surprised Anthony hadn't made it more interesting for him. An abduction from the hospice and a murder in order to gain transport; it was a little tame, really. Tap walked for a few minutes to collect his thoughts, but was interrupted by the sound of a phone ringing over by the warehouse.

"What the fuck's that?" Tap asked. He followed the sound over towards the warehouse. The old brick building was the only point of interest situated on this waste land surrounded by an ageing, metal link fence. There was a black door visible at the side of the dilapidated building, which was covered in graffiti.

"It's coming from inside!" Tap shouted. "Get out of here!" he snapped at the uniform as he ran forward with Slug.

Tap kicked the door, which flew open with ease, and immediately swung back against the wall in case of possible booby-traps. When nothing happened, he peered cautiously round the door, pointing his gun into the building. His attention was momentarily distracted by feeling something wet under his hand, which was placed against the door. The graffiti appeared to have been done very recently, because it was not yet dry. On closer inspection, it became apparent that the pattern, which looked like Chinese figures, was written in blood.

Francis was sitting in an old arm chair inside the building. He was not tied or bound, but the heavy damage to the side of his head firmly proclaimed him to be dead. The phone, which was still ringing, was neatly tucked into the damage on the right hand side of the victim's head. The green screen, which lit up every time the jingle repeated itself, displayed seven missed calls.

Tap made his weapon safe before putting it away and removing the mobile phone from its gory holster. It was damp with blood at the base, but had been strategically placed on a cushion of dark hair to prevent any major damage. Having wiped the blood away on Francis's jumper, Tap put the phone to his ear and pressed the green button to answer.

"Hello Anthony!" Well, who else could it be? A chilling, childish giggle filled the detective's ear.

"Yes Billy, it is I! Long-time no speak, mate, eh?" Anthony chuckled.

Billy nodded to his colleague, confirming that their man was at the other end of the line.

"It depends, Anthony. It depends on what sort of time span you've got left to play with, doesn't it? Has it been a long time for you? It's been short for me!" Tap fired back.

"I seem to have all the time in the world so far, Billy, because you haven't caught me yet have you?" AJ countered simply.

"Where are you then, Anthony?"

"Shaftsbury Avenue, car park!" Anthony returned promptly.

"Yeah, right…!" Tap spoke without much thought.

"Okay, ask Dennis then if you don't believe me. Dennis, where are we?" Another voice spoke into the phone, confirming their location. The voice sounded frail, frightened but definitely male.

"See?" Anthony was back on the line.

Tap laughed again, for Slug's benefit as much as anyone else's, because it looked as though Jenkins wanted to play games.

"Okay, excuse me Anthony I just have to confer with my colleague. Have you met Slug? It don't matter, I'll introduce you later. Hey Slug, Anthony is in a car park on Shaftsbury Avenue! I know that only narrows it down to about three hundred fucking car parks, but can we get someone down there? Nah, fuck it, get everyone down there, please!" Tap was being sarcastic of course, his smirk confirming that Slug was not really to follow those instructions. Tap held his free hand up as though conducting an orchestra.

"The NCP car park where Shaftsbury Avenue meets Old Compton Street!" Anthony retorted. This was game-playing at its best. Tap was a little takenback, in fact he was quite shocked. Of course, how much of this new information was true was as yet unknown. He signalled to Slug that he needed a pen, which Slug located within seconds and handed over, together with a pad to write on. Tap scribbled down the new information and handed it back to Slug, who nodded in agreement. He knew what he had to do, and he set about the arrangements straight away.

"You've gone a little quiet all of a sudden, Billy. I hope I haven't rendered you speechless?"

"No, no; the day I'm speechless will be the day I'm dead, Anthony. No, I've just been thinking, that's all."

"'Course you have, Billy; you've been thinking about Dennis. Like who the fuck is he? That's what you're thinking, isn't it?"

Tap thought that Dennis was obviously some poor bastard who had got mixed up with the psychopath; a car park attendant or something. But now Anthony had brought it up, he felt obliged to ask. He hastily moved the phone away from his ear as a terrifically loud bang sounded at the other end.

"Dead, Billy, very fucking dead; that's what Dennis is! You had another question Billy? Fire away. I must apologise for the heavy breathing, because I'm making my getaway. So be quick, don't want you to catch me now, do I?"

Tap was totally gobsmacked. He pulled an invisible shooter from his waist band and pretended to fire at the floor, indicating to Slug that they had another casualty. Now it was time to upset the psycho. Tap had played along nicely so far but it had only resulted in another corpse, so no more Mr nice guy.

"That's one question sort of answered," he spoke slowly into the phone, "but the one that was bugging me was getting back to this time issue. Now, I was thinking that you and me got all the time in the world, ain't we? But I was thinking of that lovely young lady of yours; she ain't gonna be so lucky with this old time business, is she? Looking at a box within a matter of weeks, I hear. You really need to be looking after her, Anthony!"

"I am fucking looking after her!" Came the rapid reply. He had obviously touched a nerve there. "That's why she's with me now, so I can look after her. You cunts haven't done fuck all for her, have you?" Anthony snapped.

Tap was unsure how he fitted into the 'you cunts' category, since he was a police officer and not a medic.

"You've lost me, Anthony. What have we got to do with your bird's treatment? We're Old Bill, mate, so what the fuck you on about, son?"

Anthony was breathing heavily. He was in the street now, although he must have been close to the surface in the first place to have got phone reception.

"Police, civil servants, society, you're all responsible for the state she's in, and as for medical science and the National Health; well that's a fucking joke an' all. You're all guilty!" Anthony shared his anguish; his broadcast cracked up for a few seconds but the traffic in the background grew louder again as it shared the air with Anthony's heavy breathing.

"And what about you Anthony…? How long have you got left? You sound ill, son. I've read your diary. You've got a nice little hit list there; all those doctors who've done you an injustice. Forget all the smack and whores, eh? No, you blame those who were trying to help you!" Billy tried again for a reaction.

"I've got long enough, Billy; long enough to do what I have to do!" Anthony replied, after hawking and spitting.

"Who's first on your list then, Anthony, Your GP or psychiatrist? Which one's first, then?"

Anthony was silent. This copper was confusing him. His agenda had been simple; to take care of and protect Haley in her final days. What the fuck was this cunt rabbiting on about, doctors? The matter needed some thought, so he fed him a line to be going on with.

"Maybe it's you, Billy. Maybe it's you!"

The line went dead as Tap swore into his mobile. No one threatened him! He was well fucking pissed off. The phone Anthony had used had more than likely belonged to Dennis, unless Jenkins had got himself a charger for the one they had first spoken on, George the Yardie's phone. Without matching up the phone numbers he couldn't say at this stage. It made sense though, because that would explain why Anthony had made no fuss regarding the call being traced this time, like he had the last time. After all, he had given them the location anyway and so knowing the whereabouts of the phone was a waste of time, unless Jenkins had used it elsewhere. Tap doubted it; the phone had probably been disposed of already but Tap would keep Francis's phone anyway, just to be on the safe side.

"Let's go then!" Tap ordered his one-man team to leave the scene. "Get Doughnut down to the car park an' all!" he added as he climbed into the passenger side of the Subaru, having warned the three uniformed officers on site to take care of the scene in their absence. Don't touch anything until forensics arrived; it was simple enough, nothing too difficult. Following orders, Slug pressed a button on his phone and waited for his colleague to answer.

"Get up, fatty!" He ordered, before explaining Doughnut's task for the morning. Message delivered, he climbed into the driver's seat and brought the engine to life. The wheels spun until traction was achieved between rubber and gravel.

"Don't damage the crime scene, I just told them!" Tap scolded. "Then you go and wheel spin all over the gravel! Go across the grass, you fucking animal!"

Tap pondered the unanswered questions. How had Anthony and his patient left the site? He could see why the killer had chosen the piece of land because it was in the middle of London yet still secluded enough to not be seen, but how had they got away? They surely hadn't walked or caught a bus. They must have had a car waiting, or got a taxi. Was Dennis a taxi driver? All he could do was get to the car park for the next piece of the puzzle. Surely AJ would have left them a little something to be getting on with!

"What do you reckon then, Gordon? I've made you a coffee; here. It's decaff I'm afraid, because I can't have caffeine; it fucks me up! You ain't gonna drink yours anyway, so it ain't gonna bother you really, is it? Haley's here. She's in bed, tired, see, from the journey and that. We've had a busy morning, Gordon; well busy, in fact. I told you earlier on, didn't I, that I was gonna get her out of there and bring her back here? And I did!" Anthony boasted as he took a swig from Leigh Anderson's coffee mug.

Gordon was where Anthony had left him, but then he wasn't likely to be moving anywhere. The only thing that looked different was the blood scrawled across the wall and the open stab wound that had been used as an inkwell; they had both dried, and the wound had scabbed over with congealed blood.

"I did it in style as well, I think. I'm sure they'll agree. Yes, Billy will like this one. I'm a kind of celebrity now, Gordon. I've seen my work in the newspaper and I suppose it's only a matter of time now before I'm on the telly. Probably am already; haven't had a chance to look, to be honest! It's a bit of a touch really because I've always wanted to be famous - for something good, ideally, but there we go, it's not my fault is it?" Anthony spoke with sincerity, believing what he said to be true. "I'd just like to say, Gordon, to clear the air you understand that in a way I wish I hadn't killed you. Well no, I had to kill you because of what you are and what you've done, but I could have done with having you as a friend, you know? It's your fault that I killed you, though, because you shouldn't have let me see this." He indicated the pictures of naked children. "I thought I'd killed you for a cause for our cause, mine and Haley's, but I didn't really. It seems I'm just fucking killing anyone who gets in my way now, and that's wrong, Gordon. I mean, I've just killed some geezer, just now in Shaftsbury Avenue, a taxi driver, he was, I'm sorry, Gordon, I keep assuming that you know what I'm talking about. I'll start at the beginning, shall I?"

The dead man stared at him in his rickety wicker chair in the far corner of the room. The light shone in from the patio window that led to a balcony, illuminating Anthony's words of wisdom on the wall above the bed. He needed to talk; he needed a partner in conversation, even if he was dead and the discussion was a little one-sided. Haley was now in her new bed - her dream bed, the one Anthony had provided just like he promised. She had asked a lot of questions about the flat, of course she had, but she wasn't feeling too clever at the minute. She was in fact very poorly indeed, so her guardian had managed to avoid answering too many questions for the time being. To lay his lover fears to rest, Anthony had explained that he had borrowed some money from his business to finance this surprise; to fund her dream, or in a sense to finance her final days. Haley knew in her heart that this sounded suspiciously like bullshit, but she was in no position to argue because she was clearly slipping away; the strength that the journey had taken out of her was evidence enough of that.

"It was funny really, Gordon. I got to the hospice and saw Haley, like I always do. She was pleased to see me, very pleased in fact, because yesterday I promised that I'd walk her. Oh shit, that sounds like she's a dog or something, doesn't it? I mean push her in a chair, out of there to freedom. You know what I mean, don't you Gordon?" Anthony enquired and even expected an answer for a few seconds, before shaking his head. "Yeah, you do know. You're still listening, I reckon. All of you are, all my, well, my victims, I suppose. There's nothing you can do about it, though, is there? No, just listen; that's all you can do!" he mocked.

"She looked lovely. She'd got a nurse to do her hair and make her all up and that; she had made an effort, which was nice. I wheeled her out into the garden. It's been a nice day. Yeah, well, I took her round the back to the kitchens and we went through a gate to this van I'd sorted out for our escape. It was one of those Volkswagen things, I had to nick it, obviously, and of course tragically someone had to die. I don't know his name, some Mick, he was. I'd seen him pulling up earlier on and when he got out of the van I belted him with the butt of my gun and he fell to the floor like a sack of shit. I had to make it a clean job and that because I had to go and get Haley, so claret on the clothing was not an option, if you know what I mean? I just gave him a little whack to put him down, but he was still groaning and stuff on the floor so I stamped on his head until the cunt stopped moaning. Trouble is, I had another fucking corpse on my hands then, didn't I? So, do you know what I did?" Anthony asked as if the remains he was talking to actually had some real interest in the matter. The enthusiasm in his voice rang chillingly in the air.

"I only put it in the van, didn't I? Yeah, took the fucker with me. There was nowhere to hide it, you see, so I unfolded the back seats of this van into a bed and put the body in the space underneath it. That was that, the body was hidden away a treat. I put Haley in the back, on the bed of course and then put her wheelchair in the space in front of the bed you know, the bit behind the driver's seat, clever, eh?" AJ reminisced. He remembered not being able to fold the chair and how he had struggled getting it into the van. A bag which they had hidden underneath the chair, covered by a blanket, was causing the problem but Anthony didn't have time to fuss so he simply forced the chair in whole. He was as high as a kite when he had rescued his lover, due to the fact that he had had a second helping of his powdered breakfast after killing Francis.

"This fucking coffee's horrible!" He remarked, chucking it onto the carpet. His left leg shook uncontrollably, causing the wicker to creak in time with it. "I always do that, don't know why, anxiety maybe? Maybe it's the demons shaking their way out. Don't even realise I'm doing it most of the time. Fucking should have seen this Limo thing, though, mate. I hired it out of the paper; it was well smart. It weren't stretched or anything like that it was just flash. Bentley, it was! Would have cost me over three hundred nicker to rent it. I just fucking shot the cunt instead, though. Three hundred quid is taking the piss really, ain't it? You don't pay for shit when you've got one of these, do you Gordon? It's fucking nice, ain't it?" he admired the gleaming silver killing machine, having removed it from the table at his side. He never let it out of his sight when he was away from Haley, especially in his other flat where he now sat talking to the owner.

"I haven't shot anyone yet with it, have I? Just hit a few with it; might as well carry a fucking hammer. Oh no, I have, I shot Tara, didn't I? That was a mercy killing, though, because those fuckers had already chopped her all up anyhow, so I did

her a favour really! Oh, fuck and Limo driver, so I've done two people then. That's not a lot, is it? That's two bullets, ten left, then. Excellent!" He remembered Tyrone telling him that there were twelve rounds. "Bet you've fired some guns, Gordon," he went on. "I bet you were in the…" he paused to think, "airforce, I reckon! I bet you flew planes, didn't you? You lot were lucky, you got to fly planes in them days. In them days you had national service and could make something of yourself, regardless of your background, eh? And you got to shoot people and it was perfectly okay. How fucked up is that? I'm shooting people now and look at all the commotion it's causing. Where's my national service? Where's my licence to kill? I ain't got one, have I? I've had to make my own!" he lamented bitterly. He imagined Gordon standing next to a plane, moustached, with a child in his arms, and that brought his attention back to the corpse in front of him.

"Kiddie fiddler of the sky. That really is a filthy habit you've got, Gordon; it'll be the death of you one day, my friend!" he joked. You had to see the funny side. Anthony roared with laughter, only stopping to clear his throat when it got too painful and he was forced to spit the contents of his mouth onto the nearest wall.

"Oh, you are a card, Gordon! I've gone off the track a bit, ain't I? We were talking about that Limo, weren't we? Well, not a lot to say about that really. Dumped the camper van and the dead Irish feller at an old piece of land that we used to fuck about on as kids. Torched the van, I wanted Billy to see it, you see. I'm hoping it'll wind him up, you know, now you see it, now you don't! Evidence up in smoke. Well, it would piss me off so I hope it does the same to him. I rang him, you know? Yeah, rang him up and… sorry, I'm jumping the gun again, ain't I? I'd better tell you where the phone was. You see, I'd sat Francis in an old chair in this disused warehouse and… I put the phone in his fucking head! Yeah, where I'd stamped on his head it was all caved in, and that's where I put it. So, when I rang him up from this car park I was at, he picked the phone up from this hole in the geezer's head. Now how fucked up is that? Anyway, we had a chat and that and I told him where I was. Well, he couldn't have got there any quicker than I could leave! Billy was getting a bit cocky in my opinion so I give him something to shut him up. Yeah, it fucking did an' all. I got this Limo driver, Dennis, to confirm the address of where we were at and then I shot him straight in the head, point blank. Big mess, I'll tell you that. Like shooting a jar of beetroot it was, fucking bang! Had to leg it a bit sharpish then, though. I was spewing me guts up and clearing this shit out of me throat all the time. You probably noticed that I grunt a bit? Sore throat, you see; bad lungs, mate, you know?" The corpse didn't, of course, but nevertheless Anthony was having a good time reliving the experience with his slowly decomposing listener.

Anthony suddenly realised that he had missed a bit, and recapped accordingly.

"The Limo, you see, picked us up from the warehouse and brought us here. I wanted Haley to arrive here in style, seeing as she'll more than likely never be leaving here again; not unless I get it early or something. We were driven through London like the King and Queen. Haley loved it, I could tell. The Limo dropped us off here and I introduced Haley to the flat. She fucking loved it, all white and clean like she had dreamt; it was perfect. Once she was settled into bed, she was feeling a bit poorly, you see, I got a lift with the Limo driver down to Shaftsbury Avenue. I paid him for it at first, anyway, but he paid in the end because I snatched all the cash I'd given him back out of his pocket once I'd done him. Well, he didn't need it any more, did he? That was that then, Gordon. I did a runner out of the car park and came back here. Bought a charger for the phone on the way back, though, so we can have a little chat with Billy once the battery is charged up. Sorry, am I confusing you? The phone that I left in the Irishman's head, that weren't the phone I got from the Yardies, yesterday. No, I'm keeping that. The one I left was his, the Irishman's! I just phoned Tap's office, got his mobile number off this girl and then called him, as easy as that! I tell you what, I'm just gonna check on Haley and then I'll be back and tell you all about Tyrone and his mate. Sit tight!" Anthony laughed as he rose from his wicker chair and slipped his faithful handgun into the waistband of his jeans. Sit tight, had to laugh, sit tight!

Haley was awake. She was reaching for the glass of water that her helper had left for her on the bedside table, but to actually reach the glass was proving quite difficult.

"Here you are I've got it." Anthony assisted. Gently, he held the glass to her lips as she drank, his hand shaking slightly as he did so.

"Are you all right, Anthony?" She asked. He replied that he was fine; he'd just had a busy morning that was all, lots to organise and get sorted. "Have you got my medication yet, Anthony?" She asked quietly, settling back down onto her pillow. Anthony was frightened by how frail and weak she looked; in need of professional help.

He shook his head, smiling, and lied that he was going to have to travel all the way across London to get the medication. He explained that he knew a chemist who would supply what he wanted without a prescription, but he just needed to make sure that she was all right before he left.

"They can wait until tomorrow if you like, Anthony. I have enough in my bag to see me through the night. I put it under the chair, have you got it?"

Anthony had indeed got the bag; it was in the kitchen, minus the tablets that now littered the side board.

"I've got the bag, and your medication. I'm going to go in a little while and get some more for you. It's best to go now, just in case they have to order them in or something because you've only got enough for one night. So, what do you think of the flat, then?"

Haley loved the flat, but it was the question of how Anthony had acquired it that she was unsure about. She smelt a rat, and it was a big fucker.

"There's a lovely view of the park from the living room, I'll show you later. I'll go and get your drugs in a minute and let you rest. Maybe tonight we can watch some television together. That would be nice, wouldn't it? Watch telly in our own place; it's what we've always dreamed off, isn't it?" Anthony pleaded. "Yeah, I'll let you sleep and I'll get the drugs and some take away. Chinese, yeah?"

Chinese was fine, just nothing too spicy; spicy was not good for her condition.

"Okay then, I'll be off then, yeah?" Anthony had no idea how he was going to get the drugs. Smack, Coke, Pills - Anthony could get any of those, but prescription drugs, now that was another matter. That reminded him; the supplies of the old brown powder were starting to dwindle as well. Better see Ritchie, because Anthony couldn't go to work running on empty; that would be ridiculous.

In the living room, Anthony pulled on his leather coat, after retrieving his shooter from the kitchen, where he had previously hidden it before seeing Haley. He tucked the weapon into the waistband of his jeans, striking a pose while looking at himself in the mirror. His gaze suddenly broke, as he hastily retrieved the firearm again, cowboy styli, and aimed it at his reflection.

"Bang!" He said, before returning the weapon to its holster. "I'm a fucking Bad Boy!" He said aloud, straightening the lapels of his jacket. "A real fucking Bad Boy!" He coughed and spat the newly-formed contents of his throat at his artwork on the wall.

"Here, have some of that!" It was a good shot; right in between the words: 'Effective Punishment'. Let it be known, there was a new sheriff in town!

*

"Well, will you look at the fucking state of that?" Tap asked his sidekick as the pair stood in the car park in Shaftsbury Avenue, staring at an ageing white luxury car. Doughnut had to agree, although the novelty had worn off slightly for him as he had already been here about five minutes keeping the headless corpse company.

"It's fucked the interior in that, ain't it? You'll never get that off!" Doughnut reminisced. He was right; a gunshot fired point-blank into the head of someone sitting inside a Bentley does tend to make a mess, although of course that would apply to any car, not just a Bentley.

The corpse was leaning back casually against the cream leather driver's seat, well, as casually as one can without a head. Tap was studying the corpse at close range but backed off in response to footsteps on the concrete floor from behind. Slug was on his way over, but Tap's shaking head caught his eye. The shaking head said it all to Slug; he was being advised not to look at this one.

"No, stay there, Slug. Comb the floor for clues or something, but just don't come down here puking your guts over everything." Tap advised him.

Tap noticed that the smearing of blood over the white bonnet appeared to create a pattern.

"Make sure we get a picture of that!" He ordered.

"What?" Doughnut asked.

"That symbol, it's the same as the one on the door of the warehouse we just came from, where we found the chef. It must mean something, I suppose. Just take a fucking photo of it for me, okay?"

"Messy, very messy!" Doughnut shared his opinion. Tap agreed, but was forced to remark that it was still nothing compared to the mess that would occur if his main man Doughnut took one in the guts. Doughnut took the abuse with a smile.

"You haven't seen me having a shit yet!" He retorted. Tap had to agree, because thankfully he hadn't, but he had to admit he was impressed by the prompt comeback.

"Who is he, then?" Doughnut asked, indicating the headless corpse.

"Dennis. Dennis the Limo driver," Tap replied, sharing what little he knew of the man. Judging by Doughnut's look of confusion, more information was required.

"Jenkins sprung his girlfriend from the hospice this morning. He killed, or kidnapped and then killed this chef, stole his van, and then used it to get away. He then torched the van and put its owner inside this warehouse. That's where we found him, although we don't know whether he was alive before he got there. From then on; well, fuck knows. We can only assume that Dennis here was called to collect Jenkins and his piece and this is where they ended up, although I would imagine that they dropped her off somewhere first. In fact they definitely did, because when I spoke to Jenkins on the phone he was running and his bitch ain't in no fit state to go jogging. Saying that, neither was he by the sounds of things. Perhaps they need a little fitness advice from you, Doughnut.

"So he's rung you then, since last night?" Doughnut asked. Last he heard, Jenkins and Tap had had a little discussion but then there had been nothing throughout the morning. Tap explained about the phone in the chef's head.

"Twisted fucker, this bloke, isn't he?" Doughnut remarked. "Well, what's the crack then? What's he after?"

Tap shrugged.

"I think he's pissed off with the way he's been treated. He's ill, you see. I reckon he's got the lurgy, although he denies that. Whatever, he ain't well and in all fairness he has been treated like a cunt by the NHS, but I think he's taking the complaints procedure a bit too far. Look at the facts up to now. Kills a couple of Yardies; why? We don't know for sure, but it looks like the dad owes them money. Tyrone then gets shot when selling him arms, and two more Yardies are shot at the family home. Oh, and a prostitute, but I think she was fucked anyway. He did her a favour, I reckon. Then we've got a chef and a taxi driver dead, now that he's sprung his bird from the hospice; a fucking hospice that she could have just walked out of anyway. It don't make a lot of sense. I think he did have a plan but it went tits up. I think he hit the Yardies in his shop for their cash. He then got guns but didn't want to part with his funds, so bye-bye Tyrone. After that, he went back to the flat for some reason, saw his family being attacked and flipped out. He probably felt guilty that they were attacking his family because he had knocked them only a few hours before. We've then got the chef, killed for his transport and the same with Dennis; transport and to prove a point." Tap paused, ruminating.

"I reckon he's finally cracked. He's been going to these doctors, health workers and that, and they've failed him for whatever reasons. Now the guy was understandably pissed off, but he's lost it now and is on a mission to seek revenge. You've got to read the diary, man, this geezer is proper sick. He's been to the doctors and said to them, 'hey, look guys, I need help, I'm ill!' And what have they done for him? Sweet FA!"

"What, revenge on the doctors and that?" Doughnut asked.

Tap nodded, but Doughnut was not so sure.

"Okay, so why didn't he take the diary with him? It didn't seem important enough for him to rescue it from the flat, did it? And why is he so keen to get his bird out of the hospice? After all, she's there for a reason, ain't she? Doughnut pointed out the flaws in his boss's theory.

"The diary? Well, that's simple. The Yardies were there, and you can't do battle with a fucking great book under your arm. Anyway, he didn't need the diary when he had the names in his head. And as for getting his bird out, he needs to hide her, don't he? Because as soon as he starts his war we're going to crash straight down on her, ain't we? No, he's hidden her well out of the way and the only man that could have told us where she is, other than Jenkins, is sitting in that car with a headache. No, I tell you fat boy, he's on a mission. Read that diary, it's all in there. That's what this is all about, I'm sure of it!" Tap was not as certain as he sounded.

"Can you clear this shit up, Slim?" Tap asked. Of course Doughnut could. By 'clear up' his boss meant he was to manage the boys in blue, who would follow a set procedure. The work was simple: get the evidence bagged and tagged, get all the statements written and then film and photograph the site before getting the body and car removed to a storage facility. Laborious and time consuming, but not difficult.

Tap told Doughnut he would be back at the office; he felt a little siesta coming on and all contact was to be made via Slug, who was currently waiting at the barrier of red tape running from one side of the car park entrance to the other. He was reading the paper.

"It's made the local!" Slug informed his colleague as Tap approached. Tap was pleased to hear it. "Your name's in there!" Slug continued, looking impressed.

"Have they used William or Billy?" Tap asked. But it was neither; he had been described as Detective Sergeant Tap. That was good enough. He was going to catch this cunt Jenkins, and it was going to be any day now.

"We're gonna get a phone call!" Tap informed his colleague. "He's taking care of his lady friend at the minute. He's been out to work, out on the prowl, and he's done what he set out to do this morning. Now he's taking care of his own. She obviously has needs; she's at death's door, ain't she? Now, he must have her medicine 'cos he wouldn't be stupid enough to kidnap her without it, would he? So now he's taking care of her before he takes care of business!" Tap surmised aloud.

Slugs nodded his agreement; it did seem to make sense.

"And the business is what?" He enquired.

"I don't know!" said Tap, unwilling to share his theory for now. "We'll have to wait until he calls."

Waiting sounded good; waiting meant a few hours' kip for Tap and he couldn't wait to get back to the office. Waiting was good for the time being, as it would allow his batteries to recharge until Anthony started phase two of his attack. Doctors and nurses, Tap guessed; they would be the next to suffer, he was convinced of it.

*

Slug drove as they set off back to the office. He glanced at Tap as something caught his attention.

"Don't cause a scene, but if you look in your mirror you'll observe that we're being followed. They've been with us since we left the car park. Want me to shake them off? Or shall we give 'em a tug?" Slug asked.

Tap shook his head as he pulled down and adjusted the vanity mirror situated in the sun visor. They were being pursued by a Mercedes, a new jeep-type thing.

"No, leave them!" He said, reaching for his phone and punching a number into it.

"Whiskey four seven six, Romeo uniform Michael," Tap said into the mouthpiece. "Grey Mercedes," he added. "Get it off my back, now!"

Tap then made another call, to the Yardie top boy, Boyd, who was following them. "I fucking told you, when I know where he is, you will! Have patience, my friend!"

Boyd acknowledged that he was indeed running out of patience, but with all due respect the matter was getting a little out of hand. He had four men dead; those deaths had to be avenged, and Tap was being employed to do it.

"It's all under control, a matter of hours now, trust me!" Tap said, soothingly. "But in the meantime, just keep your monkeys off my back or they'll be sorry. Bye for now!" Tap terminated the call.

"Fucking cunts…!" He commented for Slug's benefit. "They've got no patience, those fuckers; everything has to be done yesterday. Who do they think I am?" He broke into a smile. "There she goes, gutless cunts!" Tap laughed as the Mercedes skidded to a halt before performing a U turn under Boyd's command. Boyd knew they would get a tug any minute by uniform, so it was time to bail out.

Good, thought Slug to himself; the last thing they needed this morning was a display of might in the middle of a busy high street. No, Boyd had made the right choice. He had to be patient to counter Tap, who was not!

Joanne looked as fit as fuck as usual, and Tap pinched her arse as he entered the office. It was a fine arse, fine all round. Sexual discrimination? Don't be silly, not in this office!

"Has he rung?" Tap asked, already knowing the answer. He studied his assistant as she worked the fax machine. He was going to have to have a go on her again soon; he made a mental note to that effect as he awaited her reply.

"Have I rung you?" She asked in return. "And no, I haven't left the phone unattended either!"

"Oh, well!" Tap suddenly felt very tired. He was also hung over and coming down all at the same time. Slug was left in charge as he went into the back room for a rest. There was a bed there, which they all used on occasions when going home was not an option.

"Do you want to do us a tea, Jo?" He asked.

"I'll bring it in a minute," she promised, as her boss winked knowingly at his right-hand man. Yeah, bring it in girl, the wink stated. Slug smiled back with respect as Tap went into the back room and the welcoming bed. It was Anthony's move now!

Chapter Five

Any pills…?

Okay, he needed Haley's medication, but he also needed his own. He needed chemicals to sustain life. Anthony weighed the situation up and it was clear to him that at this moment his need was greater than Haley's. Haley couldn't help herself; she could hardly move, let alone walk down to the chemist's. Anthony, however, was fully mobile and apart from being slightly insane, could still function normally as long as he was medicated. So, the simple hypothesis was to medicate those who could then continue to help others. That was that then; it was time to see Ritchie Roach.

Being the most wanted man in Britain was a bit weird; no, bollocks, it was totally off the wall. Pulling on a bobble hat, minus the bobble, as an improvised form of disguise, Anthony took a tube. London stank in the rain, and especially down Soho's darker alleys. Anthony could identify the smell; it was piss. The same smell that used to greet him when he had had a shop to keep. Speaking of the shop, it was a fucking right state now. Anthony saw it as he went past, swearing under his breath as he saw the wooden panelling that surrounded the devastation. He could just see over the top of it where the insurance company, or whoever, had been forced to pull the whole building down - and next door, for reasons of safety he imagined.

The naughty ladies did their best to hide from the rain, sheltering in doorways. The lights around them shone brightly as if taking full advantage of this downpour to advertise their goods. At least they didn't have to parade around outside in the wet; they had been rained off. Pimps watched from the shelter of coffee bars and kiosks, keen for the weather to cheer in order to line their pockets. Rain meant loss of earnings, lack of punters and damp women. A damp whore did not sell well.

No, fuck off! Anthony wanted to say as he passed one such pimp in an alley way leading out of flashy-light land. But he didn't say it; it would only end up as a roll-about-on-the-cobbles type affair and Anthony would have to pop the pimp. Whores were not on the agenda.

Things had started to change rapidly, although AJ's plan was all still based upon making Haley's last weeks on this earth her best. Despite that, Anthony couldn't get Tap out of his mind. It was as if the detective was with him, taunting him continuously. Their last conversation kept repeating in the killer's mind, especially the bit about the doctors. Anthony's doctors and a hit list, the diary. Fuck me, Anthony thought. The diary was a log of what he had been through. Okay, he was pissed-off with the Health Service, anyone who had been through his experience would be, but at some level he understood, or rather accepted the fact that he had fucked his own head up with years of abuse of ecstasy, cocaine, alcohol and of course the final nail, smack. These four things had probably caused the majority of his problems, along with his family life and a whole bunch of other crap, but the damage was done and now needed fixing. Now his current medication, smack, did not fix, but it certainly kept him alive. It was fair to say that the drug numbed the pain that would have eventually led to a suicide. This was his mission for the next hour, to gain more medicine and hopefully a little knowledge about where to pick up Haley's prescription.

He was an interesting feller, this Ritchie Roach. He got the name at school because apparently everything he possessed in the form of paper had a corner missing to make a roach out of. Ritchie lived in a squat which had previously been an abandoned cinema. Anthony knocked on the door, but Ritchie didn't answer. Some other wanker pulled open a letter box which was positioned high up on the door and at the wrong angle. One eye could be seen staring at Anthony before the flap snapped shut again.

"Cunt!" Anthony cursed the owner of the eye, touching cold steel in anticipation. Blow the fucking door off, it was simple! Yeah; it was simple but also noisy, messy and a waste of ammunition. Thankfully he did not have to resort to it, as the door opened with a click. With another click, Anthony prepared to kill again by pulling back the block of his handgun in anticipation for a shoot-out.

"Hello, Anthony. Come in son," the wanker greeted him. There were two men in the main entrance to the cinema, one of whom was Ritchie Roach.

"Two for Debbie does Dallas, a milk maid and some stardust!" Anthony joked, having stepped inside.

Ritchie laughed, surprised that Anthony remembered going down the Odeon on Saturday mornings for the film foundation films.

"Stardust man!" He reminisced, smiling and shaking his head. Anthony smiled back, pleased with his attempt at camaraderie. Ritchie confessed that the only stardust that he had these days was of the Angel variety, PCP. He noticed Anthony glancing round the filthy foyer with disgust.

"Yeah, cleaner's day off!" He joked. The squat was messier than usual today, since last night had been busy. Ritchie's doorman sat down on the stairs as Ritchie himself perched on the counter of what had been the snack bar. He and Anthony were long time business associates: Ritchie sold, Anthony bought. Ritchie of course knew exactly why his client was here.

"How much do you need, mate?" He asked. One of his better customers, Anthony usually took two hundred quid's worth. This was good for business and especially for discretion, because instead of having some filthy smack head knocking on his door three times a day, it was more like once a week.

Anthony thought it was probably a good idea to stock up well, and was able to do this thanks to the three grand in neatly-folded fifties that lined his pockets. *Yeah, buy more rather than less,* Anthony was thinking; after all, the element of risk involved in his current enterprise was, shall we say, quite high? He might end up under siege or something and would need a heavy supply to see him through.

"Five hundred quid's worth. What can you do me for that, then?" He asked at last.

"Fifty!" replied the greasy-haired businessman, promptly.

Sounded good to Anthony; fifty grams of the brown stuff. It was agreed. The pale-faced dealer shrugged his shoulders matter-of-factly. "Sort him out, Jules!" he instructed his henchman, lolling back casually on the counter and fingering his shoulder-length rats' tails.

"So AJ, how's it going, then? You're in the paper, man. Them Yardies been giving you shit, man, and you didn't take it like the rest of us. Respect man, you the man!" Ritchie praised in a lick-arse sort of way. He was actually quite impressed, and Anthony liked this new approach to his situation.

The blond-haired, spotty doorman was concentrating deeply on his work. The tools of his trade and the produce were laid out on a huge glass coffee table, along with a set of measuring scales. The wraps had already been measured; all he had to do was count them as he worked through Anthony's order, but having got to twenty he was starting to struggle.

"Jules, man, what have I told you? Count them into tens!" sighed Ritchie. "Fucking hell, you're bound to get muddled up counting to fifty after this fucking gear. It's good, man; in fact, it's the best I've ever had, I reckon!" Ritchie bragged.

Anthony nodded mechanically; Ritchie always said that. Maybe he was so bolloxed all the time that he didn't realise he'd developed a catchphrase.

The drug dealing duo actually lived in this part of the cinema, leaving the actual auditorium to the rats and the sewage which flooded it. A huge telly was suspended from the ceiling in order to keep them entertained while they lounged around all day smacked out of their heads. As Jules counted the wraps, Ritchie lay back on his canvass mattress, situated on the candy counter, and flicked through the channels one at a time. Jules had now produced three piles of ten; only two more to go. There were three sofas in the room, one either side of the coffee table where Jules worked and another under the wide-screen, next to a stereo, a games console, a video and a DVD player. It had to be seen to be believed, Anthony thought.

Suddenly, he spotted something on the television. It was him, Anthony.

"Go back!" He snapped. Ritchie turned, uncomprehending.

"The news, man! Go back to the news. It was me!"

He had not just been on the news; he was the news. He had made it, big time.

"Fucking hell!" was all Anthony could say, awestruck as he watched the report of his activities.

The cameras were outside the car park in Shaftsbury Avenue where some prick had left a green 'Scooby' parked in the middle of the pavement. Two detectives left the car park but said nothing to the cameras; they just spoke to each other as they got into the Subaru Impretza. One reporter attempted to stick his camera into the passenger side of the sports car, but it was soon pushed away by Tap, mouthing the words 'fuck off' to the camera.

"There he is!" Anthony exclaimed.

"Who?" asked Ritchie disinterestedly.

Anthony pointed to the screen. It was that copper, he explained, Detective Sergeant Tap, the one who was after him.

"Haven't you heard of him?" He asked.

Ritchie looked blank.

"No mate, never heard of him. Looks a bad boy, though!"

"Oh, he is. A bad and Batty Boy!"

"Really…!" Ritchie feigned interest, although he couldn't really care less about the sexuality of some supposedly celeb copper. It was more Anthony's situation that drew his attention.

"You're gonna have to take him down, man. He wants you bad, you can tell!"

This must have been guess work, unless Ritchie had some strange ability to read people's minds from the TV. Anthony had to agree, however; Tap did look a bit of a bad ass. He glanced across at Jules and his rapidly-growing piles of folded paper. Thinking about it, Anthony was unsure why the duo didn't just give him fifty grams in a plastic bag, but then what would Jules have to do all day? Ritchie had to give him something to occupy him or he'd go mad. Plus, heavily-cut brown powder looked better in grams; it disguised a lot of the cutting, and plastic bags were nowhere near as aesthetically pleasing. No, keep it under wraps, like Ritchie had for the last fifteen years. Jules must have reached at least forty five now, so he reached into his coat pocket. A sideways glance from the Roach indicating that he was wondering which way it was going to go, but fortunately Anthony removed a wad of notes from his pocket instead of a gun.

"It's okay, Anthony, this one's on the house!" Ritchie offered unexpectedly. "You've been a good customer of mine, geezer, and I've made good money off your custom. Look, it don't look like I'm gonna see you again now, does it? So I'm, like, giving something back, man. Plus, I respect what you're doing. I get shit off them all the time, innit? Now, you know who takes care of me and yeah, they keep the Yardies at bay, but for how long? Longer now that you've put them back in their place. Fuck me, Anthony, I pay thousands a week in protection and you just took out four of my biggest problems in one morning! So there's your cut. Take it, man, there's plenty more where that come from. Enjoy it, brother, we're behind you, man!"

Ritchie was almost pleading. He seemed genuine enough, and Anthony could see his point. The fact was, they both knew Anthony could have just taken the drugs anyway - not to mention their whole supply and the money - and their lives, if he had wanted. Yes, Anthony would accept this gift. He needed something else, though, before he went, so he explained about the drugs he needed for Haley.

"Yeah, no problem, AJ," said Ritchie, his face showing relief that it was a request he could easily comply with. "I know where you can source what you want. You can do it two ways: I can get you a prescription written up in a matter of hours; but to be quite honest with you mate, the second option is your best. It's a bit of a trek, but you won't be disappointed. What is it you want, anyway?"

The fucking list, where had he put it? As Anthony searched his pockets, he let his coat swing open to reveal a huge, shining death machine. He produced it at last and read off the catalogue of drugs, none of which Ritchie had heard of, but that didn't matter.

I'll give you the address of where to go and you'll get sorted out there. Jules, writing device please!" Ritchie asked politely. Jules stared at him vacantly. "A fucking pen…!"

"Okay, where do I go then?" Anthony asked, writing the details down as Ritchie gave them. "Fucking Tooting!" He exclaimed in disgust.

"Yeah man, Tooting! It's a bit of a trek but you'll get your gear. Worth the train fair mate, without a doubt."

AJ sighed with resignation. If there had been anywhere closer, Ritchie would have told him; Anthony had faith in his man Roach.

"Okay, nice one Ritchie. Do I need a name?"

A shake of the head confirmed that he didn't.

It's a Chemist's shop and the owners seem to change overnight, but they're all part of the same scam. One man controls the whole deal. If you get off at Tooting station, then turn left, it's just there. There's a hospital on the right hand side of the road, St George's or something. All right?" Ritchie concluded, hoping that this psycho would fuck off now out of his life.

Anthony was pleased with his visit to Ritchie Roach, and especially by the gift he had received; it made him feel almost human again. He nodded to the two men in thanks for their hospitality.

"Nice one, boys! I'd like to say I'll see you again but I think you'll agree it's unlikely."

Jules unlocked the door while Anthony did the bottom of his coat up, having inserted his newly-acquired package of drugs into the inside pocket, which already held three grand cash and a mobile. It sat there just right; nice and snug.

Stepping out into bright daylight and a warm breeze, Anthony left the cinema. A good day to die and all that! Fuck it, if today was the day then so be it, but first Haley needed her medication. He walked to the tube station with hope in his heart. Fucking Tooting, though, he still couldn't believe it!

*

Settled into his seat on the train, Anthony's mind went back to the scenario at the old cinema. Something about it was making him feel uncomfortable. Things had gone too well, especially compared to the last two days which, let's face it, had been a complete fuck up. Then today, all his luck seemed to have turned around. It was as if someone else was controlling the show.

The train banged around on the tracks and Anthony fidgeted with impatience. At Euston a welcome distraction boarded, female, obviously, but with a suspect boyfriend. The couple sat on the seat opposite Anthony, who stared out of the window but used the reflection in the glass to study them since he had nothing better to do. After eavesdropping on their conversation for a few minutes, it became clear to him that they were not a couple in the conventional sense, but something else. Brother and sister? That seemed the most likely relationship, and by all accounts they had another family member of some kind who seemed to be in some kind of trouble. As they talked, the girl became upset and started to cry.

"Are you all right?" Anthony blurted out. The girl was young and pretty, no more than eighteen or nineteen. She had wavy brown shoulder-length hair and such a pretty little face. It was a shame she was going to fuck up her make-up with the waterworks. A short skirt and crop top covered what Anthony really wanted to see.

"She's upset," replied the brother curtly in response to Anthony's solicitous enquiry.

The family had money, Anthony thought; the boy's expensive taste in clothes testified to that, dressed as he was from head to toe in designer denim with a bright white shirt underneath.

Anthony abandoned his good Samaritan bit, since the message to keep his nose out came across loud and clear, and concentrated once more on counting the stops to his destination. He used the map on the ceiling for reference: four more stops, excellent! There was a newspaper on the spare seat to his left, showing a picture of him on the front page. It had been taken when he was a lot younger because his family hadn't had a camera for years. *Bad picture, Tap!* Anthony had to laugh under his breath. Tap was losing and it felt good.

He eavesdropped some more, discreetly, because there was fuck all better to do. He cleared his throat as quietly as he could and swallowed the contents in order not to cause offence. So what did we have? The person they were talking about was sick, another brother, it appeared to be, and at a guess it was a car accident. No, a motorbike accident. They were probably going to Tooting as well, because that was the only hospital in the area apart from the loony bin.

"Is he in St George's?" Anthony asked before he could stop himself.

The brother flushed with anger.

"What the fuck's it got to do with you?" He snapped.

"Easy, my friend, just showing a little interest in your business. I hate to see a pretty lady cry." Anthony replied quietly, with staring eyes that warned against any further threatening behaviour. "You're not from London, are you?" The country accents had given that one away.

The girl touched her brother on the leg, indicating that she wasn't happy about him being hostile to the natives.

"We're from Norwich, and yes, our brother is in Tooting," she said softly. "He had a motorbike accident but he's okay; he's just in a bit of trouble."

Anthony nodded in agreement. This fitted in with the bits of conversation he had overheard.

"Yeah, getting caught with a load of gear doesn't do you any favours, does it?" he commented laconically.

"Who said anything about drugs?" The brother cut in again.

Anthony chuckled.

"Don't mouth off about your business on public transport if you don't want any fucker to overhear it!" He said wisely.

"Was it a lot of drugs?" He addressed the question to the cute young girl.

She nodded, going on to explain that her brother hadn't actually known he was carrying drugs, it was a package and blah, blah, blah!

"Yeah, right," Anthony butted in. 'Course he didn't know; they never do, do they? "So, he's in big shit then?"

Tears fell from the big blue eyes.

"Oh yeah, he's up to his knees in it!"

Anthony laughed and the brother wanted to know what his fucking problem was. Anthony laughed again as he picked up the paper beside him.

"Bet he's not in bigger shit than me!"

The couple stared in disbelief at the face on the front of the paper and then at the face opposite them. Both mouthed the word 'shit' at the same time. Of all the people to sit next to on a train in London, they had picked him! And they say bad luck always comes in threes. For fuck's sake, what was next?

"So what do you want then?" Cutie stuttered, deducing that he wouldn't have revealed his identity unless it was for some good reason.

But Anthony wasn't going to share his plans with her, although he would offer the couple some assistance if they played ball in his little plan. Yes, if they scratched his back, he would scratch theirs.

Chapter Six

Like lambs to the slaughter

Anthony led the way so as not to be distracted from the job in hand by that pretty white arse in its short white skirt. In doing so, he was forced to deposit the contents of his rapidly rotting throat into almost every bin they came across. Gina and her brother put it down to a summer cold or something. When Anthony suggested going for a drink, Gina readily agreed to it despite her brother's obvious reluctance; as he had boasted, Anthony may be able to help them. By all accounts he was a vigilante, an angel of mercy attempting to clean up the London gangs. She had watched a documentary on him this morning. Whatever, he was a law unto himself and the real law was not going to help her brother, so she would have to manipulate this killer for her own benefit.

They went into a café three doors down from the train station and sat down at a table in the far corner of the room, out of the way and as far from the front door as possible. Gina and her brother sat opposite Anthony. The waiter came over to take their order and Anthony asked for coffee and an ice cream, big fucker with all that shit on top, and maybe a flake? The waiter shook his head.

"What, no flake?" His customer was forced to ask.

Not only was there no flake, there was no fucking ice cream either because this was a café; a greasy spoon, not Mr fucking Whippy!

"Just a fucking decaffeinated coffee then for me!"

Gina only wanted a coffee as well, a proper one though, and big brother ordered tea.

"What, nothing to eat?" Asked Anthony in surprise. "You've come all the way from, where was it? Norwich, that's it, and you're not hungry? No, bollocks to that, you can't leave London without blocked arteries. Three of your special breakfasts please, sir. The works, mate!" Anthony ordered.

The chef nodded; the bollocks it was, and it would be about five minutes but he would bring the drinks straight over.

"Lovely!" Anthony commented.

"So, what's the deal then?" Big brother enquired when it had gone quiet.

Anthony didn't answer. He was staring out of the window. They could only see through a bit of it because they were in the corner of the café, but it was enough for Anthony. Gina wondered why he hadn't taken a seat at the front of the café if he had wanted to stare out of the window.

"Oi!" Big brother persisted, and his sister tapped him on the leg, warning him to leave it. Anthony turned momentarily, putting a finger to his lips as he did so. He had seen something out of the window, something that had knocked him for six. All this business about him being guided by God, the Devil, or fuck knows what else, had started to flood back to him as he stared in wonder out of the window at a green Impretza.

"The fucking bastards!" He swore in amazement. It had gone for now, but for how long? Suddenly everything made sense. He was convinced that he was being guided, led, driven, whatever, this meeting with the brother and sister was just a gift. He would have been in the chemist's by now if this gift hadn't come his way; he had been set up by Ritchie Roach and he hadn't even seen it. But someone had; someone had saved him.

Anthony continued to stare out of the window, but brought his attention back to the couple seated in front of him.

"The deal is simple, my friend. You do a job for me, and then I'll do a little job for you. It's as simple as that!"

"What's the fucking job, then?" Asked the boy, "and what spooked you outside?" He ignored Gina, who was pinching his leg to warn him against being so hostile.

"Thank you very much," said Anthony as three cups of hot liquid were slopped onto the table. It was time to sell them the plan. "Easy-peasy, your end is; simple as fuck! You see that chemist's over the road?" He pointed out of the window. "I've got a list of drugs I need from there. Perfectly legal drugs, all prescribed; all you have to do is collect them for me. See, simple!"

Big brother stared through the window as Anthony spoke. It looked easy enough, which meant that there had to be a catch.

"Well if that's all it is, why can't you do that yourself? Why can't you walk straight in there and get whatever it fucking is that you want?"

Anthony opened his coat and removed a package from the inside pocket. He opened it and allowed them to examine the contents.

"Drugs…!" Gina shuddered. This was why her brother was now in St George's; fucking drugs. "No way, no fucking way. I'm having nothing to do with that shit!" She cried.

"No, no," Anthony placated her, "this is my business, my little habit if you like. Yeah fuck it, I'm an addict. That's not your business, though. It's simple: me and her stay here, you get my prescription and come back here, then it's off to hospital to free your brother. You've seen what I can do; you've seen what I'm capable of, it's on the news and in all the papers!" Anthony boasted, discreetly touching the shining weapon in his jacket as two of the breakfasts arrived. The conversation suddenly died as the waiter went back for the third plate.

"I can't get this prescription myself because I'm barred," Anthony went on to explain when the coast was clear again. "I got nicked a few weeks back using a dodgy prescription. I had a pad of them and… well, that's another story, but I need the drugs from there urgent. My girlfriend is very sick, she's got leukaemia and she's in bed at my flat. She was in a hospice, but, well, you know what they're like."

The brother and sister actually had no idea.

"Well, they're shitty places to die. The doctors have done all they can for her and now it's my turn, but she needs the medication. She only has half a day's worth left so I need it now. So you take my list, get my prescription and come back here. I'll come with you two to the hospital, I'll wave this around a bit and it will all be tickity-boo!" He indicated his inner coat pocket.

"Do you want some sauce and shit?" He asked, grabbing three different varieties of sauces from the sticky table next to them. "Eat up!" He pushed away his own plate, obviously having a poor appetite himself.

"When you say 'wave your gun around a bit,' are people going to die?" Gina asked, breaking the silence.

Anthony chuckled.

"No no no. No heroes, no dying. There'll only be a guard watching your brother, nothing too heavy if what you say about him is true."

Gina sat up indignantly, cutlery poised.

"Of course it's true! I told you, he was delivering something for someone and got arrested. That's all, he's not a drug dealer!"

Anthony put his hands up playfully as if to protect himself.

"This accident that your brother had, was he trying to get away from the police? How did he come to have a crash?" He quizzed; guessing that the bloke must have known he had something to hide, otherwise he would have stopped for the police when they tried to pull him over. Gina didn't know, or rather didn't want to know. Big brother agreed to Anthony's terms; he would do it to help his brother. He obviously knew a little more about his brother's activities in the drug world than Gina did. It would be interesting to know just how deep this guy was in it, but maybe Anthony would find out later. For now, though, a fucking green Impretza had just rolled past again, and this time it was parking. Fuck!

*

The chemist's shop looked busy today. There was a silver Mercedes jeep, brand spanker, parked outside with four men in it, all black, almost certainly Yardies. The green Impretza parked on the opposite side of the road and its passenger climbed out to fire abuse at the passengers in the Merc through the open window. Tap drew a long breath as he put his mobile phone to his ear and dialled a number while watching his colleague get out of the sports car.

The driver of the Merc jeep panicked; he didn't like this man Billy Tap. Fuck that, he was out of here because the detective was ringing his boss, Boyd, and the next call he received would be from Boyd himself. As he reversed he hit the car behind him, shunting it backwards, and as he pulled off he caught the near-side rear of another car. Oops! Tap gave the finger to the fleeing Jamaicans as he finished his call, having had a pretty heated conversation with the man on the other end of the line.

Anthony watched with amusement, but the smirk was wiped off his face as the policeman and that skinny little cunt that was always with him walked towards the café. He stayed cool for the benefit of his companions. The high-backed bench seat he had opted for shielded him from the view of people entering the café.

Tap and his companion sat down and ordered a couple of coffees, before Tap stood back up and went out the back to use the toilet. On the way back, Gina caught his eye and so he gave her a cheeky smile before taking his seat again. Tap was pleased with himself; his hunch had proved to be right. It had been easy to find out where Anthony Jenkins was getting his gear from, and from there it had been a simple step to have a word with Ritchie Roach, who was well known to him, and force him to set a trap. It looked like Ritchie had been working for all sides, though, because the Yardies had obviously put the frighteners on him too. They wanted Jenkins badly, but unfortunately their gung ho approach would not work in this particular game of cat and mouse.

"Now, I'm not being funny," the boy was saying to Anthony, "but if I do this for you, how do I know that you will help my brother? You might just fuck off and leave us once you've got what you want."

Anthony was not in the least bit offended by such a slur on his integrity.

"You're right. Fuck me, you need some security. Well, I tell you what. This café is our rendezvous point. You do the chemist's job for me and come back here - I'll leave a slate open for you! Me and your sister will go and get your brother. That'll take ten minutes, max. It's only over the road, innit?"

"I don't know, I don't really want my sister witnessing a murder for anyone's sake."

"I don't just go around killing people willy nilly, you know," said Anthony, affronted. All the people I've killed were bad people wanting to do bad things to me. I had to do what I did for my own protection. The police guarding your brother won't be hurt. You have to remember, my friend, the mind is greater that the sword!" Suck on that, Anthony thought. It was good bullshit, but bullshit nevertheless.

"Okay, let's do it your way." Big brother agreed.

"You haven't got enough pockets in your jacket; you'll have to borrow mine," said Anthony, removing his gun from its holster and placing it on the chair next to him. The smack was also laid upon the chair and the money went into the back pocket of Anthony's jeans. That just left the phone, fuck, he needed a handbag or something.

"Give us your jacket!" Anthony asked; quite politely for him as he passed his own jacket across the table. The exchange was made as Anthony took the boy's denim jacket. The leather one fitted big brother better than it ever had Anthony and the denim one also seemed to fit Anthony better than its real owner. It had been too tight for big brother really. With a few buttons done up at the bottom of the jacket, Anthony slipped his faithful handgun down the waist band of his jeans and prayed that it wouldn't go off and leave his love truncheon a withering mess on the floor. Yeah, of course it had a safety device, but Anthony didn't know how to activate it and wasn't sure he wanted to; the weapon had proved it could kill at a second's notice and that was good enough for him. Gina offered to take the smack, but that was out of the question as far as Anthony was concerned. Instead, he shoved it into his left hand jeans pocket, feeling the pinch as he had pushed his phone into the other side. It was a bit of a squeeze, but no matter.

The table fell quiet for a moment until Anthony spoke.

"Okay, are we ready then? Here, you might as well have the hat as well. At least it will keep you disguised a little." And Anthony's little clone was all ready for action.

"Are you ready?"

Big brother had the list.

"Okay then, let's do it. You head over to the chemist's and we'll follow, okay?"

Okay, I'm out of here," big brother announced heroically as he stood, smiled at his sister as if for the last time and vacated his seat. As he left the safety of their table, he noticed for the first time the two men sitting near the door. One turned to him, the one facing him, as he went to reach out for the door handle. A funny-looking man he was, posh-looking somehow, and he hadn't even spoken. His eyes were keen as they stared at him.

Big brother reached the door and opened it. Slug's gaze followed the man as the door closed behind him and he came into view again walking across the road towards the opposite pavement.

"Tap!" Said Slug quietly.

Billy had been reading the latest write-up in the paper. This latest update had come from Stacey. She had bigged up the situation a treat, just as he had asked her to, in order to whip up public feeling. He would get his arse kicked by top brass, he knew that, but not now; maybe later when their lunatic friend had been captured. Which would not be long now, Billy Tap was sure of it.

"What, Slug?" Tap responded.

Slug was staring out of the window at the youth, who had just left the café to walk towards the pharmacy and was cautiously crossing the road as he spoke.

"Bobble hat, no bobble. Black leather, blue jeans, that's what Ritchie said, wasn't it?" Slug double checked.

Tap looked up from the paper.

"Yeah…!" He confirmed.

"Crossing the road now, he just came out of here. Fuck, I bet that's him, bobble hat with no bobble!" Slug kicked himself for not remembering the hat bit earlier, but the youth hadn't looked like a killer and was seemingly unfazed by his enemies sitting at the other side of the room. After all, he knew what they looked like. Surely he would have killed them?

Tap grabbed his walkie talkie.

"Suspect crossing the road and heading towards rendezvous, he must not make it to the shop. I repeat, must not make it to the shop!" he frantically ordered his back-up team. The detective on the other end of the communication device asked if that was a green light.

"Affirmative…! And remember, I want him alive!"

As the words travelled though time and space, Billy Tap stood and walked to the door with sharp-eyed Slug in tow. They could see their suspect just making it to the pavement on the other side of the road.

Anthony grabbed Gina by the hand and led her down a little corridor towards the toilets out the back. They ran through an alley way and out onto the street. Gina didn't know what the hurry was, but Anthony knew only too well that time was precious. He knew exactly where they were heading as they ran up the road towards a familiar green sports car. He was going to have that, thank you very much. The doors were unlocked and Gina fastened her seat belt as Anthony found the black box and turned the ignition on using a piece of the steering shroud that he had broken off. The engine fired and, more importantly, the stereo came to life. *Coppers* Anthony thought as he turned the stereo up as high as possible. Although the car was brand new, it had no alarm or immobiliser because somebody had lost the only key fob to it when it had first arrived.

"Why have you got the radio on so loud?" Gina shouted. Anthony replied that he was a little deaf, which wasn't true because he could hear his scapegoat back at the chemist's perfectly clearly, even with the music turned up high. There was a lot of shouting going on just up the road behind them and he didn't want his passenger to hear it if possible. Fortunately Gina didn't seem aware of it as he pulled away from the kerb and roared off down the road. Thank fuck she didn't look out of the back window or into the wing mirrors, because there was a right commotion going on behind them. It was kicking off big time and Anthony would bet the three grand in his pocket that he'd be explaining gunshots any minute now.

"Stop, armed police!" Anthony could just hear in the distance behind them, followed by a rapid succession of four gunshots. *Oops* he thought to himself. He had not exactly meant that to happen, although there had been a huge risk that it would, but then big brother was obviously at fault in not taking heed of the warnings.

*

Tap ran across the road, oblivious to his car's disappearance and to the fact that whoever was lying there on the ground dead or dying was not his intended target. Slug followed close behind, also unaware that they had a long walk home.

"Oh fuck!" Tap swore in disbelief as he saw the face of the victim who lay shaking upon the ground. Well, three quarters of his face, because that was all that was left. Tap was not taking responsibility for this fuck up, absolutely no way. The leader of the supposedly crack squad employed to do Tap's dirty work also seemed keen to pass the buck.

"Clayton!" Tap roared.

Clayton was a typical copper who had seen no other world but the blue uniform since the tender age of sixteen. Almost twenty five years he had served now. He was now bollocking his junior officers for the fuck up, which was apparently their fault.

"What's this?" Clayton asked one of the two men standing to attention in front of him, holding up his hand.

"A hand?" the bright lad on the left hazarded a guess as it swept across the top of his helmet.

"An arm. And this?" the other lad was asked, as a foot found its way into his nether regions.

"Yes, very good," said Clayton, pretending to be impressed when the right answer was dutifully returned, "so we do know what arms and legs are, then. Now, let's take another look at our target. Let's see: we have the right arm unmarked, but the left arm is hit. The left leg is also hit, and the right leg is hit, and then the fucking head is hit! Who said shoot him in the fucking head? I gave strict orders to disable the target, not blow his fucking head off!" Clayton was bright red now, as were his students.

"He was reaching though, sir!" Protested the one who had taken the right hand flank. Clayton turned fiercely towards him, as red as boiled lobster by now.

"I know he was fucking reaching. The only problem is, he hasn't got a fucking gun on him, has he? This was true because Clayton himself had checked. The corpse would, however, be found with a handgun on it to avoid the inconvenience of having to pay out compensation to the guy's family, not to mention the tiresome fuss the press would make of it if they got their hands on the story. Heads would have to roll, and Clayton wasn't planning on his going anywhere.

Tap clapped his hands as if enjoying the show, but Clayton simply shook his head with regret as he apologised for his team's fuck up. Tap merely shrugged his shoulders.

"I take it you'll be taking care of the paperwork?" He enquired. The orders had been to disable the gunman with a shot to the limbs and it had been up to Clayton to make that happen.

"Why ain't he armed?" Clayton asked. "You said Jenkins was a fucking nut case!"

"Jenkins is a madman; a total fucking lunatic. He is also heavily armed. There's only one problem, you haven't shot Jenkins!" Tap smirked.

"Well who the fuck is it, then?" Tap suddenly felt vulnerable, as if all eyes were on him. Anthony Jenkins, the madman, was here somewhere watching him, maybe planning a sniper attack. Maybe that had been the purpose of the decoy. Tap ducked for cover as he removed his firearm once again from its holster.

"Are you all right? Slug enquired, and was rewarded with some choice language.

"Get down you cunt, he's here!" Slug didn't know what his partner meant, but he dropped to his knees anyway.

"Who, Jenkins?" he guessed as he watched his boss shuffle across the road and back through the parked cars before coming face to face with the bloke who had served Anthony in the café.

"Are you all right, son?" Reggie asked.

"That kid who just came out of your café, Reg, was he alone?"

Reggie told him that there had been another boy with him, and a girl.

"Was this him?" Tap showed Reggie the photo that he carried of Anthony, and Reg instantly nodded before explaining that the pair had departed out of the back of the café just before the shooting started. They had used the back door which led through the alley way.

"Thanks Reggie, you've been a great help, mate. I think I'll get off my knees now." He stood up awkwardly, looking a little sheepish. "Oh, one last thing, what was the guy wearing when he left the café?"

"A denim jacket," Reggie answered promptly. "And she had on a white skirt and a sort of pink top; fuck all, really."

Tap was impressed as he suddenly remembered the bird in the café; the plot had gone from a little watery to bastard thick in a matter of minutes.

"I'm back onto you, Jenkins!" He threatened. "See you, Reggie, and thanks for your help!" Tap reached into his pocket and pulled out a handful of used notes which he handed over to Reggie, who took them after a token protest. If things kicked off against him or Clayton now, the key witness had accepted money from a policeman and would be about as useful to an enquiry as an ashtray on a motorbike.

Tap was distracted by a phone call from Sid, who was on his way having taken the videos from the hospice back to the Yard. He had briefed forensics on what they needed, but Tap knew only too well what it was like back at the station trying to get videos booked in to be analysed. He couldn't wait until such work was sub contracted to a supermarket or something, as it probably would be eventually. He sat on the step, drinking coffee and chatting to Reggie until he heard a familiar voice behind him.

"All right, boss?"

"All right Sidney, about fucking time too! Okay Sid, stay here and keep an eye on things for me. Any questions that might land us in the shit, you call me. Deny all knowledge – you're fucking good at that anyway, you little fucker! Simple shit happened here, right? The suspect left the building, orders were given to apprehend the target, target pulled, the boys in blue were on strict orders to take our man down with limb shots. The rest is lying there on the ground being shovelled up as we speak. That's all you know, and need to know. Have we communicated?"

Sid knew the score.

"As for that fat cunt Doughnut, I want him getting an army out there searching for CCTV footage of Jenkins' journey here. Fucking train, obviously! He probably got on at Tottenham Court Road or something, about an hour ago I reckon. I want footage of his new friends, you got that?"

A nod of the head suggested that Sid should fuck off now, and Sid took the hint and disappeared as Slug came up with a worried expression on his face.

"Billy, did we or did we not park the beast about eight cars along on this side of the road?"

Tap couldn't remember.

"Why?" He asked suspiciously.

"Well, it's not there now!"

Tap walked towards the site in question. The space was empty but for pieces of steering shroud - their fucking steering shroud!

"Cunt…!"

It was bad enough that they had shot the wrong bloke and let the real suspect escape, but now it looked as though he had nicked their car as well.

"This is bad news, Billy," moaned Slug. "We're fucked! How're we going to explain this?"

"Shut up and get Buzby on the phone!" Tap ordered.

Slug did as he was told. He took his phone from his pocket and phoned Buzby's private number; if it had been in the phone book it would have been under 'get out of the shit.' That was why only certain members of the police force knew it. The phone rang and Buzby answered.

"All right, Buzby, Billy wants you," Slug announced, before passing the phone over to Tap, who snatched it from his hand.

"Buzby, top man! All right?" Tap got straight to the point. "Look mate, I'm in the shit big time; not the biggest, but it could go that way if you know what I mean."

Buzby did.

"You've got a tracker system there, ain't you?" Tap enquired.

Buzby reminded him that they had loads of tracking systems. Which one did Tap want?

"Our car, the green Impretza. You know it, I nearly killed you in it a few weeks ago taking you down the pub, remember?"

"Yeah, I remember, how could I forget? What's happened, then? Someone nicked your car?" Buzby joked.

"It's not funny," Tap replied coldly. "Find my bastard car, will you?"

"What's the reg, then?" Buzby asked.

Tap didn't know, but Slug supplied the information. Buzby tapped it into the hub of the tracking system that was fitted to the vehicle.

"Yeah, got it. It's at St George's hospital. Looks like it's in the car park."

Tap thanked him for his help and informed Buzby that he was once again in his debt.

"No problem," replied Buzby. "Just do one thing for me, right? When you find the wanker who nicked your car, limb shots only please. Not the head, okay?"

News obviously travelled fast, Tap ruminated.

"St George's!" Tap informed Slug. "We better get down there quick, it's only down that road. Take that turning on the right!"

Tap was a good runner, better than Slug who hadn't run for years. The duo kept pace with one another but Tap was the only one able to talk while in motion. Through panting breaths, Billy cursed Jenkins. He was taking the piss out of them now, and the more he took the piss the harder it was going to be to keep this mess in house. They needed to sharpen up; they had underestimated their enemy. Yeah, sharpen up, but that was easier said than done!

They were outside St George's hospital, not a quarter of a mile from where their car had been stolen, but it had felt like a marathon while they were running it. Across the road was an army of huge metal railings surrounding the hospital. As they walked down the steps to the car park they saw the grey

Mercedes Jeep parked up. The driver had wound the window down and was having a smoke of some description.

"How the fuck did they get here?" Slug exclaimed, outraged.

"Well, I suppose they fucking drove, Slug. I suppose they followed the stolen car that you left unlocked, thereby facilitating its theft. They probably thought they were following us, but they weren't, were they? Oh no, they've followed Jenkins, cut us out son, and now Boyd's got straight to the end product that I'm supposed to deliver and now he's taking the fucking piss out of me!"

It sounded feasible enough to Slug. They walked around the right-hand side of the building to look for their car, avoiding the Yardies who were lying in wait on the left side. There was a strange smell in the air, and Tap's mobile phone rang just as the sound of sirens and a fire alarm hit the airwaves.

"Yes!" He snapped into the phone.

Buzby had been watching the tracker on their stolen car and the signal had suddenly vanished.

"Only two things do that," he informed Tap, "it's either been destroyed, or the signal's been camouflaged."

Tap knew exactly what the reason was behind the transmitter failure; he could smell it.

"It's burnt, Buzby, burnt to a fucking cinder just like my car. But hey, fuck it! That's saved us a few explanations, hasn't it? I thank you for your assistance on this little matter, Buzby, and I trust we can keep this little escapade between the three of us?"

Tap and Slug walked around the side of the hospital just in time to witness the fire service putting out the flames that had gutted their car to rest.

"Look at the fucking state of that!"

Slug had to agree, and remarked that it was easier to explain it being burnt to a cinder than crashed with loss of life or damage to private property. At least there had been no one in it, it seemed. Jenkins junior had obviously thought his shit through when he had planned this little escapade because he had torched the car right at the back of the hospital where the fire escapes all met each other on the staircase. This meant that people were not using the fire escapes to exit the building but were instead flooding out down the main stairs and through the main entrances effectively providing Jenkins with cover for whatever he had planned to do next. Speaking of flooding; the fire crew attending had dowsed the flames without mercy, like they do, and so the clean-up campaign was going to be dirty business.

Tap thought that Jenkins might be using the hospital for a second attempt to shop for the drugs that he had failed to obtain from the chemist's. Where was the girl, though? Was she still active in Jenkins's work, or would they find her later on, a broken game piece? Maybe, but then perhaps Jenkins had come to the hospital purely to wreak revenge on those who had done him wrong. Tap cast his mind back to the list in the diary found at the killer's flat, a photocopy of which was in his pocket. Just as he reached for it, his phone beeped to indicate that a text message had arrived.

"Cunt!" Tap swore aloud as he read the text. Slug had to twist his head around to read it as the duo watched the last remaining flames disappear under the force of the water. 'Sorry about your car!' it stated.

Tap was certain that Anthony was not in the slightest bit sorry as he fired a message back: 'Don't worry about my car m8, worry about your bird, funeral parlour next to get her a nice box?'

The reply was wicked but simple, aimed to arouse anger. He put the phone away and checked the photocopied list of possible victims. No doctors from St George's were on it, so it looked like pharmaceuticals were the reason behind Anthony's visit.

The smoke was thick around the burnt-out fire escape door, so thick that Tap commandeered two sets of light breathing apparatus. A flash of the badge gained them the equipment they needed to survive in the smoke for several minutes. The fire alarm was still ringing and Tap asked one of the fire officers if they could turn it off, but that wasn't going to happen until the building was deemed safe, which could be a while yet. Tap and Slug didn't have a clue where they were going as they climbed the fire escape and were two floors up before they heard anything. Was it gunfire, or a brief explosion? It was definitely a firearm. Only one shot had been fired, but they were on their way up to level three. Tap took out his Glock as he charged ahead, Slug following as back up. As they reached the fire door on level three, Tap nodded three times by way of a countdown before pulling open the door and storming into the building.

"Fuck!" Slug swore as Tap made his way towards their targets, who were thirty metres or so up the corridor, in a small ward. Tap could see them clearly because all the wards were glass from waist height up. His targets saw him; they had the shock of their lives when they saw who was coming for them and raised their weapons.

One of the two men looked like he had just come from the gym, wearing tracksuit bottoms with silver trainers and a padded ski jacket in bright yellow. The other guy wore jeans with a similar type of jacket, except in black and oversized boots. Both of them sparkled with more gold than was really necessary. The heavy metal jingled away as the two Yardies raised their hands, still holding their weapons. Tap had told them to fuck off back outside the pharmacy and had even warned their boss, but they obviously thought he was some kind of double yoker. Laugh now, motherfuckers!

You could smell gunfire in the air already and Tap had no compunction about adding to it. He aimed through the open door and pulled the trigger, sending a clear message to his opponents that no one fucked with him and made him look stupid. The bullet hit its target straight in the face and the wall behind the man was suddenly transformed from pristine white to blood red.

The man's weapon fell from his hands as his body hit the floor with a sickening thud. The blood carried on pumping from the head wound. The shot was a messy one; an eye, it looked like. The other man dropped his heavy knife to the floor with a clang, but Tap had already pulled the trigger again and unloaded another shot into the second victim's face. This time the bullet took the top of the man's head off, causing the body to fly backwards across the empty bed before hitting a small bedside cupboard.

Only now was Tap able to see what had been keeping Boyd's men so busy that they hadn't seen him coming until it was too late. It was the girl from the café, the one with the gorgeous face and lovely little body, although right now her face wasn't gorgeous any more. Her throat had been half-heartedly cut and her face was badly slashed by a knife blade. Her underwear was around her knees, although her skirt was still in place. With the barrel of his gun, the detective lifted the hem of the victim's skirt. There didn't seem to be any damage at first glance, so it looked like Tap had intervened before these boys had got really nasty. The girl was still alive, although barely.

Tap was aware that Boyd wasn't going to be happy, but then Boyd wasn't going to have too much time to get upset because Tap was coming for him next, just as soon as this little mess was tidied up.

"Don't look in here, Slug, check out the other rooms!" Tap ordered loudly. Slug could just make out the girl on the middle bed of the three that filled the room. Fucking hell, she had bled, although in all fairness it wasn't all hers. Slug did as he was told, leaving his superior on his own to tidy up some loose ends. Tap kicked the gun away from the first man he had shot, then picked the weapon up with an evidence bag he found in his pocket and wrapped the bag around the handgun, which he pointed at the girl on the bed. She was still alive, staring at Tap as he pulled the trigger. The detective looked away as he shot the woman in the heart rather than the face; he felt he owed her parents that much. He hadn't wanted to do it, but she knew stuff and as far as Tap was concerned she had to go away. It was for the best, anyway, because she was in a right state.

"One of ours…!" Slug shouted as Tap replaced the gun in the dead Yardie's hand without ever having touched it.

"Okay, two seconds!" Tap replied as he searched the other gangster for weapons. He found an old Colt forty-five; that would do nicely. It was business as usual for Tap as he left the room in search of his main man.

There were two corpses in a room on the opposite side of the ward. One was a policeman, and the other was, well, fuck knows. Tap studied the victim, who lay upon a bed. He'd been stabbed in the stomach and abdomen a few times, his throat had been cut and finally he had been shot. This had all the hallmarks of a Yardie-type torture, which Tap had witnessed several times before. The police officer had sustained a single gunshot wound to the face. He had been a member of the armed response unit, but unfortunately for Tap his gun was missing. This fact sent shivers down Tap's spine because the ten rounds that Anthony Jenkins had left had now possibly multiplied to thirty or forty plus. Shit, Tap didn't like that one bit. That was assuming Jenkins was responsible for this, but it looked like he was because he had written something on the wall in blood. "Dr Taylor,"

Tap read the message out loud. There was that weird fucking symbol thing again; it was like a wheat sheaf or something.

"Who the fuck's he, then?" Slug asked as his superior searched through his pockets again for the photocopied list from Anthony's diary.

"A doctor I suppose, Slug? Yeah, here he is; he practises at that new health centre on Tottenham Court Road." It was there on the list as plain as day. He knew it, Anthony was hunting the doctors who had treated him, although things hadn't gone entirely according to plan. Maybe now he was getting back to the point of the mission.

"Oh, thank fuck for that!" Tap exclaimed as the alarm bells finally stopped ringing. "Now we can hear ourselves think!"

Billy took out his phone again and rang Doughnut, who had been left behind at the car park in Shaftsbury Avenue to cleanse the scene. As he was dialling, Slug interrupted.

"You're not allowed to use phones in a hospital."

"Slug, I've just fucking shot three people and you're chanting some shit about hospital rules and regulations! I don't suppose mass murder is allowed either, but I've just fucking done it. What the fuck's up with you?"

"Three people…?" Slug queried.

"She knew too much, Slug. Her throat and face was all cut up and shit; she was fucked, mate. It was a mercy killing, you know I had to do it, don't you?"

Had they dug such a fucking huge hole for themselves over the years that this is what it had come to; silencing witnesses? Slug needed more reassurance than that.

"I've set it all up mate, it's clean as a whistle in there. Just leave it to me mate, I'll do all the talking. Now, what's going on with our buddies then?"

Doughnut answered his call straight away, distracting the two men's attention from the scene in front of them.

"Slim, how you doing?" Tap enquired, referring to the cleaning up of the crime scene. Doughnut explained that it was all done apart from the floor, which needed cleaning. Forensics had finished their bit and uniform were just sorting the floor out. Doughnut was making his way back to the office because he had a lot of paperwork to do, thanks to Anthony Jenkins, but had just had a call from Sid saying that he was on his way to Tottenham Court Road.

"I know you've got a lot on your plate, Slim, which is why I feel a real cunt adding to it, but I need you here, like yesterday. Okay?"

Doughnut agreed reluctantly, thinking of his growing pile of paperwork and reminding Tap that he would have to pick up the CCTV videos of Jenkins' train journey on the way. Tap didn't bother telling him what was going on at his end; after all, Doughnut would be shovelling it up in an hour or so. He put his phone away and rubbed his chin thoughtfully.

"So, who the fuck's this then?" he asked, indicating the corpse on the bed. Slug checked the bedside cabinet for any clues but there were none. The man was wearing a green hospital gown, which Tap lifted up with the tip of his handgun. The stab wounds had to be seen to be believed. It had clearly been a frenzied attack: nasty, very nasty.

"Big old dick, though!" he had to comment to Slug, who didn't find the comment very funny.

Tap rang the Yard and reported the murder and theft of the police officer's weapons, the latter being the main concern. He gave the dead officer's badge number, which confirmed his name as Michael Parish. They were on their way, the Sergeant on the other end of the phone promised. A single gunshot wound to the face at close range.

“Browning,” Tap suggested. If so, the killer was likely to be Jenkins. As well as the writing on the wall, the fact that the Yardies were on scene was strong evidence of Jenkins’ involvement because they had obviously followed their car in search of a lead, not knowing that it was actually AJ and this bird who were in it. They must then have followed the couple to this ward. So what did Anthony Jenkins’ armoury consist of now? Well, probably a police issue MP5 sub-machine gun and an empty Glock hand gun. He knew it was empty because the clip was still attached to the dead officer’s belt – fucking amateur! Tap formulated his theory, thinking aloud for Slug’s benefit.

“He recruited that bird and the geezer who was shot dead at the pharmacy. Fuck knows why or how. I didn’t get a good look at him before Clayton blew half his face off, but I suspect they were a couple or something. It looks like Jenkins got that bloke to do his shopping for him at the pharmacy, which means that he must have known we were coming, that means we’ve got those fucking filthy smackheads to take care of yet. He was a decoy; we were watching him when Jenkins and that bird in there did a bunk. I reckon they came here so that Jenkins could get the pharmaceuticals and shit that he needs to keep his bird alive, but why the fuck they ended up in here I don’t know. So, this bloke here on the bed must be someone to do with her and the feller that we took out at the pharmacy. Jenkins took the copper out for some reason - probably for his weapon - and then just disappeared. He somehow got away, leaving these behind. I suppose the Yardies wanted some answers, which is why this chap here and the bird were tortured. Sounds feasible, don’t it?”

Slug agreed; it did seem feasible. He asked if there was any identification on the girl in the other room, but a search of the cabinet beside the bed revealed nothing but a photograph.

"They're fucking brother and sister, ain't they? Look!" Tap exclaimed, waving the family photo which showed mum, dad and their three late offspring. Slug had to agree it looked that way. Miller was the family name and Slug had worked out that the corpse they were looking at was John, according to the paperwork attached to the clipboard at the end of the bed. Tap repeated the name a few times, eventually modifying it to Johnny Miller.

"I know that cunt!" He swore. "He was one of Mark Swaney's boys, you know Swaney?"

Slug did indeed; all four brothers. Mark was the youngest but by far the most entrepreneurial one in the family. Not any more though, since one of his couriers had been caught and was about to turn Queen's evidence.

"You don't reckon, do you?" Slug asked.

"No, this was no hit," replied Tap, "this was Jenkins, you'll have to trust me on this one!"

A rumpus was heard at the entrance to the ward; it was uniform sticking their heads round the door, unsure who had control of the situation. They looked relieved to see that it was Tap and Slug rather than those fucking psycho drug-crazed Yardies.

"Secure that door and I don't want any of you monkeys in here until forensics turn up!" ordered Tap.

Tap had had a hunch. If Jenkins had come to get medication for his girlfriend, then he was likely to be still on the premises.

"You!" Tap called a nurse over as he walked across the corridor towards the lifts. "If someone had AIDS or something and they wanted to get medication in here for it, where would they look? I mean, do you have that sort of thing here?"

The nurse said she was not really sure what pharmaceuticals were used to treat AIDS; they may have them in the drug dispensary or the pharmacy, but she didn't know for sure. Tap thanked the woman for her help and got directions to the hospital pharmacy, which was on the second floor.

The stairs seemed the best option, so Tap could keep a look-out through the windows in the hope of witnessing Anthony making an escape. One thing he did see was the Merc Jeep, still out there and high up there on Tap's priority list of items to take care of. The police were now storming the building; every Tom, Dick and Harry was coming to get a piece of this one! Dead copper; the shit really was going to hit the fan.

"Hang on a minute, Slug."

Slug turned to see that Tap had his phone to his ear and was waiting for someone to answer.

"Clayton, you at the hospital? Merc Jeep, two black guys in it armed to the teeth. Make them yours, Clayton. Suggest severe caution; men armed and dangerous. I repeat, severe caution Clayton, you know what I mean?"

Clayton thanked his colleague for the tip.

Arriving at the second floor, Tap kicked the door open and stormed into the corridor, his handgun held at the ready. There were several nurses bustling about, reassuring the patients that all was well and waiting for information as to whether they would have to lead the patients out of the hospital to safety. Tap asked the first nurse he came across if she had seen anyone strange wandering about on this level, but she hadn't.

"Where's the drugs dispensary, or chemist's or whatever?" he asked.

"Down there," the nurse replied fearfully, with her hands above her head.

"Oh, we're police, sorry!" Tap added belatedly, flashing his badge. The two officers moved cautiously up the corridor until they saw the sign for the pharmacy.

Tap stormed the drug dispensary head on, but there was no one there. Nothing in the room looked out of the ordinary, except that it appeared to be unmanned, which was a bit strange given the fact that it was full of highly desirable drugs.

"He ain't been here," Tap concluded. If he had, the place would have been in chaos. He went to the window as a series of gunshots suddenly sounded from the car park. Clayton had fired into the Jeep and was now walking slowly towards it.

"Good!" Tap commented. He just had Boyd to silence now.

"Slug, take care of this will you? I've got some business to take care of because we're taking Boyd out tonight. I want armed guards in this drug dispensary for the rest of the day, and you're clear about what took place upstairs now, ain't you?" Tap asked.

Slug answered in the affirmative. As for the bit about Boyd, that unnerved Slug a little because this was big-time. But he understood that Boyd had to go; he'd taken the piss this time.

"Wait for Slim, okay? Then get some rest. Make a call though, we need a van off one of our mates, clean right, must be clean. You'd better chill out for a bit and get the old brain matter positively charged so that you're ready for tonight. I'll have a plan by then. Eight o'clock it's going to happen, all right?"

It was clear to Slug that Tap already had a plan of some sort, he just had to implement it and arrange the necessary muscle. Slug would leave it all to him. All he had to do was wait for Doughnut, answer a few questions upstairs, sort their transport for tonight, and then he could get some rest to recharge his batteries and get his head straight, because this shit was getting out of hand.

"Just fucking walk like we're together and everything will be all right!" the denim-clad, skinny white male ordered through gritted teeth. The young woman with whom he had linked arms turned away in disgust as he spoke, droplets of his saliva spattering her face. She didn't want to be here, that much was evident. The couple arrived at a huge block of red brick flats where her kidnapper's hideout lay. His right hand gripped her left arm fiercely as she unlocked the door at his bidding, his left pushing a firearm against firm ribs. He snatched the key back from her before pushing her into the hallway.

"Press the lift button!" Jenkins ordered as he removed a white plastic bag from beneath his denim jacket. Thankfully the goods inside the bag seemed to have remained dry, despite the torrential rain outside.

The lift bell pinged loudly as the doors opened to reveal an empty lift. Pushing the woman inside, Jenkins pressed the button for the third floor and stared unnervingly at his latest victim as the lift sped upwards. She was a pretty little thing in her early twenties with dark, shoulder-length hair, her white coat just visible beneath the oversized duffle coat she wore. Anthony hadn't really had a plan in mind when he abducted her from the hospital pharmacy, except that she might be useful in helping him to look after Haley's needs. She had not been very cooperative so far, but that was probably not surprising under the circumstances. They had come this far now and he was going to take a chance on her. He just had to teach her a few ground rules first, which he started by slapping her across the face with a backhander and sending her crashing to the floor.

"What the fuck was that for?" The girl screamed, looking up at her captor, her face reddened by the blow. Jenkins pulled her upright by her hair until she was standing then moved his hand to her throat. With his face less than an inch from hers, he told her how it was going to be.

It was simple: they were going to enter his flat now when the lift stopped. When they did so, they would find Haley there. She was to say nothing to Haley unless Jenkins said so.

She was hired as a home help, private nurse, whatever, and that was the role she was to fulfil under Jenkins' supervision. As soon as her tasks were performed, she would be free to go. Haley was dying; it would be a matter of a few weeks at the most. Tears welled in the Sarah's eyes. She was scared, understandably so because this man who was speaking to her, so close to her face, was a fucking lunatic. Anthony asked her not to cry, because it was not the end of the world; not as long as she did what she was told. She had to remember that Haley knew nothing about anything and it had to remain that way, did she understand? Not really. She knew what she had to do in order to survive, but as for understanding, how the fuck do you understand this bullshit?

Sarah was led towards Gordon's flat at gunpoint, once Anthony had checked the corridor from the safety of the lift and felt it safe to manoeuvre. He gave her the key and she cautiously unlocked the door and pushed it open. The flat was dark and she switched on the light, having first obtained Anthony's permission to do so. Anthony dropped the bag of smack onto the kitchen work surface before removing his jacket, the money and the phone.

Sarah was frightened again, was this the bit where she was raped or fucked around with? She hoped with all her heart that it was only the cargo she carried that was of interest to her kidnapper. She took off her coat, and there it sat, taped to her midriff with thick brown parcel tap, the beautiful MP5. Jenkins took another knife from the knife block by the kettle, leaving it minus two now. With precision cuts, the tape was slashed and the sub-machine gun snatched away by its new owner. Still with the Browning in his right hand, Jenkins stepped back towards the back wall, his left hand holding the sub close to his chest as he tucked the Browning away in his waistband. The sub was fucking gorgeous. He was lost for words; never had he held such firepower. The only small problem was that he had not the faintest idea how to use this weapon, but then he hadn't known how to use the Browning either until he worked it out. It couldn't be that difficult. "In there!" Jenkins whispered. He wanted to keep the noise down so that Haley didn't know he was back yet. If they made too much noise she would hear through the hole he had made in the wall to gain access to Leigh Anderson's flat. He waved Sarah towards the main bedroom of the old man's flat and followed behind her ready to stifle her inevitable screams at the sight of the dead and decaying old man with his own genitalia protruding from his mouth.

"Meet Gordon!" He whispered in her ear as the bedroom door gently closed behind them. "Chill out, girl. Shh, shh, shh, shh!"

Anthony relaxed his grip over her mouth slightly as she got over the initial shock.

"Come on, he's dead, so screaming's a waste of time now, ain't it? I'm going to let go, all right?"

Sarah overcame her instinct to scream the place down and nodded slightly, adjusting her balance as her captor released his grip. Only then did she notice the pornographic pictures of the most serious nature littering the bed, and the words 'effective punishment' on the wall above the corpse, together with the artist's signature and some strange sort of squiggle that looked like a Chinese character.

"I don't understand," she stated woodenly.

"Well, what can I say? Gordon was a naughty boy. I sort of killed him by accident at first. I mean, I didn't really mean to. It weren't an accident as such, because I knew I had to kill him really, it's a bit complicated," Anthony tried to explain. He also tried to explain that he didn't really feel as though it was him doing these things; he was kind of doing them for someone else, although he didn't know who.

Jenkins joined his hostage on the floor, cradling his beloved new toy, the police-issue killing machine. It made a change to talk to someone who was alive.

"Have you seen me in the news?" The killer asked. Sarah nodded. In an attempt to establish some sort of friendly terms with her kidnapper, she casually asked him how he had come to be in such a situation.

"I just went to work as usual on Saturday morning. I'd been to see Haley that morning at a hospice that she was in, early hours that is. She looked very unwell. Well, she is, ain't she? Anyway, I got to my shop, same old shit, opened up and that, and then two fellers came in giving it the large because my stepdad owed them money. It was self-defence really. They had come to hurt me and I had to protect myself, so I did! I then had two dead bodies though, didn't I? So I torched the shop, hoping someone would think that one of the corpses was me. Didn't work, though. Well, the fire worked; it's just the other bit. So, I'm on the run, I need a gun, and so I arrange it. Tried to buy a gun, tried my hardest, but it went wrong. The dealer tried to tuck me up and so, well, bang! Anyway, went back to my mum's flat and there's two more of these debt collectors. You've heard of Yardies, I suppose?"

Sarah nodded again, unwilling to interrupt the flow of information.

"Yeah, well it was two of them. I say debt collectors, but they were actually hit men so I had to take them out before they took me out. It was on the cards really because they'd been waiting for me. I'd seen them come out of my mum's flat just minutes before I done 'em. I went up into the flat once I'd sorted them out, and there was my stepdad and a friend of his dead, all cut up and that. Mum wasn't there thankfully, but I knew then that I was on the run, good and proper! So, I fucking run and ended up here, didn't I? I found this dirty cunt and he had to go. I didn't know why I was killing him at first but when I dragged him in here and saw all this filthy shit, I knew I'd done right. Then it was time to free Haley, so I did that but someone got in the way there so I had to remove him from the equation. And another guy, a Limo driver - oh, don't ask! Well, after that I ended up at your hospital. I'd tried to get what I needed for Haley from the chemist's down the road but it was being staked out and the police shot someone thinking he was me. His sister and I ran for our lives because the police were hunting us down and we ended up at St George's. It was fucking mental, I tell you!"

Sarah did interrupt at that point, to ask about the bloke's sister.

"Yeah, I met some chap and his sister on a train to the hospital. They were from Norwich or somewhere, and we were going to help each other out with a couple of problems that we had. I only wanted the gear, it was simple, create a diversion down stairs, well, you saw the fire, and then get what I needed from the pharmacy. Simple, no one had to die. Well, I say no one but I had to kill a policeman. You carried his gun here. So, this guy who the police shot back at the pharmacy was with his sister, and he was getting Haley's medicine for me when he got ambushed. So me and his sister came to the hospital. She had another brother there and he was in this dilemma sort of thing. Now, I had agreed to free her brother from hospital, he was under armed guard for drug offences. Now, I'm not the fucking Samaritans or anything so it didn't matter if I freed her brother or not to be honest, because the only thing that attracted me to the task was the armed guard; armed meaning firearms. So, easy as taking candy from a baby, I shot him in the face, cut his gun off and nicked it. I actually nicked two, but the other had no fucking bullets in it and by the time I noticed it was too late to go back for them. See, I'd seen these geezers lurking around the place. They were looking for me because not only are the police after me, these gangsters want my arse too, thanks to my stepdad. So, I had to leave the scene quick, but first I needed these drugs for Haley and you were kind enough to sort me out. You had to come with me, though. I know you don't like the idea and I don't expect you to, but I've got no reason to hurt you if you behave. It's simple: Haley needs you. She's only got a few weeks left so it's not too much to ask, is it?"

"So, it's okay to just kidnap someone and make them do what you want, is it? And you keep going on about a 'cause'. What is your cause? Why are you doing this? I don't understand."

Jenkins gave the matter some thought. He even looked at Gordon for inspiration, but in the end honesty had to be the best policy.

"Look, if I'd asked for your help then you wouldn't have given it to me, now would you?"

"Maybe. Depends what's in it for me."

That threw him off balance, so he had to ask her what she meant.

"Well, maybe I'm not your average person. Maybe I have problems myself. Just because I'm a pharmacist's assistant, it doesn't mean I'm squeaky clean. Come on mate, this is the fucking real world, you know?"

"What sort of problems?"

"Mainly money problems." She chanced it causing Anthony to laugh with relief.

"Fucking hell, is that all? Wait there!" He left the room and returned almost instantly with a wad of cash.

"There's nearly three grand there. Will that help your money problems?" Anthony asked.

Sarah laughed in surprise. It would certainly go a long way, she admitted. Anthony smiled.

"Good, I'll get you some more then. Two weeks is all I'm asking: look after Haley for two weeks and all your money problems are sorted. Fucking hell, you'll get compensation and newspaper fees and all sorts. You'll be fucking made because on paper, I'm the craziest motherfucker that they've had in the papers for decades!" Anthony bragged.

"Okay, you say you'll give me the money if I look after your girlfriend. But how do I know you won't kill me when it's over and done with?" Sarah asked. It was a good question.

"No, no, no. If I don't get any trouble from you, if we can work together on this, then I won't kill you. Fuck, no! You're on my side. I'll give you my word. I have no reason to kill you unless you make me, and to be honest, I don't relish the thought of killing you at all. I'm not a fucking animal, you know? I've just been pushed too far and it's my duty to protect myself and Haley. You have no reason to die; your death wouldn't further the cause in any way. To kill you would simply be murder and I don't do murder, I just do punishment!" Anthony spoke what he considered to be the truth, but Sarah was left in no doubt that the man talking to her could kill at a second's notice if the need arose. You just had to read the bloody papers! But she couldn't help being intrigued nevertheless.

"What is this cause thing then?" She asked, and Anthony was more than happy to explain because it was simply a rehearsal of his memoirs.

"All I wanted from life was what most people want: a nice wife, a nice flat or house, whatever, and a nice job, my own business perhaps. It wasn't much to ask really, was it? Yeah well, being brought up in shit breeds shit, and that was me and I wanted my life to change. So, I went away travelling for a few years, Oz and a bit of South America and that - and when I came back - well, life was proper shit! The old club scene was pumping, though, so the same thing I went travelling to escape soon clawed me back into its grasp. Pills, coke, speed, fucked out of my head most weekends and using the week to recover until it was time to do it all again. But it all went wrong in the end.

"Didn't fucking come down one night, I was still buzzing days later, weeks even. The adrenaline was pumping and it just wouldn't go away; it just kept poisoning my body. I was feeling sick, I couldn't see properly, I was shaking like a motherfucker and all sorts. So, I go to the fucking doctor and it's 'Oh, have some beta blockers, you'll be all right, you've just got yourself into a bit of a state!' Fucking understatement of the year! Tried them, but they were a waste of fucking time. So, I go back and same again. Seven months this went on, and in the end I warned the doctor that it was going to be blood on his hands and so he gave me anti-depressants, which worked to a degree, and I was referred to a psychiatric hospital as a day patient. Week after week I did these fucking bullshit relaxation lessons, and all the time I kept telling them that something was wrong with me big time. Everyone else in the group had the odd panic attack when they went to a busy shop or something but as for me, well, I was completely fucked up in the head. A fucking year and a half I wasted there and then some cheeky fucker rings me up to say that in their opinion I was cured now. Well, I just fucking exploded then. I just lost it. I went straight to the hospital and shit the life out of them. I told them that if I was going, then they were coming with me because something inside me was telling me to pull the plug and I was having real trouble resisting these thoughts. So, they turned round and said that maybe they'd overlooked my case and I got to see a psychiatrist.

"I'm totally fucked by the time I've seen her; I'm probably like ten times worse than when I first went to see a doctor about it in the first place, twenty one months before. It's a long time to live with the fact that you're losing your marbles. So, I saw the psychiatrist - six months I saw her - and she helped me a lot, but she'd done about all she could and by then I was experimenting with drugs again to get through what was happening to me. Before you know it I was hooked onto the only thing that made me feel better: smack."

Jenkins poured his heart out. He felt glad to have someone to talk to, and she was really listening.

"You asked me what my cause was and I'm gonna get to that, but you need the whole picture. I used to get my drugs from Haley, that's how I met her. She became ill, HIV, like I said. I fell in love with her, truly, and all I wanted to do was make her life better, or as good as it could be until the end. I invested in my stepfather's shop, which was doing okay but the returns weren't quick enough because Haley became really ill quicker than we expected. So there we were: me a drug addict held together by my next clout and Haley riddled with AIDS and dying faster than I could take care of her. The world stinks, don't it?"

Sarah felt that a response was required.

"Okay then, so you feel hard done by and the world's against you. Your cause is to punish it, am I warm?" She asked bluntly.

Anthony laughed.

"Not the world, my dear; just society. The system, if you like - well, any fucker that gets in my way, really. Like I said, shit breeds shit and I was brought up in it. I'm surrounded by shit: drugs, crime, prostitution, fucking everything that's bad in this world, I was brought up in it. I didn't want it, but this is Britain in the year two thousand. It shouldn't be here; I should be protected from it, and Haley. Fucking hell, she had to sell her body to make a living and then on her death bed she had to sell drugs! What kind of a fucking life is that? What's the fucking point? I owe it to her to make her last couple of weeks the best they can be, and I've dedicated my life to it. That wasn't the initial plan, it's just that all this shit I've been talking about has forced me into it. I'm trapped now, and so it's to the death for me, but I will give Haley what I promised, and I almost have!

"I think I will be stopped soon, because there are people out there who are determined that I won't fulfil my task. I have a copper chasing me, Billy, his name is, and he wants me bad. He's struggling to catch me though, because I'm always one step ahead, but I think he will in the end! He has this idea that I'm in this purely because I have some uncontrollable hatred for the doctors who treated me, which isn't really true. Of course I have some resentment towards them, but in all fairness they didn't really know what they were dealing with. I have friends who are dropping like flies, and they say they want to decriminalise Ecstasy and Amphetamines! It just goes to show that those motherfuckers haven't got a clue. They're the most dangerous drug on the market! Okay, it's very unlikely that you'd die on the spot with them, but it's the long term damage that the doctors are only now starting to realise comes from the prolonged use of these drugs. It's like, enjoy now; pay later, and it's going to be the epidemic of the twenty first century, believe me! Our generation's fucked, just ask any GP how fast the mental illness cases have risen. Get the age groups and you'll see I'm right; we are the brain-fried generation and the system let us do it! There's proof everywhere. Give me ten famous people who've been diagnosed with Parkinson's or Alzheimer's, then tell me they weren't the biggest Charlie heads' in Hollywood! But now they're dying, tragically, so remember the saying: enjoy now, pay later.

"Getting back to these doctors, though, this copper is convinced that I'm going for them. He's found a diary in my flat, you see. It's just a list of appointments: who dealt with me and the outcome, it's a sort of log of my treatment more than anything, or lack of, but Billy thinks it's a hit list. He's totally wrong, but who knows? Maybe I'll surprise him. He likes playing games, you see, so why should I disappoint him? That would be cruel!" Anthony sneered. He stopped at last, and a shrug of his shoulders indicated that he had finished.

What he said made some kind of sense to Sarah. The business about the rise in mental health problems hit home quite sharply, because her brother had been struck down with severe anxiety and had been very ill for years. And yes he was one of the rave generation. It was frightening to think to the future, which no longer looked as bright as it had done.

"You understand the cause now?" Anthony asked.

Sarah nodded. There was silence between them for a few minutes, eventually broken by Anthony again.

"You know this copper who I said was chasing me? It's weird, right. I feel so close to this man; I feel like I know him. I know that sounds fucking stupid but that's how I feel, although I don't really know how I feel no more to be honest, not over the last couple of days. Last week, causing this sort of shit wouldn't even have entered my head, but I died yesterday. No shit, I fucking died and I came back, and I just haven't felt the same since."

"Died?" Sarah had to ask.

Jenkins nodded.

"Yesterday morning I overdosed. I was gone. I didn't have an out-of-body experience or anything there was just darkness before I came back. But whoever has come back, it's not me. It's someone else. Someone else is controlling me."

Okaaay, Sarah silently dragged the word out in her mind. This was heavy stuff, fuelling her initial suspicions that her kidnapper was totally fucking insane. Anthony decided to leave it at that rather than risk freaking her out even more.

"No more talk," he said briskly. "Come on, I'll introduce you to Haley. Not you though, Gordon, you filthy cunt; you stay there!"

Chapter Seven

Do you think I'm sexy?

"There's that Ann bird; pick her up, Slug!" Tap gave an order as darkness came fully upon them. The nearly new blue transit van slowed down as if kerb crawling. Slug was driving as usual. Tap sat 'looking up to no good' on the middle of the passenger bench seat, staring out of the window. Ann looked like a hooker, but suddenly resembled a scared rabbit as she saw the van turn up. She didn't have a problem with vans as such, just vans with that cunt Billy Tap in them. Ann was standing beside a dustbin, into which she threw a lighted cigarette. The blue transit clipped the kerb as it pulled over, causing the passenger to complain. She looked ill, anorexic or malnourished, but without her clothes on the pin-cushion elbow joints gave the real game away.

"Get in!" Tap ordered, as he opened the passenger door, making it clear that this was a request that was not really worth arguing about.

Ann didn't waste her time arguing, but tossed her bag over her shoulder before crossing the pavement towards the van from which Tap, her nemesis, stared out through the open passenger side window. He opened the door as she approached and pulled her up the step by her jacket. Ann looked a little nervous as she sat on her half of the bench seat, although she didn't actually have a clue what was going on. She had spiked a vein in the bus shelter only minutes before and life was quite adorable at the moment, although she suspected that that was about to change. Tap leaned across her to shut the door against the elements.

"Drive, Slug!" He ordered as the prostitute smiled and leaned forward to catch a glimpse of the driver, who she recognised. Leaning back again and dropping her bag on the floor, Ann laughed with resignation. She was in trouble and she knew it; she was in Billy Tap's care now. Languidly, she put her feet up on the shelf that was moulded into the dash. She had kinky boots on, well, that was what Tap called any footwear that touched the knee, and she allowed her denim coat to fall open as if in invitation. Tap didn't really dig tartan, but the skirt was short enough below a bare waist decorated with a jewel-encrusted ornamental belly button stud. Tap wasn't interest in anything above the waist, the tits needed a small fortune spending on them and her face needed weight. Nah, he wouldn't! Well, he probably would, but not at this moment in time, certainly wouldn't cross the road for it! Getting back to the tartan though; Tap lifted the material up at the hem and took a quick peek underneath, only to reveal 'big old pants' as he called them. Why the fuck someone paid for this, he had no idea; she could at least have put some decent knickers on, or gone without. It was like going to buy a car which looked the nuts, all bells and whistles, so you take it for a spin only to find out that under the bonnet it's a one point fucking one with a body kit and flash wheels. Anyway, whatever was under Ann's hood, she must have made money from it or she wouldn't do it.

Tap turned his nose up as she pulled aside her underwear in a pathetic attempt at seduction. It did nothing for him, other than to prompt him to ask Slug to remind him that his neighbour's fern tree needed a good trim as it kept tapping on his balcony window. She ought to at least keep her workplace tidy! Ann was obviously known to Tap and Slug, but they had left her alone lately because she had a little dirt on Tap. In fact, at one time she had had a fucking skip load, enough to sink him, but she had wisely kept her mouth shut. Shame she couldn't do the same with her legs!

"Put it away, love; it's a fucking health hazard. We'll have to call the environmental health department in if you carry on!" Tap joked. She made him feel queasy, which was saying something because you could carry out a full autopsy in front of Tap while he dined and it wouldn't be a problem.

The history was that Tap had fitted someone up not so many moons ago, and Ann was involved because she had coaxed the guy in question to where Tap wanted him before leaving the rest to the officers. The scam had involved an under-age girl and Tap's target had taken the bait; hook, line and sinker. What Ann hadn't known at the time was that it was an internal job; a case of the police taking care of their own rotten apples. Trouble was, there was a risk that she might talk under pressure from other interrogators. One other minor point was that her pimp was our friend Boyd.

The transit van drove around some of the quieter London back streets, dimly lit and well off the tourist trail. It didn't look like a particularly rough area, but by God it was. Tap leaned back casually, and Ann too relaxed in her seat as if completely chilled with the situation. She wedged herself in position by pressing one of her feet against a shelf in the footwell and the other on the dash, the tip of her boot touching an antique jewellery box which had been placed on the dash.

"Like that, do you?" Tap asked, breaking the silence.

The prostitute shrugged. In truth, she did like it, as Tap had known she would. This little jewellery box was like silver to a magpie where a Tom was concerned. Tap's theory was that prostitutes left home at an early age; every prostitute had a mother and every mother had a jewellery box. When you opened the jewellery box, it played a tune, reminding whoever had opened it of home, family, mother and normality.

"Open it if you like," he offered. Ann couldn't help but do so. It was quite heavy for a jewellery box; ever so smooth though, and shiny, with a finish like mahogany. The box played a tune when the lid was opened; oh how it sang, and it was music to her ears as a little ballerina popped up and spun round in all her glory. Slug had to take his hat off to Tap as he glanced sideways at Ann while trying to keep his eyes on the road at the same time. Slug hadn't liked the plan and had strongly tried to oppose it a few hours before, but he had to concede that it was a good one and had locked his conscience firmly away. Tonight was going to be messy, Slug knew, very messy. However, if you play with fire, you get burnt from time to time. In fact, if this plan fucked up they were going to be char-grilled.

The chimes of the musical box echoed in the cab of the stolen van, mesmerising the young woman. There was an expensive-looking necklace in the bottom of the red, velvet-lined container. She picked it up and straightened in her seat to hold it up to the light. There was not much, but enough to make out the exquisite silver art work.

"You like it?" Tap asked.

Of course she did. She took another look in the box, but there was nothing else there except red velvet. The dimensions of the box weren't quite right somehow; the space inside seemed too small for the size of the box. Ann searched to see if she had missed a drawer or a compartment, but she hadn't so she wasted no more time on the matter.

"Try it on!" Billy offered.

Suspicious, she guessed that there must be some ulterior motive behind this sudden change in Tap's manner, but hoped that it might just be that she had to fuck him or something. Fuck them both, maybe, which was no big deal to her. She would gladly fuck him for this exquisite piece, she had done it for a lot less. She had even done it for a fucking cigarette before now, but times had been hard back then.

“Go on!” Tap repeated, having sensed her caution.

So Ann hesitated no more as she held the jewellery up to her neck and turned her head slightly to the left, indicating to Tap to fasten the clasp. It looked nice, not a million dollars, but it was old and it was expensive.

“You can have it if you like,” Tap offered, whereupon Ann asked what she had to do to earn it. Tap laughed; they were so suspicious, these Toms! “Not a lot,” he said softly.

It was simple, really; all she had to do was deliver some money to Boyd, her employer. Tap had the money here. He took it from the inside pocket of his black leather jacket and passed it across to her with leather-clad fingers. Ann took the money. It was in a white envelope. The flap was open and she couldn’t help but look inside the package. Yes, there was money - a fucking lot of money.

“You can have that an’ all.” Tap offered, indicating the jewellery box. After all, it was no use to him.

The whole scenario stank like shit, but she was so fucked out of her head that she saw no problem with the transaction. All she had to do was deliver the money to Boyd, which was in turn helping her employer, wasn’t it? Because he was obviously owed the money, or Tap wouldn’t have been delivering it, would he? For her part, she got this lovely jewellery box and this more than lovely chain. Fuck, it was a deal! As if she feared that Tap might turn back on the arrangement, Ann closed the jewellery box lid and hid it deep within her capacious shoulder bag.

“Be careful with that love,” Tap said, “that’s a fucking antique, so show it a little respect, eh?”

Ann stowed the envelope containing the money away in the inside pocket of her denim jacket. There was silence in the van for a while, until the occupants gradually became aware of a noise coming from the back of it, inside the cargo hold so to speak. It was like a faint humming. Tap turned to double check that there was no window behind his head, but there wasn't.

"Can you hear that?" He asked. There was definitely a humming noise coming from the back of the van.

"What is it?" Slug asked. Tap didn't answer, although he had his suspicions. If there had been a window looking into the back of the van, he would have been able to see. He reached for his phone and pressed a button, then waited impatiently for someone to answer.

"Loft-hatch, what the fuck is going on in there?" Tap asked. "Praying? Are you taking the fucking piss out of me?" There was a brief silence, then, "I don't care where they come from, or what their fucking tradition is. If they're going to fucking pray in my time, then can they do it fucking quietly?" He banged on the bulkhead of the van behind his head. "Shut up, you fucking lunatics!" He screamed. There was a momentary silence, and then a solitary bang as someone in the back returned Tap's message.

"Are they taking the piss?" Tap asked, but Loft-hatch assured his employer that they weren't.

"Tell your mates that they can do what the fuck they need or have to do in the back of the van but, all I ask is that you just keep them fucking quiet please, okay? It's not too much to ask now, is it? ETA is about five minutes, so be ready! Now, you clear on what you've got to do?"

Loft-hatch replied in reasonably good English that he did understand, one hundred per cent, and at Tap's request repeated the basic fundamentals of the plan.

"Okay, you are taking the door, yeah?"

Tap agreed; he was taking the door.

"Yes, you take the door; we take the house. If they're tooled-up and not me, Slug, or your boys, we shoot them. If they're punters, we do what you said to them and if they're female, we put them in the van. Correct?"

The plan had been formulated in this way and specifically defined on the basis that, out of the four men sitting in the back of the van, only one spoke English. The gang which Tap anticipated would be their immediate enemy was Jamaican. They ran several brothels, at least ten of them in and around London. The one they were heading for tonight was in a pretty plush area in a huge house, and the majority of the punters were wealthy business men. Maybe the odd innocent punter who happened to have the wrong colour of skin or decided to arm themselves may die, but Tap was okay with that because there were always innocent casualties in a war. Tap was taking Boyd out tonight, and he knew where he was and how to get him.

Loft-hatch was from the Middle East. He got his nickname from an incident a few years back when Tap had been called to a huge old house in London where it was reported that a number of known terrorists were hiding out. He had been in charge of a squad to storm the safe house, which surveillance teams had been watching for several weeks. Tap's team had raided the house and found to their surprise that every fucker inside it had topped himself. They'd known they were being watched, so right at the last minute when it was evident that a raid was about to take place they thought they'd ascend to that better place in the sky a little earlier than planned. After all, according to their religious beliefs, this life was pretty shitty compared to what was on the other side.

So, there were poisoned suspected terrorists, drug overdosed suspected terrorists, one in the car in the garage, all gassed up, slit wrists and so on: the works. There was also one hanging from the open loft hatch, dangling from a rope that was attached to a beam in the roof. Tap had been walking round the house trying to come to terms with the sudden lack of punters to nick, when someone shouted upstairs that they had a live one. So, they cut the twitching body down and found he was indeed still alive; thus Loft-hatch had been born. Loft-hatch went to hospital and had various treatments for a neck that was now two inches longer than it should be, before he was imprisoned and eventually sentenced to be extradited back to where he came from, where he faced charges of attempted terrorism. Attempted? Yeah, Loft-hatch had been shot and wounded several years before during an attempt to blow up a bus full of people. He had run onto the bus, shouted his cause and then pressed the detonating device in his hand. Unfortunately, or rather fortunately for the passengers but unfortunately for him, nothing had happened and the would-be suicide bomber made off with his waistcoat of explosives still intact. Of course, with a lunatic running down a busy high street wearing a whole lot of danger, the army and police had had to be a bit careful where they shot him. They got one arm and one leg, but he still managed to get away somehow. It was hard to say whether he was the unluckiest man in the world or the luckiest.

So, Loft-hatch had fled to England to further whatever plot; he was not the brains behind the job, just the brawn. So, one day he was being transported to the airport in the back of a truck ready to be extradited to where he came from, when it turned out that he was next to Ian Selby! It couldn't be just some two bit low life, could it? No, it had to be fucking Selby, didn't it? Now Mr Selby, as most called him, when not calling him 'Sir,' was a fucking head-case who was being dropped off at the Scrubs en route to the airport. This bloke was absolutely chicken-fucking-oriental. The prison service were using a multi-drop system to get the prisoners where they needed to be, so they were asking for trouble really, which is exactly what they got. Selby had been a very pro-active member of a known local terror organisation and he had contacts on the outside who were very happy to help him get out. So, the truck driver had left for work that morning, kissing goodbye to his nearly-new wife and their three month old kid, leaving them in the tender care of a few of Selby's old buddies. And so it was no wonder that he had pulled up in the middle of nowhere and handed over the keys.

So there was poor fucking Loft-hatch, free again and stranded in the pissing rain, in the middle of nowhere, in a country that was not his own. He had managed to get a lift into town and rob a shop, using the money to get a train back into London, where he sought sanctuary with his own kind until his services were required again in the great-war. Selby was shot not long after by some of his political opponents and the two other prisoners who had been freed were found in the local pub. They had attempted to hijack it but got pissed in the process and when the police arrived three hours later they were found rolling about on the floor in a pool of their own urine and vomit. Never underestimate the local ales!

Loft-hatch stayed out the way of the police for a while, until the beloved he believed in called again, and Tap was once more summoned to the scene of a suspicious 'suicide.' He was looking down into a bathtub in a flat in Brixton containing the naked, brown-skinned body and an electric heater, when suddenly the body twitched and Tap nearly shit himself. All the coppers in the room jumped back in amazement. Loft-hatch had minor burns to his hands and his hair was a bit of a mess, but under the circumstances he looked in pretty good nick.

They had found him when a neighbour had alerted the warden at the flats that all the electrics had gone off in the building. The fault was traced to Room 14, and so the caretaker opened the door and looked into the flat where Loft-hatch lay in the bathroom. The fucking lunatic had switched the electric fire on once he was in the bath, in an attempt to electrocute himself, and he succeeded to a degree. Until the electrics in the whole building fused, that is. He was unconscious for about two hours and then boom, he woke up to find a room full of police; how freaky was that? Almost as freaky as finding that, standing there looking down upon him, was the same copper who had kicked the fuck out of him when he had last tried to top himself by hanging.

There were no extradition proceedings this time, because Loft-hatch now had a spanking new name, passport and identity, and therefore no criminal record. This was fucking perfect from Tap's point of view, because now he owned him. What a touch! And own him Tap did, to the extent that when any little jobs like the one they were about to do tonight needed doing, then Loft-hatch was the man. In fact, here was the ideal man because although he was a highly-trained terrorist with a military background, he was still fully malleable. What he personally lacked in being able to actually pull-off his missions, he made up for in being able to recruit and train soldiers much better at the actual dirty work than he. When it came to storming a building or similar activities, those he trained were second only to the SAS because he had been trained by one of their previous members. Loft-hatch wasn't very active in terrorist activities in England, but he had become a good fund-raiser for his cause and needed the help of the police on occasions. This was quite handy, seeing as Tap was a man who liked offering a helping hand.

So, Loft-hatch was on the books. All he had to do to earn his keep was to grass a few colleagues up when they got a bit out of line, take out the competitors, that sort of thing. Of course, he also had to keep Tap up to date with the pulse of the streets as far as his organisation was concerned, and he also had to do the odd dirty job now and again, jobs that only a well-trained lunatic could do. This was Loft-hatch's night.

He had his own crew with him this evening, new recruits who spoke little English and cared about nothing but their religious beliefs. Tap had dealt with religious fanatics in the past and they were the toughest cookies to crack. You could forget interrogating them; you could try torturing them - Tap had, on many occasions - but still they say nothing and their lack of English was an added bonus.

The traffic was typical of London at seven o'clock, stopping and starting at varied intervals. Sitting in the back of the van with his small army of three men, all dressed in black, Loft-hatch felt a tingling sensation on his left nipple. It was created by the phone in his jacket pocket. On answering the phone, it became clear that they were very close to reaching their rendezvous point, so Lofty warned his crew that the time had come. Putting the phone away, the terrorist leader watched as his crew carried out a last-minute weapons check. Micro-Uzis were the gang's preference, the chosen weapon of their homeland, although these were in fact Chinese replicas. These weapons were the cousin of the world famous Uzi 9 millimetre, just a smaller, more refined version and ideal for the assault that they were about to perform. The state-of-the-art firearms were double-checked, re-adjusted and then left attached to their owners' wrists by their muzzle straps. These were an optional extra to help support the weapon. Glock hand guns were double checked, spare magazine locations tested. Knives that would put the shits up a Kebab man were checked in their locations around the killers' bodies, and various other killing devices such as garrottes and grenades were double checked. The van suddenly came to a halt outside a huge white house.

Loft-hatch listened carefully as he heard the transit van's passenger door open and people step out. One of his crew members started to mutter something but he put a stop to that with a palm raised firmly; he needed silence. Why Slug couldn't have got a fucking van with a window looking into the cab, Loft-hatch didn't know. One person almost immediately got back into the van and closed the door. Lofty had heard a conversation between a man and a woman, something about her knowing what she had to do, blah, blah, blah! This was Tap giving his little helper some final tuition before she too took her part in the assault.

Yeah, she knew what she had to do, well, sort of, she was staggering a bit and probably didn't have a clue what was going on around her, but she was just about up to the task of walking to the door and knocking on it. Tap watched her through the passenger window of the van, hoping she would get the timing right. She was walking down the drive leading to one of the main entrances. There were actually two drive entrances; the same drive met the house before turning back and heading towards the road again, twenty or so metres further down from the other. That made the drive look semi-circular from a bird's eye view, leaving an island of established trees and shrubs between the road and the drive. Yeah very posh, very secluded, ideal for a brothel. Even more so for closing one down, Tap style!

He wondered if she could possibly make any more noise on the gravel path if she tried. She was stumbling a bit over the stones, making hard work of it, resembling a weary lost soul traipsing towards salvation. Tap felt no pity for her; she had earned none. He climbed out of the van and walked along the side of it, reaching out and opening the side door of the van as if releasing some unstoppable force from its depths.

The small but deadly band of brothers climbed out, now wearing black masks. Even Tap stood back momentarily, impressed by the menacing sight of them. Loft-hatch got out first, but waited for his men to disembark before leading them into war. Two of them disappeared into the small island of trees and shrubs and the other two took the shrubbery that bordered the front of the house, each taking one side of the porch-type construction that housed the recessed front door. The trained killers never touched gravel, and once they had disappeared into the jungle they were nowhere to be seen. It was more than apparent that they had done this before. Even the prostitute hadn't seen them, but that was the idea. Granted, they could probably have approached the house equipped with tambourines and bells around their ankles and she wouldn't have noticed, because Tap had given her one for the road and she was drugged up to the eyeballs.

Fair play to the girl though, she had done as she was told and was waiting for some kind of signal before she made her final approach to the front door. In the meantime, she just stood by the solid metal gate at the side of the house, which was shielded by a well-constructed brick surround. The combination of gate and brick construction severely limited access to the gardens at the back. There were pit-bulls patrolling the grounds, and the heavy door would not have looked out of place in a prison.

The signal that it was time for Ann to move onto phase two of the plan would come in the form of a vibration from the phone that Tap had given her. She held it in her right hand and cradled her bag with her left. The bag had a strap but it was a chilly night and Ann hugged it to her. She had been instructed never to let go of the phone, even when she entered the house. Unbeknown to her, this was because it constituted a vital piece of evidence which would have to be destroyed. Ann waited patiently for the go-ahead to commence work, hoping that Tap would hurry up. After all, what was he fucking waiting for?

"Oh, fuck!" Tap swore. He had just laid some kind of device on the dashboard of the van. It was a small box thing with a number of green lights on it and a red button encased under a small plastic lid. The detective was setting the object up, ready for use at a moment's notice, when he suddenly saw something that sent a shiver down his spine. The front door of the house opened, just when Tap really could do with it being closed! He took some deep breaths to steady his heartbeat as he watched a white male leave the house through the complicated door system. From inside the house you could see a wooden front door open as a seriously heavy-duty metal one closed behind it.

He was in two minds whether to leave his army put and let the seemingly unaware punter leave peacefully, or take him down now. That was no good; they didn't have time to fuck about while this punter got in his car and messed about before setting off, so he had to go. Tap thought quickly. He was hampered by the fact that he had a very unpredictable prostitute dancing around by the back gate, trying to keep warm, which was a potential for disaster. His phone had been buzzing about on the dash for a few seconds, and he picked it up when it gyrated too close to the small device that sat next to it. The mysterious black box now had its red button fully exposed, the small plastic cap sitting open above it. He put the phone to his ear and quietly spoke two words, his mind made up.

"Do it!"

Loft-hatch jumped out of the island of trees like a madman and wrapped a choke wire around his unsuspecting victim's neck as he dragged him backwards into the jungle surrounding them. There was no noise, no real struggle because the wire had almost cut the man's head off. Lofty had overdone it a bit; this was evident as he tried to extract the garrotte from the meat into which he had forced it. The razor-sharp wire was then put away for the time being, still covered in blood.

His first task completed, the leader of the assault team rang his boss to confirm, while the gang waited in silence. Ann, who had got the signal from her vibrating phone, finally walked up to the front door of the house with eagerness to get on with the job and also to get inside and warm up, because it was fucking freezing out there. The door-bell rang, one long jangle. For a couple of minutes there was nothing, but then the outer door opened, leaving the inner door still closed as the prostitute was recognised and greeted. She stepped into the small recess created by the two doors.

Ann explained to the doorman that she had some money to deliver to Boyd. It was from Tap who needed a little favour doing. He would have rung Boyd by now, so Boyd would know what the money was for. The man on the door was professional so he searched her briefly to check that she had no added extras attached to her; like a wire or something. Satisfied that she wasn't carrying anything suspicious, he signalled for her to enter the house just as a huge explosion erupted without warning, filling the hallway and taking out the whole reception area. The heavy steel door was now sitting in the jungle next to Loft-hatch and his compatriots on the other side of the island.

"Fuck me!" He exclaimed, when he realised how close he'd come to being taken out himself by the flying door. The huge steel projectile was literally less than half a metre from him, having just split the tree next to him in half as a corner of it pierced the bark like a bullet, and was now wedged straight in the middle of it.

So where was Ann then, and her friend on the door? Well, the vast majority of them littered the driveway and some sat in the trees of the jungle, but overall there was very little that hadn't been burnt to a crisp or sent into space. Amongst the debris on the drive, Loft-hatch could see what looked like a head or half of one anyway. It was definitely Ann's, or definitely a white woman's at the very least, because it had earrings and there was a silver chain melted into what was left of her neck. Not a pretty sight by any stretch of the imagination! The air was filled with a strange smell, and parachuting debris slowly fell back to earth. The jewellery box hadn't really been the gift it had seemed.

Well there it was: no porch, no highly sophisticated door security system, no fucking stairs, which was a bit of a bastard, really, just devastation. Even from where Tap was sitting they had felt the blast rock the van. Single fire was coming from the house; the windows lit up with each large bang that filled the air. As ordered, Slug started the van up again and accelerated across the road and up the driveway. They screeched over the gravel as the brakes were applied and came to a halt right in the thick of things. Tap donned a balaclava as he got out of the van, closing the passenger door behind him.

It was fucking mayhem inside the house: loads of shouting and shit, gunshots, fire, mini-explosions, sparks. Tap's Glock was firmly in his right hand as he waited anxiously for some punters to leave the building. Loft-hatch was to take out anyone who got in their way, except one man. Come on Boyd, come to daddy!

Before long several women emerged from the house in various states of undress, one wearing nothing at all, Tap waved them into the back of the van. Three men soon followed, shuffling through the flames, their balance impaired by the cable ties that locked their wrists together behind their backs. The girls climbed in the van without the slightest complaint; as far as they were aware they were being nicked, and it was a pleasure after the fright they had just had. As for their clients; well, they were obviously not so keen to be nicked and they wouldn't be for the time being, not until the real police arrived anyway. Instead, Tap forced them to the ground one by one, where they lay face-down. Another three girls ran through the doorway of flames and were escorted to the safety of the transit van. Another punter then arrived, via the second floor window. He looked dead, having landed on his face, and Tap dragged him over to join the others.

The first of the masked warriors left the building almost as confidently as he had entered it. He carried a girl in his arms. She had been shot, but was still breathing. The wound was to her stomach and it looked messy and very painful. Thankfully for her, she was unconscious and Tap slid open the side door of the van to put her with the others.

Two more of Loft-hatch's crew emerged prisoner-free, marching out of the house pretty much unscathed, although their clothes were a little burnt around the edges. They had stormed the building in darkness, apart from what flickering light came from the plastic explosives. The laser sights attached to their firearms showed burning plaster, wallpaper, dado-rails, and of course what was left of the staircase, the majority of which was lying in a big pile on the floor. Years old it was, probably as old as the house, and had been made of solid wood so was just starting to smoulder away a treat. Underneath the staircase had been some kind of reception desk, and the receptionist was still there, dead, of course.

One of Loft-hatch's men had simply run up the pile of stairs and shot both of the men who had appeared at the top, since they fitted the criteria of being 'gangster'. This had resulted in frantic screams from several rooms on that floor. The assassin on the first floor had crouched down and helped Loft-hatch up beside him and the two men had given each other some sort of hug before shouting something in gibberish and running to opposite ends of the landing. They had been born and bred to fight, and heaven help any who got in their way.

In the meantime, the two remaining soldiers down below stormed the living rooms and kitchens. In the living room there were bodies littered around, some dead and some wounded as a result of the shrapnel that had flown from the blast in the hallway. They simply shot everyone, dead or alive, since there was no time to check what was what. In the kitchen they found a huge sheet of plastic laid out on the floor with two headless corpses lying on it. One of the corpses had also had its arms and legs removed, probably in an attempt to get it ready for disposal. All the parts were there; the heads lay in a pool of rapidly-thickening blood, looking up at the Ninja styled hit-men with a mask of total horror still painted upon their faces. Not knowing how these corpses fell into the plan, the two killers grabbed a head each and left the room with them, re-entering the hall with their loot. One of the heads had long, greasy hair, which made it a lot easier to carry than the other, which had short blond hair and therefore had to be carried by one ear.

The two armed killers decided to run outside and stick the heads on the floor next to the man who was paying for this little exhibition. Under the circumstances it seemed the best thing to do; after all, they were white folks, the heads owners, that is. Tap knew immediately who they belonged to, a pair of fucking traitors, so he flicked each head in turn with his foot, sending them into the air before they landed with a thud on the gravelled drive about two metres away.

One of the downstairs crew used a fire extinguisher on the stairs, making it easier to retrieve the girls, who were handed down from the upper floor into the raised arms waiting below. Eventually, there were no more girls or punters left upstairs, which just left Loft-Hatch and his right-hand man with one final prisoner. They were not to kill him that would be their employer's prerogative. Loft-hatch had had to beat his head against a burning wall several times, though, before chucking him off the balcony and onto the broken stairs below. The fall broke arms and ribs, and burnt his face badly as it came into contact with the smouldering wood. As Boyd managed to haul himself to his knees, he was picked up by Loft-hatch and dragged outside. The goods were a little fucked-up now, but still breathing. This was the part that Tap had been waiting for all day; to look into Boyd's eyes, ask a few questions and then shoot the cunt in the face.

Tap didn't even notice the two remaining soldiers climb back into the van. The only thing that mattered to him was the demise of Boyd, who had now been forced down onto the hot gravel and was being guarded by Loft-hatch. Boyd's punters watched the downfall of the man whom they had never actually met, but who had provided girls for them to play with. It looked like a gang thing to them, a takeover bid or something, who knows?

"You couldn't fucking leave it, could you Boyd, you cunt?" Tap said, pulling off his balaclava. "Keep out of my way, that's all I said. Keep out of my fucking way and I'd bring you what you wanted, then none of this had to fucking happen! It weren't fucking hard, was it? I mean, all you had to do was sit back, relax, and it would have been job done. But no, you couldn't do that so you start causing me grief, and I can't have that, Boyd. You gotta go, son, you were getting in my way and that ain't gonna happen!" Tap preached as he stared into Boyd's eyes from a crouching position opposite his victim. One hand rested on his left knee, the other cradled the Glock 21. Boyd looked pretty beat, basically because he was. He tried to argue the toss that Tap hadn't been coming up with the goods; they weren't arriving like he promised. By goods, he meant this lunatic Jenkins, the one who had taken out Boyd's foot-soldiers and was at the bottom of all this fucking mayhem. Tap had to agree that things had not moved along as quickly as he would have liked, but it was only a matter of hours now, just hours, before Anthony Jenkins was taken out of the equation.

"And I'm gonna do him a lot worse than I'm going to do you!" Tap promised. Taking a backwards step, he fiddled with his handgun before smashing the butt of the firearm three times into his victim's face. Teeth broke, you could fucking hear them, not to mention see them as Tap dropped back down to Boyd's level. Oh yeah, messy, very messy, fucking painful an' all; but there we go, pain was the name of the game. As far as Tap was concerned, he had suffered a great deal of pain today, and Boyd was going to pay for it.

While this was going on, Loft-Hatch took the opportunity to point out that Tap's blue-uniformed buddies were going to be here any minute and could they please get a move on?

"Okay Lofty, let's get it over with. I wouldn't stand there though if I was you, mate!" Tap suggested.

Loft-Hatch stepped aside as Tap wedged the barrel of his handgun into Boyd's mouth. Boyd tried closing his mouth to make Tap's task a little harder, but with nearly all the front teeth missing the gun was still able to penetrate. Knocking his teeth out had been a sensible precaution, although to be fair Tap had poached the idea from a crime scene he had once come across and adapted it to his own method of killing. With the weapon firmly in place and a gentle kiss planted on the victim's forehead, Tap leaned back a little before pulling the trigger.

Human flesh and blood atomised in the air as it met the flames that were now rising from the whorehouse. The fire was really picking up, as was evident from the sweat running down Tap's brow as he moved away from the recoiling corpse.

"Chuck him in there!" Tap ordered, indicating the fire, and Loft-hatch obediently bent down to pick up the body.

"Chuck them two heads in while you're at it. Fucking animals, your old boys, fancy chopping their heads off!" Tap laughed, fully aware that Loft-hatch's compatriots had not been responsible for the barbaric act, not that they were incapable of it.

He well knew who the men were and who had chopped them up; it had been Boyd. Way before Tap had arrived at the café, the place next to the pharmacist's where the shooting of the Anthony Jenkins impostor had taken place, he had received a call from a Mr Roach. Yes, the man Ritchie had called Tap to tell him that Jenkins had crossed his path in search of drugs, and was this information of any value to Billy? And was it; yeah, just a bit! So Tap had assured Ritchie Roach that he was interested in paying good money for such information. Well, not money as such, more like a kilo of speed that was knocking around at the station. Good shit an' all, pure base; the leftovers from a raid that some biker gang had suffered. This information had allowed Tap and his armed colleagues to lie in wait for Jenkins. Ritchie had sold out Jenkins to Billy Tap, but it had turned out to be the worst mistake of his life. Not selling out Jenkins, that is, but trusting William Tap!

At the time of making the decision to do business with Ritchie, the fucking smackhead freak, Tap had been planning on keeping the informer and his sidekick alive. This was to Tap's personal advantage more than anything, because good dealers were nice to have on the books for future use. Only trouble was, though, Ritchie had a big gob. He might be useful in the future, but on the other hand they might not have a future if Mr Roach turned Judas again. So, the kilo of speed was delivered and Ritchie was as happy as a pig in shit, especially when Tap phoned the dealer later on and told him that he had managed to find a buyer for the drug. Tap would take a cut, of course. Naturally, the buyer was Boyd, who was welcome to keep the speed and whatever else he wanted from Ritchie's Aladdin's cave, he just had to make sure that the two bodies left over would be disposed of. Hence, the reason for Boyd's men cutting the corpses up in the kitchen.

The flames now started to lick around Boyd's corpse and Loft-hatch again reminded his boss that it was time they did one as he watched Tap strolling around, admiring his handiwork.

"Do you know what, Lofty? You're too fucking impatient, you are." Tap waved Loft-hatch into the back of the van. "Get in the back of there, Lofty, where you belong, you fucking lunatic!" Tap swung into the front passenger seat beside Slug, who promptly floored the accelerator pedal.

"There, that's a bit better, ain't it? One down, another ten thousand to go!" Tap commented, referring to the number of brothels in the country. "Left here, Slug…!"

The van screamed down a side road adjacent to the property they had just bombed. As it did so, Tap flicked on the radio and began to tune it in. Before long the speeding getaway vehicle had become one of hundreds on a busy road, along which police cars and riot vans were screeching in the opposite direction.

"Better late than never!" Tap mocked, patting his driver on the shoulder. Slug had held it together tonight. Tap fiddled with the stations and started to gyrate in his seat as Rod Stewart's 'Do you think I'm sexy?' filled the cab. Yeah, 'course you fucking do', Tap sang, while laughing like what he was.

"We done it, Slug, fucking done it good an' all, mate. That was good policing, because that's how you have to deal with these people, see? We should be in the fucking Bill mate, we'd clear up Sun Hill in no fucking time. I tell you, Slug, when I'm fucking Prime Minister, you're gonna see a lot of that because that's how you've got to deal with these people. They don't reason to anything less. Yeah, we done well, mate. That's pro-active policing. We're the future, Slug, we're the fucking future!" Tap bragged.

The vibrating of Tap's phone in the inside pocket of his leather jacket brought the duo back down to earth with a bang. It was a text message, not from one of Tap's many conquests, unfortunately, or one of his mates. No, it was from you-know-who. Tap held the phone out for Slug to read the message himself.

"Bastard, he's fucking with us!" Slug spoke for them both. Tap agreed it did seem there was a game of wanker on the table and they hadn't the best of hands. The text message read: 'Very humorous, just make sure it's not you they're measuring up.' Then the phone buzzed again as another message arrived. 'What, you gone shy on me now?' the next message read. This seemed like a response to the message that Tap had sent hours ago, three or four hours to be precise. There must have been a delay or something - bad congestion on the airwaves, fucked transmitter, or just shit service from the provider. This really pissed Tap off, because his phone often did this and the number of sexual conquests he had missed out on due to these major inconveniences was bordering on ridiculous.

"Fucking phones are shit." Anthony had obviously sent the second message a good while after the first, not realising that Tap hadn't received the first one. Another buzz filled the air.

"Fuck me, how many more?" Tap exclaimed. This message was only fifteen minutes old, so it was probably the last. 'OK shy boy, get some sleep and tomorrow we play,' the message read. Tap's lack of response had obviously got Jenkins a bit rattled. A final message buzzed through: 'your appointment is at 10 tomorrow, don't be late!'

By appointment, Jenkins meant with Dr. Taylor, Tap felt sure, thinking back to what had been written in blood on the wall of the ward where Gina's brother and the policeman had been killed. Jenkins had laid down the gauntlet and Tap was more than willing to accept the challenge.

"You're fucked tomorrow, Anthony my friend!"

He wondered what they were all doing now. There was Jenkins and his bird, and uniform still hadn't found that missing pharmacist, so it seemed pretty obvious that they were all together. He didn't realise that he had thought aloud until Slug replied.

"Dunno. Having a Chinese?"

"Having a fucking Chinese?" Tap repeated, staring at his driver in amazement. Slug struggled to keep a straight face at the wheel, but Tap had also started to see the funning side, and they both began to laugh uncontrollably, with a slightly hysterical edge to their laughter.

"Cunt…!" Tap gasped. "Fucking Chinese…!"

"Are you going to ring him then?" Slug asked eventually, when the mirth had subsided.

"No mate. He wants me to call him, that's what he's waiting for, but I'm not going to give him that satisfaction tonight. Besides, a duel has been set up now; the doctor's place tomorrow. It's all gonna end there!" Tap felt quietly confident.

Slug wondered which phone Jenkins had been using to send the text messages and Tap replied casually.

"Well, it's the fucking Paddy's with the hole in his head, in it?" As soon as he had spoken, Tap thought again and checked his phone just to make sure. The number was neither the Paddy's, nor George Belazaire's. This was a new number! No, shit - actually that wasn't strictly true. It was just the last two texts that hadn't been sent from the Paddy's phone.

"Slug, you're a little darling; a little treasure glistening in this otherwise dark world. Now I know why I let you hang around with me! Anthony's got a new phone."

"Yeah, and so what?" Slug asked.

Tap sat back silently in his seat, deep in thought. He watched the world go by from behind the protection of the tinted glass as the blue van drove through London, courier speed. The city was disappearing rapidly as they clocked up the miles; they were obviously leaving the Smoke.

"He could have stolen one!" Tap mused. "Or, he could have bought one. What's stopping him walking into a shop and doing that then?" Pay as you go. Once you'd bought one of those, no one knew you had it. Tap brought the number up on the phone's display and read it out to Slug.

"Can you remember that for a few seconds?" He asked.

They were pulling over in about five minutes to lose some of the cargo; Loft-hatch and his mates, to be precise.

*

The van stopped somewhere in the countryside, outside London at any rate. It was time to get rid of those fucking head cases in the back of the van, so Tap climbed out to unleash the beasts. They may have been beasts an hour before, but now they had transformed themselves into well-dressed foreign gentlemen who casually strolled out of the back of the van and walked over to their Toyota jeep parked nearby. They carried bags with them, which had previously held the ethnic clothing that they currently wore, but now contained the blood stained attire worn during the slaughter at the brothel.

Garbed in black and lacking their headgear, three of the trained killers climbed into the Toyota after Loft-hatch had blipped the key fob and lit up the skies with an orange glow.

"Good work, mate, just make sure you clean up properly!" Tap warned, indicating the need to burn the clothes, debrief the men and lose the Toyota. The job would be done properly, Tap was sure; it always was when Lofty went to work. Tap had to admire the gang; they were solid, not to mention loyal. You didn't often get that in gangs anymore; every fucker was usually out for himself these days.

The whores in the back of the van had been handcuffed with police-issue tie straps so they couldn't play up when it came their turn to be unloaded later that evening. Once he had delivered them to where they were going, Tap's conscience, or what little there was of it, would be clean. They would still be whores; they were just being recycled, more meat for a different street.

Tap slid the side door of the van closed, plunging the girls into darkness again. He had explained to them where they were going and assured them of their safety, but they probably didn't believe him. Whatever, they made little fuss for the time being, although some of them complained that they needed the opportunity to relieve, refresh and poison themselves. Tap agreed that he would also like to do those things, and indicated that within the hour they would all be able to.

"Forty five minutes, girls, and then you can do whatever you fucking like. Piss on the floor if you need to. Bye for now!" Tap compromised.

To be fair, a bit of piss weren't going make much odds to the state of the van floor, not with all the claret that was there already, sloshing about. The girl that took the bullet looked in a bad way. One of her colleagues was crouched down beside her, keeping an eye on things and stroking her forehead. She weren't going to make it, not leaking like that. But then this was war, people get hurt, tragedies occur. It's just the way it is. Tap was heard climbing back into the passenger side of the van before that door closed too, and a faint vibration through the floor indicated that they were out of there.

"What is it, then?" Tap asked.

Slug was temporarily nonplussed as he watched Tap fiddling with his mobile phone.

"The number, Slug; the number!" Tap reminded him.

"Oh, the number!" Slug suddenly remembered, passing his hand across to Tap, the number having been hastily scribbled on the back of it with a biro. Tap pressed an auto dial number that was stored in the memory of his mobile and waited for someone to answer the phone.

"Buzby?" Tap asked. He read the number off Slug's hand down the phone as Buzby wrote it down.

"I want to know what phone that number relates to. It's going to be a pay-as-you-go, we know that, but if you can get a few people out of bed and find out who's sold it, it would be most appreciated. And it's not just important, it's fucking really important, so jump to it my son!"

Tap was delighted to hear that an hour should be long enough to complete this task.

"Good to hear it. Top man Buzby…!"

Just as he rang off, another call came in. It was Doughnut, very fed up. Tap had had the call waiting signal and had prayed, fantasised, that it would be Anthony Jenkins, but it wasn't to be.

"Slim, how's it going, big guy?"

It was going well, as it happened, apart from the fact that every time he had called Tap's phone there had been no answer. Tap replied airily that he had been in a bad reception area for a few hours.

"So what's the latest then, Doughnut? You done what I asked?" Tap already knew that he had, otherwise he wouldn't be reporting in because it wouldn't be worth the shit he'd get for failing. Doughnut had finished his work several hours ago, and yes, the job was complete. Tap actually knew this already because he had phoned Sid earlier on in the evening and got an update on their goings on. It had been a bit of a saga and hadn't gone entirely to plan, but they had several minor results.

When Doughnut had gone to collect the film footage, he had been held up by the rush hour commuters and it had taken over an hour to obtain the first tape from Tottenham Court Road. Tap simply couldn't have this, so he had had to make an executive decision and tell Doughnut to forget the Tooting tape. Instead, Sid had been and got it because the crime scene he had been guarding had been wrapped up quite early. Doughnut had then arrived at Tooting with the tape from Tottenham Court Road and had made his way straight to the hospital to take over there, while Sid had reluctantly made his way back to the Yard in order to get the two tapes analysed.

Since the two people who Jenkins had met on the train were actually dead and Jenkins himself wouldn't be coming in alive, the video tape evidence was actually going to be of use to an inquest rather than a trial. Sid hadn't got the outcome that he wanted, but he had got a fair result. There had been a number of hurdles to cross, train company bureaucracy and all that - but in the end, Sid had got a result of sorts, including some camera footage of Anthony Jenkins boarding a train alone at Tottenham Court station just as Tap had forecast. Doughnut had also seen footage of Jenkins, this time leaving the train at Tooting along with two other people: two people who had very recently died at Tooting hospital. What he didn't have, though, was footage of the trio meeting on the train itself. This was basically because some little cunt had sprayed over the camera - probably vandalism damage, because Sid had cleverly got the security guy at Tottenham Court Road to check the film footage right back to that morning and the camera hadn't been working then either, so Jenkins was innocent of that at least.

"Are you at home now?" Tap enquired. Doughnut was indeed at home with his family; he had got a lot out of the idle bastard over the last few days. It had been an eventful night and Doughnut and Sid were better off out of it. He had kept the business concerning Boyd away from them, although when they heard the news the next day they would know who had set it up. They knew better than to question Tap or his right-hand man about the night's events, however, since it didn't always pay to know other people's business.

"Give it a rest tonight, Doughnut. Have a break and be up early tomorrow because we've got some business to take care of. Meet me at my favourite fast food vendor on Oxford Street tomorrow morning at nine, and be properly tooled up an' all! Sid knows where to go. He's dropped off the tapes and he's on a date with some chick now, but I've told him that he's on call tonight if Jenkins starts playing up. Nine o'clock tomorrow morning, Doughnut, and don't be late!"

Doughnut had a habit of being late and tomorrow would probably be no different, which was why Tap had told him to be there forty five minutes before it was really necessary.

"Tomorrow, Doughnut, Anthony Jenkins goes down. Don't be fucking late!"

Chapter Eight

Pear-shaped

The van carried on through the suburbs, hitting urban sprawls every ten minutes or so. Soon there was nothing but countryside - trees and shit, nothing to write home about. Tap felt a million miles away until they hit a small village that immediately felt like home. Tap had been here before, a good few years ago now, but he had been a regular visitor back in those days. The detective was excited; he was reuniting with an old friend. Not an old flame this time; this woman knew better than to get involved with Tap. Besides, she was a classy bit and he had known her late husband. Since when did Tap give a fuck if someone was married or not? When her husband was Bradley O'Brien, that's when! Tap tried not to think about those days much, they were wild; everything had got a bit out of hand.

*

Bradley O'Brien had been big-time in his day, about as big as it gets. Usual scenario, he was a fucking nut-case, but of course to those who knew him he was the salt of the earth. In reality he had been a vicious cunt who had run his patch accordingly. He had had two wives, they say. A total player this feller was, a fucking legend! Anyway, that's another story. Getting back to the other, to put it briefly, the walls of this geezer's kingdom had just seemed to fall down around his ears during the last year of his reign. There had been some dispute between Bradley O'Brien and his brother and it had all gone tits up in the end. The friction within the camp had all come to a head one night at O'Brien's mansion, the very same mansion to which they were now travelling. The brothers killed each other in the end, but then every other fucker was killing each other that night; it was some really fucked up shit and it had all happened at this house in this tiny little village in the middle of nowhere. Kimberley O'Brien had been the only one to survive in the end. Everyone else in that house on that day had perished; over a hundred people, they say! O'Brien's other wife, Karla, was unfortunately not so lucky because she too had fallen victim to her brother-in-law. The two girls went way back; they had grown up together, and as well as loving each other, they had loved the same man. It sounds impossible, but it really did work.

After the shit had hit the fan and Kimberley had escaped the killings at the house, not to mention the police, she had stayed in hiding for a while. An emotional wreck, she had gone back and stayed with her mother, who she hadn't seen for years. The slate was wiped clean and the past was put behind them. Kimberley had been pregnant, you see, and mother was going to be a grandmother. She had bought a house with loads of land for her parents, and for well over a year she had remained a recluse with her retired parents.

Once the paparazzi had milked the story for all it was worth and the fuss had died down, Kimberley came out of retirement. A new woman, she had a lot of money tucked away and she decided to start using it to do some good for a change. The majority of it was drug money and the rest came from racketeering, dodgy motors, emptied banks, and so on and so forth.

Kimberley had taken everything of value from the house when she had left it after the final battle. Okay, it was hers anyway, but that wasn't why she had taken it. She had taken it purely to make sure that the police didn't get it when they raided the house. Tap had been on the payroll with the

O'Brien brothers, although indirectly through his boss at work, a detective known as Gallagher. The latter had worked very closely with the gang, very closely indeed, so it was no surprise that when they went down, he had gone down with them. And Tap? Yeah, could have done, could have done very easily, but he didn't. A top man in the Met had decided to be lenient with him, the reason being that Tap had dirt on him; a little insurance package that had every angle covered. Gallagher had ended up taking the rap for it in the end and had been shot down by armed police when they tried to arrest him. In fact, Tap had been the one who had pulled the trigger. But then Kimberley was not to know that, and neither was anyone else apart from the Police Commissioner from whom Tap had his protective cotton wool coating, and who, coincidentally, was due for retirement. Not that there was any risk he might want to clear his conscience; Tap had made sure of that.

Many years before, Tap had been quite friendly with the Commissioner's son, so friendly that they used to sleep together, and not in a tent-at-the-end-of-the-garden kind of way. Tap had been a bit of a player in the gay celebrity scene back then and had introduced the Commissioner's son to it all. Fuelled by Charlie, Tap's new plaything had ended up getting fucked right, left and centre. Before long he was in the bedrooms of the stars, packing more meat than his local butcher's. More coke, more perverted shit, videos, mass orgies - it went on and on. A star had been born and Tap had the video evidence with which to prove it when the Gallagher and O'Brien affair was happening. So, Tap had tapes of the Police Commissioner's son doing all kinds of shit that really did no one's career any favours, apart from that of the newly promoted Detective Sergeant Tap, of course! The deal was simple: the Commissioner gave Tap the red light to deal with Gallagher as he saw fit, which was not a problem to Tap – it was just a shame that all promotions at work weren't so simple! The Police Commissioner's son still held his passion for gay sex, but had since learnt to keep his antics a little more discreet, especially as he had since risen to quite an elevated position in the government.

So, the Police Commissioner was about to retire, gracefully if possible, but Tap wasn't about to let him do that. No, the old devil had been into prostitutes in a big way over the last few years and not too many people knew that. His wife knew, Tap knew and so did some of his colleagues down the nick, but nobody said anything because everyone had their own back to cover without stirring up shit for their leader. So, Tap hired one of his light-fingered scallies to burgle the Commissioner's house; just money and jewellery, nothing else. Tap was put on the case and solved it in a matter of days, returning all the jewellery except for a silver necklace. The insurance was paid, a hefty whack by anyone's standards, and the police were obliged to keep an eye out for the exquisite piece that was still missing.

It would be interesting to see what explanation the Commissioner had to offer when the scene-of-crimes department finished cleaning up Boyd's little whorehouse and found the antique piece of jewellery stolen from his house attached to the still-smouldering neck of a well-known prostitute. It was going to be bad enough explaining that one, but the fact that she was a key witness to another crime that included one of Tap's other colleagues and was about to be reopened, was definitely going to arouse the suspicion of those waiting for the Commissioner to put a foot wrong. It was not going to look good. Not for anyone except Tap, that is.

There was a nice little pub in the village, also a little corner shop and a school, but fuck all else really. The village was tiny, in marked contrast to the driveway of the house that belonged to this girl Kimberley. It was miles long, with a security post right at the end. You would have expected some police or armed forces reject to be manning the post, or at least someone with a bit of clout, but instead there was this girl who was barely in her twenties. She obliged the van to stop at the gate by refusing to lift the barrier until she was ready. A phone call seemed to be the deciding factor and once she had made it the barrier was raised automatically on the press of a button.

Tap liked the look of this woman; she was a pretty little thing, dirty as well, one would imagine, because at some point in her life she had more than likely been one of the girls in the back of their van. Before she had been rehabilitated of course. The guard looked no match for a man of Tap's stature, but unexpectedly he didn't offer her any grief or abuse. Maybe it was because she was almost certainly armed, but it was also partly due to the fact that Tap wanted nothing derogatory of his character to leak back to Kimberley. He liked Kimberley, he liked her a lot, it was just a shame she didn't feel the same about him. Kimberley Jones didn't do coppers; she used them, she manipulated them to do what she needed them to do, just as she had been taught by her late husband, but in truth she fucking hated them.

Kimberley took the money that she had saved from her marriage, which was growing nicely thanks to some wise investments, and used it to rehabilitate as many streetwalkers and whores as were willing to take up the opportunity. Some couldn't help but fuck up their last chance, but for every one that failed, three would make it to the other side. The house was like a cross between a health farm and a prison. You arrived, you were briefed, and then you were asked if this scheme was right for you. If it was, then your gear was provided by a doctor, assuming you were an addict, and then you were cleansed thoroughly before being offered clean clothing. You were then counselled, and if you responded, you moved on to stage two. If not, you were dropped back to where you came from with a little money in your pocket and no questions asked.

Stage two involved rehabilitation. A room and meals were provided and all residents mucked in with the chores. It was just like a posh prison really, although you were free to leave at any time. Drug users were slowly weaned off their habits and a future was planned for each individual case. Training and a certain level of education were provided. If successful at this stage, Kimberley placed the girls into positions within organisations which she owned. Overall, there were a lot of success stories. There were a few failures as well, but on the whole Kimberley's charity was doing well. This was Kimberly's new life, a life into which she hoped her three year old son would follow, because all this was for Daddy. The whole organisation was dedicated to the man whom Kimberley had adored and her best friend who had died with him. Tap's involvement was that he got a couple of grand for each of the girls; it was expensive, but if two grand assisted in saving the life of a single prostitute, then it was worth every penny to Kimberley.

The biggest house Slug had ever seen now loomed up in front of them. Tap made no comment; he only had to think back to when he had first seen the place. It had been like Fort fucking Knox in those days, still was, probably, although the security was probably a little more advanced now. It was a little more discreet now, because the savage pit-bulls and armed guerrillas that handled them made up some of the most frightening scenes that Tap had ever witnessed as a runt in CID.

Another security check was made; nothing heavy, just the weapons and a quick look in the back. Again, a woman dealt with the situation. She was a big girl, though, unlike the previous one. Tap judged her like he did every woman and decided right on the spot that he wouldn't, not a fucking chance, not after ten pills and a gram of Charlie! She had a bit of a big arse for him, amongst other things, and he didn't do big arses. Apart from a geezer's arse, of course, because they generally were bigger. He rolled the thought around in his mind a few times, though, just to make sure that his judgment was the right one.

They had to give up their weapons before they could go in, as firearms no longer had any place behind these walls; those days were gone. Tap had a spare, of course, and Kimberley knew he would have, but she didn't force the issue because she knew that Tap was only here to get his money. Besides, he knew exactly what she was capable of because on that terrible night of her husband's death, it was rumoured that she had killed ten men.

And what a beautiful woman she was. It was rare that Slug felt aroused at just the sight of a woman, unlike his partner, but on this occasion he could definitely feel a stirring in his trousers. As they drove on towards the house, she was walking down a huge set of stone stairs that led to the first floor of the house, bordered by a wall of matching stone. The house was four storeys high if you included the ground floor, which housed garages, kitchens and so on. The living area was one storey up for added protection and was only accessible from the outside by this one set of stairs. The two guests watched with amazement as Kimberley came down the final steps. Wearing a white dress, she looked like an angel descending from above.

The duo got out of the van and Slug stretched, sore and stiff from the amount of driving he had done that evening, as he watched Tap greet this vision of loveliness. She was absolutely beautiful. Tap gave the woman a hug, but she broke from the embrace as quickly as she could without being impolite. Tap understood; she was a one man woman, and the man was boxed-up in the grounds somewhere.

Kimberley opened the sliding door of the transit van and was disgusted by what she saw, although she held her tongue, speaking only to suggest that in the future Tap might spare a thought for his cargo and treat them a little better than animals. By now, various members of staff had started to turn up, more women, but this time dressed in nurses' uniforms. They helped the new arrivals from the van as Kimberley Jones looked on with disapproval.

"Look at the state of them, Billy; they're all cut and bruised. And why have you tied their hands? You did that with the last load and they've still got marks on their wrists. Is it really necessary?"

Tap apologised and blamed Slug's driving for the cuts and bruises, promising that for the next batch he would hire a Limo with air-con and a mini bar, so as not to offend. He also pointed out that the girls didn't know where they were going until they got there, so he couldn't risk letting them have their hands free as they drove through the centre of London. Perhaps she could produce a pamphlet and a short film to inform them of what they could expect on arrival? It was clearly a conversation that Tap and Kimberley had had before. Tap wound it up by cheekily asking if she was going to offer them a drink.

The house had a swimming pool inside, with Jacuzzis and a hot tub. It also had its own little night-club, all under a domed glass roof. The place was simply amazing; out of this world.

"Be my guest, Billy, you know where it is. Tina's got your money in the house. I'm sure you'll want to say hello; she's in the front room." Kimberley hoped that Billy would not opt for the hot tub, because if he did she would have to change the water before she used it again.

Tap felt the memories flooding back as he walked towards the stone steps of the house with his side-kick in tow. Kimberley was helping the staff unload the girls from the van and tell them what was going on. Her warm voice seemed to offer them reassurance as they looked round in bewilderment at their splendid surroundings.

The girls looked a good batch; all reasonably clean and healthy, albeit a bit thin and pale. They all wore clothes, apart from one who was starker's. Some wore more than others, although all were reasonably decent. The explosion at the front door of the brothel had given them enough time to spruce themselves up a bit, because making yourself look presentable during a raid was always a priority.

Having briefed the girls on where they were, Kimberley welcomed them each in turn, looking straight into their eyes as she did so. She was checking their pupils for any signs of restriction or dilation, a better indication even than needle marks. If the girls had any little habits, then it was crack cocaine, which was smoked rather than injected. The pupils did look rather large on the whole, but then it was dark. If they were hooked on crack, then they had a tough time ahead of them and at least one or perhaps two of the girls wouldn't make it. Crack was a tough cookie to crack! Heroin was a bit of a bastard as well, but crack was definitely the tougher of the two. However, nothing was impossible and Kimberley had had a fair degree of success with both.

Tap watched her rounding up the girls from his vantage point as he ascended the stone stairs with Slug. Good luck to her, he thought. At the top of the first flight, he could see Tina looking through the living room window.

"Fucking gorgeous bit of stuff…!" He couldn't help commenting. Slug couldn't dispute it, but in his eyes Kimberley was the better of the two, her long legs and fuller breasts, probably plastic nowadays, just put her in front, as well as those lips that looked like they could suck a golf ball through a hose pipe. Tina, on the other hand, was more petite, with tits to match. Her legs were shorter but in proportion and she was a few years younger than Kimberley, who was only in her late twenties but starting to look a bit weathered nonetheless.

Tina was curled up in a ball on a huge white sofa, big enough to be a bed. She had been one of Kimberley's first rescue projects, and had happily stayed on after her rehabilitation was complete to act as her assistant, since she had no other family or friends. Her main tasks were to assist in the therapy sessions, since she had been through a tough time herself in the past. She held out Tap's envelope containing his money without taking her eyes from the television.

"We'll help ourselves to a drink then, shall we?" Tap asked sarcastically, in reply to which Tina just laughed and nodded.

Tap muttered under his breath as he walked across the huge, wood-floored hall towards a door in the corner, which led to the night club.

Okay, hot tub it was then. As hot-tubs go, this was the nuts. You could sit in it and control it with a water-proof remote control that also worked a huge TV screen coming down from the ceiling. The domed room was basically an extension of the house and encased the whole of the back part of the house, from the roof down. The ground floor of the house retained most of its original features, including the hugely impressive stone staircase that spiralled down from the night club above, gradually widening down to the swimming pool before flaring right out at the bottom. A stone banister completed the effect. A number of other doors at ground floor level led to a gym, sauna, toilets, changing rooms and solariums, and outside in the domed room was the hot tub, jacuzzi and swimming pool. Running off the back of the house, a stone wall partly surrounded the pool area and provided a support for the domed roof. This was partly for privacy, and more importantly for protection.

In the night club was a bar, sofas and glass tables, as well as some arcade machines, a fizzy drinks machine and of course a cigarette machine. Tap remembered that the bar was well stocked and they helped themselves to a couple of beers each. There was another bar downstairs, but it was a healthier alternative being for use by the toms on re-hab who used the pool and other facilities. It hadn't always been like that, though; Tap could remember parties here when the bar next to the pool was stacked to the brim with booze. They had been wild, the wildest he had ever seen, which was saying something. Fucking hell, there had even been waiters employed just to hand out the fucking drugs, and that was just the delivery service because there was a table full of pharmaceuticals upstairs for one's perusal. Dangerous days!

The pool had had some water slides back in those days, big spiral ones, which on many occasion were frequented by drug-crazed, drunken, naked ladies. As Tap remembered, the gang used to invite party girls from the London dance scene to the events, where they would get all fucked up on drugs and basically offer themselves on a plate. Tap's plate was always filled. The parties had been off the scale and Tap missed them as he reminisced to Slug about some of the darker scenes that he had witnessed back in those days. There had been the gang bangs, the free-for-alls in the pool, spas and saunas, not to mention the dance floor. Tap had been around a bit, but he had never witnessed anything to compare with Bradley O'Brien's parties.

Slug listened with interest and wide eyes, courtesy of a metal tray, a small straw and a gram of white powder that he had just shared with his partner. If it had been anyone other than Tap telling him these stories, they would have sounded like bullshit. The detective had seen shit that most people didn't even know existed. Some of the people he talked about were the lowest of the low, but they were interesting nevertheless. The stories flowed, the beer had turned to Champagne and Tap had pissed in the hot tub several times; the party was well under way. Kimberley had popped in once to check up on her guests and see if they were okay, which they certainly looked like they were. Tap hopefully invited her to join them, but one of the new recruits was going off on one and Kimberley was going to have to spend some time with the girl.

"I'm off to tend to the needy, you know where everything is. I'll leave you in peace. Tina's up there if you want anything," Kimberley said, then reminded Tap that his phone was ringing as she walked towards the stairs at the back of the room and climbed up them into the night club.

"Phone, fuck, the fucking phone!" Tap climbed out of the hot tub in just his white pants, Slug, having made him leave his shorts on. He tiptoed towards the wooden chairs near the stone wall behind them which acted as a support for the glass domed roof. Taking care not to slip on the specially-designed floor tiles that were meant to be non-slip, he snatched his phone from off the top of his clothing. It was Buzby.

"Funny fucking hour…!" Tap shouted down the phone.

"Yeah, sorry Billy, but I've been a bit busy. Something's come up."

"Tell me."

"Well, it's like this. A few hours back, someone held up a phone shop on Faroe Street - armed raid and all that - and they stole one phone!"

"They stole one phone?" Tap repeated. It hardly sounded like the crime of the century.

"This geezer, bold as fucking brass, walks into a mobile phone shop and starts waving a shooter about. He nicks one phone and about three grand that he made the manager get out of the safe, and then fucks off!"

Tap shook his head and waved a wanker sign in the air for Slug's benefit.

"So, he didn't just take one phone then; he took three fucking grand as well. That is not one phone Buzby, its one phone and three fucking grand. There is a big difference!"

Buzby asked him if he didn't find it rather strange, one phone, regardless of the money.

"Perhaps he just had a call to make!" Tap yelled down his mobile.

Buzby replied that he was right; the bandit did have a call to make. He had called Tap's phone.

"You what…?" He really should have worked it out by now, but Tap was coked-up to the eyeballs, not to mention pissed, and he needed a little assistance.

"The guy who robbed the shop, he texted you," Buzby patiently explained. "So who was it, then?"

But Tap was saying nothing for the time being, except to ask if anyone else knew about it yet.

"'Course they don't, I know better than that!" Buzby replied indignantly.

"Good, let's keep it that way then, eh? You can't trace the phone if anyone asks. I want to keep this between us for a little while, Buzby, you know the score! Where's the shop?"

Tap knew it; it was right by the park on Faroe Road, not a problem.

"I want you to call Sid for me, mate, and make sure he gets uniform to put a bod on that shop overnight. He's on a date, so he may get a bit arsy about it, but just tell him I said to do it. We're on our way now!" Tap ended the call and turned to Slug.

"Get out the bath, Slug, and get dressed! Jenkins is taking the piss out of us. We've got to get back to London; I hope you can fucking drive."

Slug couldn't drive, not legally, but then he didn't have to drive legally because he was a copper and he could drive how he liked. Personally, Tap thought he drove better when he was pissed anyway. He looked a bit out of it, but one for the road should bring him round nicely.

The dynamic duo managed to get dressed and up to the night club for some more sherbet before staggering to the van, but it all went a little tits-up after that. A slight mishap between the van and a fucking huge stone gate post left the gate post just fine but the van a write-off. Fleeing the scene, the pair managed to stumble back into the house, climb up the stairs and collapse on a couple of sofas, where they slept like babies until the morning.

At first, Kimberly had just wanted Tap to leave the house as quickly as possible, but as the night wore on it became clear that the two men were going nowhere, so the next best thing was to make sure that they were silent and immobilised. Sleeping tablets dropped into their drinks seemed to do the trick. She was sorry about their van, but it was probably nicked anyway.

*

Jenkins re-entered his flat, or rather Gordon's flat. It was late evening and judging by his attire it was cold outside, although at least it had stopped raining. He carried with him a bag bearing the logo of a product relating to the mobile phone industry. Hoping to find everything as peaceful as he had left it, Anthony cautiously entered Leigh's flat via Gordon's and the hole in the wall. He was wearing a ridiculous-looking long, black leather jacket which looked very ill fitting, but then that was probably because there was something underneath it. Jenkins chucked the bag onto the sofa before undoing the leather jacket and revealing what it was that was causing the coat to bulge: a Heckler and Koch MP5, and a very long carving knife. He had learnt recently that when he removed this coat, he had to remember that the knife was in the inside pocket because he looked a real twat when it fell out onto the floor. He laid the coat across an armchair near the bedrooms and put the blade back in the kitchen where it belonged. The sub-machine gun kept it company under the sink, temporarily. The Browning was staying in AJ's possession though, probably until the day he died, and so it remained in the waistband of his trousers, covered by his shirt. Jenkins reached for the bag that he had tossed onto the sofa. It had three bundles of cash in it, which he placed beside the unconscious Sarah, more interested in the mobile phone and the phone cards for now.

Leigh's front room was dimly lit; the scene nice and cosy, just how he'd had left it. Nothing had changed, except that Sarah was mostly on the floor rather than the sofa, and she was lying in a pool of her own vomit. He had left her in the recovery position when he went out forty-five minutes or so earlier, so she had him to thank for the fact that she had not choked, as well as the fact that she was in that state in the first place. Welcome to heroin. She was better off in a coma for now, so Anthony left her and went to spend some quality time with his lover.

Haley looked contented, lying there in the metal-framed bed with its clean white sheets. The white walls and ceiling made the room look kind of clinical, but Haley didn't care - at least she was not hospitalised. She was awake when Anthony entered the room, and he was glad of that because he hated waking her when she was resting.

"Are you all right?" He asked his sweetheart.

She smiled bravely and assured him that she was feeling good – well, not good, just a bit better than normal. She was indeed looking quite perky and Jenkins was pleased, because this had to be down to his master plan. He had got her this wonderful flat, a personal nurse and shitloads of the drugs that she needed: it was a good job as far as he was concerned.

"Do you want the TV on?"

Haley didn't, but she was busting for a piss.

"Just give it to me!" She demanded as Anthony struggled with a funny-shaped potty, attempting to slide it under the covers.

"I thought the nurse would be helping me with things like this, anyway. Where is she?" Haley asked.

"She's asleep. She's been at work all day so I said I'd help you for a while until she's had some rest."

It sounded like a strange set up to Haley, but she let it go; she was too tired to expend much thought on the matter.

"So, who is she then? Where did you find her?" Haley asked. Anthony carefully pulled the bedpan from under the covers as he contemplated his reply. Clearly, the truth wasn't an option.

"She's the daughter of a friend of mum's. She's been working abroad or something and she's come back to make a little money before she does the off again to wherever. I can't remember where it was, she's a fully qualified nurse and all that, knows her shit an all, apparently. I'm just gonna pay her to look after you for a while," Anthony improvised. He was pretty sure that Haley would smell a rat, she always did, although as the days went on it seemed that her mind was beginning to focus more on other matters.

"For a while until I die?" She asked wryly.

"Yes Haley, until the end," he replied tenderly.

Anthony did not understand the difference between a nurse and a pharmacist; as far as he was concerned, they both wore white coats. Sarah had tried to explain to him that she wasn't even a qualified pharmacist, just an assistant, but it had fallen on deaf ears.

For years, Anthony had been dreading the day that Haley departed from him. She was the only decent thing in his life and soon she would be gone. There would be nothing left to live for then; life was shit enough as it was. He hoped that his pain and suffering would be gone afterwards. There would be no more ill health, no more struggling to make ends meet in the filthy streets of Soho. More importantly, though, he would be rid of that ever-increasing feeling of not really wanting to be here in the first place. He felt like he was part of some experiment to study what happened when someone forced as much crap upon another human being as was physically possible in order to find out when they would finally snap. Why had he been dogged by crime, drugs, prostitution, poverty and all the rest of the shit that had made up his youth? He had never asked for it; it has been forced upon him and had turned him into the person he was. He wasn't meant for this; his brain could not take the pressure of today's world and the speed at which it turned. It was time to rest, and rest he would. He just needed to make sure that Haley had the best time possible before they could rest together for the whole of eternity. Would they get peace then? Would they be left alone to look after and love each other? They'd better, Anthony thought. Having seen what he was capable of bringing about in this world, the other one had better watch out!

Anthony and Haley chatted about some of the good times they'd had in the past, Anthony stretched out on the huge white double bed beside her as they talked. Haley reminded him about the time they had done this and that, nothing spectacular, but it meant a lot to them. It was just simple things like trips to theme parks, Southend, and of course the nightclubs. They had really had it in those days; Haley remembered some of the best days of her life. Did they need long-haul trips or tropical islands or golden sandy beaches? Did they fuck! They had found something better, and it was called Ecstasy! Okay, Anthony was paying now for his days on the pills, but in a way it had been worth it.

"Do you remember the night that we were in the Cross and I went over to the middle of the dance floor to see if you were all right, because you were trying to buy a hot-dog off some bloke? He was dancing away and you thought he was a hot-dog seller, so you were telling him to put onions on your hot-dog and a bit of sauce as well. At the same time you were trying to count some change in your hand to pay him with?" Haley reminisced, giggling. Anthony started to chuckle too.

"That was after about six pills though, Haley. I was pretty fucked!"

"Yeah, you were, you kept eating my hair that night and trying to take my glasses off!" Haley reminded him. Not that she had ever worn glasses; it was one of those strange optical illusions you sometimes get when pilled out of your head.

"Everyone seems to be wearing glasses when I'm on Ecstasy, and their faces are always melting," AJ confessed.

Haley reminded him of the time he'd kept seeing the two Mario Brothers amongst the crowd, one red and one blue, and the pair laughed again before falling into a companionable silence and their own private reminiscences.

"Those were the best days of my fucking life!" Anthony sighed.

"Me too," Haley agreed. "It was brilliant."

It was true. For these two there had been no need to travel to some far away destination, nor to spend a fortune. No, you just bought a club ticket and a handful of 'little ones' and you'd be guaranteed the best time money could buy. There was no doubt about it; you simply could not enjoy yourself in life any better than a night on Ecstasy. The only problem was that with life so good on pills, what happened when you couldn't enjoy yourself any other way? What happened when a year of clubbing turned into two, then two turned into eight, and so on? What happened when a night down the boozer or a tacky club just simply wasn't enough anymore and you needed a minimum of three thousand people and a pocket full of pills to have a good time? Then because you wanted it, you kept chasing it. You knew things were going wrong, but a good night in a club, on pills, would make you feel better. At least the week went quicker in anticipation of the next weekend.

Here's a simple fact of life: fuck with your brain, and it will fuck right back with you. The brain is delicate, and long-term chemical interference would do it no favours. You wouldn't notice it at first; just a few weird things would start to happen and you would start to feel that you couldn't be bothered to go out. You may start to withdraw slightly, but you'd blame it on being too fucked last week, or on getting old. Your brain would start to make a few wrong decisions, or you would start to be increasingly dissatisfied with life. Once upon a time you had been happy with an average job, a few beers down the pub at the weekend, a shag now and then, or maybe a steady bird. Life had been simple back then, life had been great, but not anymore because you were poisoned and your brain knew that there was more out there. The computer in your head now understood that it could do better; have more. You couldn't have a steady relationship anymore because there was no one good enough, not now you'd been a heavy clubber and seen girls through the eyes of ecstasy: they're fantastic, the most beautiful women in the world. They were all on pills too.

Anyway, the story did not end there. Years went by and you thought nothing of the time you spent off your face. You've given up now. You may have a girlfriend, you may or may not be happy with her, but then the time you spend with this woman will never be any good without the chemicals. She probably feels the same. The years go on and the harder it gets. No matter what you do, it's never going to be as good as it was. You can't go back though - you've done that old life to death. It was good, but towards the end you felt that things were going wrong. Okay, you weren't addicted or anything, were you? Not to the drug, no! Just the scene, the people, the clubs and everything it stood for. Well, you can still have that without the drugs, can't you? Can you? Can you fuck! It's gone, and without the pills, it simply ain't coming back.

Oh well, you need it, so you get into cocaine. It's nowhere near as intense as when you're on a pill - it's a cunt to use socially, and it does your nose no favours either, not to mention your bank account. Dental and respiratory complaints will start to haunt you now, but hey - no pain, no gain! On pills, you could have lasted all night on the sixty quid that you just spent on that gram of Charlie. That was enough for more pills than you could handle in a night, and you'd have been fucked out of your head, not just slightly aroused, like on over-cut cocaine. The years pass as relationships fail. Sex is never as good as it was when you took Ecstasy. By now you may be feeling a little depressed or anxious, depending on whether your preference was Ecstasy or Amphetamines. You may start having the odd panic attack, or just a feeling of loneliness, paranoia or insecurity. You want more from life, but it ain't going to give you that. Instead, it's going to give you something else; something unpleasant, something called mental illness. It's a reality for a lot of people, just look at the waiting list in your local clinic.

The government have started issuing warnings about Ecstasy now, not that it kills you any more, that's all gone, because although there is a very slight risk that it could, it is highly unlikely. You hear some people say that we should decriminalise ecstasy, because it's safe. Well, get them to spend a day down the local health centre, or a mental hospital, and they'd soon change their minds. Check out the figures for suicides, count the number of tramps and homeless, check the queues at the surgeries and listen to the warnings that the government are now offering, because there is an epidemic on its way. Anthony had read an article in a major newspaper stating that ecstasy caused brain damage. Well hallelujah, only twenty years too late!

So, like Anthony, you go for treatment. What do you get? Not a lot, because the GPs aren't ready for this epidemic; they can treat depression and anxiety to a degree, but this strain is not one that they recognise. It's a bit different to the norm - it's more severe than most, and above all it's unique. You can do all the relaxation exercises in the world, they will try and make you, but it's a fucking waste of time. They'll give you anti-depressants, but they won't work properly. They'll test every part of your body, but they won't find the cause because they can't see it; they can't see the damage you have done to your own brain. Only you know the extent of the damage. There is no life after ecstasy for some, and only the strong will survive. Unfortunately, Anthony was not strong on the inside; he was the living dead.

"Them were the days, aye?" He mused. "Do you regret them?"

Haley had to think about that one.

"I regret it sometimes, and I regret what those times did to you, but it's only one instalment in a lifetime of regrets," she said at last. Upon Anthony's prompting, she tried to be more specific. There was so much.

"Well, I regret my youth, especially making my parents disown me like they did, but then they never really understood about drugs. To them, everyone is a junkie if they take drugs. I can't blame them, though, they just didn't understand."

Anthony had to agree. He had been more fortunate in that his parents had tolerated his actions, but then it was pretty much the norm where he lived because his upbringing had been very different to hers.

Haley had approached London in a way that many young people do. She had abandoned a life of stability in suburbia by leaving her home town of wherever it was. Anthony could not remember, to be honest, in search of the bright lights and adventure. Somewhere near Bristol, he recalled, because he had been used to taking the piss out of the way she talked. He remembered when he had first met her. She had been a drug dealer with a difference, being absolutely beautiful. Well, in Anthony's eyes she was anyway.

He had been running around London like a fucking lunatic, trying to score gear. The Colombians had been starting to widen their market into Britain and the market was flooded. Although they normally sold Coke, they had also started growing poppies for export because their climate was well suited to it. Now, with a network already set up for Cocaine, the Heroin started to flow in thick and fast. This wasn't a problem until the Triads, Turks and everyone else involved in supplying the drug started getting the arse and competing for their own piece of the market. The result was dead smack heads, because in an attempt to keep their custom, they were not cutting the Heroin as before and it was top quality - good-shit – too fucking good for some, because Heroin addicts were dropping like flies.

So, the police stepped in: more resources leading to more seizures and less smack on the streets. Good for the likes of you and I, but a total bastard for anyone who relied on the gear to perform their daily role.

Anthony had tried his normal supplier, but found him being led away from his apartment in handcuffs. Fuck, this was a nightmare. He contacted dealer after dealer, five to be precise, but none of them could help. Number six could, although it wasn't who Anthony thought it was. The person who answered the phone should have been Nigel, a last resort in most cases, but to Anthony's dismay, it wasn't him. He assumed that the girl who answered the phone, and then the door and barricade to the squat, was Nigel's bird, but she wasn't; she was his replacement. Nigel had tried the 'good stuff,' which was why he was lying dead in a corner of the squat.

Anthony couldn't believe it. He asked how long Nigel had been like this and Haley, this woman, said that he had collapsed that morning. In reply to Anthony's question as to what she was going to do about it, she replied that she was going to move squat. That was a good idea, Anthony agreed, but in the meantime did she have gear to sell? She did, and the two became quite pally as Anthony made his first purchase and filled his veins with a weaker mix of brown powder and water than he usually did. He was out of it for a while, just like his partner, but the two awoke from their drug-induced slumber about two hours later. Nigel's mobile phone battery had drained out completely by now so the shop was shut; even knocks on the door were ignored. The pair stayed in the room for nearly a day, during which time Anthony made love to her several times. She had told him about the HIV and made sure he used a condom, but Anthony didn't care anyway because smack made the world a beautiful, safe place.

Their relationship flourished, and before long Anthony was getting a flat with his loved one. Condemned she may have been, but perhaps there was hope, as medical science was moving along quickly and new drugs were being invented day by day. Life was still shit but it was tolerable for a while, because although the couple didn't have a pot to piss in, they still had each other. They had their share of arguments and dirty laundry, like any normal couple, in fact probably more so as Haley struggled with the acceptance of her death sentence. Despite all the tantrums and kick-offs that Haley threw her lover's way, Anthony was never nasty to her. He had suffered at the hands of nastiness himself for most his youth, and the only good thing that he had to say about his stepfather was that he had opened his eyes to what a real nasty bastard was. This is why Haley loved Anthony so much, he had never let her down. Not until these last few days, that is, but she wasn't to know that.

Life became frustrating for Anthony because every time he thought he was taking a step-forward, he was sent crashing backwards again due to something or other. Inevitably, Haley started to get worse. It was on the cards, written in the skies, Sod's law even, and no surprise to anybody. As she deteriorated, Anthony started to lose it. It was bad enough watching the disease suck the life out of her, but to add to that he had to cope with the fact that he had basically pissed his own health down the drain as well.

First, he had a really bad abscess in his leg which nearly caused him to lose it, so he did himself a favour and came off the gear for a while. It was hard, but he just locked himself away and rode through it. Haley was ordered to keep him locked away until the cold turkey was over. It was a painful time, but worth it because he had seen the light. Haley was impressed, so much so that she followed suit. It was even harder for her, but Anthony assisted in the therapy. She actually took two to three weeks to come round, before finally being released from the bedroom that they had modified in order to restrain each other. The pain was worth it in the end, though, and once the deed was done it only took a few months for Haley to recuperate. So, with the smack habit gone, Anthony started getting into the club scene. Years went by until his health once again started to deteriorate. Anthony was in self-destruct mode again, but he never saw it coming.

Anxiety this time, fucking severe as well, he was as rotten as a pear with it. One night he was 'doing it large', the next he just never seemed to come down. Haley had done almost as many pills as her lover in the same period of time but she seemed unaffected, although she had started to notice other small problems with her body as time rolled on. Weight loss was the first cause for concern, although that was partly due to stress and worry because by now, every time Haley had a cold or something, she became petrified. This was understandable, because her days were surely numbered now. Her view was that if she was going to go in seven years anyway, she might as well go in five instead and have a good time while she was still here.

So, Anthony became a day patient and saw psychiatrists and shit, but as everybody knows they weren't much help. Despite being clean for three years, Anthony knew that the only thing that could help him feel any better was the old brown powder, so it was time to hunt down the dope man. Time to get the old needle and spoon out again? No, not this time. Anthony liked his new mobility, not to mention being able to feel his limbs again, and so with the old veins out of action it was time to chase the dragon, which he did for the next few years.

"I also regret getting into prostitution, of course. I came to London in search of that pot of gold, but mine was full of shit. I don't regret coming to London though, and do you know why?" Haley asked.

Anthony shook his head.

"Because, I met you, stupid. You're the best thing that's ever happened to me and I'm just so sorry I can't be there for you much longer. I would have been a good wife to you, looked after you, and let's face it, you need looking after, don't you?" She joked.

Anthony turned towards her and nodded, smiling. It was a shame they'd never married, he thought, pondering on the afterlife.

The afterlife? Yeah, exactly, what if there was life after death? Surely that would count for something if there was one, marriage, that is. Surely if you'd taken your vows in this world, then they would still be valid in the other. Another fucking world - had he gone mad? He was pretty sure there wasn't one, but there was always a chance he was wrong. Let's face it, you don't usually sit down and dwell on such matters until your box is calling. Although it was only Haley who was condemned, he was going to be on the next bus after her, even if he had to buy the ticket himself with a bullet. Thinking out loud, he shrugged and commented that he wished they had got married.

"You'd be a widower then," Haley observed. "It might cause you problems when you meet the next girl."

"The next girl…?" Anthony sat bolt upright on the bed and repeated Haley's last comment.

"Yes Anthony, another girl. There will be one, and you must make sure there is. We've had our time and it was fabulous, I couldn't have hoped to meet a more special person, but it wasn't to be. Once you've sorted out that cough, Anthony had just cleared his throat and swallowed the rotten lump, "you will be able to move on. You've got to get off them drugs, though. Move forward with your life, Anthony, make it pure and make me proud. I'll be watching you all the way; I'll be your guardian angel, but you must promise me now that when I'm gone, I'm gone! I don't want you mourning for me forever, because you didn't do this to me. God did, so I know I'm being called and I must go. I don't want you ever to forget me but I mustn't haunt you, you don't deserve that!" Haley begged. In her eyes, Anthony Jenkins was everything she had said and she loved him with all her heart. They both started to fill up with tears, cuddling silently together.

Anthony would have liked to sleep, but with so much on his mind it wasn't going to happen so he just lay there at Haley's side until she had dozed off. The idea of marriage was playing on his mind, but as Haley had said, it would surely benefit neither of them now. He knew there was something else he was supposed to be thinking about, too.

Oh yeah, that was right, it was time to play a game of wanker with our friend Tap. A plan began to hatch in his mind. The basics of it were already there, it just needed updating to fit in with recent events. He needed a mobile phone, so he carefully removed his arm from around Haley and slowly climbed off the bed.

The way forward was to set up a meeting some time tomorrow, so that hopefully for the first and last time Anthony could come face to face with the hunter who was tracking him down. Belazaire's phone battery was completely flat by now, he had been using the dead Paddy's phone to abuse Tap by text. He was starting to get a little edgy about the absence of a reply to the last one, however. It was time to send another message, but this time on his new phone, the brand-spanker that he had just acquired down in the phone shop across the road.

The shop that Anthony had been studying for a fair part of the afternoon, through a crack in the living room curtains, boasted a whole range of state-of-the-art communication devices. Anthony knew he had to get himself one, because since he'd sent the last text on the dead Paddy's phone, the paranoia had begun to set in at an alarming rate. The absence of a reply was too much for a man living on the edge. He had been wearing out the carpet in the flat by pacing up and down the front room.

The makeshift nurse had given her patient a dose of her pills and made sure she was comfortable. When Sarah came out of the bedroom, she saw Anthony peering out of the window through the gap in the curtains, into the rapidly-darkening street. He had told Sarah to turn the lights down low, which was a bit of a pain because she was trying to study the information she'd got from the hospital about the drugs she was administering to Haley. Fortunately, Jenkins had allowed her the use of a small table lamp next to the sofa on which she was sitting. He was preoccupied now, mumbling stuff to himself, and seemed almost to have forgotten she was there.

The lack of response from William Tap had set Anthony's mind working on a number of possible explanations, but for the life of him he could not decide which one was the most feasible. The theory that the police knew where the flat was and were currently planning to raid it was the most sinister of them all, and he tortured himself with this one for a good hour before deciding to go on a little reconnaissance mission.

The only problem was that Sarah might do a runner, despite the deal he had offered her. He couldn't very well tie her up, because she would never trust him then. No, the best plan was to take her out of the picture for a while. Having made his decision, he sat down on the sofa by the window, next to which was a little round table with a lamp on it. In the lamp was a light bulb, from which he removed the screw-in base. Next, he added a little brown powder to the light bulb and heated the base of it while carefully gripping the neck. When smoke started to issue from the open end of the light bulb, Anthony drew in puff after puff in order to gain his high. Blown away for a few minutes, he fell back onto the sofa, eyes rolling and ready to chill out, but his mind was having none of that; they had work to do!

He added more powder to the bulb and called Sarah over, asking her if she wanted a little something to help her relax. She hadn't done smack before, but had stolen quite a bit of methadone and used that. She thought about it for a few minutes before replying that she didn't mind giving it a go, as long as she didn't have to do it intravenously. After all, she had fuck all, better to do.

Her decision fell in perfectly with Jenkins' plans. She sat next to him on the sofa as he flicked the lighter on in preparation for heating the base of the light bulb. He put the bulb right in front of her mouth and asked if she was ready, to which she nodded in reply. The powder became fumes and Sarah sucked away on the open end of the light bulb, inhaling as though it was pure, clear air. Jenkins warned her that a lot of people were sick on their first few attempts at making friends with 'brown'. The warning came too late, however as Sarah honked her guts up all over the white carpeted floor before slumping back in her seat as paradise took over. The drug was fast-acting and Sarah felt good, despite her recent nausea. There was some blood on her lip where she had been careless with the sharp end of the light bulb, but it was only a superficial cut. The vomit on the floor stank and was only going to get worse, but Jenkins didn't care because he was off to work in a minute; he had a little bit of shopping to do. He pulled her feet so that she was lying full length and then thoughtfully turned her onto her front, if she choked on her own vomit he would be back at square one.

Jenkins emerged onto the street outside, armed to the teeth. He wore a long, black leather coat, Matrix style, which probably gave the impression that he was either a fucking nut case or a sad fuck who wanted people to think he was. He had borrowed the coat from Leigh Anderson's wardrobe and it fitted him perfectly, although it had a slightly futuristic look. He had fastened it shut, and underneath was a small arsenal. He had the Browning automatic in the waistband of his trousers, just to the side of his bollocks in case it went off by accident, and a carving knife located in a deep pocket inside the leather coat. He had made a shoulder strap for the police-issue Heckler and Koch MP5. The design was improvised, two leather belts and a heavy silver hair clip, but it allowed the gun to be adapted for inner city warfare. He put the strap around his left shoulder and neck, allowing the weapon to hang down the left hand side of his body.

The plan was to go into the shop, close the front door and then open the front of the coat and produce the German sub-machine gun. Jenkins would then take control of the situation. If anyone caused him a problem, then they were taking a bullet. At the moment he didn't even know if he was going to make it into the street, let alone to the shop, because part of him was convinced that Tap and his band of merry men were waiting for him to make his move. In preparation for warfare, he had adapted Gordon's kitchen with the help of a full-length mirror on a stand and practised his war stance, drawing his weapons one by one from their hiding places as quickly as he could. He didn't look bad, he thought, even with this big girl's coat on. So, off to war it was! Come on Tap, you cunt, let's fucking have it!

Waiting to be shot down in the street makes you sweat and Jenkins was sweating profusely like he'd just been given numerous back-to-back life sentences with no parole. It was windy outside with a slight chill factor, although it was going to get worse as the night went on. At least it wasn't raining.

'Unbeatable prices on all networks,' said the sign in the window of the telecommunications shop over the road. Interesting stuff it was, but Jenkins decided that he'd better not stand there staring at the window all night from across the road in case it aroused suspicion. The rush hour was at its height at this time, and people moved along the pavement in front of him and slightly below, due to the fact that he was still standing on the second set of stairs that led down from his new flash apartment. The traffic on the road was at a standstill, so Jenkins simply walked around the cars that blocked his route to the phone shop. He stared in at the window for a few moments, trying to look as though he was just choosing which mobile phone to purchase. A straightforward purchase however, would not serve the purpose of getting Tap's attention.

Jenkins waited for the two customers in the shop to leave, but then two more walked in. The first couple left, leaving two customers and the assistant. This was two more people than Jenkins had anticipated, but he could be waiting all day so it was all systems go, go, go…!

The shop assistant was called Andy, according to his name badge, and he was busy clinching a deal as Jenkins walked into the shop. He would look up in a minute or so and greet his next catch, but for now he was dealing with a profitable sale; a young couple wanted two phones on business tariffs. Under Andy's careful guidance, they were choosing a tariff that met their needs and lined the salesman's pockets at the same time. The shop was decked out in a pseudo-futuristic style, the walls lined with silver display cases. Cardboard cut-outs stood beside the exhibits, apparently depicting the type of person best suited to each style of phone. On one of them, a family man and his two children were at the peak of a roller coaster ride and one of the kids was speaking to someone on a mobile. It was obviously a modern family because of the absence of a mother, who was presumably out working to support her children and househusband. Or maybe she was out turning tricks, or in hospital with some incurable disease. Whatever, the single parent was taking care of business.

An astronaut floated around in another picture, but how the fuck he was managing to use his phone through that huge helmet was anyone's guess. That just left the tit with the Ferrari full of clacker. Nice clacker too, but he shouldn't be letting them put their feet up on the seats. Instead of rattling away on the phone outside an American-style diner, he ought to be asserting some of the authority he undoubtedly had in order to possess such a car and lifestyle.

Jenkins attracted no attention walking into the shop, but he soon made heads turn when he locked the door behind him and then reached up to press a button inside a purpose-built wooden box above the doorway. He was not an expert on how those shutter things worked, but the buttons had to be hidden somewhere up there. Andy's face was a picture as he heard the cogs turning and the motors starting to spin as the unfolding metal shutter began to clang and bang around outside.

"Excuse me?" He blustered.

"Why, have you shit yourself?" Jenkins asked with a cheeky smile, starting to unbutton his coat. He let it fall to the ground and stood there in a black T-shirt and jeans, courtesy of Leigh Anderson again - with a stolen police issue sub-machine gun in his hand, a Browning automatic handgun tucked into his waistband and a twelve inch kitchen knife that had just fallen out of his coat pocket. The blade played a tinkling tune on the tiled floor as it bounced.

Soon the shutters were all the way down and Anthony asked the sales assistant to turn up the lights. He also asked whether anyone else was around. Andy assured him that there wasn't, his hands raised above his head.

"You two, sit on that desk!" Jenkins ordered. The couple looked round, their blank faces suggesting that further instructions were required.

"The desk behind you, sit on it!" He repeated, raising the MP5 with his right hand and pointing it towards the hostages.

They got the message. Tight jeans and 'fuck me' boots hindered the woman's progress onto the counter, but with a hand up from her husband she managed it. Jenkins noticed that they were married, seeing the wedding rings on their fingers. He had this marriage thing on the brain lately.

"So, how long have you been married then…?" He asked.

The expensive-looking blonde seemed taken aback by the question, as well she might. Her good looking husband glanced at her, then at Jenkins. The clean-cut couple reminded Anthony of Barbie and Ken.

"Look, it's not a hard question, is it? Watch! Andy, you're not married, are you?" Jenkins asked, having first checked the assistant's left hand for a ring. Andy shook his head, and Jenkins asked him what he thought of the single life.

"It's cool!" the salesman confessed. Jenkins laughed.

"Kool and the gang, is it? Good, I'm glad you enjoy it, Andrew. Let's hope we can keep you on the circuit then, doing your thing!" The veiled warning was received and understood immediately.

"Now, the safe, Andrew," he went on, "perhaps you could point me in its general direction, and maybe even open it for me? I don't want to hear that someone else has got the keys, and I don't want to hear that it works off a timer. I don't want to hear anything like that, to be honest. I'd just prefer to take the money and not have to waste any of my bullets. I've got a budget, you see, so I have to be responsible with my ammunition. Saying that though I could just carve you up with this knife. Maybe start with your ears, or something, and just work my way through you. But we don't want to do that now, do we? We just want the safe open, so you've got two minutes starting now, Andrew!"

The salesman liked his job; he liked the shop and he had quite a deep feeling of loyalty towards his employers, but on this occasion they could go and fuck themselves. Andy read the papers like everybody else and he knew that the lunatic who had come to rob him was no fucking Muppet. He could talk the talk, but he could also walk the walk. He had the juice, every paper in the fucking land said as much.

The married couple, on the other hand, lived in cuckoo land. Of course they had heard there was some psychopathic lunatic loose in London, but that was nothing special. They watched Andy, who right now was moving a cabinet over the left hand side of the shop, exposing a safe built into the wall behind it. Having opened the safe, he pulled out two bags of cash in the form of notes. Three grand there was - he had counted it himself this morning and it was all ready for collection. A grand of the money was for that horrible man who came round once a month for the fee he charged for 'protecting' the premises, and two grand was set aside for a delivery of 'moody' mobile pay-as-you-go phones and SIM cards that were arriving tomorrow. He handed the cash over to Jenkins.

"So what's it like then, married life?" Anthony had asked casually, as he too watched Andy delving into the safe.

"It's like being a fucking animal in a cage, all right?" Ken said bitterly. "It's hard enough meeting someone in the first place, and when you do, it's just as hard holding on to them. Of course, before you marry her you've got to go out of your way to please her and make her feel special, you do the best you can, give her everything she wants, but it's never fucking good enough. Then you marry her, and the more you give, the more she fucking wants. You don't know if you're going to be able to keep hold of her, because there are so many people out there just waiting for you to make a big mistake so they can offer her a way out. They've probably got more money than you have, they're probably a bit younger, or whatever. There's no loyalty any more. What is it then Rachel? Come on, what is that Burgess has got that I haven't? Come on, let's fucking hear it!"

Barbie had started to suffer some major face leaks by now. Fake tan, mascara and all sorts of shit had started to give way like mud banks in a torrent. The scenario was ridiculous; Barbie was getting a slating from her probably soon-to-be-ex-husband and the two of them were totally oblivious to the fact that their audience, which consisted of a shop assistant and a heavily-armed lunatic, were staring at them in disbelief. Not to mention the security camera! Jenkins had only just remembered about that, not that it really mattered at the end of the day, as Tap already had enough evidence on him to write a book.

Maybe he was mellowing a little as the days rolled on, but Anthony didn't feel like killing anyone just then. People died in his cause because they had to, but these people had actually been helpful, especially Andy. The couple had helped in their own way, by providing entertainment and educating him about the state of matrimony. Right now they were looking like they were going to come to actual blows, so Jenkins got back to business.

"Andrew, I need a mobile phone. Pay-as-you-go I want, nice one too, but not too hard to use; fucked if I'm gonna sit there all night learning how to use it!"

Andy was on the ball in seconds, running around the shop looking for the best deal he could find for his customer.

In the meantime, Jenkins carried on watching the show. It seemed that Barbie worked with the guy she was shagging, and to add insult to injury he was also loaded and treated her like this and that…ah fuck it, he'd heard enough.

"Enough!" He ordered, but they were so wrapped up in their argument that they didn't hear him. He sighed, reversed the MP5 in his hands and hit Ken across the face with its butt.

"Fucking hell…!" Ken screamed, leaking claret like a sieve.

"Your wedding rings, I want them, now!" He requested coldly.

Ken struggled to remove his, pulling at the ring that had probably not been taken off his finger for years, but Barbie didn't even reach for hers. It was probably shock rather than ignorance, but whatever the case she soon handed over her platinum ring when Jenkins enquired if Burgess would still chuck one in her if she had a nose splattered across her face like her husband's.

Anthony took the rings and put them in his trouser pocket as Andy arrived at his side with a boxed mobile phone and a handful of phone credit cards. It looked as though he was going to achieve his mission without killing anyone on this occasion, a phenomenon that would doubtless astonish Tap. No one was going to die today. He would have to wait until tomorrow for that. Oh yes, there was something special in the pipeline for tomorrow's news; something very special indeed, and AJ was going to fucking love it!

Jenkins waved Andy back behind the counter as he dropped the cash onto a display box. Taking a step back and lowering the MP5 as he did so, he put on the long black coat again and took the Browning from his waistband, this being more easily manoeuvrable while leaving the shop. Besides, he didn't know if he had sussed that machine gun out yet, it had so many switches and shit, but to let it off in here would be asking for trouble.

"Andrew, I hate to take the piss but could I have a bag please?" He asked. He dropped the phone into the bag that was promptly handed to him by the sales assistant, followed by the money. It was time to take his leave.

"I'll be seeing you then," he said cheerily, "oh, and don't worry about the rings. Report them stolen and you'll probably get them back in a few weeks, if you still need them! Anyway, you take care of Burgess, mate, and your missis. And I think you should stop taking care of Burgess, love, and start taking care of your husband. Then you'll probably both start getting along a little better. Think of it this way, you could have both died today - some lunatic could have come in here and blown your fucking heads off. So hold that thought and move on. Andrew, the back door please. I take it there is one?"

A wave of a handgun ensured that Andy showed him into the back room, which contained stacks of phones in boxes, a PC and a messy desk. There was a heavy fire door at the back of the room. Being uncertain what was waiting for him beyond that door, Jenkins signalled to Andy to open it. After a few seconds, during which nothing seemed to be happening, he cautiously peeked out. There was no one there.

"Nice one Andrew!" was his parting comment as he shook Andy's hand before stepping outside onto the pavement. His purpose in doing this wasn't entirely to express his gratitude for Andy's help, but was also a little insurance measure just in case there was anyone out there; it could have been handy to have hold of a hostage for a few seconds. It wasn't long, but long enough to make out any background noises which might indicate an ambush.

Jenkins walked out of Haley's room and back into the darkened living room. Fucking dirty bitch had puked again! Sarah, that is. He walked over to her and kicked her gently in the side. There was no response at first, so he lifted her up out of her pools of vomit and sat her down on the sofa. Fucking hell, she looked like someone had chucked a kebab at her at close range, with extra chilli sauce! One eye opened momentarily and then shut again as she slipped back into that dark but wonderful place. Let's face it, there aren't hundreds of thousands of heroin addicts for nothing now, are there? A wonderful tiredness had taken away all of Sarah's problems and left her in paradise. Nothing mattered, nothing needed attending to and nothing hurt anymore, so why the fuck would anyone want to wake up from this? She could get used to this; just shoot up and let those shitty days fly past.

Sarah smiled slightly as Anthony forced open her right eyelid.

"Wake up!" He ordered. He waited for some sign that she was ready to come back to earth, but it wasn't happening.

Picking up a half-empty bottle of beer from the small table to the right of the sofa, he emptied it over her face. The cool liquid ran down her face and into the ample cleavage that bulged out of her white coat, making her sit upright in shock as it continued its course all the way through the gap between her breasts, beneath the under-wire of her bra and down her stomach.

Focused as he was on his mission, this had no sexual effect on Anthony at all. The only woman for him was the one dying in the next room, and she was the whole world to him. Also, a heavy smack habit doesn't do your sex drive any favours. Even when Sarah stood in a fit of panic and started to remove her uniform, undoing the buttons one at a time from the top to the bottom as fast as she could, Jenkins didn't bat an eyelid. She dashed off to the bathroom wearing little more than her white plimsolls.

"You need some clothes, I take it?" He called after a few minutes. "There's some clean clothes in a basket in the spare room. Don't go in Haley's room rummaging about, though, because I've just got her off to sleep." AJ warned, which came as a relief to Sarah because Haley would only start asking her a load of strange questions again, like she had earlier. Anthony had told her all the lies she was to use and she had done as she was told, but it got hard work trying to remember what to say. Oh well, the clothes were clean, thankfully! There was underwear, although the bra size was far too small so she wouldn't bother. The jeans and t-shirt should fit a treat. She showered before putting on the clean clothes, and when she came out Jenkins had a present for her.

"We're quits now," he said, throwing a wad of money down on the sofa, "but don't worry, I'll give you a little bonus at the end if the pot's looking well pissed in. After all, I ain't gonna need it where I'm going!" The last sentence was mumbled as he turned away, and she didn't hear it.

The cause had been so simple up to now; just shoot any motherfucker who got in the way. But now; well, Anthony had to decide what cause he was fighting. Was it to help Haley, to give her the best two weeks that he could before her time ran out? Or was it to prove something to William Tap, to show him who was running things here; who was the man in charge. Whatever, he was going to take Tap out tomorrow and that would be the major thorn in his side taken care of. He could then commit the rest of his life, one hundred per cent, to looking after his lover. Tap must die tomorrow so that Haley could live another day.

Jenkins was hungry. He hadn't eaten for a good day or so and the pains in his stomach were beginning to affect his concentration. It was going to be a takeaway, but what? He was open to suggestions; anything but pizza. He ascertained from Sarah that her preference would be Chinese. There was a thought; he hadn't had Chinese for ages. As if back in the real world all of a sudden, AJ looked through the local paper to find an advert for a Chinese takeaway and ordered a meal for two, giving the address of the flat for delivery.

"Your man better come in via the Dulwich Road though, rather than South, because something's happened outside my flat and the Old Bill have shut the road off, all right?"

It was Captain fucking Chaos outside, kicking off big time! More Old Bill than you could shake a stick at were pulling up like something out of an American movie, sirens wailing and lights flashing. It gave Anthony a real kick to look down upon his handiwork. This was his doing, he had made this happen. Power was a great toy to play with and Anthony felt that he had more power than the national grid at that moment. Billy, this is all for you! His happiness suddenly turned to spite as the name flashed through his mind. *Tap, Tap, Tap…fucking bastard! Where's that fucking phone?*

It was where Anthony left it, on the sofa next to the money. It was in a cool little box, all neatly wrapped with its own little compartments. There it was; the greatest weapon in the art of modern warfare, because if you can fuck with the enemy's mind, you had struck the first blow.

"Ah bollocks…!" He cursed realising that the batteries weren't even fitted into the phone, so it was probably dead. He managed to stop himself from smashing the phone to bits in a rage and took some deep breaths. All he had to do was fit the battery. That was easy. Then he fitted the charger to the phone, which was a bit of a bastard but he figured it out. Then he plugged the socket for the charger into the wall, and nothing happened.

"Give it to me!" Sarah demanded, drying her hair with one hand and reaching out towards Anthony with the other. Jenkins obliged and handed over the phone because he wasn't one to look a gift horse in the mouth. He watched as her long, nimble fingers made easy work of the complicated machinery, then took the phone as she handed it back to him, having put in the date and time.

"Texting your old mate, then?" She asked sarcastically. She was starting to feel quite at ease with Anthony and even beginning to like him a bit. He was nothing like the other men she had encountered in her life, and was even starting to feel a little put out that he hadn't tried to fuck her yet. Back in the bathroom she had made a point of checking herself before she stepped in the shower, just in case she had been violated and hadn't noticed because she had been so fucked out of her head. But Jenkins had obviously been the perfect gentleman.

He punched in the words, 'OK shy boy, get some sleep and tomorrow we play,' typing in the number from memory. He had memorised Tap's number in case he was ever without a mobile and needed to make a call. The number then went into the memory of the new phone, along with Tap's name. After a few moments, he sent his final message, 'your appointment is at 10 tomorrow don't be late.' He sat, face devoid of emotion. *Tomorrow, Tap, we will settle this.*

Chapter Nine

Wrong!

"Billy!" Slug screamed. There was no answer, so Slug started to shake his colleague violently while his mobile phone sang away in some inside pocket. Typical that, fucking typical! He rummaged frantically in Tap's pocket, but of course the thing stopped ringing just as he found it.

"What do you want Slug, except for fucking castrating?" Billy asked, finally awake now. "And what time is it?"

The men looked at each other in horror.

"Nine thirty, Slug, we're fucking late! What happened? I can't fucking remember."

Slug didn't really know either, he just knew that they must have caned it because they both looked a complete mess and his mouth was as dry as a Pharaoh's flip flop. He needed fluids, and plenty of them.

"We're proper late, Slug, proper fucking late! Jenkins is going to be at Tottenham Court Road Health Centre at ten and we ain't, not by any stretch of the imagination. We've fucked-up mate, big time!" The reality of this monster fuck-up began slowly to sink in. His head pulsated as though struck by hammer-blows as he struggled, foal-like, to his feet. Too much sherbet, they must have done at least three grams between them, together with alcohol. He had no idea that Kimberley had poisoned them too, which was just as well.

"Your phone, Billy!" Slug snapped as he walked over to the bar. He was getting pissed off with the noise it made and the fact that it always heralded more grief. He found orange juice and cola behind the bar and helped himself, while Tap searched for his phone and demanded a neat vodka. Slug cringed at such a filthy thought and was nearly sick as he poured the drink, smelling the poisonous vapours. Tap was talking on the phone, trying to explain why he was late, but his story was all muddled up. He grabbed the quadruple vodka and downed it in one. That did it; Slug was sick in the sink behind the bar. Tap was a fucking filthy cunt, how could any man do that?

Tap took a can of coke and opened it with one hand as he listened to what the voice on the other end of the phone had to say.

"No, you're not going to do that, Doughnut! You get out of there now!" he ordered. "Listen to what I'm saying, and do exactly as you're told. You get out of there now and you do one. I don't care where you go or what you do, you just get out of there. Jenkins is too clever for you, Doughnut! Whatever it is you're thinking of pulling off, you'll lose. Trust me! Is Sid there? Put him on the phone, Doughnut, now!"

Doughnut didn't dare argue any more. This was the harshest Tap had ever spoken to him and he was glad to hand over the phone to Sid, who took a couple of deep breaths before putting it to his ear.

"Sid, I need you to leave the health centre, okay?" Tap asked calmly. "I want you to abort this mission. It's twenty to ten, Sid, and our appointment with Jenkins is not until ten o'clock, so you might still have time to get out of there. This is what I want you to do. This is a direct order, Sid, and if you don't do it I'll reprimand both of you."

"What about the doctor?" Sid asked lamely. Tap's response indicated that what happened to the doctor was not his concern, but in less polite terms.

The truth of the matter was that the two detectives on the scene were the only two who were going to be there, full stop. Like most of their recent jobs, this ambush that they had planned was being carried out hush-hush. The boys upstairs back at the Yard didn't even know what was happening; they couldn't, because a police raid on a building full of innocent members of the public just wasn't on. On the other hand, if Tap had just happened to be there when it all kicked off; well, he could have worked a bit of well-rehearsed bullshit around that, just like he always did.

But the fact remained that Sid and Doughnut were currently left without back-up. Sid suggested that maybe they could stay there, let Jenkins arrive and then just act like patients.

"I'll be truthful with you, Sid," said Tap, "I think he's already there, mate. He's always one step ahead of us. Just get out of there mate, and quick!" With that, Tap silenced the phone with the press of the button. He just had to pray that he was wrong now.

*

"Well, what do you reckon then?" Sid asked his colleague, who was leaning against the wall next to him. The red plastic seats in the waiting area weren't designed for someone with an arse the size of Doughnut's. There was a long corridor from the front entrance with a reception desk to the right, just after the main door, then directly opposite that was the waiting area, the left wall of which backed onto the street. The right hand wall of the waiting area formed a partition between the waiting area and a small room. All the usual things were going up and down the corridor: nurses, patients, trolleys, cleaners, wheelchairs and all that type of clinic stuff.

The chairs in the waiting room ran around the walls with two rows sitting in the centre. They were all fixed firmly to the floor so that people couldn't pick them up and throw them. Sid was on the right hand side of the front row. The two police officers thought that this seating position gave them the strategic edge.

Doughnut simply shrugged in response to Sid's question.

"For fuck's sake, Doughnut!" Sid whispered through gritted teeth.

"I'll go with whatever you say," Doughnut added, after a moment's thought. That figured, Sid thought, looking round at the other people in the waiting room.

There were old men, old ladies, even the living dead were wandering around aimlessly, not really knowing what was going on but being steered in various directions by people who did. Among them were some healthy-looking people – two birds, fit as fuck, obviously come in for…well, Sid checked his thoughts; he must have been hanging round with Tap for too long.

Sid was not the only ethnic person in the waiting room; there were two something-or-others. He had no idea where they were from but they couldn't speak English, although Sid would have bet his left bollock that they had the health service and benefits system worked out. Sid readily admitted he was a racist – these people got his back up, but in his position he had to keep his mouth shut.

That was just about it for the waiting area, apart from a blind man sitting next to Sid. He glanced at him with pity; he'd rather be in a box than lose his sight. The guide dog didn't look much use, either. Sid wasn't a great dog lover, but this one looked kind of stressed, fidgeting about all over the place. Maybe it wanted a crap or something. The blind man wore a long black coat and a matching flat cap with dark glasses concealing his sightless eyes. He held the standard white cane. Sid couldn't help noticing that he looked quite young, and although skinny was wiry in build. He kept a sturdy grip on the long metal handle attached to the dog's white harness, as the animal tried to run round him in circles.

"Are you all right mate?" Sid asked, and the blind man turned towards him as if trying to see him.

"And who are you?" He asked.

Sid was taken aback by the question, so the blind man answered it for him.

"You're a policeman, aren't you?"

Stunned, Sid asked how he had known.

"You talk very loud; not too loud for everyone, just too loud for a man who sees through his ears!" A philosopher as well as a clever sod, it seemed.

Okaaaaaay, thought Sid, a little freaked out by the blind man. He looked for some support from Doughnut, who merely shrugged again. One day, he'd shrug at the wrong person, Sid thought. The blind man must have sensed his movement, because he spoke again.

"You are not alone then. Who is your friend?"

Now this blind man was a real nosy fella, and Doughnut had to chuckle at his colleague's predicament. Sid couldn't be rude; everyone feels sorry for a blind bloke.

"No, I'm with some silly fat bastard called Doughnut who does nothing all day but eat and shit. He's very fond of dropping his guts in the car, just when you least expect it, and finds it amusing to lock the electric windows as well, fucking animal!" is what Sid would have liked to say as he thought back to their journey over here, but sadly he couldn't say that.

"I'm with a colleague!" Was his actual reply. He was no good at being put on the spot and found it hard not to speak the truth. The blind man nodded, and asked which one of them was ill. Sid thought quickly.

"Oh, yeah, he's got bad guts, pains and that. My colleague, I mean.

The blind man nodded again and turned his face back to face straight in front of him. That was that then, Sid had done his bit and now it was someone else's turn.

"What we going to do then, Doughnut?" Sid asked again, as quietly as he could. Doughnut thought it might be better if they did one, and Sid was about to agree when he was interrupted once more by that pain in the arse blind bloke. He turned to him again, struggling to remain polite.

"Pardon, sir?" He asked.

The blind man repeated his question while at the same time trying to keep his dog under control.

"Your friend - are you not going to wait for your friend?"

This was doing Sid's image of blind people no favours at all.

"What friend?" He asked.

"Your friend Jenkins. I heard you on the phone, you said you were waiting for Jenkins."

Sid took a couple of deep breaths, before replying in level tones that they had been waiting for someone, but it didn't matter anymore because it looked like he wasn't coming. The blind man nodded, and Sid patted him on his left shoulder as he stood up to leave. This was becoming an extremely weird conversation.

"We're gonna go now, my friend. Hope your appointment goes well!"

Sid and Doughnut set off across the room towards the door, talking amongst themselves until their conversation was stopped dead in its tracks. The blind man had spoken again, dropping the dog's reins as he did so.

"And good luck with yours!" He said, the words echoing down the corridor as the dog did what Doughnut and his colleague should have done ten minutes before and got the fuck out of there. The dog shot out through the front door, knocking a porter flying and sending the cups and shit that he was carrying crashing to the floor. Even with all that racket, the sound of the plastic cane making contact with the floor was clearly to be heard. Sid turned slowly to face the blind man, who was apparently blind no more.

The hat had been discarded and the dark glasses that had disguised his blue eyes now rested on his forehead. Sid knew straight away that he was fucked; he didn't even bother reaching for his weapon. He and Doughnut just stood there like statues as they faced the very man they had been warned to avoid. His long, black coat, nylon this time, and stolen from a real blind man, fell open as Jenkins stood, revealing the armoury beneath. The sub-machine gun was in his right hand and the Browning in his left.

He was still a bit unsure about how to use the MP5; there was a lever switch thing on the left hand side of the weapon with three positions marked by letters of the alphabet: S, E and F. The letter S was at the top of the switch's travel. The E and the F were in red and the S was in white. He assumed that the white S stood for 'safety' and the two red letters would be automatic fire and single shot modes. He couldn't work out what the E and F stood for, however, because the words they represented were German. Whatever, Jenkins had moved the switch to F – F for fucking mayhem, hopefully, because he was praying that when he pulled the trigger, bullets were going to spew out just like he'd seen on the television. He really hoped that the F did not stand for 'fuck, wrong button,' but there was only one way to find out. That was why he had his back-up plan in the form of the tried-and-tested Browning.

In front of him, Sid and Doughnut had their hands up and behind him the waiting room had rapidly emptied.

"Where's Tap?" He asked. "You can speak, by the way." He added insult to injury, thinking how unpleasant it must be for a copper to be in this situation. Think of all the people they'd done this to, thinking they were all that! And now look at them - the fat boy looked like he was going to shit himself.

"He's not here; he's been delayed," Sid replied woodenly.

Jenkins turned to Doughnut and repeated the question.

"Where's Tap? "Come on, it's not a very hard question, is it? You fucking know where he is, don't you? You're just fucking me about. That's why I'm here in the first place, because you and your boss think you can fuck me about. All this bullshit about me coming here to wreak revenge on doctors who I haven't even seen for years, you lot are fucking making it up! You haven't got any better theory about what I'm doing so you've come up with that shit. What you got to say about that, then? Come on, I want to talk, it's fucking therapy, remember!" Jenkins spat out the words, his face red and his voice becoming hoarse until he spat out the restriction in his throat onto the floor.

"Well come on then, you cunts, let's have it! If I was in custody now you'd have a fuck sight more to say to me, wouldn't you? But the shoe's on the other foot now, my friends, and that shoe has just trodden right in the shit!"

Sid decided to speak.

"Well, why you here then?" Sid asked carefully.

Jenkins laughed at first, before walking closer to his captives. When he was a metre or so away, he answered the question in a shower of spit.

"Because you fucking wankers invited me. Your boss kept on about what my plans were, my big fucking plans, but he didn't know the half of it. All I wanted was for my girlfriend to have a decent last few weeks of her life in a place that she could call home, but you couldn't have that. I mean, it weren't much to ask now, was it?"

The answer to that would be yes, as far as Sid was concerned, but he didn't dare reply to that effect. Instead he asked what Jenkins expected them to do when he was killing people right, left and centre.

Jenkins laughed openly.

"People?" He repeated. "You call scum like that people? I'm in my shop, minding my own business, and two cunt's come in there shouting the odds, giving it all the large about cutting me up and shit. And for what? Because my pisshead father owed them a few grand. Fuck me, if they'd asked nicely I'd have told them where the cunt was and they could have kicked the fuck out of him instead of trying to kick the fuck out of me. If the Yardies hadn't got him back in the flat, then I fucking would have done, the shit he's caused me. Shame about the bird though, Tara, I'd known her for ages, but wrong time, wrong place I suppose. You know that weren't me, don't ya?"

Sid agreed that he did, for arguments sake, although technically Jenkins was talking bollocks. Okay, the Yardies had indeed killed Jenkins senior and cut the prostitute up to within an inch of her life, but it had been a bullet from a Browning automatic that had finished her off. Now probably wasn't the best time to bring this up, though.

"I did their hit men, though. Did the cunts proper, an' all! You know, an eye for an eye and all that, innit? They done me a favour with me stepdad, but let's just say I did it for Tara. Yeah, that'll look sweet in the papers! So, you see my point so far, don't you? I haven't killed any 'people' up to now, have I? Only the dregs of society, and that's what they are, they're just shit, they ain't people, they were the fucking scum of the earth!"

It was clear that he had more to say, but for now he paced the tiled floors, never taking his eye off his catch and always keeping them in the firing line of the German killing machine. The Browning automatic in his other hand was waved about freely as though he were conducting an orchestra.

Sid started him off again by pointing out the fact that, although Tyrone, the two-bit arms dealer, fitted the category of scumbag, what about the Irishman and the Limo driver?

What the fuck had they ever done? Jenkins paused for thought for a minute before he nodded in agreement. He had to admit that Sid had a point.

"Honestly, I think it was the gear. I was caning it a bit and I weren't thinking straight. I had these fantasies about…well, I don't know what they were about, I just lost it. They'd served their purpose, hadn't they, so they had to go. Don't ask me why again because I don't know. I've learnt from it, though, don't you worry; they didn't die in vain. The trouble is, you see, even I don't really know what I'm fighting for any more. I did, but you lot have put paid to that. It's like now, innit? I shouldn't be here, and why am I here? Because you cunts are playing with me! You think I'm some toy that you can just fuck about with. You make up some bullshit fucking theory that I'm meant to be working from, and so here I fucking am, and I'm well up for it!"

Sid didn't know what to say next. Jenkins wanted a row, this much was clear.

"What about last night, then, at the phone shop?" Sid stuck his neck out. He watched in disgust as Jenkins emptied the contents of his throat onto the floor with a professional flourish. Jenkins smiled, acknowledging that he had been caught out and shaking the Browning in his left hand as a mark of respect.

"Well, it's like I said: I was all fucked up and angry before, but I'd had a chance to calm down by last night. Plus those people were cooperative. I told them what I wanted, they gave it to me and it was all tickety-boo, no one had to die! I nicked a phone because I had to call you cunts! See, you've been fucking inciting me again. I needed a phone, and so I had to get one." He illustrated his arguments with flourishes of the Browning.

"So, what about the three grand then?" Sid went on, somewhat recklessly in the circumstances, "Oh, wait a minute

- I know, you had to nick that because we were after you and you needed cash, right? Oh, fuck me, it's our fault again! I was there, I took the statements, and you terrorised those people into doing what you wanted. I saw the state of them afterwards, so don't give me any of your bullshit!" Sid was treading on thin ice now, and Doughnut gave him a look that said 'shut the fuck up!'

"I know you were there, Mr Policeman, I was watching you. I was disappointed that Billy never showed up though - I would have liked to have seen him; it's been a while now. Okay then, I did nick the three grand, but the reason I didn't kill those three Muppets back in the shop is so you lot didn't get a chance to print a load of shit about me. You just had to print shit about me though didn't you that's why the papers read 'psycho robs phone shop, terrorises customers and manager.' That's bullshit, bullshit and fucking bullshit! I didn't terrorise them, I was in and out in minutes. You want to see me when I fucking terrorise someone! What if you'd actually told the truth to the papers? Anthony Jenkins robs shop in order to fund the medical care his girlfriend needs to stay alive. She doesn't want to die in a shit hole fucking hospice; she deserves better than that. And why is she in a fucking hospice anyway? I'll tell you why - because you cunts can't keep the streets clean of what put her there. Fucking drugs, that's what! I tell ya, I can get a pizza right now in ten minutes, but I bet you anything you like that I could get drugs here within five. Now that's wrong, why aren't we protected from that? Why is Haley dying of AIDS and why am I as fucked up as I am? I'll tell you why, shit fucking drugs everywhere, shit police, and fucking shit health service. That's why! I tell you what put the fucking British legal system in there as well, because that's fucking crap too! Look at you cunts; you couldn't catch me if I tied bells to my ankles and ran round naked, I take the piss out of you lot at every opportunity. You, you were at that shop yesterday, asking questions, giving it all the large, walking around like the big I am, and I'm sitting there watching you. Where's your boss then? Has he shit it, let you two cunt's take the fall instead, or what?" Jenkins had to pause for breath there, and to rid himself of the fluids that had suddenly risen from his throat into his mouth.

Sid should have kept his mouth shut really, but there was something he needed to know.

"If you saw me at the shop, why didn't you take me out there and then?"

Doughnut nodded as if he thought it was a good question.

"What do you mean? Do you mean take you out and fuck you? Take you out to the pictures?" Jenkins asked, laughing. "That would have spoilt all the fun, messenger boy! You wouldn't be here now if I didn't want you here. Besides, one doesn't shit on ones doorstep now, does one?"

Sid's mind started to work very fast at that last comment.

"Anyway, I've had enough of the chit-chat now, boys, so do you mind if I give you what you've got coming? You know, shoot you?" Jenkins laughed.

Sid went for his gun in desperation, but he never had a chance. His leather coat was unfastened, but his police-issue Glock was still in its holster, located under the detective's left arm. As he reached for his weapon, he threw himself across the floor at the same time, but it only bought him a second or two.

The corridor lit up as Jenkins pulled the trigger and flames were generated from the barrel of the sub-machine gun. He just held the trigger and the weapon did the rest, shooting anything that it was pointed at until the weapon clicked empty. It was a beautiful smell, the smell of gunpowder burning as a fine mist of smoke bellowed from each of the gun's orifices. There was also the satisfying sound of dead shells being expelled as they were cast out of the weapon and clattered onto the floor. Jenkins watched with a sense of pride and amazement as the cartridges bailed out from the side of the weapon and jingled around merrily on the tiles.

Doughnut had turned his head away as the corridor filled up with smoke; he couldn't watch as he waited for the bullets to pierce his skin and wreak havoc within his heavy frame. Strangely though, none had hit him, not yet anyway, so he looked back towards his partner and the gunman once the shooting had stopped.

Sid had obviously been the main target. He lay on the floor, literally six metres back from where he had been standing before his heroic dive. The velocity of the bullets had sent him back a few more metres as they hit him: two in the stomach, two in the legs and one in his right arm. Jenkins had been aiming for the guts but he could only hold that position for two bullets because of his lack of expertise with the weapon. The rest of the bullets had just hit anything - walls, ceilings, floors, whatever was in their way, basically. A white haze of plaster and debris mixed with the sunlight coming in through the tiny, high windows.

Sid's hands were clamped over his stomach, shaking with shock.

Jenkins undid the buckle on his makeshift sub-machine gun holder, pulled the strap through from under his coat and discarded the now useless weapon.

"That makes your stomach ache pale into significance, don't it?" He joked to Doughnut. "Open the jacket on your man there and step back!" he ordered. He wanted Sid's coat fully open so he could reach in and take his gun without having to fuck about.

Doughnut obediently crouched down beside his colleague and stared into his face. It looked bad. Sid's eyelids were fluttering as he tried to talk and his body was shaking violently now. Doughnut cautiously opened Sid's coat as instructed.

"Stand up and step back!" Jenkins ordered. Doughnut dare not disobey, and did as he was told.

"Print this in the papers, you cunts!" Jenkins forced the barrel of the Browning automatic under the dying detective's chin as he knelt beside his victim, who was struggling for breath.

Now would have been a good time for Doughnut to have tried to jump him if he was going to, but he simply didn't have the balls, so he stood helplessly aside as the killer straightened up again, holding Sid's Glock. The Browning automatic was no longer required for the time being, so Jenkins made it safe before hiding it away in the waistband of his jeans. He took the time to study his new toy, a big boy's toy. It looked the part, black in colour and contemporary in every aspect. The Browning wasn't bad, but it was getting on a bit and was nowhere near as cool as the weapon he now cradled in his hands. He was going to have some fun letting this little baby off! He squeezed the trigger ever so lightly and felt the safety device release.

"What we gonna do with you then, fat arse?" He asked, as if genuinely seeking Doughnut's advice.

Doughnut shrugged; he simply didn't know what else to do. When he tried to speak, he simply stuttered like a scratched record. He hadn't stuttered since he was a child, but the shock was bringing it back. He didn't see it coming, even when Jenkins told him to check his colleague's pulse. Obediently, he bent down and picked up Sid's limp wrist, feeling for some indication that the blood was still coursing through his veins. As he did so, Jenkins swiftly knelt behind him and shot him up the arse. This was justifiable vengeance, as far as he was concerned, against those who hunted him. They were worse than he was, because they carried out their atrocities under the protection of the law. If they wanted to leak this one out to the papers, they were welcome!

He had wondered whether the bullet would travel in a straight line and actually blow Doughnut's head off, but instead it had emerged from his neck, severing his spine as it did so. The head flopped lifelessly and the body stumbled forward in an uncoordinated fashion before collapsing face down upon the cold tiles of the hospital floor. Jenkins stared in wonder at the blood that pumped freely out of the bullet's exit wound. Curiosity was giving way to guilt, which he could feel by the burning of his arms underneath the skin and the incipient hunching of his shoulders. Whatever damage had been done inside the big man's body was hidden by the jacket and the skin and muscle that lay beneath it. Just to be on the safe side, he pumped another couple of bullets into Doughnut's body as it lay there twitching.

By this act, Jenkins' message to Tap was simply, 'up your bum!' He had used to say this to his mother when he was little, and she had replied, 'fuck you, you little cunt!' *Yeah, well. Anyway Tap, up your bum, you wanker, up your fucking bum!*

The catastrophe that had befallen his colleague seemed to have given Sid a second wind, fuelled by adrenaline. He spat blood from his mouth, some of it Doughnut's, and coughed violently as he fought to speak before it was too late.

"You got something to say then, mate?" Jenkins asked him. He crouched down close to the dying man to hear his reply, while at the same time retrieving Doughnut's firearm from the holster beneath his coat.

"I'm fucking dead, am I?" Jenkins laughed out loud, looking up to the ceiling as he did so. "Speak up, you cunt, I can't hear ya!"

"You're fucking dead, Jenkins, but not as dead as your fucking bird. You've been stitched up, you fucking idiot.

'Course Tap's not here. We know where you're staying and Tap's there now! And what do you think he's doing to your sweetheart, eh? Fucking hell, I bet he's doing all sorts of nasty shit to her right now! You fucking sucker, we're just decoys! So run along home now, Jenkins, run home to your sweet heart, but it's too fucking late! Tap will be waiting for you and you'll pay for this. You will pay fucking dearly, I promise you that!" Sid smiled one last time as he died.

Deep in thought, Jenkins stared down at him and watched a pool of blood that had formed in Sid's mouth gradually rise until it covered his teeth. The odd air bubble emerged, but other than that there was nothing. Sid had given up now that he had had his say. The pain was over and it was time to cross over to the other-side, where Sid's religion suggested there was something better.

Jenkins wanted to hit his victim or something, maybe shoot him again, but it seemed that there was no point. Sid's last words echoed in his head. The adrenaline was beginning to surge through his system; several times more adrenaline than he should have had. He stood up quickly, feeling dizzy for a few seconds, before shoving Doughnuts handgun into the waistband of his trousers and reaching for his mobile phone. He called the flat, but it rang four times and then the answering service cut in.

He gave a muted scream, and blood stained phlegm flew from the corners of his mouth. This was bad news; he had purposely left the Irishman's phone in the flat so that he could keep in touch with the nest. But then, of course, Sarah could just be having a shit or something. He tried again, but the same thing happened.

"Cunt!" He screamed, stomping about like a lead singer in a heavy metal band. He had to decide what to do next. Should he kill the doctor to teach Tap a lesson? First he would have to leave a message. He bent down and brushed the fingers of his right hand through the mixture of the two dead men's blood on the floor, having first swapped the Glock from one hand to the other. He was going to get the job done, right now. Stepping up to the wall, he wrote the word 'wrong!' above the tableau of bodies that he had created.

He then ran to the hospital door, half expecting the road outside to be lined with police, but it wasn't. There were a few, but none of them looked armed. When he had planned this escapade, he had worked out that he would have plenty of time to do what he had to do and then get the fuck away from the crime scene before the armed response teams arrived, but Sid's talk of the hunters having one up on him had seriously unnerved him.

What the fuck was that? Jenkins was over by the door when he heard a familiar tune fill the air. It was a phone, of course, playing a recent chart hit as its ring tone. He skipped over towards the noise and eventually tracked it down as coming from Sid's pocket. Patting the pockets, he felt a lump in one of them and removed the phone, the tune growing louder as he did so. He looked at the phone's display, but there was just a number; no name. Shit, should he answer it or not? He decided he would.

"Hello?" He said.

"Sid?" Came a woman's voice. Jenkins thought quickly.

"This is Chief Inspector Mills of the Metropolitan Police. Can I ask who's calling please?" he asked sternly, in the sort of voice he expected a Chief Inspector might use.

The woman replied that she was Stacey Payne and she was trying to get hold of the man who she knew only as Sid.

"Yes, I know Sid. I am actually with him at the moment. Sid's actually in hospital at the moment, he's been injured."

There was a moment's silence, the woman then spoke again.

"Was it Jenkins?" she asked quietly.

"I cannot disclose that information, Miss Payne. Let's just say that we've found Sid and his colleague, and they're in a bad way. Detective Sergeant Billy Tap is on his way to the scene at the minute. I was first here and I'm waiting for him to come and decide where we go next with this." These were good lies, very good. He knew he had to drop Tap's name into the conversation somewhere in order to open up some doors, and it sounded as though he had struck gold.

"That's who I'm really trying to get hold of; Billy. I'm looking after a friend of his and I just need to know what's happening. Can you please get him to call me as soon as you see him? It's really important. We're a bit scared to be honest, especially now you're telling me Sid's been hurt! Look, I know all about Jenkins and, well, I'm a single woman and connected to Billy. I'm really worried now to be honest."

Jenkins might not have been the brightest of stars ever to shine, but he knew when somebody was trying to spin him a yarn and wanted to get in on the action. why, he had no idea. Perhaps she was genuinely concerned for her safety, and that of whoever it was she was looking after for Tap. The very thought of this, Tap having someone guarded, made Jenkins smile as possibilities of revenge flooded through his mind. This was fucking perfect.

"I'll get Tap to call you as soon as he arrives. If you're really concerned, I might be able to send an officer round to your house to look after you until you can talk to Billy. How does that sound?"

Stacey gave the matter some thought. She didn't really need protection - Jenkins didn't know about her or what she did. The only thing that really interested her was getting closer to the action. Billy had been letting her down a bit over the last day or two as far as ground-breaking stories were concerned, so if she could get a police guard and get involved that way, there might be opportunities. Stacey gave her address.

"I should be able to have a guard there in about twenty minutes, madam, but in the meantime lock the doors and don't answer to strangers. Billy will call you just as soon as he can. Bye for now."

"Stupid, fucking bitch…!" He commented as he pressed the red button to end the call. He kept the phone, putting it in his pocket in case he needed her number again. Anyway, now it was time to leave in order to meet the woman who he presumed was looking after Tap's girlfriend. Tap's girlfriend, that was fantastic. Fancy being able to get hold of Tap's girlfriend, it was fucking marvellous. *So, Tap thinks he's going to hurt my Haley? Well, Tap, maybe we can do a trade: my Haley for your friend.*

Police sirens were wailing closer now and he had to laugh when he saw the crowds on the other side of the glass doors. They all wanted a bit; all wanted to see what was going on. Well, let them see! Jenkins kicked open the main door of the hospital and walked out into the High Street. The crowds that had gathered suddenly splintered off into groups, leaving only the brave and the stupid remaining close to the scene.

"Fucking run you cunts! Run while you can!" He screamed.

Some people actually just stood there, watching the gunman make his journey towards them. It was as if he was re-enacting some scene from a play or a film. Some onlookers took sanctuary behind parked cars, letter boxes, phone boxes, trees, shrubs, anything. Why they didn't all run he had no idea. The police were not so stupid, though; they kept a distance.

At least the real blind man had been taken care of though; he was resting in the bosom of some middle-aged woman who had obviously found him in his hour of need. Jenkins had seen him earlier taking a wrong path. Well okay, he had taken the wrong path because Jenkins had been steering his guide dog down it by feeding it chocolate. The path had led to an ally way round the side of the building, where there was a small, open-faced shed. Although the blind man could sense some kind of danger, he had not been able to sense the smack in the mouth that Anthony Jenkins gave him. Jenkins had, however, managed to catch him as he fell and at least stop his head hitting the ground. He had then stolen his victim's coat, hat, glasses and dog before setting about his task. He was dressed for the part, but there had been no time for a rehearsal.

Anyway, it looked as though he was in good hands now. As he passed him again, Jenkins removed his jacket and threw it on the ground at the blind man's feet, apologising for its blood stained condition as he did so. Casually, he walked over to the bushes where he had felled the blind man and removed a sports bag containing some fresh clothes.

Jenkins raised one of his new guns and aimed it into the crowd, which had reassembled at what they considered to be a safe distance. It soon dispersed again, leaving just the woman with the blind man and a few coppers. Well, this was for the coppers, Jenkins thought as he took pot shots at the unarmed policemen while walking along, sports bag over his shoulder. SO19 were on their way but they wouldn't be quick enough because Jenkins was getting closer and closer to the subway and no one was going to find him in there. He would be long gone before the transport police, not to mention the armed response unit, got anywhere near him. The Glock dispensed round after round until it was empty, discarded, and the other stolen police issue killing machine put into action. How many bullets did these things have? Jenkins didn't know but the bullets must have been rapidly dwindling as he aimed shot after shot at the four policeman who attempted to take refuge behind cars, wheelie bins or just about anything else that might offer them some protection. All of a sudden the shooting stopped as Jenkins disappeared into the underground station.

The second Glock was soon empty, so also discarded. Rather than the Browning automatic, he opted now for his trusty twelve-inch carving knife which had been hidden away in the waistband of his combat trousers. He had improvised a makeshift sheath for it, and now as he drew it out he waved it around in front of him, parting the sea of people and creating a clear path for himself as he did so. As he passed through, the crowds closed up again behind him.

Now he remembered that he had had no chance to call Haley again as he had left the clinic and his phone wouldn't work down here. He walked up to a ticket booth, the knife in front of him and his face expressionless, and as if by magic a free ticket appeared on the wooden counter. He would like to have cut the attendant up, because this was the first time he had received service like this from one of those wankers, but the man was protected by a glass screen.

As he turned onto the platform, a rumbling indicated the impending arrival of a train, bringing lots of new people. There were two ways he could deal with this: either stand with his twelve-inch carving knife on full display and scare the shit out of the new arrivals, possibly causing a state of panic, or worse still a coup or overthrow, or he could hide the knife and let people go about their business as usual until they met the congestion upstairs. The knife had to go back into obscurity, back into the safety of the sheath, where hopefully it would remain for the duration of the journey home. Jenkins stood like a statue as a blast of cool air filled the station, signalling that the train was only seconds away.

New arrivals poured onto the platform: students, suits, mothers, babies, schoolchildren, immigrants, vicars, a Rastafarian. Jenkins stared at the masses, but only a minority of them stared back because they had business to attend to, and who the fuck was this skinny little tosser anyway? Only front page news, the most wanted man in Britain!

As Jenkins boarded the train he said a little prayer, asking for Haley to be protected from evil. *She had better be all right, Tap! Oh, she had better be, for your sake! I'm on my way now, on my way to end this!* The doors closed. The train was not that busy; Jenkins could have had a seat if he wanted one, but he didn't. Instead, he leaned up against a glass passenger shield next to the door. This was the best place for him to stand because he didn't like tubes, especially when he was as wired as he was now. He needed medicine soon; sweet, sweet medicine, and it wouldn't be long now until he could get it; not long at all.

There was a newspaper lying on the seat next to him with his photo on the front page. Front page news and no one even recognised him; he could tell as much by slyly looking around the carriage - no one gave a fuck! It wasn't the best picture in the world, admittedly; he had had longer hair then. Jenkins knew that he had to be careful from here on because the end was coming; he was too exposed to the public now, this much was very clear. The cause had gone and all that really mattered now was seeing Haley again and taking out this thorn-in-the-side detective. Little else held a place in Jenkins' thoughts for the next ten minutes or so. He knew where he was going and what he was going to do. More innocent people had to die in order for Jenkins to reach his goal, but reach his goal he would. This was for Haley, if nothing else, because Jenkins wanted revenge. That's all he really gave a fuck about now, revenge, and he was hell bent on it.

"I hope you're all right, baby." He whispered to the reflection of Haley that he had conjured up in the glass of the door. He reached out to touch her but she was cold, just cold glass.

"Piss off, just piss off, right, unless you want to fucking drive?" Slug bellowed at his passenger. There was some gravel on the road and that's why he had skidded to a halt. This car had anti-lock fucking everything, it stopped on a pin head, and Slug was going to take a while to get used to the vehicle's high specification. Tap was pissing him off, but there was nothing new there. This car was the bollocks, Merc, with all the toys: leather interior, convertible roof, they hadn't had time yet to play with all the gadgets.

It was Tina's car, courtesy of Kimberley Jones, albeit indirectly. Silver in colour, four weeks old, it had a seventy-five grand price tag. It was kind of on loan, Tap having bullied it out of Tina. Kimberley hadn't been there when Tap had woken up and was running round the house panicking. He looked a mess and stank like a brewery; Tina had seen them get on it last night through a window on the upstairs landing that looked down into the domed room.

Tap had come running into the TV room in a state of panic, telling some rambling tale about his mates being in trouble and a lunatic on the loose.

"Hold it, I'll call Kimberley and you can tell someone who gives a fuck," Tina commented, reaching for her mobile phone. Kimberley was at her husband's grave at an old church inside the estate. She didn't like being disturbed while she was there because this was her time alone with her loved one. She was accompanied by her late husband's dog, Fugly, and like most white English Bull Terriers, fuck was it ugly! Tina was relieved when her friend answered her mobile. Normally she wouldn't have, but on this occasion she knew that Tap was around.

Tina apologised for the interruption before explaining why she had been forced to seek her advice. Tap's van was knackered after hitting the gate post and they needed a car to get back to London. They were in a hurry and panicking because one of their mates was in trouble or something. Kimberley didn't need the gory details - they could take the Mercedes, the SL whatever it was, the silver car, because that was a moody one anyway. As with most of Kimberley's cars, it had been stolen, on this occasion from a famous motor show. Prior to receiving, it had been ringed, so they could do what they wanted to that car because it owed Kimberley nothing. It had been a gift from some old friends in the trade, a present for a favour.

"If anyone asks though, Tap nicked it!" Kimberley warned Tina.

Tina handed the keys to her pride and joy over to the detectives. Technically it had been her car, Kimberley had let her have it, but now it was Tap's, and she knew it wasn't coming back. Not in one piece, anyway. Whatever, it was almost worth losing a seventy-five grand car just to get rid of these two pricks. They were only here because they were on the take, and take they did, in the form of Tina's fucking car. She stood in the driveway as Tap and his chauffeur drove off into the distance with gravel flying everywhere. Tina made a small wish, and it was granted when Slug made it past the gate posts without hitting them.

"We'll get rid of this fucking van then, shall we?" She shouted as the car roared away, and a thumbs-up sign appeared briefly out of the passenger side window.

"Pair of cunts!" Was her only comment as she walked back towards the house with her mobile phone to her ear. It was time to ring a man who knew how to shift metal.

*

"Fucking shifts a bit don't it?" Slug had to admit that he was impressed. Tap shrugged in reply before reminding his colleague that it didn't matter how fast it was, not unless it was a fucking time machine, because that's what they needed! Teleportation was about the only way they were going to get back to London as quickly as they needed to. In a nut shell, it weren't gonna happen. Tap confessed that he feared the worst for their two colleagues; there was going to be a row if Doughnut hadn't taken his advice and got as far from that health centre as was physically possible. This was assuming they had survived; somehow, Tap knew that his two foot soldiers hadn't done as he told them. He knew them too well, the fuckers!

It was five to ten and a storm was brewing. Tap opened his inside pocket and proved that cars were not the only things he could steal off Kimberley Jones. He had a bottle of something nasty, blue shit it was, or rather that's what he called it; the label said vodka. A swig of this caused him to swear, a look of pain on his face. He asked Slug if he wanted some, but Slug reminded him that he was responsible for their lives while he was driving so blue shit was not the one, not just at that moment.

"I don't suppose you want any sherbet then, neither?" Tap offered.

"Nah, bollocks to that do you know how much this car is worth?"

Tap laughed. Yeah, he knew how much this car was worth – fuck all! Even if it was legit, it had been bought with drug money so who gave a fuck what happened to it?

Slug kept the speed to what he called fast/sensible, even though Tap had named it slow/pussy. But he would have said the same if they had been leading the Grand Prix, because he had just powdered his nose on the inside and was now enjoying a high that had become all too familiar these past few days. He could no longer smell the luxurious red leather, just the dirty, bitter smell of the cocaine powder that lined his nostrils. He sniffed as if he had flu, clearing his sinuses in order to prevent any of the powder mixing with mucus and sliding back down, because not only was that a waste, it was fucking annoying! He fiddled with the CD player and swirled blue shit around his numb teeth. He found an R&B CD that wasn't too bad and put it in the player.

Sitting back comfortably in the leather seat, Tap asked Slug what time he reckoned they were going to get back. A good hour was an optimistic estimate, and Tap shook his head as if their situation was hopeless.

"We fucked up, Slug, we fucked up big-time. Jenkins is too clever for those two fucking idiots. If they didn't get out of that health centre when I told them to, then Jenkins will have them for fucking breakfast. What do you reckon? Do you reckon they would have gone?" Tap sought some reassurance that there was a chance Doughnut would have listened to him, but Slug's only comment was that they were big boys who could take care of themselves. Tap laughed and shook his head.

"Big boys? You're having a fucking laugh! They're probably fucking dead already! I've got this feeling, this horrible fucking feeling that I get, and when I get it I know I've already found the answer to the question. They're not going to make it through this, Slug. They won't leave that health centre. They'll try and impress me, be heroes, and Jenkins will simply take them for the pair of cunts they are!"

Traffic had begun to build as the car of the decade roared down the North Circular. Tap stared at bus stops, through shop windows and inside the cars and buses they passed; anywhere where he thought something worth fucking might be hiding. He was on one: coked-up and almost pissed. He had been using this time of enforced idleness to catch up with a few people. He had phoned Stacey but couldn't get hold of her, she was probably out of range or something. He left a message for her to call him. Doughnut and Sid were unobtainable; Tap had called them at least thirty times each, as Slug had pointed out, causing Tap to retort that if he wanted a bitch to nag him, he would get fucking married.

Conscience: that annoying time between sleep, drugs and alcohol. As central London approached, the office buildings increased in number. Tap thought this was the fucked-up part of London; the bit where no one actually lived, just worked; a ghost town at the weekends but a bustling hub of misery in the weekdays. Money, money, money, some liked to earn it, but that was too much like hard work as far as Tap was concerned. He preferred to steal it, one way or another. Tap loved crime-fighting in the City almost as much as he liked hunting scum in the red light districts. Maybe there was a sense of pride in taking down a corporate legend or one of their thousands of wannabees who did their dirty work. Tap had some respect for real criminals, of the thieving variety, that is, they took a chance and they either got away with it or they got caught. The ones who hid behind a corporation though, he had no time for, setting up pensions they couldn't honour, making extortionate contracts and interest charges, embezzlement. Tap had dealt with a lot of corporate garbage and he wasn't fooled by the sheer size and glory of these offices, the apparently well-heeled personnel and the plush receptions where people wouldn't piss on you if you were on fire. These streets were just as bad as the streets where Anthony Jenkins prowled, if not worse.

The number of exquisite glass buildings began to decrease, giving way to their older fore-bearers rising from the shadows. It was almost like driving through a theme park, starting with modern skyscrapers and taking a trip through history as the buildings became older and older. Tap didn't feel at home here; he felt alien to this world. Just get him back to his filthy streets; he knew where he was then, back where he belonged.

About ten minutes had passed since he had called Doughnut. In the meantime, they were driving deeper into central London.

"It's got to have been five minutes since you rang Doughnut, ain't it?" Slug asked, breaking the silence. Tap had to laugh. He rang the number again: engaged, as before. Tap gave up on the call and pressed the red button on his phone. A few minutes passed, then suddenly the phone rang and Tap saw with joy that it was Doughnut's number in the display. Switching the music off, he pressed the button and asked the fat, useless cunt where he had been. But instead of the familiar nervous babble, there was silence. In the background, Tap could hear the sound of the streets; cars, voices, footsteps. He knew straight away who was on the other end of the phone. It was his enemy, his nemesis, Anthony Jenkins! For just about the first time in his life, Tap didn't know what to say.

In the silence, Jenkins also listened carefully to the sounds on the other end of the line. There was nothing much; just the roar of an engine and the sound of air pressure. But to Jenkins, the fact that there was road noise in the background meant that Sid had been lying; Tap was still on his way.

"That must be you, Billy?" He said. "Hello mate, I've got a joke for you! A fat white bloke and a skinny Asian fella walk into a pub, and the barman says… only joking, Billy; they didn't walk into a pub at all, they walked into a health centre. Yeah, that was right, and the doctor said…well, what do you reckon he said then, Billy?"

Tap frantically tapped Slug on the arm and pointed to the phone to indicate that it was Jenkins, which fell on deaf ears.

"The doctor said fuck all Billy, because he was sensible enough to have got the fuck out of there when Anthony Jenkins arrived. Oh Billy, I've got to apologise, I fucked your plans up, I'm afraid, fucked 'em up good and proper. You were thinking I was going to take the doctor out, but I ended up taking your buddies out instead! It seems that the doctor meant nothing to me in the end after all! Never mind, we live and learn. Fuck, did that fat motherfucker go bang! I shot him up the arse as a kind of social experiment, or a testament to you, I suppose, and he just blew up like a fucking blood-orange. Messy, fucking messy mate. Classy, though. Well, I wanted to do something juicy that you could put in the papers again tomorrow - you know, big me up a bit, 'cos you like doing that, Billy, don't you? I let your Asian mate watch, an' all. Gave him a couple in the old guts first, left him writhing about a bit on the floor like a piece of shit, and then…nah, nah, nah, I'm not gonna tell you anymore, Billy, 'cos I'm busy. I've got a few house calls to make, you know how it is? Not talking then, Billy? Thought you had something to say about everything. You haven't got a theory about what I'm going to do next though, have you my friend? Never worry, just read the fucking papers! Where the fuck are you anyway? Your buddy was giving it all the crap about you being at my humble abode. He said you'd found where I'm staying and were entertaining my missis, then he died! You ain't, though, are you? Because if you was, you wouldn't be in a fucking car now, would you? Bet you'd love to get hold of my missis, though, just as much as I'd like to get hold of yours, aye? Who knows what's around the corner, Billy, who fucking knows? Anyway, it's been really nice talking to you but I can tell you're not in the most talkative of moods, so I'll leave you in peace. Peace that is, not pieces, like your boys back there! Bye for now, Billy, ta-ra!" Jenkins hung up the call, sounding a lot more confident than he felt.

Jenkins was sure he was right about Sid lying; he had been clutching at straws while at death's door. Tap had obviously been in a car, which meant that he couldn't be at his flat. But Tap's silence had unnerved him. He must have been doing it on purpose, employing tactics. Tap was good at this, keeping

Jenkins hanging on tenterhooks. He had no idea that his opponent was actually falling apart at the seams rather than employing any strategy to outwit him.

Going through Tap's mind was guilt, shock, anger and near enough every fucking emotion going. Then add a gram of white powder and half a bottle of fuck-knows-what. Slug was asking what was going on.

"I take it that was Doughnut, then?" Tap was silent once more as the severity of his fuck-up started to sink into his pickled brain. Doughnut and Sid were dead and it was all his fault; not Slug's, just his, because everything Slug did, he did for Tap and no one could blame him. Slug shook his arm. What the fuck was up with Tap?

"No, it weren't fucking Doughnut, Slug. It was Jenkins."

Slug just managed to avoid a bus that was pulling out in front of them.

"Well, what's he fucking say, then?" He screamed. He whacked his foot down hard on the brake pedal, bringing the gleaming silver Mercedes to an almost instant standstill. Horns blasted, people shouted. Slug flung open the door, ran around the front of the car and opened the passenger door. A man in a car behind them opened his driver's door and got out, but thought better of it when he saw Slug's face and the firearm in the holster under his jacket.

Tap remained catatonic, even when Slug pulled him from the car and slammed him firmly against the side of it. Adhering to the rule that you never fight a man when he has a bottle in his hand, he removed the bottle of blue vodka shit and threw it across the road towards the car driven by the have-a-go hero.

If there had been a scale of how pissed off he actually was, Slug would be nearing the top of it. Usually the milder of the two, Slug was shaking Tap around like a rag doll and encountering no resistance whatsoever. People wound their windows down from the safety of their cars and listened to the foul-mouthed abuse.

Slug used some of his police-taught judo to put Tap on his back, at the same time using some of street know-how to kick him as he went down. The blow to the arms was not meant to hurt, and it didn't; it was just meant to emphasis Slug's frustration. Tap held his arms in a posture of submission as his back hit the floor. He was off his tits, totally confused and vulnerable, so Slug refrained from punching him on the nose as he had been planning to do.

"Speak, you cunt! Tell me what the fuck Jenkins said! Are they dead? Are they fucking dead, Billy?" Slug screamed.

Tap was waving his arms about as if swatting flies, as an audience began to appear from behind the cars. He attempted to communicate while nodding his head: they were dead; Jenkins had got them. Slug knew as much already. Tap was useless, fucked-up in the head, so it was going to be down to him to call the shots now and to do that he needed some answers, and quickly.

"What's he going to do next, Billy? What did he say?" Slug begged for some feedback before turning to shout at some nosy bastard who was getting too close to the scene. The observer backed off; these two men looked like trouble, one sitting on top of the other as though he was shagging him. Tap shook his head and Slug shook him about a bit.

"Think, Billy! Where's he going next? What did he say?"

Tap couldn't remember. He only remembered fragments of what Jenkins had said. He had said something about a doctor, and something about him thinking that they'd found where he lived with his girlfriend. This made no sense to Slug, but the effort of using his brain was forcing Tap to come round a bit, enough to be able to push Slug backwards.

"Get off me, man!"

Slug stood and leaned against the back of the car, getting his breath as Tap pulled himself to a sitting position. Suddenly, the two men became aware of the fact that the crowd around them had grown considerably and was now fronted by two of their uniformed colleagues armed with pepper spray.

"Don't fire that shit, we're police!" Slug said politely, but they weren't going to have any of it. The fingers on the spray bottles were twitching, so Slug turned, crouched, and ran behind the sports car, reaching for his badge and gun as his did so. Then he extended his arm, holding his handgun, into the face of the young black officer who pursued him.

"Are you prepared to listen now?" Slug asked, eliciting a wary nod. "We are detectives and here is my identification. Would you like to see it?" Slug spoke slowly, with emphasis. The rookie recognised that he had indeed made a bad call as Slug's ID was flashed past his face.

Slug put his identification away as he climbed into the car. The road was clear for miles in front of their new Mercedes. Having checked that the two uniformed officers had abandoned their cause, Slug re-holstered his firearm and fired the engine. Tap had already taken his seat in the passenger side. The tyres squealed as the car roared off towards central London, destination Tottenham Court Road.

Stacey Payne had a quick shower while she was waiting for her bodyguard to turn up. Her flat felt like a prison now, a cell for her and André to hide in until their release date became clear. Work kept calling her, asking her for more of the same type of information with which she had supplied them yesterday, but unfortunately the material was not forthcoming at the moment. She hadn't been able to do a lot over the past sixteen hours or so, but had passed the time by making sure that André was clear about his sexual orientation. There wasn't anything else to do, really. Stacey was really angry with Tap: not only had he lumbered her with the youth, he had also failed to keep in touch with her regarding his own whereabouts, not to mention the whereabouts of Anthony Jenkins, or more importantly, what the killer had been up to since she had received her last instalment of the chaotic saga. Eventually she had got fed up with waiting and had made the call to Sid; she was going to get the missing pieces in the Anthony Jenkins jigsaw one way or the other!

Andre was entertaining himself with a play-station game as his host and teacher got herself ready. Slyly, the boy occasionally spied on her as she fluttered around the room. Fuck, she looked good! Although blonde-haired, she in no way resembled the stereotype, being very intelligent. The hair colour was not real; it was simply there to attract attention and help her get whatever information she required from the opposition. It usually worked very well, and it would work today, she felt sure. To go with it, she decided to dress in fuck-me style: fuck-me boots, fuck-me short skirt and fuck-me tight top with a leather coat to finish; and fuck me, did she look awesome! Good enough to extract information from the hardest policeman on the force. Sex sells; sex is magical; sex makes the world go around, especially the world in which Stacey Payne was involved. She would get a result she bragged to herself. It would be as easy as taking candy from a baby.

Immersed in the shower, she had not heard Tap's phone call. When she was ready, she decided to settle down to one last quick game on the play-station, after fixing herself a stiff drink, and so had forgotten to check her phone.

*

Tottenham Court Road was filled with police, more police that you could shake a stick at. Slug had called into the Yard and warned them that they were on their way, but for the first time in years they were encountering a situation that had gone way over their heads. The top-men were not happy with the way the last day's events had been handled, because there had been a lamentable lack of feedback from Billy Tap. Now, that in itself was not unusual, but this case was, and so common sense should have prevailed. But since it was Billy, he got a lot more leeway than most.

Pulling up at the health centre sent a shiver down Tap's spine. He had come down a bit now and the reality of what they were approaching had begun to sink in. Rather than being totally off his box, he was now very quiet, intensely nervous and clearly paranoid; maybe even remorseful. The gleaming sports car was the envy of all the policemen who controlled the area around the health centre. How the fuck those two had ended up in a car like this they would never know.

On the way, Slug had made numerous calls to men and women in the know, making them aware that they were on their way to Jenkins' latest crime scene. They had been investigating a lead out Buckinghamshire way, had got stuck out there and… it was a long story, and he didn't go into too much detail. He knew he would have to later on, he would be ordered to, but hopefully by then he and Tap would have had a chance to get their stories straight.

Slug was an angry man: angered by his colleague's performance, angered by the man who they chased and of course by the death of their colleagues. There was going to be payback for what Jenkins had done and Slug was no longer taking a back seat in the hunt. These were Slug's initial feelings as the two arrivals entered the health centre, and they were hugely intensified by the time they left. They didn't stay long, the scene was horrific. Slug didn't know how, but he knew that he was going to put a stop to it, and now. Tap had seen the carnage and put a brave face on it, but the suggestion that they leave came from him. His excuse to one of his superiors was that he was too closely linked to the two men, through friendship as well as professionally, and it was better left to someone more neutral to deal with the scene of crime stuff. They knew who had carried out the slaughter anyway, so there was no point in hanging around.

Tap's main interest was in the ballistics report. A team was sweeping the room now in order to find out what weapons had been fired, because he was hoping to be able to get some idea about Jenkins' remaining firepower. Three weapons had been found on or close to the site; that much had been established already. One was the stolen police sub-machine gun from back at the hospital and the other two were standard police-issue Glock's. This meant that Jenkins was armed with only the Browning at the minute, and his ammunition store was rapidly depleting. Slug told ballistics that they needed to know if any Browning shells had been found. There had been none so far, but it was still early in the investigation.

Naturally, Tap's bosses wanted some answers as to where the two men had been all night. Tap was cagey in his response, but promised that they had been on police work and currently had Jenkins in their sights. At that point, Slug interrupted his colleague, who looked extremely pale and ill, and apologised for their sudden need to leave but they had to follow up a lead straight away. As they left, Slug glanced around the scene once more for any clue as to where Jenkins' next destination would be. There was nothing though, nothing except the two bodies and A whole lot of blood. The words 'wrong' and that fucking stupid symbol on the wall didn't aid them one iota. In fact, it gave them about as much assistance as the rest of the blood that had plastered the whole room: walls, ceilings, floors, it was fucking everywhere.

Tap walked out before Slug had finished speaking to their superiors and Slug found himself having to explain to their top man that he was suffering from grief. His superior officer replied suspiciously that Tap looked more like he was pissed, which of course was nearer the truth.

Outside, Tap was looking at the blood on the ground that had been left by Jenkins' footprints. It led down into the tube station, although by the time the trail reached the top of the steps it was so faint as to be barely perceptible. Slug informed Tap that he had just promised their employer that they were going to get Jenkins that same day, and that by evening he would be in captivity. Tap simply laughed and asked just how he planned to do that.

"With plenty of black coffee, something to eat, and you stopping feeling sorry for yourself and getting your act together!" Slug replied firmly.

There was a coffee shop over the road that did an awesome English breakfast, so it seemed as good a place as any to start. The coffee shop was half empty, its few customers being mainly suits and a couple of old ladies. Tap had stared at everyone in the room, one at a time, in order to make sure that he wasn't sharing a restaurant with Anthony Jenkins again. Slug took the lead, and Tap listened for once.

"I tried Doughnut's phone again earlier, but there was no answer. Who were you ringing earlier when you left a message, was it that reporter girl?" Slug asked, thinking hard for any tiny little lead. Tap nodded.

"Couldn't get hold of her, but I only really wanted to check that she still had André with her - I don't want him running around on his own at the minute, going round my flat and shit, just in case Jenkins finds him. I've been avoiding her because I owe her a story on what's been going on lately and she's gonna give me a load of shit that I don't really need at the minute."

"Maybe I should give her a call, then, just in case there's a problem," Slug suggested. "Let's face it, our leads are basically fucking zero! We need to go and check out the phone shop as well, because there might be something there. Sid checked the scene last night, but he wouldn't have had chance to do a report. What do you reckon?"

Tap agreed that they didn't have much else to go on at the moment and handed his mobile phone to Slug so he could make the call.

"It's down as Lois Lane," Tap informed Slug, who was searching the phone's memory for the number. Slug scrolled through the numbers until he found the Ls, then slowed down until he found the one he required. Yes, there she was, Miss Payne! He pressed the button, and this time the call was answered.

"Billy?" Came a female voice, sounding out of breath. She had taken a while to answer the phone. Slug explained who he was and asked Stacey if she was OK, which she confirmed.

"Tap's here with me; he's just tying up a few loose ends," Slug lied.

"Is it to do with what happened at the health centre?" she asked, to Slug's amazement.

"How the fuck do you know about that?"

Tap snatched the phone out of his hand.

"Stacey, it's Tap. How did you know about that?"

Stacey told him that she had spoken to his boss, having rung Tap numerous times and received no answer, so she had rung Sid as a sort of third resort. This man had answered and said that he was…

"Who…?" Tap interrupted.

"Detective Mills, I think he said?"

"Detective Mills," Tap rolled the name around his head, looking at Slug, who shrugged. Neither of them had heard of a Mills in the hierarchy. The only Mills who Tap could think of was Haley Mills, Jenkins' girlfriend. The thought sent sudden shivers down his spine.

"What did he say, Stacey? It's very important."

Stacey repeated what the man had said to her, as best she could remember it.

"He said he was your boss, and I told him I was concerned that I couldn't get hold of you. I told him I really needed to get in touch with you urgently. I bigged it up that I was really concerned for my welfare because Jenkins is still running around and I'm responsible for a big story on him. I'll be honest, Billy, I ain't gonna lie to you, I was trying to get in with the police because I need more information. You promised me it and then…"

"Shut up!" Tap interrupted. "Did you tell this man where you are?"

"Yes!"

Tap swore down the phone.

"Get out of the flat now. Don't get your things, don't make yourself look pretty, you just get out of that flat now and you take André with you. I take it he's still there?"

Stacey promised that she would do as instructed, realising that, far from having police protection on the way to her, she was down in the snake pit. André was with her, she confirmed, in the front room. Tap suggested that she try and keep their little problem to themselves for the time being. But where should she go?

"Anywhere, anywhere that's full of people, the main thing is to get out of the flat before it's too late! Have you got a gun?" Tap asked.

"For fuck's sake, Billy I'm a reporter, not a fucking mercenary. I'm fucking pissed off with you, Billy. How could you put us in this position?" Stacey demanded.

"You put yourself in this position, Stacey, you and your thirst for knowledge. It'll be the death of you unless you do what I say, and do it now! We're on our way - we'll be at your place in ten minutes max. Don't wait for us, though, you hear?

Just get out of the fucking flat and run. I don't care where you go, you just fucking run, and when you get wherever it is that you're going, you tell me where you are."

With that, the phone went dead, indicating that Stacey was doing as she was told.

Billy Tap stood up.

"Come on, Stacey Payne's, quick!" He once again took charge of the situation. A lesser man than Slug would have been pissed off to be once again demoted, but he was just glad they were getting back on track. He had picked up on the gist of Tap's conversation with Stacey, swallowing his food hastily as he did so and washing it down with lashings of lukewarm coffee. It had become clear that the chase was now back on, so heaven knew when their next meal would be. Things were definitely looking up.

Tap chucked twenty quid across the counter to the prettier of the two waitresses. She was smiling seductively but he didn't even notice. He had things on his mind, dark, horrific things, a vision of Stacey Payne and André Bach being slaughtered. He nodded at the girls behind the counter and indicated with a point of the finger that they were to keep the change, then the two of them stepped out of the house of grease and into the street. Tap prayed that he wasn't psychic.

Chapter Ten

Cherubim Collide

The Merc was still warm from its last performance; you could hear components making a 'tinging' noise as they cooled down. Slug jumped in the car and lit its fire again with a turn of the key, causing the engine to roar. The destination was Stacey Payne's, and they needed to get there as fast as humanly possible. Although this car was limited to 155 miles per hour, that was not really an option through the centre of London. The traffic started to move a bit but soon came to a standstill again.

"Left here…!" Tap ordered. He stood up in the convertible, which had its roof down, directing the traffic with the use of the horn and the point of a finger in the absence of a blue flashing light. He didn't much care where he directed it, as long as it was out of their way as they cut right across everyone's path en route to the park.

"The park…!" Exclaimed Slug.

The car was no four-by-four but it had bags of low-end grunt and Slug used it, straight through the side of the park via an open gate. The traffic that they would have still been sitting in was to their right as they zoomed across the grass, scattering picnics and canoodling teenagers as they went. Fucking hell, Tap loved this job! They were making good time on their journey, but a huge metal fence presented an obstacle at their exit point. It was padlocked, so Tap took his handgun and fired one shot into the sky. This caused everyone to scream, but more importantly to move out of the way before he fired another shot at the padlock; then another, and another, until the chain fell free.

The once-gleaming, but at this time heavily panel damaged and filthy Mercedes now had a perfectly clear path ahead of it. Heavy metal gates do a beautiful machine like this no favours at all. Slug had to take his hat off to German engineering because even after hitting the gates at quite a high speed, she still drove a treat. Inevitably, after driving some distance with a total disregard for the law, sirens suddenly appeared behind them. As they approached Tap waved his badge about at the officers, only to realise that his firearm was still firmly gripped in his right hand. He rapidly switched it to his left and continued to wave his badge, but they were coming to the end of the footpath on which they were driving. While negotiating his way through the park, Slug had managed to make a call on his mobile telling head office what they were doing and asking for the cars now pursuing them to go ahead and clear a route for them to get through to Stacey Payne's address. This seemed to have worked beautifully, because as they came to the end of the footpath a gap in the traffic was being held open by the police car immediately ahead of them.

Tap still refused to be seated, but stood in the car like an ancient Greek in a chariot race, waving his arms and shouting the odds. The chase was back on.

After a little more than five minutes, the convoy suddenly stopped. It looked like someone had run into the road and was jumping about in front of the lead car.

"Fuck it we're nearly there, Slug. What the fuck's going on?"

Tap got out and walked over to the driver's side of the leading police car, where a man was speaking through the window to the driver. He stormed up to the man and demanded to know what the problem was. The man, who was smartly dressed, held up his hands defensively as if to indicate that he didn't want any trouble. He explained that there was a commotion going on nearby and…blah, blah blah.

Tap wasn't interested; he had no time to get involved with street crime. The man went on to explain that there had been gunshots, well, they sounded like gunshots, down there, through that alley, more than likely on the next street, though.

"People were screaming that someone had been shot. Look for yourself. Look at the people over there!"

It was probably nothing. They had received no calls regarding a shooting and so Tap walked passed his stolen vehicle and called the suit to follow him in order to pay a visit to the car that followed the silver beast. An ugly-looking copper wound his window down. Tap turned to his customer with an expression of regret.

"Look, I can't stop, I ain't got time, but these guys will take a look."

The policemen in the last car agreed with him - they would check out the man's concerns. With that sorted, Tap bid the good citizen farewell and hastened back to his own car, where he took up his previous standing position and waved the front car on.

The plan was to get to Stacey Payne's, get into her flat, take control and wait for our friend Jenkins to turn up. Imagine that: Tap and Slug sitting there on the sofa with a cup of coffee, Jenkins walks in and they had him this time, Tap was sure of it. He just hoped Jenkins wasn't already there.

*

Stacey Payne's flat looked quiet, very quiet, but then it usually did up there from right down at the bottom of the long staircase. Tap and his convoy had pulled up outside the small Victorian block of flats with the sirens switched off. These flats looked the part: if you had one of these, then either you had money or you'd bought at exactly the right time. In Stacey's case it was a bit of both.

Tap walked straight through the middle of the river of people flowing down the pavement. Starting with one side of the traffic, he told everyone to walk back from where they had come from; they were not permitted to walk in between the cars and the house.

"Go on, do one! Walk around the car. Go on, fuck off!"

People were stunned by such language from the tired-looking man, but they cottoned on quickly that there was probably a good reason for it and obeyed without Tap having to explain any further. The firearm in his right-hand might have also had something to do with it. Two uniformed officers wielding sub-machine guns held back the flow of human traffic and protected the access to the building. Slug pulled a frightening-looking handgun from his holster, removed the safety and then climbed up the stone stairs with his main-man beside him. The peak of the climb was well within their sights: that bright red front door ahead that allowed access to the flat. The two climbers were unsure if they were going to make it to the top of the stairs without meeting an ambush, which was one reason why they had created a clear run-up in the street, in case they had to bail out swiftly if the need arose.

The door was locked. Tap considered ringing the bell, but decided instead to search among the ivy to the left of the doorway for a key: he knew it was there somewhere because he had used it several times himself. Thankfully, there it was, but it had taken two minutes or so to find it. Tap began praying to no one in particular as he inserted the key in the lock. Bingo, the door opened.

There was no one waiting for them; at least, the coast seemed. Cautiously Tap and Slug entered the hallway. So far, so good. If there was going to be an ambush, Tap would expect it to be in the front room, putting himself in Jenkins' shoes. Slug shut the door behind them.

Tap could smell Stacey's scent in the hallway, although how he could smell anything after the amount of nose-candy he had inhaled that morning was anyone's guess. They checked out the bathroom first, Tap sitting on the floor directly in front of the door and reclining back. Slug then hid himself away from the door, along the bathroom wall. Tap nodded, Slug turned the handle, and then Tap kicked the door open with his foot while still leaning back as though halfway through a sit-up. There was no one there.

Slug peered into the bathroom cautiously, offering no more than his nose for target practice, but clearly there was no one hiding within his range of fire. He could see into the two far corners of the room by means of the mirror on the wall dead in front of them, just above the washbasin. Tap picked himself up off the floor and dusted himself off. He was not going to use the same method of attack for the front room, basically because it was too big and the approach would leave one of them exposed from both sides. Also, it was clear that if Jenkins was already in the front room he would be well hidden. There was also the main bedroom at the back and the kitchen to the left.

Oh well, in for a penny, in for a pound! Tap did what he did best, proving that he had more balls than sense. He simply walked towards the toilet, turned to face the front room door, pointed to the door handle and started his three-metre sprint. Slug knew the drill and opened the door as Tap reached it. There was no war cry, no words of warning; Tap simply stormed the front room with his faithful Glock. As Tap burst into the room, he seemed to spin in the air like a ballerina, checking out his surroundings as they whizzed past his eyes, before tripping over the coffee table and falling flat on his arse.

"Twat!" Commented Slug.

Tap was sprawled across the floor, one leg still on the coffee table and the other in a magazine rack.

Slug entered the room cautiously, his gun held high in front of him. Turning to the left, he sized up the kitchen area before jogging to the other side of the room and giving the bedroom the once-over. Thankfully, Jenkins wasn't there - not unless he was hiding under the bed with all the used underwear that seemed to be lying everywhere. Someone had obviously had a good time last night.

Slug sat on the bed for a while to allow the adrenaline to subside. He had to laugh as he watched Tap try to get up off his backside, removing the magazine rack from his foot before he did so.

"Lucky he weren't fucking in here!" Tap warned as he finally managed to stand, rolling his shoulders back and forth as he did so. Lucky for who, though, Slug was unsure.

"Jesus, man, I think I've broken my finger!" Tap exclaimed, studying his reddening hand. "I forgot about the fucking coffee table! That bloody hurt, you know that?"

Slug laughed.

"Good, perhaps you won't be such a silly boy in future then. Running in here like John fucking Wayne, you're lucky Jenkins wasn't in here, mate, or he'd have kicked your arse! But he isn't, so what's next then?"

"Well, we wait here for him I suppose, because he's got to be on his way. Stick the kettle on; let's have a lovely cup of Rosy. I tell you what though, mate, I've definitely fucked this finger. Do you reckon it's broken?"

"Are you going to ring Stacey, then?" Slug shouted from the kitchen as the kettle boiled in the background.

Tap reminded him that Stacey had said she was going to call him when she had found somewhere safe to hide. Just as Slug arrived back in the lounge with two cups of tea, his phone suddenly went off in his pocket. It was amazing how often that happened: Slug's theory was that the phone signals were picked up by our slowly-frying minds just before they reached the phone.

"Who is it?" Tap demanded as Slug took the phone out of his pocket.

It was Doughnut's wife, according to the display. What was Slug going to say to her? Obviously no one had told her yet and he wasn't going to be the one to do it, not this time, so he left the phone ringing.

The mood in the room turned sombre again as they sipped their tea. Then a noise on the stairs, a creaking noise, as of someone approaching, had the men slowly reaching across the coffee table for their weapons.

*

That was her: she'd said flat three. Who's that little fucker with her, though, her son? She was in good nick if it was, because he was at least fifteen years old. Pretty woman she was, very pretty, dressed nice too; sort of sexy, only a gnat's cock short of tarty. Her knee-length boots looked heavy as she tackled the stairs, holding her mini skirt down at the front until she had descended far enough. Once at the bottom of the stairwell, the woman swung her tartan bag across the shoulder of her fashionable leather coat and took the hand of the young man who followed her.

Less than a minute before, Jenkins had been walking around the corner of the flats where Stacey Payne lived. It was easy to see how he'd got this notion into his head that there was someone guiding him. He had actually been dithering about a bit outside and was just about to climb the stairs when, like a gift from above, the door started to open.

He had had his plan all worked out on his way there: he would walk to the door, ring the bell and Miss Payne would answer, simple. The only problem was that the paranoia had started again, now that the buzz of the last two murders had started to wear off. What if Tap and his boys were there now, in the flat? What if Tap was not out of town, but was actually with this Payne woman? What if he had made her call the fat boy's phone back in the hospital? Maybe Tap wanted those two coppers out of his way anyway, and Jenkins had fallen into his trap?

Instead of climbing up the stairs as he had intended, Jenkins tried to act casually as Stacey passed him coming out of the flats and walked directly across the road as if nothing had happened. To say that he was shitting it would be an understatement, because he half expected Tap to be running down those stairs after him any minute now, guns blazing. Jenkins waited for policemen to pile out of their unmarked cars, to jump out from alleys and shops, but they didn't - there was no one. The shock of what could have been caused Jenkins to double up in pain, his throat feeling as if it would explode any minute. He had some serious respiratory issues to contend with, having held his breath unconsciously. He had medicated his aching body en route to Stacey's flat, which was just about enabling him to hold it together.

He mounted the pavement through a gap between two parked cars that shouldn't have been there. The mass that had built up in Jenkins' tortured throat, thanks to the sudden flood of air entering his dying lungs, had to be disposed of, because it was not welcome. The sticky solution had to be deposited somewhere, checking that no one was behind him, Jenkins released the concoction of bodily fluids from his mouth with a swift, heavy projection.

Stacey had paraded down the stairs like a queen, with André following. He seemed unaffected by what was going on around him, probably because he had no idea. As far as he was concerned, Stacey was taking him to meet up with his lover again. Stacey was a very attractive woman and a few pedestrians watched her negotiate the stairs down from her flat in the hope that her short skirt would blow up, well, there was always the chance! Jenkins, though, wasn't interested at the prospect of a flash of panties; her clothing and accessories would only please him once they had been sliced with his knife and stained with the blood from her wounds. That was what he was going to do: slice Stacey Payne up with a knife; slice her up until she drew her last breath. Tap had done well for himself; Stacey Payne was a beautiful woman, all the more fun for him in relieving Tap of her. The kid was going to have to go too - fuck knows who he was - but it didn't really matter because when Stacey Payne got it, then so did her luggage. He hoped Tap and Stacey were married, but he doubted it. It seemed improbable. Although innocent in terms of his cause, she provided Jenkins with a means of getting at Billy Tap, just as he would use Haley to get at Jenkins. Shit, Haley, time was moving on, he reminded himself. He would have to call home again soon, he had tried twice earlier on, but there had been no answer.

With this thought now in his head, he reached for his phone in his pocket. As he did so, he never took his eye off Stacey Payne and her blond companion as they walked hand-in-hand along the pavement in the same direction as Jenkins, although they stayed on the other side of the road. He walked as slowly as he could in order to remain as far away as possible from his subject. She looked nervous, but was clearly doing her best to hide it from the youngster who held her hand.

He took his eye off his target for a few seconds, just long enough to allow him to select a number from the phone's address book. The mobile back at the flat rang, but no one answered. Jenkins spat foul language through his teeth. This was bad, no news was definitely bad news on this occasion. He kept the phone in his hand for a while as he continued to follow his subject, fuck, did she walk fast - but then she was shitting-bricks by the look of things. She skipped across the urban highway and right into Jenkins' path. This was good, because she obviously hadn't recognised him. Suddenly, his phone rang and Stacey looked round, but paid no attention as he answered it.

"All right, calm down, take some deep breaths - now what's the matter?" Jenkins asked.

"Knocking at the door, about two minutes ago, I could hear them trying to open it, fucking hell, someone's trying to get in the fucking place, and…"

Sarah was not making much sense, a little, but not a lot. Jenkins asked his ally to slow down and take a breath. Which door? At first, he assumed that Sarah meant Leigh Anderson's front door, the door to the pretty white flat that she had left behind in favour of a few weeks in the sun. He thought about it, it couldn't be Leigh Anderson returning early because she would have been able to unlock the front door of her flat and walk straight in, so whoever was knocking was clearly knocking at Gordon's door.

By now, Gordon had started to pen and ink, Sarah had actually mentioned the smell coming from the dead man's bedroom and through into their flat via the new doorway that Jenkins had created between the two residences. When the bedroom door was shut, all was well, but the smell recurred every time Anthony visited Gordon for a chat. Sarah had suggested that the hole be blocked up, and Jenkins had finally agreed because he had found a spare front door key while rooting through Leigh Anderson's things. That meant that he could activate the dead-locks on Gordon's front door, barricading his usual access, and he was able to use his own front door at last.

"What door are they knocking on, Sarah?" Jenkins asked calmly.

Sarah didn't realise the relevance of the question at first; did it fucking matter as long as it was one of theirs? It did, actually, so he asked again.

"Which door was it, Sarah?"

After some thought, she replied that they'd been knocking on both doors.

"Okay, which one did they knock on first? Think it's important!"

Jenkins paused the conversation momentarily. Stacey had just walked across the road, looking back to make sure she wasn't being followed. She must have been satisfied that she wasn't, because she turned left and continued down the pavement. She hadn't clocked him; that was for sure, otherwise she would have panicked. She seemed a little calmer now as she walked with her young friend, their arms linked. She probably thought that every step she took along this filthy pavement carried her further away from the danger of which she had been warned: little did she know that her destiny was barely twenty paces behind her, the phone still glued to his ear.

"Sorry about that. Which door, Sarah?" Jenkins asked again as he reached the other side of the pavement before turning off in pursuit of his quarry. The answer was exactly what he had envisaged: someone had been knocking on Gordon's door. The only problem was that Gordon wasn't in - he was in heaven, or wherever, and whoever was knocking on his door was probably one of the very same people who was going to be arguing over his possessions in the not-so-distant future. Then again, it could have been a postman, someone to read the gas meter or a Jehovah's Witness.

Sarah also told him that Haley's condition appeared to have deteriorated. She couldn't say what was wrong, because she didn't have the medical knowledge.

"How bad…?" Jenkins asked, with little hope in his voice. The answer was what he expected: she was very bad. She was coughing a lot, with blood and all. She looked blue in colour, had been sick a few times and seemed in pain. Although Sarah had no real medical training, she couldn't see Haley lasting the day, but she didn't dare say this to Jenkins.

"I'll be home real soon," he said. "I've just got a little something to attend to - half an hour, max."

It was time to teach Tap a lesson! He quickened his pace, as he had some ground to make up.

His subject turned all of a sudden to check out her surroundings. She saw behind her the same man who had been talking on his phone earlier. This small individual with the baseball cap had taken exactly the same route as her. He didn't look right: he was unshaven and dressed all in black apart from his jeans. Stacey turned back casually as if she had not noticed anything untoward, although her pace speeded up considerably. André noticed, and looked up to her for reassurance. She smiled at him, but her grip on his elbow strengthened.

"Just walk a little faster André, please. And don't look back," she added as he glanced behind them. But he had seen enough. They were obviously being followed by that weirdo in the baseball cap.

"Who is he?" He asked.

Stacey said she didn't know, probably just some perv eyeing her up from behind. It happened a lot, she said.

She suddenly had the idea of going into a shop, there would be people in it and she could call Tap to come and rescue them. André nearly tripped when Stacey suddenly changed direction, heading across a huge pedestrianised area leading to a number of very fashionable-looking shops. The shoe shop, next to the launderette, looked the best bet, because it had two sales assistants. The bell rang as the two of them walked through the front door of the shop, which was situated on the left hand side of the establishment with a large bay window on the other side. Stacey offered a fake smile to the two assistants. One of them was thin - Stacey wouldn't go as far to say pretty, but she had a fashionable figure and was blonde, so men probably found her attractive. The other assistant was moving shit about behind the counter, obviously doing nothing but trying to look busy. The one behind the counter, more sturdy in build, looked lazy and didn't respond to Stacey's courteous smile.

The shop was very arty-farty, with shoes around the walls from either side of the counter. A seating arrangement filled the middle of the floor. The counter was on the left–hand side of the shop, with a door behind it leading to the back room.

Stacey said 'hello' to one of the assistants, who was now hovering around her like a fly on shit, taking her eye off her victim only once to glance at the agitated-looking man who was pacing up and down the frontage of the shop.

"He can come in and wait, you know?" Kate offered, her badge having given away her name. She obviously assumed that Stacey and the man outside were together.

"No no, he can't come in, don't let him in, he's been following me. Listen carefully I need you to call the police for me. Ask for a man called Sergeant Tap, quick though, because if I go out there I'm dead!" Stacey gibbered.

The bloke outside was by now staring in through the window. What was this fucking woman doing bringing her dirty laundry in here, for fucks sake - the laundrette was next door!

"Ring him, please, Detective Sergeant Tap, quickly!" Stacey whispered urgently as she lay a hand on the other assistant's arm and gently but firmly guided her towards a rack of shoes on the far wall. She proceeded to point to various items of footwear, pretending to be engrossed, but although she had her back to the door, she still knew exactly when it swung open and her life flashed before her eyes.

*

Jenkins had felt as agitated as he looked, standing there outside the shoe shop. People had been starting to notice him acting strangely, so a decision had to be made. Still looking through the window, he formulated a plan of sorts. The boy was seated on some kind of footstool and the woman was looking at shoes. The assistant with her kept bending down to point out various styles, and every time she bent down, her underwear was exposed above the waistband of her trousers. Why didn't women's trousers fit any more? Jenkins wondered vaguely. Was it fashionable to show your pants off these days? The other sales assistant had suddenly disappeared, but she had been there a minute before. Oh, there she was, Jenkins could see her head now, just level with the counter. She seemed to be hiding. Phone, that's what she was doing, using the phone to call the police. He had to act fast.

Undoing his leather jacket and thereby revealing a white T shirt emblazoned across the front with the words 'Porn Star' - another of Leigh Anderson's fashion items, he pulled the handgun from the waistband of his jeans. In addition to this, the knife was, as always, located in its makeshift sheath in an inside pocket of the jacket.

The door swung open with force, the Browning automatic poised to kill in Jenkins' outstretched arm. A pull of the trigger dispensed a bullet that sent the sturdy shop assistant, who had just stood up in surprise from behind the counter, hurtling backwards as the flying metal hit her squarely in the chest. Her body wiped out an entire shoe rack before coming to rest on the floor, grunting and shaking. This was no clean, Hollywood-style death: this was real. The girl was spitting and gargling blood, and there was a fountain of it pumping steadily from her chest, which had been torn wide open. Panting like a dog after a hard run, she had only seconds left.

Jenkins couldn't see his victim and didn't even bother looking for her behind the counter. He was in killer mode now, and looking around to see who was next. Kate tried to run before the next shot rang out, but not quickly enough. Jenkins went for a head shot this time, a clean kill, with no choking, gargling and all that palaver to piss him off. The bullet went straight into the side of her head. It never ceased to amaze him how much mess such a tiny piece of metal could make once it had made contact with the human body. Stacey, who had been standing right next to Kate, was now frantically screaming as she tried to wipe away the mess from her face and chest. The hot, sticky fluids had hit her in the head and chest and were now dripping down inside the collar of her jacket to soak her V-necked white top underneath.

This was horrific, this was fucking gross: but the twitching, almost headless corpse at which she now stared at in disbelief was even worse. Geysers of red fluid sprang up from various parts of the open skull, jellifying as it came into contact with the air.

It appeared that André was next on the agenda, as Jenkins wedged the gun inside his wide-open mouth and pulled the trigger. Shit! It didn't go off! Fucking thing was jammed or something.

"Bastard...!" He swore as he pulled the weapon from the youth's mouth and swung out with a fist into the boy's face. The youth fell sideways and slumped onto the seat. *Fuck it - they do this, don't they, bloody guns?* Anthony remembered something he had seen in the movies. *Yeah, that's right – they do that if they're not looked after!* A dirty gun will not perform, and this gun was fucking filthy. Jenkins pulled the sliding block on the top of the weapon back and then forced it forward again. It was jammed; something was stuck. An intact bullet fell out. Looked like he was just going to have to wing it. With the blockage removed, and therefore wasted, Jenkins pulled the youth up from his prone position, his top lip swollen and his teeth blood stained.

"Open your mouth!" Jenkins ordered, and André obeyed, his blue eyes looking up pleadingly into the killers'.

Jenkins pulled the trigger and the now-familiar sound filled the room as a chunk of blond-haired scalp swung up from behind the youth's skull, brushing Jenkins' hand as it did so before falling back down to where it belonged. The only problem was that where it belonged was no longer there; it was missing. Shoes sat on their rails filled with the youth's brains and the blond skull-cap changed its colour to red, having dropped into the brainless skull.

It was too much for Stacey. She wanted to scream, but no sound was coming out of her mouth. Both she and Jenkins seemed to have frozen momentarily, as if he had suddenly realised what he was doing. Had rage taken him over to the point where he didn't really know what he was doing any more, or was he simply insane, or just pure evil? He didn't know. He felt a sort of remorse, but he ignored it. Heroin would assist with that once he had finished his work.

With the three innocent victims out of the way, it was time to start with the one he had really come for. For some reason he felt compelled to say a few words before he killed her. After all, what was the point in doing it if she didn't know why? She had brought all this trouble upon herself by being Tap's girlfriend, and so she had to be verbally reprimanded for that at the very least, before she was silenced for eternity.

He swapped the Browning automatic from his right hand to his left and took out the knife.

"Are you married?" He asked, staring at the sharp edge of the knife which he had held up to his face for examination.

A terrified shake of the head confirmed her single status. Her eyes were streaming with tears, which rolled down her blood stained cheeks. She was standing totally rigid with her hands at her sides as if she had given up. No one was going to save her now: not one of the idiots who were peering through the window to see what all the gunfire was about, not Tap, no one.

"Why you got a ring on then?" Jenkins asked as he walked over to the window and looked out at the amassing crowds. For a laugh, he opened the door, waved the gun about and then stood there laughing as he watched the crowd of about ten or twelve people 'do one' at a pretty impressive rate. They were fucking brilliant these guns, priceless for their entertainment value alone!

He locked the door before returning to his work, knowing he had to get on with it. Stacey's answer to his question was muffled by snot and drying blood.

"So I don't get hassle from men," she sobbed.

Jenkins nodded his head understandingly.

"Oh yeah, Tap wouldn't like a lady of his getting pestered. I'm not pestering you, am I?"

Stacey shook her head mutely, since 'about to murder' and 'pester' were two different things.

"Billy's pestering my girlfriend, you know. He's trying to stop me looking after her. I've gone out of my way to make sure she's comfortable, she's ill you see, as you probably already know, but he won't allow me the courtesy of my girlfriend not being pestered, and that's not fair now, is it? Is it?" he repeated when he got no response.

"This isn't fair either, Anthony, what you've done, is it?" Stacey asked recklessly, feeling that she had nothing to lose now. "I mean, why these girls? Why André? Why me? What's your problem? How are we connected to you and your girlfriend? Your problem is with Tap!"

Jenkins laughed, because Stacey had just hit the nail on the head.

"That's it, you see. You think I'm the bad person, but what about your Tap? He wishes harm on my loved one, the man said as much himself, he's warned me what he's going to do to her when he finds her. See, he thinks he's going to stop me doing what I have to do in order to keep her alive, but he won't. And as I think I've proved, I'll do anything to carry out my purpose, anything! See, the tables have turned now, haven't they, because now I have you and I'm going to do you harm because it's an eye for an eye, love. I've just beaten Tap to the golden prize, that's all, because I fucking got you first!" his voice rose to an insane scream.

The audience had gathered outside again, peering through the window. Jenkins would have liked to shoot them, but ammunition was now a precious commodity. He had expected Stacey to be frantic with fear now, but the cheeky fucking bitch was actually laughing.

"You find it funny, do you?" He asked, gripping her by her thin cotton top and making sure that her bra was within his grip as he pulled the bundle of material towards him. He ran the knife down the scrunched-up clothing, top to bottom, struggling only slightly with the underwire of her bra. The knife sliced through the cloth, lace and thin metal like butter, leaving the woman's breasts partially exposed. Jenkins wasn't interested in a cheap thrill, however, he just wanted to see what he was about to open. The silver ornamental ring in the woman's belly button was a good place to start.

Stacey suddenly laughed no more as it became clear what was about to happen to her.

"Wait, wait, wait…!" She begged as Jenkins stared at nothing but what he intended to rip out: the belly button, with the ring still attached. This was going to be a nice present for Tap; he could put it in a little box, like the ones jewellery comes in.

"You want Tap's girlfriend, do you?" Stacey threw her cards on the table.

Jenkins hesitated. Was she just stalling for time? Deciding she was, he pushed her backwards onto the footstool where she landed with a thud.

"It's not me!" She screamed, arching backwards as he put the knife to her stomach as if he were about to carve the Christmas turkey. But curiosity was too much for him and he stopped: he simply had to find out what she was talking about.

"You want to know who Tap's lover is?" She asked quickly, when Jenkins allowed her to sit up, albeit with the knife held to her throat. "He's there!" She exclaimed, pointing down at the blond boy upon the floor.

Jenkins was stunned: Tap, a bender, a batty boy, it didn't make sense. This was so fucked up that it was surely the last thing you would come up with at the point of death. And if it was a lie, a last ditch attempt to save herself from the man who was about to hack chunks out of her, then Miss Payne deserved to live because that was a top call.

Stacey had expected to have to explain matters further, to plead her case to the jury, but it seemed there was no need. Jenkins just stared at the boy in disbelief. The kid didn't look queer, he looked normal, but then Tap didn't look queer either. He looked like a ladies-man, if anything. Jenkins was not unfamiliar with the world of homosexuality, after all, he had grown up in the arsehole of London, had walked through Compton Street nearly every day, he had gay friends, probably! But this newsflash was a genuine shock to him, especially as he had thought he was the one running this show. Clearly, he was not. His shock was tinged with relief that he had actually achieved one of his goals after all, Tap's lover was dead, even though it hadn't gone according to plan.

"You didn't know, did you?" Stacey asked.

Jenkins shook his head as he put the knife away in his jacket.

"Where do we go from here, then?" She persisted, greatly daring but a little more confident now that the knife had gone.

Jenkins remained silent as he stared down at the corpse. He turned to look at her.

"Nothing has changed," he said expressionlessly. He had to kill her; it would be unfair not to, now that the others were dead. What made her so special that she should live?

"I can help you!" Stacey blurted out desperately. "You said yourself that Tap was making you out to be the bad person, when we all know he's no angel. He's drawing you into this conflict, threatening your girlfriend. I can help you. I can show the world that there's more to you than the police want people to believe. I'm a reporter, we can do an exclusive interview and you can tell the world your side of the story. You owe this to yourself, Anthony you owe it to your girlfriend."

She was hoping that her desperate bid would save her life, not to mention give her the story of the decade. Even now, half naked, within the grasp of the most wanted man in Britain, she was still chasing the big story.

AJ paced the room, taking a moment to look through the window where the crowds were growing. The police were surely on their way, so it was time to take care of business one way or the other.

"What paper do you work for?" He asked, casually swapping his gun from his left hand to his right.

Stacey named one of the biggest of the nationals, and he nodded in apparent agreement, as though impressed. In fact he had noticed that this paper seemed to have been disclosing his antics a little sooner than the rest and there could only be one reason for the fact that they were hours ahead of all the other Fleet Street rags.

"Tap's been feeding you the information about me then?" He asked, already knowing the answer.

Stacey felt no need to lie; this was what had happened. Jenkins again nodded his head as he turned back to his victim and smiled in a way that would frighten even the hardest of cases, the image enhanced by the weapon grasped firmly in his hand.

"That would be nice, wouldn't it? Me, and you on the front page, taking on the world, imagine that, fantastic. I could tell the world all about me, and you, well you'd be made for life. Only trouble is I haven't got a life, you see, so why would I want to tell people about the life that I'll soon be leaving behind? I'll be gone, done and dusted, because they won't let me live. I'm done for!" Jenkins spoke the truth because Tap wasn't going to let him live; it simply wasn't an option.

Rubbing her head to help her think straight, Stacey tried to persuade him that this would not be the case. Tap was a nut-case, yeah, but he wasn't a murderer, not as far as she knew, anyway. In any case, if he did think something was going to happen to him, wouldn't it be better to tell his story as soon as possible? Jenkins laughed.

"Okay Stacey, we'll make that front page together; we'll show the world what me and you are made of, then."

Stacey smiled; she had the bastard, he had fallen into her trap like most men did. They just couldn't resist. But she had underestimated her foe, the man who she had scorned in the national press. Millions of people now saw him in a worse light than they would otherwise have done, thanks to her reporting. He couldn't let that go unpunished, no way!

"I'll make a deal with you, Stacey," Jenkins said chattily, pushing André's body off the footstool so he could sit down beside her. It seemed that the only dry places left to sit were those that had been protected by the felled bodies, and he was getting a bit sick of having to change his clothes all the time. He reached out with his left hand towards the woman's half-naked chest and a faint smile appeared on her pretty face as he softly touched one of her breasts – maybe all he wanted to do was fiddle about with her a bit. His hand moved downwards towards her nether regions. She didn't know where he was going or how far he wanted to go, but as far as she was concerned he could take her out to the back room and fuck her for all she cared, as long as he let her live and she got the story.

Jenkins was well aware that he had permission to explore: this little whore was a rancid piece of dirt with 'fuck me' written all over her, but Jenkins wasn't interested in sex. After all, why have sex when you've already reached the ultimate orgasm, courtesy of the art of murder! Jenkins had crossed the line some time back. Now he fondled Stacey's ornamental ring which sparkled in the artificial light, then stood as if he intended to get closer to her. Stacey had had her guard down and he grabbed her throat with menace, spitting through gritted teeth to make it abundantly clear that any deal was off. Stacey panicked now that the monster had turned on her and started kicking her legs in an attempt to fight off her attacker. She was a very supple young woman and managed to catch the psychopath on the side of his head a few times with one of her fuck-me boots; not hard, but just enough to set off the chain reaction. Jenkins stepped back; he was playing games no more as he aimed his beloved handgun at Stacey's belly button, adorned by the silver ring, and fired one shot at the target.

"Have that, you fucking bitch!"

Stacey gave one loud scream which seemed to draw the cry into her rather than send it hurtling around the shop. Stacey's body automatically curled up into a half sit-up before slumping back down again. Her belly button was gone; it had imploded into her stomach. There was a hole where it had been before it disappeared, about the size of an egg, but there was not much blood. All the layers of muscle that had made up Stacey's near-perfect belly had sort of burst like a sausage does when the skin splits. Pain had now started to take over from the initial shock of the wound and Stacey stared up at the man who had shot her as he leaned over, proud of his work. Lowering his face to within an in inch of hers, he spoke.

"You've got your wish then, Stacey, front page news it is; just me and you girl. You didn't think I was stupid enough to fall for your bullshit, did you? That's the problem with you lot; because I do what I do, you all think I'm stupid. Yet none of you can stop me, let alone fucking catch me. You hear that? That's sirens; the police are on their way. So what do they do? They fucking tell me in advance! Now that's fucking stupid, Stacey, isn't it? Anyway, I'd better dash but I'll make another deal with you, yeah? If you survive that, then I'll do your story, okay? Yeah, just hold on baby. I don't think you'll make it, but you never know. Either way you've got front page news, girl, because you deserve it! Anyway, bye for now and I hope we meet again. Oh, and no hard feelings!" He joked as he made his way across to the counter at the other side of the shop.

To keep Sarah at home in her position of trust, Jenkins was going to have to give her what he had promised, more cash, which seemed the only language that she spoke. These shoes may have been posh, but business seemed to have been slow today and there was little over a grand in the till. What was that - four pairs of shoes at the most? It was better than a kick in the bollocks though, so he took the money out of the till.

Now, having shot everyone and robbed the place, it was probably a good time to leave. A turn of the back door handle confirmed that it wasn't locked, but he left it ajar for now and jogged back through the river of blood to retrieve a mirror, complete with its stand. Taking care not to slip, he smiled and winked at his only victim still alive. Stacey had no idea why he was taking a mirror across to the back door but she was more concerned about staying alive for now.

He positioned the mirror in front of the back door so that when it was opened, it would allow him to see inside the back room without being exposed. The back room was empty, except for shoes. This was good; there was probably a safe in here somewhere but unfortunately there was no time to find and empty it, nor was there anyone left alive who could help him with that. Never mind, the back door to the outer world was in sight. Jenkins made his walk to freedom.

Stacey was in a lot of pain now: her stomach hurt and she couldn't move her legs. When she tried to a trickle of blood flowed from somewhere near her spinal cord and down the edge of the footstool. She needed to force her back down onto the padding of the seat to restrict the flow of blood; the bullet had obviously passed through her body and was probably lodged in the seat somewhere.

The sound of police sirens filled the air; she hoped there was an ambulance with them. As the time ticked away, the pain increased. Foolishly, she tried to tense her stomach muscles but that caused all hell to break loose inside and she felt something give way, the pain simultaneously doubling in its intensity. There didn't seem to be much blood coming out of the hole at the front, but judging by the amount of blood pooling on the floor it was all dripping out of the back. Tiring of the situation, she started to feel weaker and weaker as the minutes moved swiftly on. Was it cold today? She couldn't remember, but she assumed it was because there was definitely a chill in the air that was sweeping right through her.

There was a commotion at the front door, which was locked. Stacey's eyes were half closed as she watched them shatter the glass. She wanted to watch her saviours arrive but her vision was blurred. She could feel people lift her arms, feel her pulse and pull at her eyelids, blinding her with a light. She was weak and tired; she just needed a rest that was all, just a few minutes. She would be okay then, she would just let them do their work - work their magic, and then they would wake her. That's what they do, you see; they wake you when the worst bit's over.

*

"Hello?" Asked a nervous voice as its owner reached the top of the stairs.

There was no reply except for the sound of a gun being loaded.

"Come in," said Slug. The uniformed officer was welcome and was waved into the room once a visual check had confirmed that he was what he seemed. Stranger things had happened that week. The uniform, complete with moustache, was definitely the real thing. He had been nicknamed Tache, for obvious reasons in the hour since Tap and Slug had made his acquaintance.

"All clear then?" The newcomer asked.

Tap met the question with an expressionless stare: if it hadn't been clear, the place would be strewn with bodies. He was playing with his finger, which still hurt. He held it up in the air and asked Tache whether you could still move your finger if it was broken. Tache had no idea. The finger did look sore, though, all red and swollen.

"What can we do for you, then?" Slug asked after taking a sip of his tea.

It was not tea and biscuits today, but tea and cocaine. Tap had talked his sidekick into it, persuading him that they had to remain alert and cocaine was the best thing for the job. Tache had some news, and he was bursting with self-importance.

"You know squad sixteen?" he asked. Since this question was met with blank looks, he went on to explain. "The car that was following us, that went off to take care of that business down the road?"

Slug nodded.

"Well, we've just had a call in from squad sixteen and they're currently surrounding a shoe shop just around the corner from here. Four shots have been fired inside the building, according to eyewitnesses. SO19 are waiting for your permission to storm the building. Word has it that your man is in there, this Jenkins feller, and they need you down there as quick as possible."

Tap's face had brightened at the mention of the word "surrounding," but had become grim again on hearing of the gunshots. Four gunshots meant death. Jenkins was in this neck of the woods to do one thing, and one thing only, and that was to find Stacey Payne and teach Tap a lesson.

"If it's Jenkins who's responsible, then he won't be there now. Four gunshots means four dead people. He'll be long gone; he's too clever to stay around. Did the eyewitness say who was in the shop? Say, for instance, a blond girl mid-twenties or a young chap, eighteen-ish?" Tap asked.

Tache didn't know, and neither did anyone else as yet. The quicker Tap got down there, the quicker they would all know. Tap took out his phone and flicked through the list of numbers, blocking out thoughts of what might have happened to André, and, somewhat less importantly, to Stacey. He wasn't too upset because he had always kept them at arm's length emotionally: the relationship he had with each of them was no more than an arrangement for their mutual gratification, based on Tap getting sex in exchange for information, or in the case of André, for helping him get established in London. They had become fond of one another though, he couldn't deny that.

Jenkins was down in the phone's memory as Jenkins 3, which was the third phone number from which he had called Tap during their great chase. He selected the number. The phone rang and Jenkins answered almost immediately. He didn't speak, but remained silent in the hope of intimidating Tap. It didn't' work. Tap listened carefully to the silence, hearing traffic in the background, cars and shit, police sirens, possibly an ambulance, Jenkins was close by but, more importantly, he wasn't trapped inside that shop.

"What you been up to in the shoe shop, Anthony?" He asked casually. "What's all that about, eh? You should be home with us, mate, with me and Haley, not taking the bait like a fucking amateur! Come home to Daddy, your comeuppance awaits you!" He taunted before cutting the line dead.

His theory was simple: Jenkins was at the shoe shop, or had been, therefore was almost certainly still in the vicinity. That meant that he wasn't wherever his sweetheart was, because she was over the other side of the city. He had deduced that from the fact that the majority of the other killings had taken place over there and he was betting that Jenkins had carried those out on his home ground, where he felt more secure. Tap knew he was playing a game of guesswork, and he knew that Stacey was probably dead because Jenkins had targeted her as his girlfriend. That just left Haley: the object of both men's desires now, although for different reasons. Haley was the ultimate prize now and the race was on to claim her. The only trouble was he had no idea where she was hidden. Jenkins would be heading back to the nest now.

Jenkins was growing complacent now, Tap reasoned, and this would be his downfall. He had become the hunter now rather than the hunted, but his target had shifted from society in general to Billy Tap in particular. Jenkins had become disillusioned; his hate had now made him dangerous. Tap knew that Jenkins was beginning to lose the plot completely, the savageness of his killings were evidence of that. All he could do was tease him, enrage him, draw him onwards by bluffing and hope he would fall into the trap and let something slip.

"Raid the shop!" Tap ordered as his phone started to rang. It was Jenkins, so he left it ringing to antagonise him further.

"Storm the shop; approval gained from DS William Tap!" said Tache into his radio. Now they just had to wait until SO19 had worked their magic.

Tap recalled that Jenkins' breathing had sounded pretty rough on the phone, and shared this information with Slug.

"Good, hope the cunt dies!" was Slug's response.

But Tap didn't want Jenkins to die, not just yet.

"When he dies, it will be from me putting a fucking bullet into his head, Slug, and not from natural bloody causes. Jenkins is mine, mate, all mine, so let's go and find him!"

"Okay then, where do we start?"

"What's the only crime scene we aint visited yet?" Tap asked cryptically.

"The phone shop…' How's that going to help us?"

"It's the only place we haven't checked out ourselves. That place is significant, I don't know why, I just have this feeling - you know? Besides, we've got fuck all other leads now, have we? He'll be long gone from the shoe shop by now, I know that much. Fucking shoe shop, only Stacey could have gone shopping for shoes at a time like this!"

"Aren't we going to check it out, though?" Asked Slug.

"Okay, we'll go to the shoe shop first, but I ain't going in there. I've seen enough blood and guts for a few days, and I'm only interested in ballistics reports. I want to find empty shells, four of them, preferably. I bet you any money that the bullet casings we find will have been fired from a Browning automatic, and that's all we need to know, Slug."

Jenkins' armoury was depleting fast and that could only be good news.

*

"It's only round the corner, Slug we might as well leave the fucking car here. Won't be able to park it anyway, look at the fucking traffic!"

The two detectives made their way down the steps that led to Stacey Payne's flat. Tap hadn't even bothered asking if there were any survivors on the scene at the shoe shop, because there weren't usually when Jenkins had been around. People stared at them in awe; they were obviously the police, but they didn't have uniforms so they must be something special. Tache and a colleague went ahead, creating a path down which Tap and Slug could walk without having to rub shoulders with the little people whom they protected. Tache pointed across the road and to the left, just in case Slug had forgotten, which he hadn't, despite the fact that he was deeply engrossed in a telephone conversation.

Slug was obeying instructions and phoning the officer currently in charge on the site of the shoe shop massacres. His demands were straightforward: locate the shells, not the bullets, because they'd be there all fucking day finding those, just the shells. Also, he was to confirm whether there had been four gunshots: this was very important, and Slug emphasised the point both with his words and the altered tone of his voice. It would also come in handy, Slug suggested, if they could find out what Jenkins was wearing. Someone must have seen him.

Jenkins had left the shoe shop via the back door and had found himself in a small courtyard at the back of the shop. At the other end of the courtyard lay a gate, which would have been an ideal exit point, but it wasn't to be. A roof partially covered the courtyard but for the last two metres or so at the back end where the gate and far wall lay. As he was about to open the gate, which was already slightly open, a car was heard screeching to a halt on the other side of the fence. A car door opened, emitting the sound of a police radio.

It was the enemy: the army sent in to put a stop to Anthony Jenkins' nonsense. How many bullets did he have left? He regretted the ones he'd wasted on taking casual pot-shots, but it was too late for that now. Jenkins made a mental note to try and recap when he got chance and remember, if he could, how many times he'd fired the Browning. Rations were short now and a police shoot-out would render him bullet-less, which was not a good way to be. He remembered something he'd heard once: a good soldier fights with his brain rather than his brawn. Words of wisdom indeed. He could out-fox the police: he had done it before and he would do it again.

Whatever he did, he would have to do it quick. He jumped into the nearest of two large metal containers behind the laundrette. They seemed to be filled with stinking bed sheets and were at least six feet tall; industrial-sized containers, in fact. They had obviously been delivered by a truck or something and were probably from a hotel. Whatever it was, it had a lot of beds, or a lot of people shitting them up.

Frantic feet could be heard outside the laundry container; that would be the police sizing up their assault on the back entrance. From what Jenkins could make out, there were three men out there. The man leading the firearms unit was unsure whether their target had vacated the premises yet. Jenkins lay silently in the well of sheets, listening. It seemed they were assuming he had already got away.

"That bastard was always one step ahead!"

He swelled with pride: it was nice to be appreciated from time to time. The situation outside the container was tense, but inside all was calm and tranquil. He stayed out of sight under a bed sheet where it was safe and warm. It became even warmer when he carefully heated the bottom of his trusty light-bulb with a cigarette lighter in order to administer his medicine, apparently oblivious of the fire hazard.

Cooking up the wonderful golden brown powder reminded him momentarily of the double-crossing fuckers who had sold it to him, he'd have to pay them a visit at some point, although they'd probably had no choice anyway. He tugged away on the top of the light bulb as he heard the three officers talking outside.

"Alpha one, proceed with caution, shop front secure. Repeat, officers inside building, proceed with caution!"

In other words: 'your buddies are already in the shop and so don't go blowing the fuck out of them. Leave that for someone innocent, someone reaching down to scratch their arse or something.'

The two armed officers made their assault on the building while their senior covered their backs.

Jenkins put the lukewarm light bulb back in his pocket. He was chilled out; sleepy. He shouldn't have a care in the world, but he had, more than one, it was fair to say! The gear was strong but he was determined not to render himself in a coma for the rest of the day and sleep through all this mayhem. He had had just enough powder to take away the pain that had begun to affect his efficiency and a bit more to counter the cravings that had started to wreak havoc with his deluded brain. As always, the powder gave him a new lease of life but there were side effects: sleepy eyes that kept closing; failing concentration. He cleared his throat quietly as often as he could, just so he had something to do to keep himself awake. Even so, it seemed that the drug was winning. And it probably would have done if it hadn't been for his phone.

Wrapped snugly in his filthy sheets, he had given no thought to switching off his phone, so when it rang he scrambled to locate it before anyone heard and switch it off. Snatching the gun off his lap with one hand, he threw back the sheets above him with the other and prepared himself for the inevitable. Had they heard it? He listened carefully for footsteps and thought he heard some. He was trapped in there. There was probably a policeman standing right outside, pointing his gun at the only exit point. The question was, did he jump out of the bin and attack, or did he simply wait until he was found? His instinct told him to take the fight to the police, jump out of the bin and blast his way the fuck out of there.

"You fucking idiot!" Jenkins cursed as he pulled the trigger, still unsure whether he was tripping or something because surely no one was stupid enough to do what this copper had just done, peer over the side of the bin. The sun was bright, hurting his restricted pupils. Despite the distortion to his vision, he clocked a white face looking down at him; a face that shattered into a million pieces as the trigger was fired. Blue eyes disappeared into a haze of glitter; freaky wasn't the fucking word for it. Trippy, more like. The face just seemed to disintegrate into the atmosphere, leaving behind it a stunning bright light. The intense glare then disappeared, leaving only the painful blue sky to contend with. Where was the shower of blood though? Jenkins didn't understand. The shattered policeman was still alive, because he could hear him screaming outside the bin.

The copper was on the floor, rolling about and picking at his face - there was something in it, glass or something. He didn't see Jenkins jump down from the safety of the can, swearing as he got something stuck in his hand. It looked like a bit of glass; it had broken the skin and drawn blood but it came out easily enough, and he tossed it away.

Totally confused, thanks to a mindful of nonsense Jenkins rolled his victim over with his right foot so that he was facing upwards. Having done so, he couldn't believe what he saw. The policeman had been hit in the face, but not by a bullet. No, by about a million pieces of glass instead. He had used a mirror on an extendible pole, about the size of a saucer, to look inside the bin. It was a clever but simple use of technology and usually worked, as long as the person you were trying to catch wasn't blessed with the luck of the Devil. Jenkins hadn't planned what happened; it was simply his good fortune that had sent his bullet into the mirror, which had promptly shattered and had been positioned in such a way as to send the glass flying straight into its owner's face.

The wounded officer attempted to cover his face with his elbows but the man who had done this to him was having none of that; he wanted to see the damage he had inadvertently caused. With his feet, he kept the protective elbows from shielding the face. The damage was fucking spectacular: shards of glass were sticking out of the man's face and eyes like the spikes on hedgehog's back. As much as the victim wanted to close his eyes, he couldn't, because the razor-sharp protrusions prevented him from doing so. His dazzling career was over, it seemed fair to say.

Bored of kicking away the elbows, Jenkins suddenly turned to stamping on the officer's stomach instead. Despite his bullet-proof jacket, the blows winded him and forced him to use his elbows to protect himself, leaving the face exposed. This was just what Jenkins had intended, so with the sole of his shoe he made sure that the job was a good one by sadistically stamping on the broken face until the screams turned to silence.

Barely seconds later Jenkins was taking cover behind the laundry bins as the officer's colleagues came piling back into the yard, having heard the gunshot. They opened fire immediately. Jenkins had had the presence of mind to take the dead officer's weapon before taking cover, so he put the faithful Browning away in his sweaty waistband for the time being and used the new one, firing a shot towards the gate just to try it out.

"Come on then you fucking bastards!" He screamed.

A marksman Jenkins wasn't, but a lucky bastard he often was these days. Thirty four bullets later the shooting stopped as the two officers ran out of ammo and were forced to reload. During this brief cessation of return fire, Jenkins hit the enemy for all he was worth, bursting out round after round. As a result he had definitely hit at least one of them, because he was lying on the ground squirming around, his body pumping out claret like a motherfucker. The other soldier of fortune was still reloading: Jenkins had missed him with every bullet. Just then, his gun expelled its last shell and that was it: click, click, fuck, click, click…!

It was time to do one, so he ran for the half-open gate, reaching into his waistband for the Browning as he did so. His lungs burned as though he were breathing fire. He made his break to safety with a couple of seconds to spare, just as the shooting started again and the thud of exploding wood filled the air right next to his ear.

Fortunately for him, he had had the presence of mind to lift a couple of other things from the pockets of the fallen police officer: a bunch of keys and something that looked like a small hand grenade, but was actually a smoke bomb. Quite handy in a siege situation, but fucking useless out in the open in broad daylight. He slipped behind the driver's side of the police car, twelve feet or so away from the gate. Crouching down low with his firearm in his right-hand, Jenkins could look back at the gate quite clearly and watched as the policeman cautiously emerged from the gateway. Holding the smoke bomb in his left hand, Jenkins twisted the top off it with his right and hurled it just to the left of his target. His aim was to create a diversion, and this it certainly did, enabling Jenkins to blow the head off his unprotected victim who instinctively turned towards the cloud of smoke engulfing the gateway.

The bullet must have hit the back of the bullet-proof helmet and then bounced back. It was as if the policeman was throwing his guts up as the backwash of his face exploded, covering the car. He had no time to feel any pain as his brain was cut to ribbons in a matter of seconds. The body of the faceless corpse fell forwards against the passenger-side front window, thud, before slipping down the glass and slumping onto the ground. Jenkins knelt to pick up the Glock that fell from its hand.

"Thank you very much, that'll do nicely," he grinned: once again, he had the power! The Browning went back into his waistband again for the time being.

It was nice to have wheels again, even if only temporarily: he could hardly get far unnoticed in this police car with what looked like the contents of a butcher's barrel splattered all over the side of it. The gunshots would also have attracted the attention of the rest of the squad at the front of the shop, so it was time to disappear. People stared from their hiding places at the end of the road, from the alleyways, their nosiness amazing Jenkins because they were prepared to risk their lives to see what was going on.

The police car fired up with little effort and the back street soon became a race track as Jenkins filled the air with the sound of a roaring engine and the screech of high-grade tyres as if attempting to break the land-speed record. He had forgotten about the dead end, and had to pull the car round by its handbrake. The driver's side rear quarter hit a wall, but no one could have turned in that space. Never mind, damaged rear quarter or not, he still had motion and he used this to his advantage. There was a right-hand turn at the end of the street which would lead back into the front of the shops and the main road.

Police officers had been running down the side road towards the stolen police car, but suddenly turned and ran the other way as it roared down the access road towards them at some considerable speed en route to the highway to freedom. It was like a game of bowls: one path and no way of escape for the skittles. Bang, strike one, another elite squad bites the dust! Armed to the teeth, the three men who had been ordered to guard the only access to the back of the shop had come running when they heard the gunshots. They had reached the top of the road when they met the enemy but had decided against standing there and waiting for him to mow them down at fifty miles an hour. Instead they ran, firing a couple of shots as they went, but they were going to have to do better than that. One skittle hit the bonnet and flew over the roof; one went underneath somewhere and the last one had his legs smeared against the wall as he clung to the bonnet, messy.

At the base camp out front, SO19 had been starting to disarm when they had heard the gunshots and consequently had to re-arm in seconds before rushing back through the shop. One team had been allocated to the back and one to the front, which made sense at the time because it didn't seem feasible that anyone could evade the death squad sent in to apprehend their prisoner.

Outside in the street there were ambulances, police cars, vans, dogs, and of course the crowds. Despite all this, there was only one armed officer present outside the shop as the car flew out of the darkness. He stared in disbelief at the car that was apparently attempting to drive through the crowds which had formed on the pavement. Fortunately, the majority of the onlookers managed to avoid the police car apart form one who hit the front of it and flew over the bonnet, nearly smashing the windscreen with her head, and another who became a human speed bump under Jenkins' axles.

The main street was in sight, just down at the bottom of the road that cut through the middle of the pavement. Jenkins reached it, albeit in a somewhat unorthodox manner, broadsiding the car movie-style. Shots were now being fired from behind, as the policeman who had almost missed the boat ran after the car, determined to repair his honour. A couple of windows were shot out and the boot flew up, but some kind of mystical force-field rendered the driver untouchable as he drove off up the reasonably clear main road, en route to freedom. Traffic had been barred from the area since the gunfire started, so the road was clear for miles.

Although it was clear of traffic, there was some lunatic running towards him down the middle of the road, so Jenkins pressed the throttle down hard in a bid to turn him into road-kill. That was before the windscreen blew out, then a tyre, and a gush of steam from under the bonnet rendered visibility zero. Whoever it was who was shooting at him, and he had a gut feeling who it was, was a good marksman.

He raised his stolen handgun through the broken windscreen: it was time to retaliate. There was nothing in the road in front of him, but a flash of black caught his eye from beyond the driver's side window. He had no time to reposition himself in order to target the movement before more bullets hit the driver's side of the car. The missiles smashed the windows and hit the dash, seats and head rests; he actually saw one whizz past his legs and another embed itself in his thigh, forcing him to release the throttle momentarily.

He was losing control of the car now, bullets ripping up the interior, as he couldn't see shit through the steam in front of him. People were shooting him through the driver's window. Bastards - another bullet scraped his arse, almost putting an end to his work. Despite the leg shot, he had the luck of the devil not to be in pieces by now. It was clear who was doing the shooting: it was Tap; Tap and his little shite of a mate who seemed to go everywhere with him. Obviously they had just been on their way to the shop after visiting Stacey Payne. *About fucking time too!* He thought.

He still had motion so he wasn't finished yet, but steam was pouring out so time was definitely a factor here. He pushed the throttle down again, hard, and a couple more bullets whizzed past his head. One hit the rear-view mirror. The car was so unsteady now that it went off the road momentarily and clipped a bus shelter, so that sparks joined forces with the plume of steam, emphasising the fact that time was of the essence. Jenkins attempted to straighten the car up and he managed it until the rubber that was left on the damaged tyre - the only bit of rubber that was giving the wheel rim its grip on the road - finally gave up and perished, leaving only the wheel's thin metal surface in contact with the road surface. The rim hit a pot hole, throwing the car completely out of control. It flew across the road and hit some pneumatic road repair equipment which became wedged underneath it and ended up being dragged half a mile up the street. The air pipes burst on the way, filling the streets with a loud hissing noise and a serpent-like object that snaked out from underneath, whipping everything that got in its way.

Jenkins was on foot from now on, but the fact that he could not walk very well only came to light once he had picked himself up off the pavement. One minute he was sitting in the driver's seat, the next he was lying in the middle of the road. When he worked it out, he realised that he must have been flung through the space where the windscreen had been. Apart from the bullet in his leg, he was also having a serious problem breathing, partly to do with the fact that his chest had been crushed by the steering wheel.

Despite the triple somersault he had executed during his exit from the car, he had somehow managed to hang onto his gun. Dragging himself to his feet, he pointed the weapon in the direction from which he assumed the attack to have come, trying to ignore the pain in his leg. Menacingly, he stared up the road, his full concentration following the aim of his weapon. They were quite close, the cunts who had shot him – perhaps it was time for them all to settle this: Tap, his bitch who always followed him around, and Jenkins himself.

This was no time for a dog fight. Billy Tap was sprinting towards his target now and was making good time until Jenkins opened fire again. He was within range, but his aim was lousy. At least it stopped the enemy in his tracks. Jenkins moved slowly backwards, his handgun still aimed in Tap's general direction. Return fire was coming he could feel it in the air, but from which direction?

And then it came; Tap and his merry-man appeared from hiding, weapons pointed in Jenkins' direction, and pulled their triggers. It was payback time, and a hoard of bullets lit up the sky. Tap actually changed clips once during the stand-off, which was indicative of the amount of ammunition he had expended. Tap was aiming at the area around the front of the police car, trying to push out of his mind the images of Stacey and the boy. As the hail of bullets hit the car, flames started to appear and the smell of petrol become pungent in the air.

Like a rat escaping a sinking ship, Jenkins was limping rapidly down the street, wincing in pain with every step. He suddenly gained twenty feet as the police car exploded, ignited by gunfire coming into contact with the petrol tank or a fuel pipe. The sound and aftermath of the two-ton petrol bomb exploding in the high street was as impressive as it was devastating: shop windows in the vicinity had been blown out, fire and theft alarms screamed in protest and water sprinklers were going off, oblivious to the damage they were causing.

Jenkins picked himself up off the ground again, his breathing loud like the thumping bass from a dance track. The alarms and the sound of breaking glass were almost inaudible as the blood pounded in his ears.

A wall of fire now separated two stunned detectives from their target and the flames and smoke made visibility poor. Squinting through it, Tap could see that Jenkins had managed to get to his knees. He struggled, Bambi-like, to his feet and continued his hobbling getaway down the road toward the amassed crowds.

It seemed as though people would never learn, but even now persisted in witnessing first-hand the events taking place in front of them instead of hurrying to safety. They soon scattered, though, when Jenkins showed that he wasn't finished yet.

His front-row audience dispersed, Jenkins was now faced only with a few rows of traffic - cars, vans, that sort of thing - that had just got stuck in the action. Most had been abandoned but there were a few people who had been either too scared or too nosy to run, or had simply decided to stay put and lie low for a while. These vehicles provided ideal cover from the bullets that were now whizzing past him again, one whining past his right ear and embedding itself in the side of a van. The shooting seemed to halt after that, which was actually down to Slug warning Tap that there were still civilians down there in some of the cars. With a sense of urgency, Jenkins cut through the jungle of metal monsters en route to freedom as people sat, petrified, inside their cars and vans. Emerging at the other side, he was now out in the open and at the mercy of fate as he hobbled down the road to freedom.

Tap now redoubled his efforts as he set off down the road again after his prey, Slug following at a lesser pace. Tap was so close to his quarry now that he could almost smell him, only fifty or so metres behind him as he kept up the chase down the main road. Every now and then he had to take cover as the streets came alive with gunfire. Tap was hindered in returning fire by the risk of hitting a civilian, not morally, because they shouldn't be stupid enough to be there in the first place, but for the MET it would be a fucking nightmare and just not worth the risk. Jenkins, however, was not hampered by such considerations.

The race led to another main road and Jenkins was going to get there first. Falling against the side of a taxi, he coughed his guts up as Tap came out of hiding momentarily from the shop doorway he had used to catch his breath and reload. As he did so, the two men's eyes met once more as Jenkins raised his police-issue Glock, aimed at his pursuer and pulled the trigger. Click! Nothing happened. Shit, we were empty! Panic set in as Jenkins watched his aggressor walk out from hiding, a freshly loaded gun in his hand. He stepped back, using the taxi to support his weight as he discarded the traitorous Glock. His lungs burned, his head spun; it looked as though he was finished.

Billy Tap was cautious as he walked towards his prey. Had Jenkins given up? Was this the end - had he had enough? Had he fuck! He was just getting his marbles back. Frantically Jenkins reached into the waistband of his jeans again and removed his faithful Browning automatic.

"Don't lock up on me, you cunt!" He pleaded out loud as he aimed and pulled the trigger at exactly the same time as Tap did the same. The Browning obediently fired out a shot just as he felt a bullet whiz past his ear and some glass or something hit the back of his head. Jesus, Billy Tap was a good shot - but not fucking good enough, it seemed. Taking out the taxi sign on top of the cab had been a cool shot, but he was at least two inches away from his intended target. Realising that return fire was imminent, Billy Tap side-stepped into the next place of safety on his pre-planned route towards his target, which was a phone box. He had seen his opponent change weapons, which meant he had to be running low on ammunition. According to Tap's rough assessment, he had three bullets left at the most.

When Tap reappeared again from hiding, it was bad news. Jenkins was mobile again, but in the taxi this time. The cab driver, who had flung himself lengthways across the passenger seat in an attempt to protect himself from the gunfire, now found the Browning automatic pointing at his head. Tap couldn't fire now in case he hit the taxi driver, so his only option was pursuit.

"Drive!" Jenkins ordered.

Tap could see the whole situation.

"Good luck mate!" He said under his breath to the driver. "Trust me buddy, you're gonna fucking need it!"

As the taxi chartered by Jenkins made its way up the road to freedom, Tap stood, tired and deep in thought as he attempted to catch his breath. He was in two minds as to what he was going to do next. The adjoining street had been road-blocked, preventing access to the one that led to the shoe shop and Stacey Payne's flat. The roadblock was still there, but there was no one stupid enough to man it after the pyrotechnic display that had just taken place half a mile or so from its barriers. A couple of panda cars lay discarded. People were free to move wherever they pleased, but the two police cars denied access to any motorist who was stupid enough to turn into the war zone.

Slug had just caught up with his colleague as the taxi that Jenkins had commissioned started to move off up the road. He bent forwards, hands on his knees, taking deep breaths. He was out of shape, and the cocaine and alcohol abuse of the last twenty four hours, together with the fry-up that morning, probably hadn't helped.

As the taxi pulled off, Jenkins could not resist the urge to offer a quick wave to the men whom he had evaded.

"We've got him now, the stupid fucker! That was the most stupid thing he could have done!" Tap exclaimed with glee.

Slug watched as the taxi drove away into the distance before the sunlight erased it without trace. He would remember that look on Jenkins' face for as long as he lived; that supercilious smile through the rear window of the taxi. Tap was right, though; there was a strong possibility that they had Jenkins now because it had been stupid of him to get into that taxi. It was a gift from the gods; they had struck gold!

Chapter Eleven

Taxi!

"That's one of Arif's wagons, init?" Tap asked. He should know because a few years back he had spent months working on a case involving those wretched bloody things. That was back in the days when to run a cab firm amounted to heavy involvement in criminal activity. One of the biggest cab companies to survive this taxi war was the firm that owned the cab Jenkins had just chosen.

"Get back to the shop, Slug, and make sure forensics have a good look around it. Not just inside it - make sure they check that fucking yard as well, and up the street. Leave no stone unturned! We want Browning shells, mate; we need to know for sure how much clout he's packing. Now, he's just offloaded two down here, and so if we find he's fired four at the shop then I reckon he's only got three bullets left. So he's fucked, unless any more of our boys hand over their weapons to him."

The two men started walking back down the road.

"Where are you going, then?" Slug asked.

"After Jenkins, mate! Don't worry, dude, as soon as I know where's he's going I'll call for you and we'll take him down together, I promise. Now get me some answers on his ammo situation, because it's time to take our friend Mr Jenkins down. All right, son?"

They parted company at that point, and a few minutes later Slug's phone rang, the display showing Buzby's number.

Tap tore down the side road that led to Stacey Payne's flat, his phone at his ear.

“Tell Arif Billy Tap wants him, and tell him now or I’ll shut you down. Fucking hurry up!”

“Okay sir, Arif will be two minutes please, he is in the workshop. I will get him now. Please, one moment.” Panic-stricken footsteps could be heard in the background, but Tap didn’t have time to wait.

“Five minutes, right? I want a call from Arif in five fucking minutes, max, or I’ll be down there within ten. You hearing me?”

The Arab on the other end of the phone did hear, loud and clear, and promised to obey.

Tap blasphemed as he saw the crowds, who fell silent as he approached from the cordoned-off area, obviously important. He ducked under the police-issue blue and white tape that had been stretched across the street and they parted to allow him through.

“Get off my car!” He raged as he approached the Mercedes. Uniformed police officers stepped away from the bonnet of the car as Tap arrived at the crime scene. Tap opened the driver’s door and climbed into the vehicle before realising that he didn’t have any keys. He got out again and went over to one of the marked police cars nearby.

“Keys, please!” He ordered. “On second thoughts, you can drive,” he amended, recognising Tache. “Come on then mate, get a move on. Chop-chop!”

Tache obediently climbed into the car next to Tap.

“Give me your ammo!” Tap ordered next, indicating the ammunition clip attached to Tache’s belt. He directed his driver to turn left at the end of the road as he stepped on the accelerator, and continued to snap directions at him as they drove.

“Down to the end and go right - you can’t go left because I totally fucked that road up half an hour ago - at the bottom of that road, turn left, then…ah, here's the bastard now!" Tap exclaimed as his phone rang.

"Arif, about fucking time! Right, listen. One of your motors XJ 19, who's driving it? Speak to me, Arif - I don't give a fuck if he's an alien, I just want to know who he is. The cab's got a tracker, right?"

Arif had been known to employ drivers who had just come straight off the boat, and his initial fear had been that one of them had fucked up. Tap's last words offered him some reassurance because it was clear that he was more interested in learning the whereabouts of the cab than who was driving it.

"He's called Sandeep. And yeah, he's a ghost. Why, what's he done then?" Arif asked apprehensively.

"Has it got a tracker?"

"Yeah, it's got a tracker, they all have. Why, Billy man?"

"Your driver's in trouble, Arif! Big fucking trouble – you're gonna be scraping his brains out from the inside of that taxi if you don't help me on this one, my friend! You heard of Anthony Jenkins?"

As it happened, Arif had.

"Good, Arif – good, mate, because I won't need to explain what danger the driver of CXJ 19 is in then, will I? Considering that his passenger is Anthony fucking Jenkins and the last time I saw them Jenkins had a gun to your man's head. He's probably dead by now but if he's not, and you want him turning back in for work tomorrow without you having to explain to immigration where the fuck he came from, then I suggest that you take a look at your computer right now and tell me where the fuck he's going."

"Fuck!" was Arif's irreverent response, immediately apologising for the blasphemy. He had known he was in the shit the minute his little helper had warned him that Billy Tap was on the phone.

There was silence as Arif did as he was asked and looked for the tracker on his computer screen. It was in his interests to cooperate with Tap so that he would maybe get his taxi back, and perhaps even the driver without damage or injury, or the need to explain why a man from Iran was driving a taxi without a passport, let alone a driving licence. Tap had pulled a lot of strings for Arif in the past, and now it was payback time. Tap could hear the keys of a computer keyboard tapping away in the background, and then the sound of a big-arse beard making contact with the receiver, resulting in momentary interference.

"Okay, he's on Fitzgerald Street heading towards Burnley Park!" Arif announced triumphantly.

"Burnley Park, toute suite, we've got a taxi to catch up with!" Tap ordered his driver, keeping Arif on the line because he wasn't finished with him yet. Tache manoeuvred the car at a sensible pace out onto the main road in which Jenkins was last seen. Burning with frustration, Tap asked him if he intended to drive like a pussy all the way to their destination. When Tache asked Tap how he would like him to drive, the reply was succinct:

"Like a cunt!"

That was fine, Tache could do 'cunt.'

"Lights, sirens?" He offered.

"No, just cunt!" Tap laughed. He was creeping in at the back door and didn't want to advertise his approach.

"Well, cunt it is then, sir!" Tache replied as he pressed his right foot down hard on the throttle.

Tap decided he liked Tache; shave that silly thing off his top lip and he'd be okay.

Still on the line, Arif carefully directed them onto the trail of the stolen taxi as it made its way down Burnley Street. Fenton Street joined Ridley Street, which met Summit Lane; they were heading for the other side of the water, just as Tap had suspected. He had Jenkins in his sights now - metaphorically speaking, of course - and Jenkins didn't even know it! All was going well, until a sudden beeping on Tap's mobile indicated that a call was waiting from Slug.

"Arif, stay on the line, I've got another call. You watch that tracker like a fucking hawk, right? I'll only be a couple of minutes!"

The line suddenly went dead, and Tap swore.

"Bastard…! I've only gone and cut the fucker off, ain't I?" Never mind, Slug was still there and he could call Arif back in a couple of minutes.

"Slug - what is it, my dear?"

He could hardly hear anything at first because there was a lot of background noise - shouting, ambulances, the usual type of things to be found at the scene of a mass murder. Slug was standing in the backyard of the laundry and his errand was going well. He had had the call from Buzby just as he and Tap had parted company. Buzby and his small crew had been doing as asked and monitoring all phone calls to the Yard in order to trace anything untoward that could give them clues as to Jenkins' whereabouts, and he was now able to tell them where Jenkins' base camp and headquarters were. This was truly a result. Buzby had done it by scanning the incoming phone and police radio calls for hours via his computer and using certain keywords to allow him access to any conversations that seemed relevant. The potential relevance of the calls was determined by the information that the computer already held regarding the case, such as street names, locations, victims' names and so on. The keyword in this instance was 'Bury Street', a street just off the Dulwich Road.

There had been a call from a very concerned woman who was checking up on her father. She had called him numerous times over the last few days but he was not answering his phone, so she decided to pay a visit, despite the fact that she lived in Bristol. Once at the flat, she had started knocking on the door but got no answer. So she called the people who owned the building so they could fetch a key, but when she tried the key in the lock she found that the door was dead bolted from the inside. Really worried now, she called the police, who rang for back-up with special equipment.

The rapidly-growing search and rescue team had knocked on the flat next door to this woman's father, the one on the left-hand side, and had found an old lady in there who couldn't hear or see shit. She was about a hundred and fucking something, and about as much use as a chocolate fireguard. They tried the other door on the right-hand side of the flat, but there was no answer. There was a strange noise, though, like someone in pain, and someone was shouting at someone else. It sounded messy, but no one was going to answer the door; that much was clear, no matter how hard this copper knocked. The daughter of the old man admitted that she had tried that door earlier on and there had been no noise back then.

That was as far as the story went for now, Slug narrating it hurriedly down the phone. He added that the 'keyword' clue had come about because there had been a robbery in Bury Street the night before, in a phone shop over the road, which was why the police had that address in their system. Because the robbery was connected with the Jenkins case, any information sent through the computer that matched this event was sniffed out and investigated further. Slug informed his leader that he had thanked the communications expert for his assistance - he had in fact praised him like a god, before reminding him that their conversation had not taken place.

"Are uniform there yet?" Tap enquired, suspecting that they might well be.

"No, not yet; I told them to hold back. There's one constable there, but that's it at the moment," Slug assured his leader, knowing full well that this was exactly what he wanted to hear.

"Good. Nice work, Slug; make sure that all those who don't need to be at those flats aren't there. And keep the front of the building police-free too, I don't want Jenkins knowing we're there. I'm gonna tell him, don't get me wrong - I just want to make sure he's got easy access to the flat before I do. When he goes in, we need him contained in that building. That's where it's all gonna end, Slug - we take him down there!"

Slug agreed, feeling somewhat redundant.

"How you doing at the shop?" Tap asked, then remembered Arif and the need for more directions. Slug was doing well; five Browning casings had already been located in the shop itself. This didn't seem to add up, because witnesses had only heard four gunshots during the slaughter of the people inside. Slug went on to explain that one casing was actually a whole bullet, but it appeared to have jammed and been discarded. Nice one; Tap liked the sound of that, because not only was Anthony Jenkins low on ammo, he also had equipment problems. That left the killer with two bullets, then.

"Nah, Billy," Slug went on, "forensics have also been checking out the back yard and they've found two Browning casings out there as well, so far. One was in a laundry basket and one was outside the back gate; they had an eye witness to confirm."

"What eye witness? I thought everyone was dead there,"

Slug went on to explain that there was a policeman who had sustained terrible facial injuries and had then been killed in the back yard, before Jenkins had been approached by the two armed officers.

"One of them was shot by our mate, then the other chased Jenkins and was gunned down outside the rear gates. Shot in the face with a helmet on, fucking messy! As for the eye witness, he kept drifting in and out of consciousness thanks to a gunshot wound under his armpit that had punctured his lung – he's not a well chappie, but he was stabilised when the paramedics got to him. As it turns out, he saw the whole thing apart from a few hazy moments. More importantly, before he was shot he saw Jenkins re-holster the Browning in the waistband of his trousers in favour of the sergeant's Glock, the very gun that shot him. Then, once he had shot the witness and attempted to shoot this geezer's partner with what was left of a full seventeen-round clip, Jenkins was seen discarding the Glock and relocating his Browning as he sprinted for the rear gates of the premises. He says that there was just a load of smoke and a single shot after that, and then he saw his colleague fall to the ground with half his chops missing."

"He's fucking good at that, our Mr Jenkins, ain't he? Pinching fucking shooters! So that's it, then, Jenkins is empty. He's run out of fucking bullets!"

If their calculations were correct, then he was completely out of ammunition and this final confrontation was going to be like taking candy from a baby. There was the prostitute, the Limo driver, the copper at the hospital; that left seven bullets at the shop and two in the High Street! That was twelve rounds, which was all the Browning's magazine could hold. Tyrone had told them that.

Slug had nearly forgotten to tell him the extra bit of news.

"She's not dead you know, Stacey I mean. She's still alive, in a bad way, but she's still hanging in there."

"And the boy…?"

Slug fell silent. There was no need to answer, and Tap didn't push it.

"Okay, Slug. Good work, son. Get your arse down to Bury Street, then. Don't do anything until I'm there though, and fucking keep out of sight because I don't want to be bagging you up today an' all, you hear?"

"I'll be there!" Slug promised. "Are you in the Merc?"

"Slug, how the fuck can I be in the Merc if you've got the bastard keys in your pocket? Knob!"

Tap turned his attention back to the matter in hand.

"We've done Fenton Street, Ridley Street and then Summit Lane - it's quicker going north though, init?" Tap asked Tache.

"Yeah. I dunno why that taxi's going that way if he's heading to Bury Street; he's well off track."

"Yeah, well - don't worry about the taxi, there's an illegal immigrant driving it so it could be going fucking anywhere. The geezer can't even speak English apparently, so how he finds his way around the Smoke I don't know. Go on then mate, do your stuff then, Bury Street, toute suite!"

Judging by the taxi driver's sense of direction, getting there before Jenkins was not now looking as impossible as it first seemed. Tap resumed his conversation with Slug.

"Chop-chop then, Slug, see you down there, and no heroics. Keep out of the way an' all until I tell you where I am, right? Ring me up if you get lost; I fucking know you and directions."

"On my way…!" Slug promised as the phone went dead, only to ring again almost immediately.

"Arif nice one! Heading for Aspen Drive, really? Arif, buy your fucking taxi driver a new map, preferably one in fucking Swahili or whatever he speaks because he's miles off from where he's meant to be going. He's meant to be heading for Bury Street!" Tap protested.

The notion that Buzby could be wrong had entered his head, of course it had, but the significance of the phone shop and the disturbance that Slug spoke of in the same road was far from coincidental. If you looked at the strategic position of that street; it was central to a lot of the places they had visited over the last few days and well within the area to which they had traced Jenkins' first phone calls. It had good tube access as well, with all the early killings taking place only several stops away. Clearly, it was all starting to add up. Arif agreed that his cabby's sense of direction was not the best in the world.

"It's not a problem, Arif, just don't contact him and warn him, all right? Leave it as it is because with a bit of luck Jenkins will notice the fuck-up and direct him to where he's going on suspicion that he's just terrible at directions rather than taking the piss. To be honest, Arif, your driver's a dead man already, I suspect. But look on the bright side at least if he's dead, he can't drop you in it, aye? Just let nature take its course, my friend, but keep an eye on that tracker because I'll be calling you back in a minute to see if he's back on track. Don't go anywhere ya hear?"

"Bury Street it is then, driver!" Tap ordered again as he relaxed back into his seat and rested his feet on the lower dash. This was it; he could feel it in his blood. He had out-foxed Jenkins this time and now it was time to gloat.

"Right, stop fucking about now mate, you're driving like my old lady!"

"You can drive if you want," Tache remarked, "if you think you can get there any quicker."

Tap laughed.

"Don't do driving, mate! Besides, if I drive are you gonna sort Jenkins out when we get there?"

Tache shrugged, momentarily reminding him of Doughnut, who had been on his mind quite a lot over the last few hours.

"Anyway, I need to rest mate," Tap went on. "I'm a well-oiled machine, you see, and I need to preserve my energy. Me and you are a team, mate: you drive, I fuck-up the bad guys. And boy am I gonna fuck this bad guy up!

"Do you know where the fuck you're going?" Jenkins asked the petrified taxi driver, forcing cold steel against his dark, sweaty skin. The pressure of the killing machine caused the man at the wheel to cringe, his face filling with terror. In answer to the question, he spouted a mouthful of gibberish. Of course he didn't know where he was going; he was the new breed of London cabby!

"Turn right here, you twat. Right! See this one!" Jenkins banged hard on the rear window, signalling the direction that the taxi driver was to take. He was sitting on one of those fold-up seats behind the driver's compartment, his left hand tucked through the glass which had been originally fitted to protect the driver when closed. The hand held the faithful Browning automatic, which was forced hard against the driver's head. Jenkins divided his attention between the driver and what may be following them. He was rattled, really rattled, because what had just occurred had been some serious shit, without doubt the closest that his opponent and his monkey had got to their target.

Back there; Jenkins had thought he had had his lot, that the man sent to stop him was going to succeed. The two men had never met, not as far as Jenkins could ever remember, but this feeling of familiarity that the prey sensed about his hunter was so strong that he felt they surely must have. He didn't understand what happened back there because Tap had simply stood in the street and watched him get away without any attempt to give chase. Something wasn't adding up, and it only served to fuel his paranoia. He was sure Billy Boy wouldn't have given up like that without a good reason, and the only reason that made any sense was that the police already knew where Jenkins' base was. But they couldn't though, surely?

"Right, just here, remember right?" Jenkins asked, slamming his free hand against the window again. Right! Yes, the driver knew right, so right it was then, straight across a set of fucking lights, causing other road-users to brake in such a way that a prayer wouldn't go amiss. Then, to add insult to injury, the driver decided to brick it half way through this manoeuvre. As the vehicle screeched to a sudden halt, Jenkins nearly fell off his tiny, fold-away-seat. Sandeep nearly earned himself a new orifice in the side of his head for that one and the air was filled with rage as the other vehicles blew their horns in retaliation.

"Look where you're fucking going, man!" Jenkins shouted. "That was close, too fucking close!" He coughed in an attempt to remove the sudden blockage that had appeared in his throat. Having located the obstruction and drawn it up to the surface, the gunman steadied himself again on his minimal seat as he deposited the new arrival into the front of the cab via the open glass window. His leg had really begun to hurt by now. The bullet hole in it was a big one and his body was leaking like a sieve, a dark red pool of blood growing on the floor. It was cause for concern; but the repair of the injury would have to wait for the time being because there were more important tasks to take care of first. Jenkins had to get home, and fast.

That near miss had been close, too fucking close for his liking, so he tried a different tactic with the driver. Taking the gun away from the man's head, he spoke softly to him:

"Steady, man! Be fucking careful because I really need to get where I'm going, okay? No gun, no pressure, just drive where I say, okay?" Jenkins spoke slowly and took particular care not to say 'right' or 'left,' because that could have led to a disaster.

Sandeep pulled off again after his emergency stop and, for once, seemed to be looking where he was going.

Jenkins had phoned Sarah the minute he had got a safe distance away from the shoe shop in the taxi, and the news had not been good. She had told him there had been people knocking on the door to Leigh Anderson's apartment and on the last occasion it had been a policeman, although just a beat bobby by the sounds of it. They had seemed more interested in Gordon's door, the next one along. Jenkins had told her to make sure that she didn't open their front door for any reason and for no one. They would have to do better than a lone copper to open Gordon's front door from the outside, even if Plod had the biggest shoulders in the world.

"What about Haley?" He had asked.

The ensuing silence had been enough. Haley was very close to the end.

Sarah was left trying to decide whether to desert the sinking ship and sacrifice her wages, and she was running out of time because Jenkins was only ten minutes away from home. If she didn't bail out soon she was going to drown, as simple as that. Haley was on her way out that much was clear; in fact the medication she was giving her seemed to be speeding up the process rather than delaying it. Perhaps the dosages were wrong, or maybe it was the wrong medication altogether; she just didn't know and it was unlikely that Jenkins did either. Far from helping Haley, they were fucking killing her.

She preferred her own company in the front room now to that of the bag of fucking bones that was howling in the bedroom. She had played ball so far, but this was all getting too much for her. It was time to bail out, because when Jenkins found out that his future wife could be dead, then no one in that building would be safe, particularly the person he had employed to look after her! On the other hand, there was the question of money. Sarah didn't know what to do; she would ponder on it for a while.

There was a funny smell in the cab and Sandeep sniffed the air like a dog. It smelt like vinegar. The driver knew that his fare was up to something because cold steel no longer drew the warmth from his temple. In his rear view mirror he could see Jenkins creating magic with a lighter and something brown in a cracked light bulb. Drugs, he suspected. Whatever it was, he ignored it because at least it distracted his assailant from the gun, which was lying on the bench seat beside him.

Familiar places flew past the cab window and Jenkins relaxed back in his seat as he watched the show. It was early evening and darkness had started to make an impression. The cab maintained a steady pace and everything else seemed to fall in line with its speed, just as Jenkins switched to a higher gear as the rest of the world carried on at its own pace. A huge set of golden arches loomed outside the window, followed by a magnificent sparkling silver lion and a massive silver star.

The vehicle came to a halt now and then, causing Jenkins to drag himself up off the seat to see what was going on. By the time he made it back to reality, the taxi had already set off again. The sound of phlegm hitting the walls and floor of the cab could be heard periodically, heralded by the filthy growl that drew the liquid up to the surface in preparation for its launch.

Nice, the buzz was very nice - but something wasn't right. The places going past the window didn't look right anymore and Jenkins suddenly came back to life again.

"Oy mate, where the fuck are you going? This ain't the way to fucking Bury Street! Have you any idea where you're fucking going? Jesus fucking Christ, all the cabbies in London and I have to fucking choose you! Left at this roundabout, that's this one! Left, do you fucking understand?" He spat venomously, banging his fist against the passenger side rear window. He couldn't believe it; what a fucking Muppet, he was gonna have to shoot this cunt because he was taking the piss now. He was gonna have to go, it was as simple as that!

"What's the crack then, Arif?" Tap asked.

"They're back on track," Arif informed him, unsure whether or not this was a good thing. It must be a bad thing, he decided, as Tap cursed the airwaves.

"How much back on track…?"

"He's just entered Drummond Street and with the traffic like it is at this time of the evening, I'd say he's looking at about a ten minute ETA to get from where he is now to where you think he's going."

"Fuck!" Tap cursed again.

Arif listened to Tap, speaking to whoever was in the car with him. They were discussing their own estimated time of arrival and, although close, it did sound like the boys in blue had the edge. Only just, though. This was a result in itself because Jenkins had had at least a fifteen minute head start on them; but then it was neither here or there really in London because traffic and fate played a bigger part in your journey times than a good map and a fast mode of transport ever did. Slug, for instance, who had set off half an hour later than everyone else, was now well on course because he had been lucky with the traffic.

"Arif, keep your eyes peeled on that screen, right? Any mishaps, if that taxi stops or anything like that - you call me, okay?"

Tap phoned Slug.

"Slug? Looks like I'm gonna just pip Jenkins to the post - only fucking just, though, by the sound of things. Gnat's cock, we're talking here! When I get there I'm going in solo. You've cleared all the bods, right?" he asked, seeking verification that all uniformed officers had been instructed to leave the site. Slug assured his leader that this had been taken care of and that they were out of sight.

"Good, because I don't want Jenkins frightened off, although he knows this is the end."

He was not the only one who thought this whole saga was going to end tonight; Slug was fucking sure of it, but as to who would be the victor he didn't know. Especially with Tap wanting to trap their prey like a snared rabbit, just so he could make sure of being the one who made the kill. Tap could already smell victory in the air, that much was clear.

"Soon as you get there, buddy, you come in and back me up. It should have all been taken care of by then though, so you just bring a mop and bucket!" he boasted.

"I hope so, Billy - I fucking hope so!"

*

Driven by anxiety and paranoid thoughts, Sarah paced around the front room of the flat. She was at her wits end; this was all too much for her. She had taken extra care in the way she had dressed herself today - hipster jeans and a tight beige top, courtesy of Leigh Anderson. Leigh must have been a size smaller on top than her, because she was spilling out a little more than she should have done above the v-neck of the top and showing plenty of midriff. She was making the most of what she had while she still could, because she knew that time was not on her side. She felt like the last remaining contestant in a reality TV programme who was just about to be released from her prison of so many days, so of course she wanted to look her best when she re-entered the real world. Clearly, if the police raided this flat any minute now, as they more than likely would, then to look one's best would be sensible; maybe then they would go easy on her. What if they already knew she was on Jenkins' payroll?

Of course, there was also the world press and Sarah was well aware that if she came out of this as a heroine rather than an accomplice, then with her breasts partially exposed and Fleet Street front-page exposure; well, the world would be her oyster! Just like on reality TV: you never knew how the world was going to perceive you on your release, but if your tits were hanging out you were in with a better chance of winning them over.

Barely minutes before she had tried to feed Haley an early dose of her medication in a last ditch attempt to calm her down, but it was to no avail. Haley was not only in a lot of physical pain, but also clearly messed up in the head. Every time Sarah tried to give her more pills, all hell broke loose. As if possessed by some kind of demon, Haley kept swearing and trying to punch and grab her nurse with everything she had, which wasn't actually a lot now. She wore a tortured look and was sweating as if she'd just received a twenty stretch in the Old Bailey. There was vomit on the lower half of her face and her night gown. It was a horrible experience to have to fight a living skeleton, but Sarah had done her best to remain calm and composed during these little fits of nastiness.

"I'm not trying to kill you, you stupid bitch, I'm trying to help you! Look, I didn't prescribe you this shit. I just got what your fucking boyfriend told me to get and fucking give you. Now chill out, will you? You're not well; you'll fucking waste your energy. And stop hitting me as well - what if you scratch me?" She hollered at her patient.

Haley did calm down for a while, maybe thirty seconds, before she attempted to lunge at her supposed helper once again. Her weakness and lack of mobility caused her to fall sideways and off the bed, striking her head on a bedside cabinet, her feet remaining trapped under the tucked-in bed sheets. Haley was bleeding from her temple now as she hung upside down along the side of the bed, groaning as she slipped in and out of consciousness. This was all getting a little fucked-up as far as Sarah was concerned; it was out of control, way out of control! As if the goods for which she was responsible were not damaged enough, they were now split and pissing out claret, infected claret at that! This was not good, not good at all. Sarah's employer would not take this well, because he truly loved this woman. It may have been a love built around filth and dirt, yet still it had prospered. This was too much. The sight of the blood seeping from Haley's head and dripping onto the floor was the last straw. This was the end, she was out of here!

She didn't have much luggage, just a bag of money which she hid inside a small satchel. Having made her decision, which she hoped was not actually a death sentence, she took one more look around the flat to memorise the place for posterity. Of course, she hoped never to see the place again, but nevertheless it had been an experience. Screams of pain or anger soon started to fill the bedroom again, indicating that Haley was awake, so she took one more look in the bedroom before she called it a day.

Haley was dangling over the side of the bed, her feet still tangled in the covers that had once protected her. Her heavily-stained white silk nightgown, that shielded onlookers from the sight of her decaying body, had dropped down over her head as she lay. She looked like she had been buried once and dug up again. Sarah did feel sorry for her, but enough was enough; it was time to bail out of this crazy situation. She shouldn't have got so involved in it in the first place but the money had looked good: a sizeable bunch of used bank notes, almost enough to pay off one of her credit cards. The fact that it was dirty money made no odds to Sarah, as far as she was concerned, it was no dirtier than credit cards when you thought of how people suffered as a result of them.

She walked briskly into the bedroom and ripped the remaining bed sheets completely off the bed, allowing Haley's legs to fall to the floor with a thud. That probably hurt, but then any movement that Haley made hurt. The twisted body remained lying face down on the sheets that had been dragged down with her in her fall. Her skeletal frame then began to twitch and shudder as she sobbed as though she had finally given up, and she probably had. The fight was gone from her; it was only a matter of time now. The only thought that remained in her mind was the fact that Anthony was not there to see her through this; but he would be, she knew that. He would never let her down. Haley cried herself into unconsciousness again and the room lapsed into silence. She was holding on, holding on for her loved one.

Well, that was that then - Sarah had done all she was prepared to do with regard to Haley's welfare. She took one more look at the condemned woman before she left the room, knowing that the sight would haunt her for the rest of her life.

"Bye Haley," she said quietly to the mess on the floor, although the words were wasted because Haley's body had shut down for the time being. Sarah didn't know if Haley could hear her, but it didn't matter really.

Now it was time to look after number one, and Sarah felt great enthusiasm for her new mission. She didn't intend to go to the police if she could help it, not for a day or so at least. Instead she would go into hiding for a while, probably until Jenkins had been caught, because when he found out that she betrayed him, she was sure he would put all his resources into hunting her down. In the meantime it would be better to hide, and when she did go to the police she would tell them that she had been too scared to do so before. Maybe she could get her side of the story to the newspapers before the police labelled her as 'Jenkins' Evil Helper'. In reality, of course, she was just the abducted pharmacist who had last been seen being escorted from the hospital premises by Anthony Jenkins. Fuck me, if she made it through this she was a national hero and the resulting exposure would surely make her a very rich woman.

Sarah swung her bag behind her as she started to fiddle with the locks on the door to the outside world. Gordon's door was done up like Fort Knox, so Leigh Anderson's was the only way out of this place. That was better because she didn't fancy going next door for another encounter with Gordon. With the turn of a handle, Sarah opened the door slowly, half expecting to be rushed by men in blue suits. There was no one there. Cautiously, she peered out into the corridor. It was clear, crystal clear! She stepped out to freedom, straight down the main corridor towards the lifts. With the lifts in sight, she quickened her pace until she was forced to stop by the figure of a man who loomed in front of her all of a sudden.

"Sarah?" He asked, smiling. He was dressed in black from head to toe and wore an impressive-looking gun holster under an open black leather jacket. He was a good-looking man, very good-looking, although he did look like a bad boy. There was something about him, something magnetic. In the holster was a terrifyingly large handgun which was similar in colour, although not in size, to the smaller version that sat on the opposite side. It was the police then, was it?

"Who are you?" She asked pretty eyes wide.

The figure before her promised that he was a friend and he had come to help. Sarah smiled in relief because that was exactly what she needed at that moment, a friend! Looking up bashfully, she was conscious that her saviour was staring at her breasts, but she didn't really care because she needed help and here he was, all six foot two of him. He could stare at her tits all day long for all she cared; for fucks sake, get her out of this mess and she'd spoon them out for him. So she felt no fear as the handsome figure before her reached out with his left hand and touched her on the side of the neck. It actually felt quite pleasurable as his fingers searched for something under her skin beneath her ear. It all happened so quickly that she only noticed slight pressure against her skin before darkness arrived, and she never even felt herself hit the floor.

Tap laughed as his naive young victim slumped down onto the corridor carpet. It still worked then, the old pressure point trick. Tap still had the magic, forget date rape drugs, you need some of this shit. Usually he preferred to punch someone in the face and knock all their teeth out in order to render them unconscious, but he couldn't do that to such a pretty young lady. He was going to have fun with her, he thought as he picked her up with one hand and slung her over his back, cave-man style, before taking her back into the lair of Anthony Jenkins.

*

"Slug, I'm in and I've had a right result!" Tap spoke into his mobile phone as he cautiously entered the flat. The door had been left carelessly ajar for all and sundry to simply walk in off the street. With a young lady slung across his shoulder and a phone to his left ear, Tap pulled the heavy artillery out from his holster and held it out in front of him. It was play time! A laser sight suddenly lit up the room at the press of a button. It would have looked more effective if the room had been pitch black, but it still looked the part even though the darkness outside had only just began to set in. Tap worked better in darkness; it was if it allowed his powers to flourish. The weapon he held at arm's length was ready to kill: Glock technology had put the safety into the trigger, so if there were any little surprises then they were taking the full brunt of a .45 bullet, guided by infra-red.

"Where are you?" Tap asked the phone.

Slug was actually just two or three minutes away from his destination, putting the silver Mercedes through its paces. With an automatic gearbox and power-assisted steering making light work of those corners, one hand was free to make polite conversation with the boss. Okay it was illegal - but hey, fuck-it, this was a police emergency!

"Good, Slug, good work." Tap filled him in on his discovery and recapture of Sarah. "Now you make sure you park out of sight when you get here, then you wait outside until Jenkins arrives, saying that, he should be here any minute. Everyone's in place outside and they've been instructed to let Jenkins walk straight in here without confrontation. But only you will follow him in, okay? I don't want any of those fucking idiots downstairs coming in here gung-ho. When you get here, you'll see a blue Citroen car and in that you'll find Tache, remember him?"

Slug did.

"He'll be able to tell you when you can come in if you arrive after our mate gets here, because he's sitting there waiting for Jenkins to show up. He's my eyes on the street, if you like. I'm just going into the flat now."

Slug took his instructions from the phone in his left hand while his right steered the speeding Mercedes through the streets of London.

"Fuck me, it fucking hums in here a bit! Hang on!" Tap exclaimed, having walked up to the end of the hallway that divided the kitchen and front bedroom. Slug heard a loud thud, as though something heavy had hit the floor. Tap had just dropped Sarah onto the floor in the front room. There was a momentary silence as Tap cautiously moved on through the room, treading carefully. With his Glock held high, laser technology lighting the room and a mobile phone to his ear, he crept further into the room like a ghost soldier.

A large hole to his left clearly allowed access to the flat next door, linking the two. Squinting in the dissolving light, Tap could see what looked like another sitting room through the DIY disaster. There were bricks and all sorts of shit everywhere in there, and piles of dust.

The living room of the flat next door looked dark and dingy, the curtains half closed. Darkness was descending rapidly and the failing light added to the overall eeriness of the effect. In front of him there were two doors, which Tap correctly deduced would lead to a bedroom and a bathroom. One of the doors was open. Tap was going to kick the nearest door to him open and storm the room with military style; just like in the old days! But first he had to make sure that the great hole behind him was safe, because that left him vulnerable to attack from the rear.

"What's it like in there? Shit hole, is it?" Slug asked. He couldn't wait to see the place for himself, if only to allow him to compare it with the vision of hell that he had already conjured up in his mind.

Tap stuck his head through the crudely-made hole in the wall and looked around inside the neighbour's flat.

"It's a nice flat, actually. It's just, well, you know… what the fuck is that smell?" Tap asked, forgetting that he was technically alone. "It's a fucking stiff!" He guessed. He knew the smell of rotting corpses.

The hole in the wall broke through into an identical lounge to the one Billy was standing in. Over the other side of the room was an identically-positioned bedroom and bathroom, doors closed; and to the left there was exactly the same hallway to the front door.

"He's been using the flat next door as well, Slug, and for some reason he's joined them together by knocking a fucking great hole in the wall. He ain't even cleaned the bricks and shit up, you know? He's just left them laying there on the living room floor. We're gonna find something fucking horrible in here, mate, I can feel it!" Tap shared his hunch as he stepped into the flat; his intention being to search it and find out what the crack was with that pungent smell that was burning the inside of his nostrils.

Looking down the hallway towards the kitchen, Tap couldn't help but notice the barricade and advanced locking system on the front door.

"He's done the front door up like Fort Knox. There's fucking bars on it, wooden planks and all sorts of shit. I don't think our Mr Jenkins ever wanted anyone to get in here you know, Slug, or out for that matter! What I wanna know, though, is why did he need this flat as well? I mean, what's the crack? I don't understand."

Slug had no idea either, but then he had given up trying to work out how Jenkins' mind worked hours ago because it only made him feel inadequate.

Walking cautiously down the hallway, Billy Tap suddenly stopped dead in his tracks. Dog-like, the soldier cocked his head slightly, directing his hearing back towards the hole in the wall where he had come in: he had heard a noise. He retreated slowly, listening out for any more sounds. When he reached the hole in the wall, his suspicions were confirmed. There was a noise coming from the first flat, from just beyond the open door of the bedroom situated at the end of the lounge. It was a moan of some sort, which was always a bad sign.

"Slug, I'll call you back, baby! Chop-chop, but be fucking careful because I know you, yer fucker! Remember, this is my show," Tap warned as if he was protecting his little brother.

Slug understood that Jenkins and Tap obviously had this little thing going, although he had no idea what it was really all about. He thought privately that Billy's personal vendetta had gone way beyond his professionalism.

Tap's phone buzzed again immediately he cut off the call to Slug.

"Yeah?" He snapped rudely. He was walking cautiously towards the bedroom, his gun poised ready to kill, the infra-red dot scanning the room ahead of him.

"You fucking what, he's stopped where?" Tap whispered loudly into the mouth-piece. "Why?"

It seemed that Jenkins had decided to dispense with the taxi driver's services, or at the very least, with the taxi. Arif had been as good as his word and had been monitoring his tracking system with a keen interest in the end result. It was looking reasonably good for Arif's employee at the moment, but that could change.

"All right, Arif, I'll get a boy down there and see if your man's all right. He might be lucky because he's only two streets away and I ain't heard no gun shots; so unless he's been carved up you might get a result. I'll make some calls, all right? Now don't ring me again, all right? Ring Slug, I'm fucking busy!" Tap killed the line because Arif had served his purpose now.

Barely two metres away from the open door of this bedroom that he had been planning to raid for the last five minutes, his bloody phone buzzed again. It was Slug, so he answered it.

"You here…?" He asked.

Slug was right outside.

"Yeah, I'm here, but so is Jenkins. He's coming down the street. He's not alone though, he's with that fucking driver - least I think it's the taxi driver. The geezer looks like an Arab or something. And I've just driven past an empty taxi. Jenkins is hurt, dude. It's where you got him in the leg, I reckon. You hit him with a forty-five so he must be in a bad way, although he's lucky to still have a fucking leg really. Here he comes, fuck, he's pissing out claret, man! Look out the window he's just coming down the road!"

Sandeep was stumbling along beside Jenkins, looking to the sky for assistance from above. He was trembling and mumbling some nonsense that was beyond his kidnapper's comprehension, a large carving knife slowly forcing its way into his Adam's apple.

Jenkins was whispering in his ear to him to shut up, and he looked like he meant it. Although he had his hands full, he managed to steer his hostage in the right direction by using his bodyweight. The pressure on the carving knife, gripped in Jenkins' left hand, acted like a throttle. The damaged leg had gone to sleep; too much blood had been spilt and it was not looking good. Well, it was definitely not looking good for the London marathon this year, put it that way! Left hand on the throttle his other waving the Browning around for all to see. Jenkins knew they were there; he couldn't see them, but he knew only too well that they were there, hiding like cowards!

"You wanna shoot him, don't you Slug?" Tap asked.

Slug couldn't lie, he did want to shoot Jenkins, but then so did everyone else. But no one dared, not until their main man offered them the freedom to do so.

"Tough shit, Slug! He's fucking mine, darling, so keep out of the fucking way and don't get in his, okay?"

Slug replied in the affirmative before the line went silent as Tap finally set about the matter in hand and prepared to storm the bedroom. Only background noises could be heard as Tap moved forwards, applying his military skill. The tip of the laser beam touched three of the four walls inside the bedroom as well as a cupboard, a wardrobe and a dressing table, before coming to rest on the corpse-like figure on the floor. Okay, we had a survivor here, this was a result. Satisfied that the room was clear, he grabbed the near-naked body and pulled it back onto the bed, turning it over as he did so. So, this was Haley. The bag of bones had AIDS, that much was clear, and she looked like she could once have been the girl in the pictures he had found in Jenkins' flat. Yeah, result! This was Haley; we had Jenkins' piece!

*

"What you doing? He's just below the window now!" Slug broke the silence by relaying an update to his leader.

His answer came when the window exploded in about fifty million pieces and a small round table flew out of the building, falling to the ground with the shards of glass. It was a coffee table; not big, but quite heavy. Ripping the curtains clear from their anchorage, Tap chucked them out of the window as well before making his appearance in the broken window frame.

"Yeah, I see him Slug!" Tap confirmed, his foot on the low window sill and the phone to his ear. He heard a sudden noise behind him and spun round, firing his weapon. Something had moved at the end of the room; something had scampered, and whatever it was Tap had missed it. Cocaine had wired him up, made him alert and on the edge, but he had still not been quick enough to put a bullet into that fucking nurse, just the wall instead! Bollocks, she was gone. She'd done one, and Tap had failed to slow her down with cap in her arse.

Sarah had been conscious for several minutes. She had watched the commotion at the end of the room and had started to crawl into the hallway just as the lunatic chucked a table through the window. When she thought she was far enough down the hall to make a dash for it, she did so, her satchel full of money still around her shoulder.

Tap was pissed off. He had failed, but at the same time he was overjoyed to be able to look out of the window and watch his target struggling up the pathway with his heavy load and diminishing strength. Jenkins had done little more than duck when the projectile flew his way, along with the razor-sharp glass darts. The glass pierced his skin where it hit him.

"Come on, you cunt, you're late!" Tap screamed down at his prey.

"I'll fucking kill him!" Jenkins screamed in reply, which made Tap laugh.

"Oh yeah, Anthony, we know that. You're a bad boy you are, son, a real bad boy! You don't want to waste him though, do you? I mean, I know you've got a knife to his throat and that, but if you chop him, then you're fucked, ain't you? You'll have no cards left, will you son? Bearing in mind you've got no bullets left, aye? You know what I mean?" Tap had to rub salt into his opponent's wounds.

Jenkins laughed back, nervously but not without confidence.

"Who says I got no bullets? I've got plenty of ammo, just you try me and you'll find out!"

Tap shrugged.

"By my calculations, you is empty boy! But hey, fuck it, come up here and party with me and Haley if you've got the fire power! Oh man, she is so thin, dude. Right lovely figure an' all! Shame she's fucking rotten, but never mind! I like thin birds as it happens, and she's proper thin - like she's just been dug up. Me, and her have been having a bit of fun you know, like you did with my girlfriend! She's very responsive, your missis; filthy bitch. Come on up and join us!" Tap invited. He could see a pale, wild-looking face staring up as he looked down.

"Do you think he bit?" Tap asked into the phone.

"Yeah, I'd say he got the message!" Slug replied.

"Slug, I've fucked up, dude," Tap went on. "I've gone and lost the nurse. I thought she was out for the count, but before I was able to shut her up she went and did one. I was going to use her to set up a little surprise for me old mate Anthony when he came up, but she woke up and fucking pegged it. If she makes it downstairs, I trust I can leave the rest up to you, my friend?"

"Yeah, leave her to me," Slug confirmed, "but I'd be surprised if she makes it past Jenkins because he's just about to go in now. I think we can rest assured that he will oblige us on this one, but I'll be following him in anyway."

Jenkins shuffled over to the front door of the building with added venom in his movements. He wanted this cunt, he wanted Tap so bad and he was gonna have him one way or another; he promised himself that! The hidden police officers gave him a free run all the way to the main door. The taxi driver looked petrified as he stared wildly around at what he hoped were police that were sitting in various cars, behind twitching curtains, and opening and closing shop doors over the road. There were two people on the roof opposite as well. Jenkins hadn't really expected a clear run back to the flat, but it was obvious by now who was orchestrating the easy passage.

Billy Tap obviously wanted to conduct the business in private and Jenkins didn't have an issue with that because at the very least it meant he would get to see Haley again, even if it was for just one more time. That was all he was really interested in: seeing Haley. Oh, and slaughtering Billy Tap like a rabid dog, but as to that he was unlikely to get past the detective's back-up, so what was the point? The mission was once again changing and the priority was now to see Haley one last time so that they could make the transition to the other world together. If he got Billy Tap on the way to that goal, then it would be a bonus.

Chapter Twelve

Thirteen

The steps were tricky, but with his hostage's help Jenkins was soon walking backwards through the door and towards where the lifts where, without warning, a lift door opened and a pinging noise filled the air. Slug peered in through the front doors, his back to a wall for protection. The look on Jenkins' face was something else as the lift opened, and standing there before him was Judas herself! Job done, Slug thought as he watched Sarah attempting to explain herself.

"The police, they're in your flat, you've got to get out of here!" she stammered unconvincingly.

Jenkins looked at the bag, which obviously contained her spoils of war. The fucking bitch was jumping ship!

Sarah screamed as Jenkins cut Sandeep's throat with the carving knife, causing him to fall to the floor while gripping his throat and gargling like a fish out of water. She continued to scream as Slug stared in disbelief, uncertain whether to intervene. In the end he didn't, remembering Tap's dire warnings. Sarah didn't stop screaming until Jenkins punched her in the face with the hand that still gripped the bloody carving knife. He managed to drag himself into the lift and as soon as he had done so he stabbed once into Sarah's stomach, then pulled the knife out again. Sarah just stood in shock, staring down at the three-inch gash in her exposed midriff. With every breath she took, bubbles blew from the wound. Sarah began to vomit; it was red and bitter-tasting.

Just as the lift doors closed, Jenkins caught a last glimpse of Sandeep squirming on the floor as the dying man applied pressure to his throat in an attempt to hold his torn windpipe together. He would not survive; Jenkins had felt cold steel scrape against the man's spinal cord, signifying that all the vital pipelines of survival had been well and truly severed but for the communication route to the brain. He pointed at the dying man lying helpless on the floor while he stumbled about in the lift.

"That's for those fucking traffic lights, you cunt!" Then he pressed the button on the lift that would take him to his final destination.

There was silence in the lift but for the sound of heavy breathing, light sobbing, and a splash of spit hitting the metal-lined walls. The journey up to Leigh Anderson's flat took a matter of seconds, and in that time Jenkins had arranged himself into a position that allowed him to stand behind his human shield, just in case. The lift soon stopped and a bell rang to signal its arrival before the doors opened automatically. The hall was fully lit; still dim, but about as good as it got. Sarah was forced to walk out of the lift. She was reluctant, but with the knife-wielding madman right behind her, she dare not risk any more puncture wounds.

"You walk, I walk behind you. No sudden movements, no fucking attitude and I won't give you anything else for them to stitch up later, okay?" Jenkins offered his rules of engagement, minus the frills. Sarah fully understood her position and nodded once, trembling with shock.

The journey from the corridor to the front door of the flat felt like an eternity. Sarah paused at the entrance while Jenkins steadied his breathing and double-checked that the safety was off. What had Tap been on about, talking about him being out of ammunition?

"Go on in!" He ordered once he was ready for combat.

Sarah was hunched over slightly with the pain of her punctured stomach. Jenkins cleared his throat and deposited the result onto the floor. Sarah had to laugh in a warped kind of way, because she now knew what it felt like to be spitting your guts up all the time, although hers were actually dripping from the sides of her mouth. She needed to sit down, or rather lie down, because she was feeling weak and suffering shock. In despair, she entered the flat.

As soon as she walked through the front door there was an almighty bang and a spray of human debris which covered the adjacent wall, floor and ceiling in a single wave. Jenkins spat out a portion of what had just covered him from head to toe, chuckling to himself like the madman he was. What was so funny? Nothing in particular; just the fact that once again he was wearing someone else, which was becoming a bit of an occupational hazard these days! He had to laugh.

He removed Leigh Anderson's leather jacket and discarded it on the floor, after first throwing away his faithful carving knife which had served him so well. He was left wearing just a pair of red-stained jeans and a white T-shirt which was also plastered in blood and God knows what else. The T-shirt still read 'Porn Star' on the front but the joke was wearing a bit thin by now, plus it was soaking wet and so Jenkins removed it and tossed it on the floor next to the jacket.

Fortunately for Jenkins, he had been positioned just to the side of his hostage when the bullet hit her head, hence the backwash of blood and brains. Sarah had been shot in the face, at quite close range by the look and sound of things. It was messy; very messy. Her almost decapitated corpse fell backwards through the front doorway, its legs having finally given up the ghost, shaking and twitching as it did so.

"Come in!" Tap invited his visitor.

Confident that Tap was not going to simply shoot him, that would be way too easy, Jenkins waded through a puddle of blood that squelched under his stumbling feet. He clutched his faithful Browning automatic in his right hand, the weapon held down by his side. Clearly, Tap was in control of the situation at the moment. He peered nervously into the lounge, his back flat against the kitchen wall for protection. All he could see was the wall that divided the master bedroom and bathroom from the lounge.

"Come in, you fucking pussy!" Billy Tap ordered.

Jenkins obliged, walking straight into the set which the detective had created. Tap was right at the back of the room, sitting on the back rest of the sofa with one foot on the arm rest and the other where you normally sit. There seemed to be someone sitting down below him, but it was hard to see at first because it was so dingy in the room. What was left of the curtains surrounding the bay window behind the sofa blew gently about in the evening breeze. It took a few seconds to allow his eyes to adjust to the room's poor illumination, but when they did, it was clear that Billy Tap had applied great thought to setting this scene. Haley was out cold on the sofa, lying there as naked as the day she was born. She was motionless. Head slumped back over the arm. Tap sat casually on her right, a huge, evil-looking handgun resting on the arm of the sofa next to his foot but with hands that were empty apart from silver rings.

"Cute! I get it now," Tap commented, pointing to the left-hand side of his own chest. He was referring to a tattoo covering half Jenkins' chest.

"The wheat sheaf…!" This was the symbol that had kept turning up at the murder scenes; a sign of his cause. It hadn't meant to be; it was just something he had seen in the tattoo artist's shop a few months back and had quite liked, so he had had it done. In particular, it was a symbol that you could create by using just two fingers. Take your ink, or some blood, and a wall or steamy window, and with a bit of practice you could create this symbol without your fingers leaving the canvas. It was the ideal calling card.

Billy cursed himself for not tearing up London's tattoo parlours in the hope of finding the artist, and hence Jenkins, a lot sooner.

"Yeah, very cute, don't worry though, mate, I'll make sure it goes on your gravestone!"

Jenkins raised his Browning automatic and pointed it straight at Tap. Clearly the detective had upset his visitor.

"Whoa, whoa, whoa, chill, man, there's no need for any shooting just yet. Not with me pants down, anyway! Just you take a few deep breaths there for a second while I button myself up." Billy emphasised his unarmed status with a wave of his hands.

Jenkins wanted to shoot this man dead, but intrigue stopped him pulling the trigger just yet. For the time being, he opted to watch the show instead. His target stood up with his hands still in the air and his genitalia fully exposed through his open jeans.

"Chill, Anthony my friend. Just let me button up. Don't want you wasting that precious ammo now, do we?" he mocked as he fiddled with his manhood and removed something rubbery, discarding it on the floor and looking to his opponent for a reaction.

Jenkins was frothing; but at the same time very cautious. Try as he might, he couldn't believe that all this was actually happening. He needed to be able to grasp some sense from the situation before he attempted to deal with it. Also, he was aware that he probably was running low on ammo, as Tap had so rightly pointed out. He was not the best shot in the world, and Tap was probably wearing body armour and capable of reaching his handgun in a matter of seconds. So, shoot him in the head then? Yeah, right - that was easier said than done. For some strange reason, this situation reminded Jenkins of when he was at school and had always been the last to be picked for the football team because when he kicked a ball, it always went the opposite way. So, for the time being, he let Tap get on with what he had to do, just in case he missed the net again.

Jenkins' face wore a look of abhorrence as he watched the man in his sights button himself up while sitting on the back rest of the sofa. The detective stared into the madman's eyes, his professional mind studying the anger that shone through them as they flicked from his crotch to an empty condom wrapper that had been discarded upon the floor, barely half a metre from the condom itself.

"What?" Billy asked, antagonising his prey further. It was time to go into overdrive; the throttle was hard down and the turbo had cut in. "What, you didn't think I'd fuck her without a hat on, did ya?" Tap asked as he stood tall from the sofa and rolled his shoulders as though fully in control of the situation, which as far as he was concerned he was, after all, Jenkins had no ammo left; he was firing blanks.

Billy put his hands on his hips and held his cool gaze into Jenkins' eyes. Jenkins stared back through the sites of the Browning. Black leather coat, black T-shirt, black jeans: the policeman looked just how Jenkins remembered him from barely a hour ago when the cunt had put a bullet in his leg.

"You ought to get that seen to!" Tap commented pointing to the other's damaged limb.

Jenkins was struggling to stand and aim his faithful Browning at the same time. He looked a mess, wobbling all over the place. Tap smiled as he took his leather coat off and laid it carefully across the back of the sofa. There was no body armour under his black T-shirt, just a holster that held another state-of-the-art firearm and a number of spare ammunition clips.

"Nice place you got here," Tap continued. He moved slightly to the left in order to grip the butt of his firearm on the arm of the sofa. Snatching the weapon up, he pointed it straight at his enemy and a red laser beam once again illuminated the room, cutting through the haze and marking out the weapon's target. The speed with which he had retrieved the killing machine was pretty impressive to say the least. Jenkins gulped before coughing and spitting out an obstruction in his throat, created by fear. The handgun aimed at him was huge, making his Browning pale into significance. Billy Tap smiled, clearly enjoying this whole scenario. He nodded towards Haley while keeping his eyes fixed on Jenkins.

"I just gave her the fuck of her life. Fuck me man, she's so tight. Is that what happens when they're all HIV'd up? Fucking felt like I was sticking it up her arse man, although I wouldn't do that to you mate; come on, some things are sacred! Besides, I think she's shit herself it's a bit messy down there. Good job I sacked your nurse because she was fucking useless by the look of things. Done you a favour there, son." Tap set about coiling the springs, but Jenkins remained strangely calm. He should have been angry, but he challenged his thoughts and worked out that this was exactly what his opponent wanted. Instead, he chuckled to himself. This was not what Billy had expected.

"What, you think it's funny that I fucked your bird, then?" he demanded.

Jenkins shrugged his shoulders, laughing like a madman.

"You say you fucked her, which I don't believe for one minute, but I totally fucked your boyfriend! I fucked him good and proper by spraying his fucking brains across a shoe shop! Bit young for you, weren't he? I can just see the look on his face before I shot him, he was fucking petrified. I don't think he felt much pain though, he died pretty quick. Not like that reporter who was with him, I shot her in the stomach and left her leaking like a sieve!" Jenkins smiled as he reminisced, but his smile soon turned to a grimace as a shot rang out in the room.

Jenkins flew back and hit the wall, his body punctured by a flying metal missile guided by laser technology. As he met the plaster, he collapsed under his own bodyweight and slid slowly down the white paintwork, leaving a trail of blood.

"What, like that?" Tap screamed. The shot had not been intended to kill but merely maim, which is exactly what it did.

Using the wall and floor for support, Jenkins peered down at the bullet wound in his right shoulder. He had hit the wall with force, dropping his firearm due to the loss of grip by a hand that was no longer working correctly. He slid sideways into a pool of his own blood and started scrabbling around with his left hand in order to regain his only ticket out of there. Billy Tap walked towards him, his face lit up through the red haze that pervaded the room.

"That ain't fucking nothing, mate, compared to what I'm fucking gonna do to her when I've finished with you. No, fuck it, I'm gonna do it to her while you sit there and watch, leaking like a fucking sieve! What's up, gone quiet? What you fucking looking for, your shooter? Hey, here it is, look! Here, let me help you, left hand, is it? Oh yeah, have to be won't it, because the other don't work no more, what a bastard, eh? Oh, and by the way, Stacey ain't dead, so you fucked up on that one. She's going to live, and make enough folds to retire for life after that interview you gave her, not to mention the shit were gonna make up an' all! So who's fucking laughing now, bad boy?" This was true as far as he knew, because Stacey had still been alive the last he heard, although for how long was anyone's guess. There was no harm in letting Jenkins have his plaything back. After all, the fucking thing was empty anyway. Kneeling in the blood next to his enemy, Tap fished around in the rapidly-expanding sea of blood in search of the missing handgun. When he found it, he moved right next to his nemesis and put it into his left hand as if mocking the man. As he did so, he took the time to study the chunk that was missing from his victim's shoulder, just above the wheat-sheaf. The gunshot wound was lubricated by a steady flow of blood and looked sore; good, he hoped it fucking hurt!

Jenkins took the gun as Billy Tap continued his speech, gripping the butt half-heartedly.

"Anyway, I fuck your bird; you fuck mine. What's it gonna matter, because at the end of the day it's not about them; it's about me and you. You got out of line and I've had to come and sort you out. Now don't get me wrong, you're here for a reason, we all know that, but you've got to know where to draw the line. You've been taking the piss mate, not to mention thoroughly inconveniencing me because I'm the cunt who has to come down and set things straight. So, here I am! Here, you having trouble with that, son? Look, you can't get your finger behind that trigger, can you? Bit heavy is it? They are a heavy gun though, mind. Here, slip your finger in there, son. Go on, ah, that's the one, feels good, don't it? You feel protected now, don't you?" Tap mocked, his words forced out through gritted teeth and accompanied by a spray of saliva.

Jenkins was confused. What the fuck Tap was going on about he had no idea: coming down, setting things straight? Inconvenienced? The bloke was a fucking madman! Still, you don't look a gift horse in the mouth so Jenkins pulled the trigger and was rewarded with the best look of surprise you could wish for on an opponent's face as a loud noise filled the room and flames brushed Anthony Jenkins' cheek.

"Fuck me!" Was about all he could say as he watched Billy Tap suddenly launch from his crouching position and fly backwards through the air, covering two or three metres of ground at least. Why this lunatic had given him his handgun back he had no idea, and clearly Tap was thinking the same as he cradled his chest in terror, aware that something had gone terribly wrong with his master plan. The hole in his chest was a major set-back. He tried to sit up, but he had lost his beloved

Glock twenty-one. He couldn't even see it now that the laser lighting had ceased to illuminate the room. He still had the seventeen but that was holstered up and he couldn't reach it, bearing in mind that he had a hole in his chest big enough to stick his fist in and his left collar bone was poking out through his skin.

Jenkins saw him trying to sit up so he pulled the trigger again and, click, click, click - fuck it, it was empty! He could hear Tap laughing through mouthfuls of blood as he gargled like a cackling fool.

"What's so fucking funny?" He asked as he groped around in the pool of blood in search of surplus weapons. That big fucker was here somewhere, the one with the laser sight that Tap had been carrying. There it was, Jenkins could see it about a metre or so away, but he could also see Billy Tap fiddling with his holster.

"Thirteen. Fucking thirteen...!" The detective kept babbling through mouthfuls of blood as he struggled to get air. Jenkins didn't know what he was on about, but he did know that he needed that spare handgun, and he needed it now, because Tap had almost freed his back-up piece. The word 'thirteen' rang in the air, distorted by the laughter of a drowning man.

"Unlucky for some...!" Jenkins felt compelled to remark as he dragged himself across the floor through the sea of blood, en route to the prize ahead of him. Reaching out, he finally managed to grip the butt of his ticket out of there with his left hand, pushing his aching body off the floor and onto his knees with the beautiful Glock twenty-one firmly in his possession. The laser sight had turned itself off during its flight through the air and Jenkins didn't even bother trying to turn it back on again, although he saw a button on the side of the sight which would probably have done it. He didn't need laser technology now - this was close range, just how he liked it. Unsteady on his knees, he pulled the trigger of Billy Tap's former handgun, aiming the weapon somewhere near the detective's heart.

"See how you like it, cunt!" He whispered as another of those frightening bangs filled the air.

He hit Tap's left elbow instead and sent the lower half of his arm flying across the room. It was safe to say that the firearm Tap had just managed to locate would be of no further threat, seeing as how it was now about six metres away, along with the arm. Tap was in real trouble now, blood pumping out of the stump of his arm like a fountain. He was also coughing weakly and it was beginning to look like he had played his last card. Victorious, Jenkins stood as best as he could and stumbled across the room towards the sofa where his loved one lay naked. After checking her pulse, he laid his new weapon on the sofa where Tap had placed it before, then stumbled off again to retrieve the only other live firearm in the room before limping back. Housing the weapon under his left armpit, Jenkins tried to ignore his own pain which was becoming hard to deal with.

"You all right, Billy?" he asked sarcastically. "Sorry to have inconvenienced you any further, me old mate. You know how it is, your days never end up as planned, not in this business. You look a bit rough though, buddy, you wanna get that seen to!" He needed a piss and didn't feel up to hobbling across to the bathroom, so he did what Tap would have done in the same situation: he unbuttoned his flies and aimed it right at his victim's mouth. The occasional trickle of blood joined the flow of urine, hitching a ride in the river of blood that stemmed from his shoulder wound. Tap had had many a man piss on him in the past. He got quite a kick out of it, but on this occasion he was having enough trouble breathing as it was. Jenkins, however, seemed to find it highly entertaining.

After delivering the golden shower, he limped back to the sofa and picked up a couple of clips that he had taken from his fallen opponent. He put one in his mouth, held it his teeth, and the other he swapped awkwardly for the standard-issue police firearm that was situated under his left armpit. Tooled up, Jenkins limped over to the window and looked down upon his adoring fans, consisting mainly of the police and reporters.

"This is for you, my humble servants!" He screamed awkwardly as he opened fire on his audience from above. The road below lit up with mayhem as those who could dived for cover, and those who couldn't took what was coming to them. Seventeen shots were fired; potentially seventeen casualties if the gun had been in more competent hands. As it was, the Glock was in his left hand and he was firing at long range, so anything he did hit was a bonus. A few unsuspecting reporters were hit by flying debris, but that was about it.

Jenkins took the clip that was wedged inside his left armpit. The little button on the left-hand side of the weapon, just above the trigger, released the weapon's spent magazine. He discarded the empty magazine and pushed the fresh one into the butt of the weapon. Awkwardly, he pulled back the slide above the chamber and the weapon was ready for another attempt.

The second burst of fire was just as spectacular as the first, although he still didn't hit anything important apart from lightly wounding a police officer. Anthony went to take the clip from his mouth and load up for the third time, but just as he pulled back and hid behind the wall in order to gain cover, the room came alive with the sound of gunfire. He didn't get a chance to look at what was exploding and hitting the side of his face at first, although he guessed it probably was the remains of the glass in the window frame. Whatever it was, it cut and splintered his cheek. Tap also received another shower, this time of building debris, which did his respiratory problems no favours. He didn't know how many police officers had returned fire but it was enough to render the whole front of the flat windowless before it stopped.

Jenkins turned as he heard a faint, hoarse whisper in the silence that followed and turned to see Haley moving, twitching, covered in a layer of broken glass and splinters from wooden window frames. She was whispering his name. He dragged himself over to the sofa, stopping once to reload a third clip into his handgun. As he did so, he heard the squeak of a floorboard and looked up to see an infra-red beam trained upon him.

"Lose the weapon!" An unfamiliar voice ordered.

Jenkins did nothing for a few seconds, but remained in his crouching position while he took the time to think. The warning was repeated, and this time he did as he was told and tossed the handgun to the floor, the weapon landing just a metre or so from the front door.

"Stand up!" The voice continued.

Slowly, he straightened himself up, raising his head until he was in a position to look into the eyes of the enemy. The laser sight created a blinding haze as it dazzled him in the darkness. Nevertheless, Jenkins recognised the man who stood in the doorway almost instantly. It was Tap's sidekick.

Tap, still alive somehow, attempted to spit out some of the blood that was drowning him as he saw the red light pass straight over his head. He choked as he did so, gargling blood in his throat.

Jenkins had been shot again, Slug could see that as he trained his sights on his target's chest, noticing the tattooed symbol as he did so and understanding its significance.

Jenkins raised his hands up as high as was physically possible, as if submitting, before stumbling slightly over to the right-hand side of the room, just a step closer to the sofa.

"I didn't tell you to move, did I?" Slug warned.

Weaponless the killer watched his enemy walk towards him and drop down into a crouching position to retrieve the surplus weapon while never taking his eyes away from the prize and maintaining the aim of his firearm at all times. As Slug reached out into the sea of blood with a white rubber-gloved left hand, Jenkins made a sudden movement again, another little hop towards the sofa.

"I told you not to move, Jenkins, didn't I?" Slug warned again.

"I need to sit down, man," Jenkins whined. "I can't stand up any longer, look, my leg's fucked!" The leg obediently buckled, bringing Jenkins yet closer to the sofa. He was close now, although not close enough to regain the use of Billy Tap's former weapon, which clearly Slug had not seen yet. He glanced towards the place on the sofa arm where he thought he had put it, but it wasn't there. Where the fuck was it? It wasn't on the floor, so it must be lying on the sofa cushion itself, by that pillow or something.

"Look dude, you got me, yeah? You got my weapon, half my shoulder's missing, my leg's fucked, I can't walk, I'm finished! Now you ain't gonna take me in, I know that, so just let me sit down on the sofa and say good bye to Haley. That's all I want, then I'm yours, yeah? What d'ya say?" Jenkins prayed for a little mercy and it seemed that the opposition was buying it.

With two guns now in his possession, Slug walked towards the sofa, pausing at the side of his injured colleague. It appeared that the two men had come to a silent understanding so Jenkins slowly moved another step towards the sofa and sat down carefully next to his loved one. Dusting off the layer of glass and plaster that covered poor Haley, Jenkins shook her lightly, praying that she was still well enough to communicate. She was curled up into a ball, her head on the far arm of the sofa and her legs pulled up in a pathetic effort to protect her dignity. How many fucking pain killers and what not she had been given today, Jenkins had no idea, but she was clearly drugged up to the hilt. While Anthony Jenkins picked glass and shit off his partner, like a monkey picking flees off its mate, Slug looked down at his colleague.

"You couldn't fucking leave it, could you?" He asked, sadly.

Billy Tap spat out another mouthful of blood as he tried to talk, but it just wasn't happening. The end was obviously near. Gagging for breath, Billy reached out for help with his only remaining arm, but there was none forthcoming. Slug stepped back in disgust, not at his partner but at the state he had been reduced to, gazing up mutely in supplication.

Slug could have made a call, got the paramedics up there to make life-prolonging temporary repairs to defer the inevitable, but he wasn't going to. Tap had been right when he had said earlier that this case would end tonight. Slug was getting fed up with witnessing murder on a daily basis and then having to cover it up. A bent copper he may have been, he had siphoned off a small fortune from his business associations through various underworld connections, and he didn't have a problem with that at all. He didn't need the money because he had gone into the police force with plenty of that from his family. No, he just wanted the buzz of the job, the feeling of achievement he got from the dynamic duo creating an empire within. But it had all got out of hand lately, what with wiping out a house full of Yardies and the murder of countless other people over these last few days. Billy Tap had lost it; it was as if he was possessed. He had always been a bad boy, but nothing like this.

Slug raised his weapon - the one he had just taken from Jenkins that had the wanted man's fingerprints all over it - and took aim at his former colleague's head. The rubber glove on his hand filled with sweat as he gripped the trigger. He glanced over towards the sofa; Jenkins looked harmless enough as he bent over his girlfriend, trying to spend a last few minutes with her. He was putting a ring on Haley's finger as he spoke a few words. He turned back to the job in hand.

One shot to the head; that was all it would take. Tap shook with anger and fear as he saw the boy he had educated aim a basic police-issue weapon at his head. Slug had been his project, a rich boy who wanted to do good. Billy had taken him on and they had done good even if in rather an unconventional manner. But to do good, you sometimes also have to do a little bad. Slug kept the farewell speech brief.

"Like you said, Billy, this is your show. And do you know what? You're fucking welcome to it, because I don't want to be a part of it any more. You need cutting down to size - anyone and fucking everyone knows that, and I don't think there's a better time than the present. Don't worry I'll clean the scene up just like I always do. And I'll send you out with a bit of dignity; that's the least I can do. Goodbye, Billy!"

Slug bid him farewell, closed his eyes and pulled the trigger. The wound was tidy, the bullet entering straight between the eyes. There was some jerking and twitching, then silence apart from the sound of a discarded firearm hitting the carpet and heavy breathing. Slug had been holding his breath without realising it and now began to gasp as the realisation of what he had just done began to sink in. It was a first for him; the murder of one's own. It was brown paper bag time, and before Slug knew what was going on a tidal wave of vomit had forced its way out of his body. He fell to his knees and collapsed sideways onto the floor, his right elbow in the island of vomit that he had created within the sea of blood.

"Fucking pussy!" Was Jenkins' comment. He could hardly believe it, the copper had looked like he had things covered there, until he fucked it all up. Now Jenkins was tooled up again, having retrieved the weapon he had left on the sofa -

which had slipped down the back of a cushion as it turned out and the copper was fucked.

The clock was ticking. He had put the rings on Haley's finger and his own, which left just enough time to deal with unfinished business before their dream became reality. Jenkins kissed his wife on the lips before he stood, brandishing his firepower once more. Fiddling with the weapon's buttons, he managed to activate the high-tech sight, filling the room with laser technology. He waved the red laser across his opponent's face as the lawman rolled over, gasping for breath. It was a pitiful sight; how the mighty had fallen!

"Fucking pussy, lose the gun!" He ordered, concerned that his opponent still had a firearm in his possession. He could hear movement out in the hallway, or at least in the corridor outside the flat. Slug dropped his only remaining firearm onto the floor as if admitting defeat. It was yet another Glock, although not of the same calibre as the weapon that aimed a laser dot on his forehead.

"Sit up and put your hands on your head!" Jenkins ordered, just before clearing his throat of a rapidly-rising deposit and spitting it into the air.

Slug held out his palms defensively as he sat up. Jenkins looked out towards the front room door where he could hear the enemy taking up their positions.

"Come on, hands on your head and then stand up!" He ordered once more. The laser sight was playing havoc with both his vision and that of his prey, so he switched it off.

It was hard work standing up from a sitting position on the floor with his hands on his head, but nevertheless Slug managed it. Jenkins nodded as if impressed.

"Over to the door, quick! Warn them you're coming though and tell them who you are, right?"

Slug did as he was told, half-expecting to be cut down by a bullet when he turned his back, but it seemed it was not to be.

"It's simple, right? I'm gonna spare you. I know, it's fucking mental, init? And why? Well, it's hardly because I think you're a nice bloke now, is it?" Jenkins joked.

Slug shrugged. He didn't know, but then who the fuck knew what went on in Jenkins' mind?

"If I spare your life, right," Jenkins went on, "then you owe me. Yeah? Just the once is all I'm asking. It's simple. In return for your life, I'm going to ask you to do one thing for me, which is to hold back your troops. I'm outnumbered, out gunned, I know that, and I ain't getting out of this one. So I want five minutes, that's all. Five minutes for your life, sounds like a fucking bargain from where I'm standing. I let you go, you go out there and you hold them back for five minutes, just for five minutes, that's all. Then you can let them in. I will have taken care of everything by then, my work will be done and we can all move on." AJ said suddenly feeling stronger.

"You leave me little option but to accept really, do you?" Slug replied coolly, since some kind of response seemed to be expected of him, he proceeded towards the door with his hands still above his head.

"Hold your fire! It's Slug, I'm coming out. Pull back to the lifts immediately!"

Now fully in control of his mission again, he was able to issue his orders with authority. There was a momentary silence then someone outside the flat repeated the order as if it were an echo. The noise of shuffling feet could be heard outside in the corridor as a nudge in the back instructed Slug to move on through the living room door and out into the unknown. He obeyed, having little choice. The hallway was long with very few obstacles apart from the open-plan kitchen. With the front door in sight, the nudges in the back became more frequent until Slug was eventually pushed outside into the corridor, banished to the world beyond the walls of Jenkins' fortress.

Raising his shoulders and pulling his head as close to them as possible with his back to the enemy, the released hostage was just waiting for the bullet now, the bullet which he was convinced was on its way, but none came. Jenkins simply took one look down towards the end of the hallway - mentally comparing the police marksmen who lined the walls like the rebel forces from the opening scenes of Star Wars, before issuing a final reminder.

"Five minutes, that was the deal!"

Slug turned to face his opponent and the two men's eyes met for probably the very last time. Seconds later, Jenkins broke the stare and retreated into his fortress, slamming the door shut behind him and leaving nothing more than the sound of rattling door locks. Slug looked at his watch: five minutes and counting, the clock was ticking.

*

Jenkins limped hastily back into the living room, using Billy Tap's chest as a springboard as he did so, just because he could. Haley had lost consciousness again but her pulse confirmed that she was still in the land of the living.

"Haley! Haley!" He called softly.

She came round and almost managed a smile.

"We're gonna go now, it's time. We're gonna go to a place where no one can hurt us. See the rings?" Jenkins asked, holding his lover's left hand up and placing it close to his own. Haley nodded and smiled again, her eyes full of pain.

"See, we're together now; together for ever. And when we cross over, they won't be able to separate us anymore. Are you ready, Haley? Are you ready to go?"

Haley nodded, although she clearly didn't have a clue what the fuck was going on. All the painkillers she had been fed by Sarah were taking her to another level.

"We'll be together on the other side, my precious, but you're gonna have to go first. When you get there, you wait for me. I'll be along shortly. No more pain, baby, no more of this shit - just me and you, forever!" Jenkins promised as he took one of the white cushions from the sofa, unzipped its cover and removed it, placing the linen-type fabric over Haley's head as if to protect her dignity. With the blindfold in place, Jenkins reached out and gripped his loved one's left hand, holding it tightly as he raised Billy Tap's handgun to her left temple. Tenderly, he leaned forward and kissed his angel softly on the lips through the cushion cover before pulling back. He never took his eyes off her. Drawing a deep breath, he pulled the trigger as his vision became blurred.

The familiar and beautiful smell of gunfire filled the air and at first Haley's hand continued to grip his as if it was supporting her entire bodyweight, but the grip quickly subsided into a few seconds' shaking and then nothing.

"Bye bye Haley, bye-bye. It won't be long now - I won't be far behind you!" he promised.

Anthony looked excited, joyful maybe that his bride had now left this world of pain for a better place. He had had two of the magic tickets and had used one of them, so now it was time to cash his in. It was time to join her, so Anthony opened his mouth and pushed the barrel of the weapon into it. The cold steel felt out of place in his mouth, the metal making his nerves tingle as it scraped his teeth. When he forced the barrel upwards, the pressure it brought to bear on his jaw was tremendous. He needed to make sure that the bullet went straight up into his brain. This was it now, it was time to meet his maker - or anyone else who was waiting for him, as well as Haley. It simply required a pull of the trigger; it was as simple as that. He tried with all his might to do it, but it wasn't happening. The weapon was in his left hand, which worked perfectly, yet the trigger could not be pulled. Anthony tried again but his finger simply would not follow the order to pull the trigger; it was as if his brain was withholding the command from his finger.

Jenkins felt a shudder of anxiety run through him; it made him feel sick to cough and accidentally spit a piece of his dying lung tissue out into the world which he was trying to leave. A voice in his head, no different to the others that he heard, was telling him not to do this; he couldn't and wouldn't be allowed, because there was another way! Fucking voices, they were a pain in the arse. It was as if there was someone else inside him, someone who kept telling him to do these evil things while his reason attempted to preach otherwise. Reason was telling Anthony that this was the end; he had got what he wanted now. Haley was safe, she was free and so he should now join her, it was for the best. Reason was telling Anthony to get on that train, get the fuck out of here, it's a fucking shit-hole down here anyway! 'Go on, do one!' it implored, but unfortunately reason was not calling the shots here. So, there was one more task then - one more thing that Anthony had to do. If it had to be that way, then so be it! He didn't really care who saw him off onto the train as long as he was getting the fuck out of here.

Right, three firearms in the arsenal. Jenkins liked that - three weapons with which to carry out his final task, and this was his final task, he knew that because no one was going to be able to protect him on this last mission. He was going to fail this one, he knew that, but he had to fail in order to succeed. Okay, two Glock Seventeen's and a Glock Twenty-one. He liked it; this was real firepower. One Seventeen was wedged into the waistband of his trousers and the other went into his left-hand. The twenty-one sat pretty in his damaged right hand because it was big and bulky and didn't hold many bullets by the look of things. They were bigger bullets than normal; his leg could vouch for that! The right hand wasn't going to do much killing, it was too fucked to assist in any real marksmanship.

The walk to the front door of the flat seemed a long one. Jenkins exercised his damaged arm, staring with interest as each movement pumped out a small offering of blood. There couldn't be much left in him now. Reaching the door, Jenkins was in the station and ready to walk towards the platform. Fiddling with the door lock signalled that the train was close, it was just pulling into the station, so he had to hurry not to miss it.

Taking deep breaths, he opened the door slowly, flattening himself against the opposite wall. The immediate hallway in front of him was clear. Jenkins peered out further from the safety of the doorway: to his left was clear, but to his right was the enemy. He suddenly noticed his heavy breathing. It reminded him of Darth Vader as he studied the rebels awaiting his arrival. The gallant crack squad were lining the two walls of the corridor, about forty metres down the hallway by the lifts. Jenkins would have liked the 'force' to have been with him, as it had been for the last few days, but it wasn't going to be. The devil's work was almost done here; there were just a few formalities to take care of before Jenkins' tortured soul went back to where it belonged.

He walked out into the corridor, weapons at his side.

"Armed police, drop your weapons!" Came a shout.

Yeah, right.

"Come on then, you cunts!" Jenkins screamed as he attempted to run down the hallway, making quite a creditable effort as he raised his firearms and started to fire away at the enemy.

It all went sort of into slow motion from where Slug was standing. Jenkins was tripping, stumbling, and falling against walls, firing indiscriminately. The direction of the bullets seemed not to matter as long as they were fired and the weapon emptied. Jenkins was half way through the clip in the Glock seventeen when he first felt a bullet pierce his skin. The missile entered his stomach, and they were right - it did fucking hurt, especially when another bullet from the same burst, and possibly the same weapon, made impact. That hit bone, Jenkins could feel it, although he could not pinpoint exactly what bone as he spun round and hit the wall, joining the exploding plaster that disintegrated under heavy fire.

Using the wall for support while still charging onwards, hell bent on death, he continued to fire at the police. He was getting a result: there were at least two officers down and considering they were armed with semi-automatic rifles he was doing all right. He suddenly lost his left ear and a chunk of flesh from the side of his face. That didn't hurt, it was just a bit freaky, all the blood and that, not to mention the gaping wound and the flap of skin that hung down. It was almost as freaky as the three bullets that hit his left leg and his groin. That was it then, no more running.

Jenkins hit the floor like a sack of shit just as he discarded his first spent firearm and reached into his waistband for his back-up piece. He had dropped the twenty-one almost as soon as the show began, so this was it as far as ammo was concerned. But it didn't matter, the end was nigh. Jenkins could feel it throughout his body. Another shot was probably about all he would have to suffer, but then look at the enemy - look at them, through the haze of shot-up plaster.

Slug was hit, but it was nothing to worry about, so he continued to fire a sub-machine-gun at their target. They don't last long though, so pretty soon he was struggling to feed another magazine into the killing machine. Slug sent out another burst of machine-gun fire; spray and pray was his chosen method of attack because you couldn't really see what you were shooting at, thanks to the haze created by the disintegrating plaster. It made the scene look eerie and indistinct, like a foggy day in World War Two. He was using a dead colleague as a human shield and the majority of the bullets were hitting his helmet and body armour as opposed to cutting him to ribbons. The return fire suddenly stopped and there was the sound of moaning and scrabbling from behind enemy lines.

The police eased off. They couldn't see much, but Jenkins must have been as good as dead: they had pumped too many rounds down this fucking corridor for him to have survived. And they were nearly right - Jenkins was dead, or as good as. He was dragging himself along the carpet in search of the only weapon in his armoury that may still have had live rounds left in it; and it was there, just there in front of him, but he couldn't be allowed to reach it!

Jenkins felt someone standing on his leg, preventing him from crawling any further, and so he gave up. This was it; the ticket conductor was here and the train would be leaving soon. Jenkins laughed like a cackling lunatic, which hurt. Slug allowed him to roll over onto his back, just as soon as he was sure that his target was packing no more weapons. Jenkins couldn't help laughing again as the two men's eyes met and stared. Slug didn't know whose eyes he was looking into as he pointed the handgun at his captive, but they weren't human, he knew that much.

"Do it!" Jenkins ordered, feeling the need for resolution at last. "Fucking do it!"

Slug looked back into the mist. He could see no one, and no one could see him.

"Do it, send me back!" Jenkins screamed, wanting to say more but the pain prevented him.

"Where's Haley?" Slug asked, knowing what game they were playing here.

"She's gone!"

Slug smiled.

"Why shouldn't I arrest you? I mean, you might live and we could preserve you for all humanity to see!" Slug suggested.

Jenkins laughed, the pain suddenly stopping the act almost as soon as it started.

"Do you really think I'm gonna live? Look at the fucking state of me! Besides, I know too much. I know about you and your mate. You won't let me live, so send me back. C'mon, I need to go - Haley's waiting for me!" Jenkins spat blood and mucus at his opponent.

Slug had to agree, Jenkins did know too much. As much as he would like to have made a public display of his dying prisoner, he couldn't risk it. So, reluctantly, he raised his handgun and aimed it at his victim's head.

Jenkins smiled.

"Do it! Send me back!" He pleaded.

The two men stared into each other's eyes. It was strange, Slug thought: if he shot him, then they would both have won - they would both have got what they wanted. The decision was made.

"Just don't be fucking sick on me afterwards, ya filthy cunt! Have some fucking respect!" Jenkins added, reminding Slug curiously of Tap.

"Give my regards to the missis, then. I hope you'll be very happy together!" Slug mocked, with a hint of sincerity, before he did what was asked of him and pulled the trigger. Jenkins was smiling, his eyes begging, then the sound of the shot rang out and a strange chill was in the air. The corridor was cold; the train was leaving; it was pulling out of the station. Jenkins was on his way to meet his loved one, to meet Haley as he began his journey to the other side. She would be waiting for him at the station at the other end, all dressed up pretty. The slate would be wiped clean and they could begin again, living life as they wanted to, not as they were forced to do.

Anthony Jenkins felt nothing but relief as the devil inside him was no more. Lucifer would have to find work for some other mug to do, because Jenkins had done his bit and he was out of here.

A love story of blood, lust, sex, drugs and revenge.
A roller-coaster ride of indulgence, greed and betrayal.

www.Bonkerbooks.com